Beside An Ocean Of Sorrow

A NOVEL BY LUCIA MANN

Eloquent Books

Eloquent Books
An imprint of Strategic Book Group
P.O.Box 333
Durham, CT 06422

www.StrategicBookGroup.com

ISBN: 978-1-60911-159-5

Printed in the United States of America

In memory of my mother, Maria Picasso, the impetus for this book.

Acknowledgements

I am indebted to all— those—*and you know who you are*—who inspired me to write this shocking story.

With inexpressible gratitude I thank my husband, Hector. Without his encouragement, *"Beside an Ocean of Sorrow"* would never have been completed. He not only suffered good-naturedly my writer's tantrums at interruptions, but also endured without complaint many makeshift meals. His steadfast confidence in my ability to weave the fabric of this amazing saga that began so many years ago remained my greatest inspiration. I'm also extremely grateful to Joan Rickard whose love and devotion to this project was unfaltering. Without the enthusiasm of these loving souls, I might well have lost the courage to research and reveal a dark past that was then and might still be rife with danger to others as well as myself. Yet write of the past I must.

Festering in my mind for over sixty years have been voices that went unheard, lives not vindicated, and bravery that was dishonored.

At last, they receive their due.

Author's Note

Beside an Ocean of Sorrow is based on the lives of real people and events. To protect certain individuals' privacy and perhaps even their safety, their names, professions, and descriptions were altered, as was mine. As the events in this story unfold, you will see there was good reason for so doing.

With an author's license, some details were embellished for dramatic purposes. Beyond such minor modifying, it's a true if novelized tale.

Of course, Truth, like Beauty, oft' lies in the mind and eyes of the beholder.

Preface

Historical Facts

On August 23, 1833, the Slavery Abolition Act outlawed slavery in the British Colonies. Slavery was officially abolished in 1838, but that did not stop the colonists, or heartless future apartheid rulers from treating the ethnic races with any modicum of humanity.

…Colonialism has lead to racism, racial discrimination, xenophobia and related intolerance, and … Africans and people of African descent, and people of Asian descent and indigenous peoples were victims of colonialism and continue to be victims of its consequences…
—Durban Declaration of the World Conference against Racism, Racial Discrimination, Xenophobia and Related Intolerance, 2001

Ten million or so Africans who crossed the Atlantic as slaves were shipped in British vessels before 1850.

Prologue

"It is natural to die as to be born; and to a little infant, perhaps one is as painful as the other."

—Francis Bacon, 1792–1871

The Union of South Africa (British Colony), 1945

In the height of Africa's summer season, December's rain should have been falling. But on this Tuesday, Christmas Day, in the wake of World War II, not a rain cloud promised relief.

As the setting sun continued to beat down like a copper mallet upon the Valley of a Thousand Hills in the South African interior, forty-five miles from the city of Durban, the air in this subtropical region hung thickly with summer's perfumes of the orange and yellow daisies, pink impatiens, *croton pseudopulchellus* (a small shrub with multiple stems and shiny delicate lemon flowers), and other indigenous plants carpeting the plains to the horizon.

But, also wafting in this garden of fragrance was a not so pleasant scent: placenta blood.

Buried in a shallow compost pit at the edge of a deserted Zulu homestead, the newborn child was no bigger than a skinned rabbit. She was barely alive. Her tiny heart thumped fitfully against her rib cage. Her breath came in labored gasps.

As life and death ebbed for this helpless baby, the remaining blood in her crudely severed umbilical cord pulsated and dribbled onto the lifeless body of her twin sister beneath her. For these tiny unwanted human beings, discarded like dirty rags, death would have been inevitable, perhaps even preferable, if not for the intervention of a phenomenon of Nature.

A gale-force wind swooped like a bird of prey from nowhere and swirling into a mini-twister, swallowed and spat out the moldy cornhusks that were blanketing the surviving child. Then as abruptly as it had appeared, the wind died down, sighing into a gentle breeze.

Its merciful task was fulfilled.

Eyelids shut against the dusting of reddish dirt layering her ashen face and long blonde eyelashes, the infant's bluish lips parted, and her lungs sucked hungrily at the needed oxygen. Flailing her arms and legs, the girl-child wailed until spent. With her last ounce of strength, she drew her knees into a fetal position, balled her tiny fists to rest under her chin, and surrendered to fate.

A shroud of silence now cocooned this child of untold misfortune.

Unlike the Christ Child, her untimely birth and struggle to survive in an unforgiving world on this godforsaken Dark Continent most definitely went uncelebrated—not unnoticed—this festive day.

Had the Creator of All Life forsaken this orphan of destiny?

No.

Her savior was definitely heaven sent.

At the edge of the cornfield, a scruffy wild dog, shoulder blades protruding from her emaciated frame, crouched behind a clump of savannah grass. Her black and pink mottled nose held high quivered as she sniffed the air. Then with her tick-infested ears twitching rapidly, the creature of the wilds stood up.

Her swollen teats hanging low, the heavily pregnant animal slunk toward the burial site.

Part One
Anele Dingane

Chapter 1

Earlier on, in the predawn hours of Christmas Day, twinkling stars were heralding the arrival of the coming festive day most Christians held sacred, showering believers and alike with boxed surprises. But for three black servants, all fast asleep except one, it would be just like any other workday… devoid of holiness or merriment. Unbeknown to the oldest of the kitchen workers, twenty-seven-year-old Anele Dingane, this day would become than just a working day. It would offer the nonbeliever more than boxed celebratory surprises. This Christmas of '45 would forever change her life.

As fate would have it, it would not be for the better.

Lying still on the edge of a grass-filled mattress in a rundown brick shack a quarter mile from the plantation residence owned by Lord and Lady Hallworthy, Anele had been awake for hours, beset with nightmare after nightmare. If she had dared close her eyelids, horrible scenes—disturbing flashbacks—would once more invade her mind. She exhaled a soft, defeated sigh. She wanted to forget, not to relive these nightmarish reflections all over again. And rarely did she have such sleepless nights—not after the grueling sixteen- to seventeen-hour workdays as head cook in Hallworthy Manor. Oh, how she loathed working at the manor, but more than anything, she hated with every inch of being its heartless owners who had forced her into servitude against her will when she was barely nine years old.

Was Hallworthy Manor cursed?

She thought so.

* * *

In the tradition of upper-class lifestyle, fifty-year-old Lord Nigel Hallworthy, a renowned London-based architect and a cousin of Queen Victoria, had designed Hallworthy Manor, a three-story palatial mansion inspired after his visit to a wealthy plantation owner in Louisiana in 1831. The 5,300-square-foot mansion, fronted with Greek columns eight feet in circumference, balconies, covered porches, slate roof, tall windows, twelve-feet-high ceilings, intricate plaster frieze, and hand-carved marble mantles, was completed by Negro slaves and Italian stonemasons in 1840.

This palatial residence was Lord Nigel's second home, as it was for other British royals and the crème de la crème of English society, who came to Africa on hunting expeditions.

Set in a 620-acre game reserve, Hallworthy estate was populated by herds of deer and, when not hunting, riders in elegant habits exercised their mounts in the morning mists.

Now in post-war times, the reserves were gone; replaced with vast fields, mostly sugar cane. Formal lawns now stretched to a backdrop of wild tangled woodland, but still maintained were the vibrant flowerbeds of pelargonium, arum lilies, and the giant protea—South Africa's national emblem—which aligned the semicircular brick driveway.

A quarter of a mile from the main residence, a dilapidated brick-and-stone outbuilding stood forlornly. Built solely for raising bloodhounds, this barn-like structure never saw any dogs. Housed within its dark musty walls, there had been another kind of wretched creature, captured from African villages—men, women, and adolescents. Nigel called them savages. Hunting them down was a better sport than shooting deer, he told his guests. He also bragged that plantation owners in the Americas had made him even richer by paying handsome sums for the shipment of strong, black slaves.

He wrote in his diary: *"To convert a savage to the proper English way of life is impossible. Even the strongest of us cannot bear their odor. I cannot have savages, who have no decent heart, living in proximity to my house, upsetting my guests. Africans are not entirely human. They are just a short step up the evolutionary ladder from apes."*

* * *

She was wide awake as anger and sadness rambled like wind-driven tumbleweed through Anele's mind. Not just for herself, but for her race, the immense human misery and injustice suffered at the hands of heartless, soulless slave traders. And the land of her birth had run red with the blood of the brave warriors fighting European invaders. Now it was *they* who dominated their land, treated her once proudly independent people like beasts of burden, without human dignity.

A volcano of turbulent emotions running through her, Anele found herself wrestling with questions she could not answer: *Why do I still tremble like a frightened child at the sight and sound of these white people who think they own my black skin… treat me with less respect than a wild cur?* She shook her head trying to dispel another disturbing thought: *There were times when I could have escaped…*

But the very idea of running away like a scared rabbit, for whatever reason, was contrary to her nature—she had the blood of brave Zulus, not a coward. Though courage ran deep in her veins, so did shame. She couldn't return home to her village in Zululand. No tribal suitor would touch her. Not after a white man had repeatedly defiled her and she had given birth to his child. Like many maidens, she longed for a traditional Zulu wedding, a good and hardworking husband, and many children.

That dream was long gone.

However, at the bottom of this deep pit of hell, there glimmered a faint hope that kept her sane: someday, somehow, she would find her missing child, a baby girl wrenched from her arms almost thirteen years ago. During that darkest moment, Anele's closest friend made her feel even more wretched.

"Anele, whether you like it or not, *they* own you now, so if you wish to survive, you have to make the most of your lot in life."

Her wounds were deep, but Anele had tried to get on with her "lot"—tried to be jolly. But smiles and laughter didn't come easy.

* * *

Tossing and turning, she finally gave up trying to get to sleep because no matter how hard she tried, her overloaded memory banks kept spewing. Now they simply switched reels from past to present. She could have wept for the ravages that time and circumstance had wrought. The once stunning African beauty was no more. She had aged a lifetime.

Slowly and gently, she ran a chapped hand over her once-unblemished chocolate-brown face. The left side was disfigured from third-degree burns, the result of an intentional scalding. Gum disease had reduced her even white teeth to broken stumps. Snow-white threads streaked her knotty black hair, and standing five-foot-ten in stocking feet, she was overweight, a condition she blamed on eating her employers leftovers—stodgy food.

Anele's throat tightened with so much bitterness she could not swallow. *Why,* she beseeched from the roots of her soul, *did the Gardeners of Life bother planting her seed when her life had no real purpose?*

Had she known that "Life" was defined by the *Oxford Dictionary* as a condition that distinguishes active animals and plants from inorganic matter, she would have most definitely argued this fact: What happens when a human life, this so called miraculous act of nature, becomes so painfully distorted by inhuman nurturing? Only then does "life" take on a brand new meaning: survival or self-destruction.

She rubbed her sore eyes and sat upright. Another deep sigh escaped her full lips. What could she do to make all this hurt go away? Pray? Will her Maker heed her sorrowful request? In her reckoning, *he* hadn't helped her in the past so why should she bother. But what the heck… she'd give it one more shot. "Namandla, Zulu God of the Invisible Kingdom of Spirits. I beg you to take this yoke off my neck. This isn't living, I'd rather be dead."

As her plea replayed over in her mind, she pulled a sour face, and then clicked her tongue in contempt. What was she thinking? That *prayer* was the answer to her problems! That her Maker would take her by the hand, releasing her from mortal chains, and take her into the kingdom of souls? Yeah right!

After what seemed an eternity, it became clear to Anele that only *she* could change her circumstances.

But how?

She tilted her head and stared up at the rusty pieces of tin serving as the shack's roof. Through a gaping hole, she looked up at the sky. Unlike the incandescent starlit heavens, Anele's coal-black eyes held no sparkle. She quickly pulled the threadbare bed sheet over her face. But sorrows marching in battalions swamped her under closed eyelids, disallowing her respite. Now an earlier incident was like an unbidden tune that replayed itself.

The scene was vivid.

* * *

Yesterday evening, at 7:00 P.M. sharp, the bell above the door in the raised brick basement rang several times. It was time to serve the evening meal to thirty-four-year-old Lord Alan Percival Hallworthy (Lord Nigel's grandson) and his Dutch-born wife, Lady Corrie, eight years his senior.

The three-course meal dished up on the second-floor dining room's long walnut table consisted of cream of tomato soup, roast chicken with new potatoes laced with fresh mint leaves, cinnamon glazed baby carrots, and an English trifle for dessert.

"You can leave now, Anele," Lady Corrie said. "I'll call you when we are done eating."

Not a thank you or, this meal looks delicious, ever passed the mistresses' lips on any given mealtime. That's how it was.

The savory victuals' aroma clinging to her clothing, Anele returned downstairs to set the younger kitchen staff—fourteen-year-old Maekela, a slender cheerful teenager and her younger sibling Isona, who, on the contrary, was short, rotund and sullen—to work. They were to scrub clean the pearl-grey enamel pots, wipe the counters, and mop the kitchen floor.

In the dank windowless scullery that housed two deep enamel sinks that had seen better days, the girls set about their chores. Behind them sat a recently purchased gasoline-powered washing machine, and next to it was a treadle sewing machine in a walnut frame.

While they worked, Anele took this opportunity to rest her aching legs from standing on them all day. She eased her ample derriere into a rocker and grimaced as she undid the laces of the undersized white leather oxfords and released her bare swollen feet. Oh, how she wanted to fling them into the garbage, along with the outdated servant's garb: a black A-line dress with long sleeves and lace cuffs, long, white cotton apron and mop cap—clothing that was unbearable in the heat, inside and outside of the kitchen.

Floorboards creaking beneath her, she cupped her chin in her hands and wondered why she waited so long to confront Lady Hallworthy about her overdue wages. Should she dare go up to their private quarters, the forbidden place for kitchen staff? Should she dare? Anele shuddered as she recalled what her predecessor, Cook Lamella, had told her: "Whatever you do, do not go upstairs to their quarters, or you'll learn the hard way." Cook added with sadness on her face, "One time, after the evening meal, I remembered that I'd forgotten to inform the Mistress about not having enough bacon for their breakfast and I wanted to know if I could cook them ham and eggs instead. So, I went upstairs in her private quarters. After screaming at me for disobeying the rules, she slapped me hard across my face several times. I never went up there again."

* * *

Nervous system jittery with angst, Anele rocked faster. The old floorboards now groaned in protest as she recalled that only the housekeeping staff knew how the other half lived upstairs, until one finally broke her oath of silence. It came as no surprise to Anele that her master and mistress led separate lives. She had witnessed the angry tirades hurled at each other across the dinner table. There was no love lost between them. Through the maid's broken promise, Anele had gleaned the couple had separate living quarters into which the other dared not encroach. They dined together only when convenient or necessary on social occasions.

Anele didn't give a hoot about her obnoxious employers or their dysfunctional marriage; she wanted only what was hers. A contemptuous smile pulled her lips upward. If she could get away with it, she'd murder them while they slept. Or better yet—the picture in her mind brought a sardonic grin—poison their food—

The bell above the swing-doors jangled.

It was time to clear the table.

Scrambling to her feet, Anele slipped her shoes back on and called out, "Maekela and Isona. Stop what you are doing! Get the clearing trays and follow me."

They rushed out of the scullery, got the trays, and followed Anele.

In the second-floor wood-paneled dining room, the twenty-foot banqueting table was empty, except for the clutter of dinner plates, side plates, tureens, sterling-silver utensils, and two fragile crystal wine glasses. Only the finest dinnerware for every meal, placed on hand-sewn linen tablecloths and napkins, was used. Anele never grasped this pomp and ceremony when less expensive dinnerware existed. This extravagance and why the dining room was situated upstairs and not sensibly closer to the kitchen had baffled her for years. Having to traipse up and down a long flight of stairs three times a day with serving trays was exhausting for all of them, especially since the dumbwaiter had been out of service for many years. Obviously, it was not a money problem. That last thought prompted her to caution her helpers. "Be extra careful. Don't drop a thing, or Lady H. will have a fit, and you won't see any wages for years."

The girls bent their knees in a mock curtsy and in unison responded, "Yes, Me Lady. You tell us this every day. And we haven't broken a dish, yet!"

"Cheeky little monkeys! Get off with you."

Anele watched the girls place a tray apiece on their heads, and gripping handles, they waltzed out through the wedged dining room door leaving Anele to her usual ritual.

She set about doing a task Corrie insisted on being done after every evening meal: polishing and buffing the table that in its heyday had seated royalty and the height of society. After this backbreaking chore was done, Anele placed in the center of the table the final touch—the huge crystal vase filled with fresh bird-of-paradise flowers. Before closing the room up for the night, there was one more task to take care of.

She knelt to check under the table. Her eyes circled the Persian rug on which the table sat, and to her delight there were not many crumbs to be seen.

"Great," Anele said out loud. *I can get away with not having to sweep up tonight.*

She gave the room a final look, deliberately averting her eyes from the oil painting—a life-size portrait of Lady Ethel Constance Hallworthy, Alan's deceased mother. Even though the dreadful woman was dead, the painted face was one Anele would rather forget. The mere thought of her previous mistress made her stomach churn and her skin crawl. The dowager's gracious façade charmed her friends, but behind closed doors, the woman wore another mask. Her soul was blacker than the black skin she detested. Not blood, but pure evil, coursed through Ethel's veins.

As if under hypnosis, Anele's fingers traced the thick ugly scars snaking down her left cheek, neck, and breast—a constant reminder of that horrible time when—

Even now, she felt herself swooning and had to take several deep breaths to steady herself. Forcing her incensed eyes away from the portrait, she flicked off the light switch, and made her way downstairs and headed straight for the scullery.

Maekela was at the sink, up to her elbows in soapsuds, and Isona was rinsing dishes. Anele leaned against the doorframe and stared at them. She was in two minds: Have them finish off their chores, or send them off to bed.

Yes. It would be wiser if they weren't here. If something were to go wrong… Anele inhaled sharply. She didn't want to think of the "what ifs." Having taken care of the orphaned girls for over a year, her protective, maternal love could not let anything happen to them. She almost felt as if they were hers.

She went over to Maekela and removed the scrubber from the older girl's hand.

"Leave the washing up to me. Take your sister and go to bed. We have to be up at four in the morning to get the Christmas food underway."

Squinting, Maekela asked, "Is something the matter, Anele?"

"No. Of course not," she replied glibly. "And when do you question my orders? Now, run along you two." Playfully, she slapped Maekela's backside and added, "Get going before I change my mind and find you something to do."

They threw their aprons into the laundry hamper and danced out through a side door into the dark of night to make the long trek back to the shack.

Anele glanced up at the electric clock. She couldn't read or write, but she could tell the time. It was 8:30 P.M. Was it too late? No, she didn't think so.

According to the housekeeper, the couple didn't go to bed until past midnight. Anele hoped this night wasn't going to be an exception. And yes, the risk was worth it.

She put on a clean apron and then made her way upstairs.

"It's now or never," she softly said, climbing the imposing staircase. The stairway seemed unending to their private quarters.

By the time Anele reached the top floor, she realized that she was unfamiliar with this part of the house and had no idea which room belonged to whom. Lord Alan was the last person she wished to encounter on this night or any night, as he was an all too real nightmare. From the very first day that she had met him, when she was nine years old, Alan had become more than just a bad dream. The thought of bumping into him sent shivers down her spine, and her courage threatened to give way. She wanted to run back downstairs, but found she could not move—her legs had turned to cement blocks. *You have to do it,* her inner voice urged. *You know you deserve the money. They owe it to you.*

Without her due, she wouldn't be able pay the white storeowner for the second-hand sewing machine he had sold her almost two years ago. He had given her until Boxing Day to come up with the money. "And not a day longer, Anele," he had said. "I'll not give you another chance to pay what you owe."

How she wished she hadn't placed her mark on the buyers agreement witnessed by Lord Alan. This long-term debt commitment— ten years—not only kept her legally chained— it forced her to beg for her pittance of a wage.

* * *

After Corrie's marriage in 1930 to the heir of Hallworthy Manor, the then nineteen-year-old Alan, the new Lady of the house took it upon herself to run the financial and operational management of the estate's affairs. With an iron will and tight fist, she governed the manor house and newly built sugar refinery while her husband supervised the day-to-day running of the sugar plantation. Subsequently, Corrie informed her household staff, "From now on, you will be compensated for your services."

Her words were hollow.

After years of working for food and lodging, Anele was offered in payment: five shillings a month—about one dollar in today's currency—that went to pay for the sewing machine.

Corrie's offer was also hollow.

She held their wages "in trust," and in turn this held *them* in bondage. Even if her servants wished to leave, they would be penniless. Where could they go with no money in their pockets? They could not afford travel fare, food, or accommodation even to seek employment elsewhere.

Nothing had changed since the slave days.

Every few months, Lady Corrie would dole out to them a small portion of their "saved" funds, with which they could purchase the barest of necessities, mainly second-hand clothing from the local market. Occasionally, Anele was able to "liberate" a few pennies from Lady Corrie's grocery money to oddments of material.

* * *

Now, stomach as tight as a sailor's knot, Anele approached the glowing light coming from underneath the nearest arched, dark-oak framed door. She knocked three times.

"Come in, Alan. The door is unlocked."

Breathing a sigh of relief that Corrie was alone, Anele entered timidly. She stopped mid-step on the blue wool rug and her jaw dropped. Never had she seen such sight. She stared in awe.

The sitting room was cluttered wall to wall with Victorian overlay, including several tripod tables adorned with porcelain figurines on hand-crocheted doilies and two brocade chesterfields draped with antimacassars. A walnut, long-case grandfather clock mournfully kept time in the corner. In the center of one wall was an Adams marble fireplace flanked by aspidistras in large brass pots

The only modern acquisitions were an electric phonograph playing an RCA Victor recording of "Smoke Gets in your Eyes," sung by Jeanette MacDonald, and a black cradle telephone resting on a rosewood occasional table.

Anele's open jaw snapped shut when her eyes connected with her employer, lounging in a green housedress, a cloud of cigarette smoke spiraling above her. Corrie, sporting a fashionable 1940's Veronica Lake hairdo, a curled lock of henna-dyed hair dangling over an eye, reclined in an oversized armchair. Wealth had granted expensive excess but had been frugal with her appearance.

The only daughter of a Dutch diamond dealer, not only was the forty-three-year-old's pallor severely pockmarked from childhood chickenpox, but her body overflowed like bread dough that had risen too high and needed pummeling. Her singular asset, exquisite violet eyes which to the servant looked like purple grapes, narrowed angrily. Anele averted her gaze and braced for a verbal thrashing. But only the tapping of Corrie's fingernails on the side table punctured the heavy silence.

She stubbed out her cigarette, straightened her back and in a flash her five-foot-two heavy-set frame sprang from the chair. "How *dare* you, Anele!" she hissed. "You know the rules. You're *never* supposed to come upstairs to my quarters. What are you doing here?"

The overbearing odor of too much Gardenia cold cream plastered on her employer's face wafted unpleasantly up Anele's nostrils. Arms stiffly at her sides, mouth dry as cinder, Anele stammered, "I'm s-s-sorry to disturb you, Mistress. I know I sh-shouldn't be up here, but—c-could I please have my wages tonight?" *There, I've said it!* She thought. Now the words rushed out of her mouth, "You see, Mistress. The man I bought my sewing machine from is hounding me—"

"Are you drunk? How dare you ask me for money! I paid you and your scullery girls only last week." Jabbing an index finger into her servant's shoulder, Lady Corrie continued her tirade, "Get out of here before I yell for the Master. If *he* finds out that you are badgering me for more money, he'll punish you."

Anele rolled her eyes. Had she heard right?

"Maybe it s-s-slipped your mind, Mistress," she countered softly. "Honest, I tell no lie. I haven't been paid in three months."

As if she'd eaten something sour, Corrie's face contorted. "One more word and you will be fired… you ungrateful *wog!* You'll not find employment anywhere, not if I can help it. Now get out of here! Don't ever again come to my quarters unless I summon you."

It took every ounce of Anele's willpower not to slam the door shut behind her. Her clenched fist longed to punch a hole in the wall or, even more satisfying, into the woman's ugly face. There was no doubt in Anele's mind that Corrie's threat about finding another job was real. No one else in the entire region would employ her. The Hallworthy woman would spread horrible lies; make it impossible for her to get work, food, or shelter. Even worse—she could end up in jail for some falsehood concocted by that Dutch shrew.

Although she wasn't going to get a penny for her labors, Anele had no intention of losing her source of bread and butter: work, leftover food, clean drinking water, and a leaky tin roof over her head were god-sent. The alternatives were bleak.

Daily, countless of her people went hungry, even starved to death. Many also slept under makeshift shelters. In the wake of World War II, domestic jobs were hard to find for not only the blacks but also for whites. Holocaust survivors arrived in droves after the war, and many scurrilous European citizens fled from Europe to save their hides and bank accounts from Hitler's hatchet men. Some, Anele learned from the whisperings of field workers, had paid big money to Alan to stay hidden on his isolated estate. When asked by refugees if he had served in the war, Alan had always responded, "The infantry wouldn't have me. I've got flat feet, and I'm color blind."

Untrue.

Money, and lots of it, paid for medical falsification and his final exemption.

* * *

Back down in the kitchen, Anele stood, arms limply at her sides, staring toward the scullery where her only possession was housed. She was angry but sad at the same time. Five long years of paying the Hallworthy finance company was more than she could bear. Tomorrow, the sewing machine surely would be repossessed. She thought of the girls and how they would react to the loss.

On their once-a-month free afternoon, the sisters strutted around the plantation like peacocks showing off their new outfits and matching bows for their hair that Anele had sewn for them. Now they would be robbed even of those small pleasures.

* * *

A lump in her throat, Anele lay on her back, opened her eyes, and refocused her gaze through the hole in the roof. Now the stars seemed to be billions of eyes mocking her—telling her that she alone was to blame for her entrapment on the white man's land.

Ah, if only…

Even Namandla, or even the whites' god for that matter, couldn't change the past, couldn't undo what she had suffered: innumerable beatings and rapes that had forever broken her once feisty African spirit.

From the tender age of twelve, she had become another of his victims. Alan had repeatedly forced himself on her, as he had done to most of his young black workers.

* * *

In 1931, when Anele was about thirteen, she couldn't hold down her food. The Hallworthy cook at the time, Lamella, had no doubt in her mind what was causing her young helper to vomit constantly. Cook had lost count of the girls made pregnant by Lord Alan and his father before him. She placed her hands on Anele's shoulders.

"Listen very carefully to what wise Lamella has to say without interrupting. You are with child. After work, I will take you to Kabila, the birthing woman who doesn't live far from here. She will give you some herbs so that the baby will not be born. No servant in this house is allowed to bear children. This baby cannot be born. Do you understand Anele?"

Anele scowled at Lamella.

After a moment's silence, tears welling, Anele stamped her foot. "Old lady, nobody is going to kill my baby! I *want* my baby even though it belongs to the white devil. I *will* run away and have it! I *will* take good care of it! I'll be a good mother!"

Lamella clucked her tongue. "Don't be so stupid, girl. Where will you run? You can't go home to your village with a white man's baby inside you. You'll be kicked out, and then where will you go? You need *money* to survive in the world outside here. You can hardly take care of *yourself!* No. You cannot give birth."

"I know several field workers who have had the master's babies and are raising them."

"That's different. They don't work in *this* house."

"Then I'll leave here and go work in the field!"

"I've heard enough!" Cook snapped. She grabbed hold of Anele's shoulders and shook her. "Anele, you will do as you are told as long as you are under my wing, or you'll end up like your sisters—" Cook loathed saying the word, but she had no choice but to shock Anele into reality "—dead!"

Anele wept.

After their work was done, Cook marched a crestfallen Anele to the birthing woman's hut. Kabila handed Anele a pouch and instructed, "Boil water, add the herbs I've given you, and drink it once it has cooled. In the morning your troubles will be over."

Kabila's foul-smelling and bad-tasting abortion concoction did not work.

Anele hid this truth and her swelling stomach by wearing one of Lady Ethel's discarded front-lacing corsets. Nine months later, she gave birth to a six-pound baby girl while alone in the shack. Lamella had left early to buy special food items for an upcoming birthday celebration and wasn't due back until later.

That happy day, Anele tenderly looked at her precious baby. Her heart said it all: *My baby girl fills a big hole in my life. I will be a good mother to her.*

Her elation was short-lived.

Anele's birthing cries had been heard by a passing field worker, who had peeked through the shack's doorway and alerted his boss, Lord Alan, who immediately mounted his steed and galloped to the shack. His face red with anger, he entered and strode to the bed. His arms outstretched, he asserted, "You can't keep the child, Anele. Give it to me."

"Don't take my baby," Anele begged. "I'll work harder for you, Master. The baby will be no trouble. I'll ask Kabila, the birthing woman, to mind her during my work hours."

"You know the rules, Anele. No husband or children are allowed to live on my property without my permission. Do not make me take the child by force—"

Like a raging windstorm, Lady Ethel, car keys gripped in her hand, blew through the doorway. "Damn you, Alan! This is the last time I'm going to tolerate your despicable behavior! I'm sure your wife won't be too happy with another half-caste bastard running about the place. Now give me the child."

Face flushing from his mother's outrage, Alan grabbed a piece of wood by the doorway and marched back to the bed. He glared into Anele's eyes, and then snarled, "It looks like you are not giving me much alternative."

The blow to Anele's head knocked her unconscious.

Alan lifted the baby from her limp arms and handed the wailing infant over to his mother. The sharp-tongued woman ordered, "Drive me back to the house, then come back here and take this black bitch to the hospital. I'll call them and make all the necessary arrangements."

Later, an unconscious Anele was dumped into the trunk of Lady Ethel's Bentley and driven to a hospital, "for blacks only," about thirty miles away.

Money passed hands.

A hysterectomy was performed.

Upon awakening, Anele's blurry eyes focused on the person standing at her bedside. "Where am I? Why am I in this strange bed with bars?"

The surgeon's eyes were kind, but his words spoke a cruel truth. "Child, I am also a victim of the white people's rules and must do as I'm told. I've had to operate on you and you will never bear a child again. What I'm trying to tell you is… if you wish to survive, you must learn to make the most of your life. You are young. Try to forget—and forgive—the evil that some men do, and move on."

Anele wanted to punch him in the mouth. His words were mere platitudes. Forget and forgive what Alan or Ethel had made the hospital do to her? *Never!* Had she a gun, she would have shot the surgeon, Alan, his wife, and his mother, and danced a jig on their graves.

Two days later, Alan turned up at the hospital to take his servant home. Though still in post-operative pain, Anele's grieving heart hurt the most. Tears streaming down her cheeks, she begged Alan to tell her what had happened to "their" child. He looked at Anele as if she was nothing but muck stuck to his boot.

"There's no use crying over spilt milk, Anele! The baby's gone. That's all there is to it!"

Anele longed for death. Why hadn't he just killed her, as he had her twin sisters? Now she was only half a woman—forever childless. Of course, she knew why—he obviously wasn't finished using her. There would be no more swollen belly to interfere with satisfying his depraved lust. Or else he would have just left her at the hospital.

* * *

Not long after her return from hospital, Alan's lust diverted to a much younger field worker, but not his verbal abuse toward Anele. He delighted in demeaning his cast-off victim: *Wog. Black whore,* were among his arsenal of obscenities hurled at her. Or he'd mock, "Found a boyfriend yet? No, I didn't think so! Who'd want an ugly, worn-out, black bitch whore like you?"

Gladly, she would have strangled him with her bare hands. The pleasure of the deed would have been worth the hanging—a rumor stopped her from killing the man she hated—that's if the story was true. It gave her hope and patience.

Through the plantation grapevine, she learned that her baby girl was *not* dead:

"Honest, Anele, as Namandla is my witness—" the young sugar cane cutter had said. "I saw it with my own eyes. The old white woman from the big house handed your baby to the Nigerian priest's wife."

"What Nigerian priest?"

"Father Batuzi."

"*Father Batuzi!* He's a Catholic priest… priests don't marry!"

"Yes, he *does* have a wife. I met her at Bible class last week. Her name is Nyasha and she's from Nigeria."

Anele scratched her head. "How do you know the baby was mine?"

"No one else birthed that day, Anele. You were the only one."

Heart somersaulting, Anele run as fast as her legs could carry her to the makeshift church at the edge of a field—only to learn from the priest's male helper that Father Batuzi had left two days earlier for Nairobi with a very pretty, and very young, Hallworthy field worker whose name he didn't know.

Numbed with the cruelties inflected upon her, Anele continued to endure this hellish bondage on the Hallworthy estate, mainly for the possibility of one day being reunited with her only child. She would gladly sell her soul to the Devil. Indeed, in a manner of speaking, she already had.

* * *

One leg dangling out of bed, Anele let out a long, slow sigh that sounded like a whistle. She was mentally and physically drained. How, she wondered, was she going to get through the backbreaking marathons of the Christmas Day meal preparations? The night and the wee hours of this day had plagued her with nightmares about things that, during the day, she shoved to the back drawers of her mind. If only her brain could be erased of its painful memories.

It was not likely.

As if it were yesterday, she was swept back to the day she and her twin sisters had had the misfortune to set foot on this unhallowed soil.

How could she ever truly forget, let alone forgive, what had transpired?

Chapter 2

Zululand, 1927

The Tswanas village, a remote Zulu settlement near Natal's northern border with Swaziland and Mpumalanga, was home to fifty-odd Nguni-speaking Zulus. They lived a simple, rural life as they had done before the Europeans inundated their land.

On a blistering afternoon in February, a naked nine-year-old girl, wet with perspiration, exited from her family's hut resembling an upside down basket. Squinting in the sun's glare, Anele eyes searched the village compound for her fifteen-year-old twin sisters, Thaka and Zhana. Normally, at this time, they would have returned from the nearby forest with firewood for the campfire meal. She wanted to tell them that she was feeling much better now, for her fever, the result of a spider's bite, had broken. She called over to a woman standing hands on hips near the communal fire pit, "Have you seen Thaka and Zhana?"

"No, and I'm annoyed," replied Mercy. "I've had to send another girl to collect wood, or we will not eat tonight."

The mere thought of food prompted Anele's next question. "What are you making this evening? I'm hungry."

The old woman sighed. "I'll make whatever the boys catch."

Anele hoped it wasn't monkey meat, yet again. This malodorous meal didn't sit too well with her delicate stomach of late. She was old enough to understand that the recent drought had starved most of their crops and livestock. So, the daily task of providing food for the village was left to the young boys.

Slingshots and spears in hand, they left the compound daily for the three-mile hike into a protected game reserve to poach. If they were lucky, their presence undetected by a warden, they targeted the dainty gazelle, gutted the deer on the spot, and hauled it back on a reed stretcher. But lately, the patrols had been stepped up, so they went hunting for whatever misfortunate creature happened to cross their path.

Hunger overcome by a more pressing bathroom need, Anele headed for dense shrubbery. There, she heard the sound of familiar voices whispering, which seemed to be coming from inside a tall clump of dried grass. Why were Thaka and Zhana hiding? Why were they not out collecting firewood? What were they whispering about? It was very strange indeed. Her first thought was to barge in and demand answers. Instead, she crouched down near the shrubbery, held her breath and bursting bladder, and strained her ears. She clapped her hand over her mouth. Were Thaka and Zhana *really* planning to *leave* the next morning without a word to anyone? But why? They knew the rules—unmarried girls had to ask permission from their father to leave the compound for any reason. Their father, Naboto Dingane, chieftain of the village, was a stickler for tradition. He had made it clear on more than one occasion: "Until you girls marry, you will obey me in every way, or I'll take a stick to you."

Anele crept closer. Now she didn't want to miss a word.

"What if we don't find work in the white township?" Thaka whispered. "How are we going to help our village if we don't get money to buy more cattle?"

"We will get work and then we will surprise Father," Zhana

assured her twin. "We will bring him lots of money to buy more goats, cows, sunflower seeds, millet, and vegetables."

Anele's mind raced like a thoroughbred horse. Yes, she too would help and join them on their crusade. She rushed into their hideout. "I heard everything," she blurted, her face flushed with excitement. "And I'm coming with you. I can work too."

Angry, Zhana, the first-born said, "Don't be so pig-stupid, Anele. You're far too young. We've heard from travelers passing through that the *umlungu* (white people) only hire strong boys and older girls to work in their fields." She smiled mischievously at her twin and added, "And maybe also find fine husbands."

Identical and inseparable, the gods had not bestowed upon the sisters countenances that excited would-be suitors. They were not pretty or tall like Anele. They were the total opposite: unattractive, extremely short, almost dwarf-like, with mottled skin, and their bellies were swollen like watermelons. And both had balked at accepting traditional marriages, much to their father's anger. They would not be married unless identical twin brothers came along. They *were* the only twins for miles.

Joined at the hip, the sisters devised a new plan. Taking over the leadership, Zhana spoke first, "Little sister, we both agree that you should take care of our widowed father when we are gone. He is much too sick to be left alone."

Taken to his bed, probably from the lack of nourishing food, Naboto was counting on his daughters to take care of his needs: bring him food, empty the urine pot, and bring him beer made from the Marula tree fruit. Anele scowled. She loved her father. But why should she be the one to take care of him? She had always allowed her headstrong sister, Zhana to manipulate her life, but this time she wasn't going to obey.

"There are plenty of single and married women to see to our widowed father's needs," Anele huffed.

"No, Anele," Zhana argued. "You must stay behind."

"Please, please, please, let me go with you."

"No."

"I'll go and tell father now," Anele threatened, "then you'll be beaten and tied up."

Zhana lunged at Anele. Hands on her sister's throat, the twin retorted, "I'll see to it that you won't see another day of your life if you dare tell father."

Thaka, the meeker of the two, took pity and came to Anele's rescue. "If *I* make her promise, she won't tell father."

Anele fell to the ground, choking and sobbing at the same time. Warm urine pooled around her legs. "I hate you, Zhana," she shouted, rubbing her neck. "You're bad. I hope you don't come back."

Anele would regret those words.

* * *

Her small breasts exposed to the rising sun, and wearing a straw skirt, several bead necklaces, and beaded headband, Anele stealthily followed the twins. After traveling for what seemed hours, she slipped on the precarious rocky path and tumbled down an embankment. Her loud shrieking stopped the twins in their tracks. Zhana kicked the dirt like a bull ready to charge. "She's in for a beating," she fumed. "That stupid child has followed us."

"No, Zhana, I won't let you beat her," Thaka responded. "I'm going back to see if she's all right."

She retraced her steps back to where Anele lay sprawled on the dirt and bent down to examine her sister's injuries, which were minor grazes to her forehead, knees, and elbows. Nothing serious— except for their predicament.

But what should she do? Take Anele back? No. They'd come this far. Without Naboto's permission, this was awkward to say the least. He'd beat them for sure. What concerned Thaka was the real reason not to go back—their father's undying hatred for the white race. He had voiced it often to them and others wishing to leave Tswanas.

Work for white people to help the village. Never! He would starve first.

* * *

In 1879, the newly appointed chieftain Naboto Dingane was thirty summers old when he led his tribesman into battle against the British. The call to arms to fight the white invaders was answered without question. Every able-bodied man and boy swore to defend his homeland and marched off from the village with their chief. This Anglo-Zulu war would take its toll on these brave men and boys.

Ambushed in the foothills of the Lebombo Mountains, they fought courageously. But their *assegais* (spears) were no match for the rifles of the white usurpers on horseback. Hemmed in, the small band of fighters finally succumbed to the odds. One by one they fell, trampled underfoot by the horses. Naboto was the last man standing when he took a bullet in the kneecap of his right leg. As he fell sideways, another projectile struck his upper body. He crashed to the ground bleeding profusely.

Triumphant soldiers callously walked over the bodies of the slain warriors, shooting anyone who twitched. Naboto feigned death. He lay face down on the reddened ground. Nearby lay the dead body of his nineteen-year-old brother, Geza. A gaping hole in his head marked the young man's end.

Naboto called out, "My brothers, speak to me. Are any of you still alive?"

There was no answer.

He called out again.

Only silence met his ears.

Was he the only survivor? Yes. And he would join his fallen brothers in death if he didn't make a move. Over to one side, he saw the many pairs of glowing eyes, jungle predators, just waiting to pounce on the fresh flesh.

Excruciating pain searing through his body, Naboto got up using his spear as a cane. He made it to dense undergrowth at the end of the killing field. Thorns attacked his feverish flesh as he looked for somewhere to rest up until daylight. In Naboto's mind, there was enough food for the scavengers not to bother coming after him.

Hidden as best he could in the deep cavity of a decaying tree trunk, he heard the night-spilling roar of a dominant male lion warning the pride: he had first pecking order. The thought of his friends being torn apart made Naboto angry. He cried for revenge. "Ikloba, Dark Spirit of the Invisible Kingdom, strike the *umlungu* from our land with your tongue of fire. Sweep them into the ocean with your breath. Bring disease to all those who have spilt the blood of our brave warriors."

In the weeks that followed Naboto's return to Tswanas, he slowly recovered. But nothing could salve his wounded spirit. Thoughts of the massacre and the death of so many, especially his brother, being the sole survivor would torment him for the rest of his life.

* * *

Little Anele hadn't intended to cause this raised conflict between her sisters.

"I'm sorr*eeee*," she apologized in sing-song, avoiding eye contact with the angry Zhana. "I'll watch where I'm going so I don't fall again. And if I do trip up, you can leave me. I'm sure some animal will find me tasty."

Thaka laughed.

Zhana didn't. The unsmiling twin urged, "Let's go now before we lose too much daylight."

* * *

It took them four days to trek the two hundred miles along the coastline to the township of Durban in the province of Natal. Walking during the day, and sleeping in the boughs of tall, Mountain Karee trees at night, the exhausted trio finally reached their destination.

Their meager rations of dried monkey meat long ago consumed, pangs of hunger and thirst were pressing on their weary bodies. It was Thaka who spotted the fast-flowing irrigation ditch paralleling the rows of tall sugar cane plants. "Water! Water!" she cried.

They drank until their stomachs rebelled against another drop. Then nature called.

Squatted in the open, the three girls emptied their bladders but cut short the flow when they heard a fast-approaching thunderous noise louder than all their village drums beating in unison—galloping hooves. An animal they had never seen before was charging toward them. Terrified, the twins stood like statues, but not Anele. She flung herself back into the ditch. Flat on her stomach, she clung to the mossy embankment as if her life depended on it.

Mounted on a black stallion, sixteen-year-old Alan Hallworthy halted his steed within inches of them. His jaw jutting, he yelled in a refined British accent, "Get off my property! *Now!* If I catch you stealing sugar cane, I'll shoot you."

The twins couldn't understand his language but, by his tone and gestures, recognized his anger. They fell to their knees, screaming.

A teenaged black field worker heard the commotion and made his way over to investigate. When the twins saw one of their own, their words spewed out like burst drainpipes. The sugar cane worker nodded and then turned to his boss. "The girls are not here to steal... they want work," Kelingo said.

As if inspecting cattle, Alan's lynx-like eyes hidden behind sunglasses checked them over. They, in turn, stared back at the sun-bronzed, high cheek-boned blonde man whose youthful handsome appearance was deceptive. For lurking behind his striking good looks was a ruthless, sadistic person, the malignant side of humanity, with a twisted evil brain inherited from his mother.

The devil himself on horseback, Alan pointed with his riding crop. "Okay. You girls follow me. I'll give you some hoes and you can begin work..." His mouth opened wide when he saw Anele's head pop up from the ditch. The twins followed his astonished gaze. "That is my younger sister, Anele," Thaka said. "She was scared. But she will also work hard for you."

Kelingo translated.

Alan pulled a face. "I don't want the kid," he huffed. "She's stick thin. She wouldn't last a day in the fields."

Dutifully, Kelingo told the girls what Alan had said. The twins protested in unison: "Please, my little sister may be thin, but she is as strong as a bull elephant."

Hiding behind Zhana's back, Anele jabbed her sister in her spine. In a small voice, she pleaded, "I want to go home. I'm scared of the white man—"

"You wanted to come with us!" Zhana stressed sharply.

Anele stamped her foot. "If I was older, I'd slap you, Zhana."

"That's never going to happen, puny child," the twin countered.

Alan's laughter sounded like a hyena's chortle. He understood Zulu. But he wasn't going to let on. Instead, he said to Kelingo in English, "Tell these ignorant bush girls that I'm in a good mood today. The skinny one can work at the house if my mother has work for her. But if Mistress Ethel says no, then send her off. I don't want her hanging around here. Is that clear?"

"Yes, Boss."

Placing a firm hold on Anele's upper arm, Kelingo told her, "You have to come with me."

"No, I won't," Anele shrieked.

Kelingo fastened his grip.

The twins looked anxiously at their struggling sister. "Where are you taking her?" Zhana asked.

"To the master's house—"

Somehow freeing herself from Kelingo's grip, Anele ran to over to Zhana and gripped her hand with such a fierce hold the twin cried out, "Stupid girl, you're hurting me!" She yanked away her hand. "Do as you are told for once. You wanted to help, now's your chance. Stubborn sister, I should take a stick to you. Go and work in the white man's house. We need the money, remember? And don't worry. Hopefully, we will see you when our work is done."

Anele chose not to respond but shot Alan the evil eye. Then, in a warlike stomp, she marched up to Alan and boldly spat a glob of phlegm on his footwear. "Ugly *umlungu!* You can't make me go where I don't want to go. I won't be separated from Thaka and Zhana. I'll work with them."

Alan's charitable conduct switched gears.

Jugular vein pulsating, face flushing dark as a summer storm, and now in perfect Zulu, he roared, "This stick insect has the nerve to hit me and talk to me like that! How shall I teach her a lesson, Kelingo? Should I whip her? Or blow her head off?"

Before Kelingo could utter a word, Anele grabbed hold of the dangling horse rein and, tugging hard, yanked the horse's head down. The steed bucked, nearly throwing off its rider. "Whoa!" Alan commanded, bringing his horse to heel. "Black bastard!" he yelled at Anele. "I've a good mind to get down and knock the shit out of you. Or better still, shoot you."

Anele didn't need a translation. Alan's face and tone said it all.

"You hurt me, white man," she taunted, "and I'll run back home and fetch my father. He is a Zulu warrior. He will chop you up with his long *assegai*. You'll bleed like a pig from this spear—"

The deliberate maneuvering of his horse sent Anele flying backward. She fell hard in the dirt. Face down, cradling her head, she sobbed.

Alan dismounted. As if he had all the time in the world, his abdomen in, his chest out, he strolled over to the sprawled child, raised the leather crop past his shoulders, and brought down it across her bare shoulders. Anele's shrieks of agony pierced the air. The twins were chilled by what they saw but made no move to help their sister. Eyes wide as saucers, they just stared. Was this really happening? This flogging was nothing like what their father doled out for disobedience. It was as if the white boy intended to beat

Anele to death.

When Anele's blood-curling screams continued, Thaka, the compassionate soul, couldn't take it. Her agonized heart bursting, she begged Alan. "Please, *umlungu-man* stop! She is a foolish child. She didn't mean to harm you or your beast."

Slapping his blood stained crop against his knee-length boots, Alan's face twisted into a grim scowl. He gave Thaka a how-dare-you-interrupt-me look and was about to say something to her when a noisy flock of sunbirds distracted him, so he didn't see Thaka's hands reach down and, in a mighty shove, push Anele out of harm's way. Alan's next strike hit Anele's savior full in the face.

Blood pouring from the gash, Thaka too let out a high-pitched screech.

Fists clenched in helpless fury behind his back, Kelingo looked down at the ground. His facial muscles twitched as though he could feel the lash cutting into his own skin.

Alan raised the crop once more to flog at whoever got in his way.

Anele scrambled to her feet and, like a rabbit pursued by a cheetah, raced toward the tall sugar cane rows, the twins following on her heels.

Cobalt blue eyes fire-red with rage, Alan's expression spoke for itself. He remounted his stallion, galloped after them, his finger on the trigger of his rifle. The inseparable twins, hand-in-hand, were his first target. He leveled his weapon and aimed. BOOM. BOOM. Smoke curled from the muzzle as the two shots rebounded. Without uttering a sound, Zhana and Thaka dropped dead. The air was rent by the frenzied screeching of pink-plumed parrots fleeing nests built in the Marula trees.

Screaming, Anele turned back. She fell on the bodies of her dead sisters, hugging them. She would have met the same fate if it weren't for Kelingo.

Every breath a gasping effort as he reached the scene, Kelingo stretched wide his arms and, blocking his employer's next aim, he pulled Anele behind his thin frame. "Please let the child live," he pleaded. "She didn't mean to say bad things. She's an ignorant bush girl. If you let me, I'll take her to the house just like you asked me to do."

In a chameleonic switch, Alan smiled warmly at the trembling Anele as if he were merely out for an afternoon ride. His voice was soft, almost tender. "Be a good girl and go with Kelingo. Forget what has happened here and you'll be fine. Work hard for Mother and you'll be rewarded." He turned to Kelingo and gestured with the butt of his rifle toward the sprawled bodies. "After you have taken the kid to the house, I want you to go and get your brother from the fields, come back here, and clean up this mess."

"What do you want us to do?" Kelingo asked.

"I don't care… bury… burn… whatever," Alan said. He scratched his chin. "On second thought, put them down the old water well. You know where it is, Kelingo."

Without a backward glance, Alan galloped off.

Too shocked to speak, Anele looked horror stricken at the death scene. Kelingo's heart wrenched with pity. "You don't know how lucky you are! Work hard and don't get into trouble. These white people are your masters now."

My masters? Never! Anele wanted to shout. But it seemed as if her tongue was glued to the roof of her mouth.

Gently but firmly, Kelingo pulled Anele away from the grisly scene. She would walk away with her life. But for this young innocent, she would soon wish she had died along with her sisters.

Shoulders sagging and chin pressed against her bloodied chest, Anele dragged her dust-covered feet on the hour walk to the manor. She was pushed into the kitchen.

Surprised, forty-one-year-old Lamella stopped kneading the bread dough. She stared at the pair as if two-headed creatures had entered her spotless kitchen.

Wiping her hands on her pinafore, she confronted Kelingo. "Why have you brought this filthy girl in here?"

"I was told to bring her here."

"Who told you that?"

"Master Alan," Kelingo replied quietly.

Scene by scene, he replayed to his aunt the heinous slaughter of the innocent teenagers. Cook wasn't shocked. She had known Alan from birth. He had his mother's evil streak. And it wouldn't be the first time Alan had caused the death of a lowly black worker or defiled a female. She hated to think how many unmarked graves dotted the vast estate. But, if reported, she knew that the white police force would only laugh the matter off. The privileged son of a titled family could never do such a thing! Alan would get away with any crime he fancied committing. Black people were dispensable.

"He should be dragged through the field and flogged," she muttered.

"I had better get back to the fields before *he* takes it upon himself to shoot *me* as well," Kelingo announced, jolting the cook back to the present. He turned to the sad-eyed child standing mutely by his side and touched her bloodied cheek. "I'm sorry that you had to go through all this, so young and all. But you will be safe with Lamella here. You can trust her. She is one of us."

Her arms limply at her sides, Anele was afloat in a silent, numbed world.

Cook's ample bosom rose up and down as she heaved a mighty sigh of resignation and regret. There was nothing she could say or do that would make the hellish ordeal the child had undergone any better. Like her mother before her, the cook had worked in the manor since she was ten.

Lamella took Anele by the hand and led her through the servant's entrance to the outside washhouse forty feet away. In the fieldstone building with sealed windows and a low, flat, sloped roof, a huge copper pot boiled on the hearth of the fireplace. The smoke from the crackling wood spiraled up through a brick chimney. The heat in the room was worse than any African summer Anele had known.

"This is where you will wash the dishes, pots and pans, and table linens," Cook said. "You will also sleep in here until the Mistress says it's alright for you to share the servant's shack with me. But first, it's time for your bath. You smell worse than the hog I butchered yesterday."

She lifted the heavy cauldron, poured the boiling water into the plugged stone sink, and then retrieved a bucket of cold water near the doorway. She removed Anele's sodden, blood-spattered skirt, lifted the feather-light child into the sink, and reached for a bar of carbolic soap. After rinsing the suds off, Lamella scratched her head. What could she put on the child? A thought popped into her head.

She rummaged through a laundry basket and extracted a garment. Miles too big, a discarded cotton petticoat belonging to Lady Ethel hung past Anele's feet. Under better circumstances, the cook would have laughed. But she nudged the child and pointed, "Sit there on that stool."

Anele did as she was told.

Giving her a wordless don't-you-dare-move-a-muscle look, Lamella added, "I'll be back in a moment."

Cook stepped outside the washhouse and slid the bolt to lock the wooden door, then made her way back through the farmhouse kitchen and up the forbidden staircase.

Upstairs on the first floor, she found her fifty-five-year-old mistress in the sunroom, tending to an array of flowering pot plants. A look of displeasure darkened Ethel's face. "You know you're not allowed upstairs without my permission. What are you doing here, Lamella?"

Lamella rushed to explain, "Mistress, something terrible has happened."

She repeated Kelingo's story.

Poker-faced, Ethel asked, "Where is the child now?"

"I've locked her in the washhouse, Mistress."

"Keep her there until I've had a word with my son." Ethel beckoned with a wave of her hand. "Follow me, Cook."

Lamella followed her employer.

From a writing desk in an adjacent room, Lady Ethel removed a work contract, backdated it by a month, and handed it to Lamella. "Have the child place her mark and bring it back to me. It will prove that she couldn't have been anywhere near the fields. But I'm not going to be too concerned about this *problem,* she emphasized. "So far, touch wood," Ethel tapped the desk. "Nobody has come here inquiring about missing black relatives." Her eyes seemed to bore through Lamella's. "And don't breathe a word of this to anyone."

Lamella nodded and took the document handed to her. She hated deceit.

By signing this paper, as she herself had once done years ago, Anele's freedom, like her own, would be forfeited. The work contract in bold letters outlined the fact that the individual would work for the Hallworthys until such time as the owner saw fit to release her. Lamella could never tell this innocent child this horrible fact—at least, not now. Anele would get to live, and not end up like her sisters, buried down a well somewhere on the estate.

Lamella's heart grew heavy when she heard the sound of mournful weeping as neared the washhouse. She undid the security bolt and gathered the sobbing girl in her arms. "Don't cry, child. Lamella is going to take care of you."

In the pain-melting warmth of the cook's embrace, Anele's once silent voice now begged, "I want to go home to Tswanas."

"Oh, sweet child, you can't."

"You can find the way to my village, old lady."

"Not so much of the old! And even if I did know where you lived, I couldn't take you."

"Why not?"

"Because, child, they'd find us…" Lamella shook her head. "We would end up like your sisters. Let's not talk about running away…" Quickly, she changed the subject. "How would you fancy a nice warm bowl of vegetable soup and a glass of fresh goat's milk?"

"No."

"It will do you good to eat, even a little something."

"No."

"Child, when did you eat last?"

Anele remained tight lipped.

Recognizing the futility of the argument, Lamella had a more pressing matter to deal with and pulled the piece of paper from her apron pocket. Guided by Cook's hand, Anele unquestionably placed her mark on the dotted line. Lamella sighed, folded the contract, put back it in her pocket, and patted Anele on the shoulder. "There is some old sheets in the corner, put them on the floor and get some sleep. I'll look in on you later."

She left Anele in the locked washroom while she busied herself in the kitchen. Another pair of hands would have been welcome, but she didn't have the time to teach her new helper. She was now behind schedule for the evening meal. When Lamella finally got through the evening chores, it was past ten. Before departing for the servant's shack, she poured a glass of milk and filled a bowl with soup, then headed for the washhouse carrying the tray. There she found little Anele curled up in the laundry basket. Lamella placed milk and soup on a shelf in the washhouse, just in case the girl grew hungry enough to swallow her anger and pride.

* * *

Lamella arrived back at her workplace at five the next morning. She unlocked the washhouse door, stepped in, and noted the empty glass standing in the middle of the floor. But no sign of the child. Where was she? She couldn't have gotten out. The windows were sealed, and the door was bolted fast.

Hiding behind the door, Anele pounced upon Lamella and pinched the puzzled-looking cook's generous behind. Her heart racing, Cook grabbed Anele's shoulder. "Child, you nearly scared me half to death! But it seems you are rested and ready for work. It will take some of that silly energy out of you."

* * *

Young Anele's long workday began in the outside washhouse. Up at four in the morning, she slaved in the merciless room until past ten in the evening. Although no stranger to hard work around her village, the traipsing to and from the kitchen with heavy trays of clean dishes, pots, and pans was a challenge for a nine-year-old. The washing and starching of table linens by hand was what she hated the most. The gooey starch always stuck to her fingers, and the smell made her constantly sneeze. But Anele never grumbled. Hard work would help stem the tide of anger that threatened to engulf her. Although there wasn't a day that passed that Anele didn't miss her father, sisters, and the life she'd left behind, she endured.

* * *

Several months went by.

On a fine April morning, Lamella set Anele to work washing the breakfast dishes in the newly installed scullery off the kitchen. Anele was happy not to have to go outside to the old washhouse. With only a cold-water faucet installed in the scullery, cooking and washing water still had to be boiled. It was Anele's job to make sure the kettle on the range in the kitchen was always on the go. On this particular day, Lamella had kneaded dough, prepared a leg of lamb, and done other cooking duties, then sat down to take a five-minute break. Sitting in the rocker, she rubbed her aching feet. As soon as Anele stepped through the door from hanging laundry outside, Cook called her over. "Child, Lamella's legs hurt today. Would you like to help me?"

"What is it that you want me to do?"

"Sweet, sweet child, I know that you are not happy to be here, but I am blessed to have you in my life. I'd like you to place the potato pan on the stove, fill it with cold water, and when it begins boiling, add a spoon of salt, then put the washed and peeled sweet potatoes…" Lamella gestured with her finger, "there in the bucket, straight into the pot. Can you do that?"

Anele gave Lamella an "of course" nod.

The pot containing the water weighed more than Anele. Somehow she found the strength to lift it onto the back burner of the coal-burning range without disturbing the dozing woman.

Prodding a sweet potato, Anele frowned. She didn't want to wake the cook, but she was unsure. She tapped Lamella's shoulder. Startled, the cook bolted upright. "What is it? How long have I been asleep?"

"Not long. But I don't know when they are done?"

Cook's sleepy brown eyes twinkled at the child. "The knife should slip through the potato without force."

Anele rushed over to the stove and stabbed one. "No," she said. "The knife sticks."

Lamella clicked her tongue. "Then they are not *quite* ready, silly girl."

A few minutes passed and Anele tried again. "They're done," she exclaimed, unable to contain the slight surge of victory. Cook's face—as broad and plain and dark as the bottom of a burnt pie pan broke into a smile. "I'm coming."

She was making her way to Anele waiting at the stove when, from behind them, came the swishing of taffeta and the strong odor of Lily of the Valley cologne. Lady Ethel glided into the kitchen. Topping her long, shiny skirt was a frilly, white lace and chiffon blouse with dainty pearl buttons fastening the neckline. The garment looked uncomfortably tight, as if it would strangle the large woman should she attempt a deep breath. A round diamond brooch pinned to her blouse reflected the light of her blue and green skirt.

Anele stared at the tightly corseted figure whose constricted waistline looked positively deformed. She did not know whether to laugh at her outrageous attire or be afraid, for immediately upon the woman's entry into the kitchen, Cook's cheerful face had stiffened.

Lady Ethel gave Anele a demonic glare. "Go to the washhouse, you filthy savage!" Her heavily rouged cheeks reddened even more. "Since when did I give *you* permission to cook *our* food? God knows *what* is under your filthy fingernails!"

Wrinkling her nose as if she had trod on something nasty, Lady Ethel snapped at her cook, "Lamella, you of all people should know better than to let this heathen near my stove!"

Anele stepped boldly forward. Hands defiantly on her hips, she said, "Don't you dare shout at Lamella! She is sick today. I offered to help her, that's all."

Unfortunately for Anele, Lady Ethel understood every Zulu word.

Furious, Ethel had raised the pan to chest level and with a mighty swing flung the contents at Anele. She tried to duck, but it was too late. The scalding water struck her with such force that it sent her reeling backward. The back of her head hit the metal bin used for vegetable peelings.

"That will teach you to be flippant," Lady Ethel snarled. "You will show me respect, girl, or I will fetch my son. He will skin you alive if I tell him you had the cheek to talk back to me." Snapping shut her teeth, Ethel flung the oven cloths and the empty pot onto the floor, and then her pointed ankle-laced boots thudded from the kitchen.

Color washed from her face, Anele looked at the scalded neck flesh stuck to her palm and screamed in shock, "Namandla, please help me! I'm dying!"

Lamella rushed to the sink, drenched a cloth in cold water, and, kneeling beside the wailing child, placed it on her burned flesh. Anele let out another blood-curling scream. The ice-cold water had seeped onto her developing left breast. Her nipple, like the rest of her burns, felt on fire. She wept in pain, "Lamella, that bad woman has blistered my womanhood."

"Whatever do you mean?"

"Look at my breast. How will I be able to give milk to my children when the time comes?"

"Oh, you poor child, it's my fault," Lamella cried. "Take your arms away. Let me have a look."

"No."

Thinking only of fleeing from this horrible place, Anele unsteadily got up. With one hand clutching the worst of the burns at her neck, she fled the kitchen to the outside, where her eyes darted frantically. She remembered seeing a fishpond not far from the washhouse. Yes, there it was! She raced toward it, flew down the steep embankment, and jumped into the pond. Thank goodness it wasn't too deep, because she couldn't swim.

The cold waters chilled Anele's burning flesh, but not her anger. She hated that white woman and her son. With a blaze no amount of water could extinguish, Anele's hate-filled heart was bursting. She'd never feel safe again. She must get as far away from this dreadful place as possible. She must! But how and when? Her home was in the heartland of the Zulu kingdom and might as well have been at the ends of the earth. Without someone to guide her, she could never find her way back home.

While tiny goldfish swam around Anele's immersed body, her young mind tried to make sense of why she'd come to this awful house in the first place. She sobbed into her hands. She wanted to blame the twins. But, as young as she was, Anele knew that she alone was really to blame. Had she stayed home and not attached herself to her runaway sisters, none of this would have happened.

A large bullfrog hopped onto a lily pad, snatched a hovering insect, eyed the person invading his feeding ground, then disappeared back into the murky water. Anele watched the amphibian with sightless eyes. Her mind saw only her father and remembered how he had always hated the white man. Anele had never understood his wrath. Now she did.

Still submersed in the pond, an eerie chill, along with the painful burning, crept over her. Like her father's, Anele's heart turned to stone.

Chapter 3

Patches of mist hovered on the hillside high above the Hallworthy workers' shanty on this Christmas morning of '45. Inside, Anele lay still, her thoughts adrift. Incredibly, the scalding incident and her sisters' horrible demise now seemed a lifetime ago—as was Lady Ethel Hallworthy's death. Four and a half years after Anele's disfigurement, Lady Ethel died in a car accident, a head-on collision, while visiting friends in Port Elizabeth. Behind closed doors, Lamella and Anele had rejoiced that day. They had held hands and done a gleeful "a-ring-a-ring-a-rosy" dance around the kitchen. Their smug happiness was short-lived, however. Ethel's successor, Lady Corrie Hallworthy, was by far the worse of the two evils. She and her cruel husband were well suited.

Anele heard the crowing of a cockerel and sighed heavily. It was time to get up and get ready to go to work.

She reached for her uniform and underclothes, a pair of rayon briefs with ribbed leg bands and a camisole that was tucked underneath the mattress. Clothing in hand, she tiptoed toward the doorway. A sleep-filled voice stopped her. "Is it time to get up, Anele?" Maekela asked.

"No, it's not," Anele answered. "I'm just going to get a breath of air, that's all. Be quiet, or you'll wake your sister. I'll tell you when it's time to get up."

Outside, slumped on the hard ground, Anele buried her face in her palms. Her thoughts skittered and tumbled like a gerbil on a wheel. Could she pull it off? What will happen to her if they find her? Would she go to prison? Or would she simply disappear like the bodies of her sisters? Reason gave her a shake: *Think about it. They'll be gone until lunchtime. I know you're tired, but think fast.*

Anele got to her feet and hurriedly dressed. She knew what she had to do before she lost her nerve. As she wrapped a bright-red fringed headscarf over her knotty hair, sadness tore at her heart. Anele desperately wanted to go back inside… whisper her goodbyes to Maekela and Isona, but she knew it wasn't wise. They had been her only family since the old cook had gone.

* * *

Shortly after Lady's Ethel's death, Anele had awoken to find Lamella missing from the bed they shared in the shack. Thinking she had already left for work, Anele hurried to the manor kitchen. Lamella wasn't there, but Corrie, clad in a brown V-neck frock, was.

"Anele, I've been waiting for you," Lady Corrie said snappily, handing the astonished girl the week's menu instructions. "You are the cook now."

Anele was more than surprised. "Why am I the cook now? Where's Lamella, Mistress?"

"She wasn't in the best of heath, you know. So I gave her permission to return to her home, to die in her own bed."

Anele didn't buy Corrie's explanation. Yes, Lamella had varicose vein problems but wasn't sick—not as far as Anele was aware. And Lamella would never have left the estate without saying goodbye to her. Why had Corrie made up this ridiculous tale? Had something terrible happened to Lamella?

Regardless, Anele had little choice but to take over Cook's duties. She had learned much from her friend and could tackle any menu put before her. Working alone in the big kitchen was hard on Anele, and Lamella's sudden disappearance had left a big hole in her heart. She felt lost, but Maekela and Isona filled that void of emptiness.

Not long after Anele had started her new position, Lady Corrie announced that help in the kitchen was on its way. Now it was Anele who assumed the guardian role that Lamella had once provided her.

Anele learned that the sisters with cobalt blue eyes had been wandering around the estate after their mother, a Bantu field worker, had died from sunstroke. Or so it was said. Their plight was announced to Lady Corrie who, for some unknown reason, because she was far from compassionate, offered the girls as helpers.

* * *

Anele hoped with all her heart that Alan's offspring wouldn't take the brunt for what she was about to do. "Ah," she sighed. "I should've done this years ago."

Trying to quell the butterflies fluttering in her belly, Anele took several deep breaths then, jaw tightened and lips compressed, she picked up the corner of her black dress, clenched the material tightly in her right hand, and started running. It wasn't bravery propelling her legs, it was the unexpected.

Halfway down the pathway leading to the manor, her lungs over-heated, a panting Anele slowed down and rested her back against a gum tree. Her head filled with questions: Could they have changed their minds and not told her? What if they were still at home? Then her bid for freedom would be in vain.

Earlier on in the week, Lady Corrie had informed Anele that, after their Christmas Eve meal, they were going to attend a party held at the home of Mr. S. J. Smith, the newly appointed Mayor of Durban. It was their intention to return around noon on Christmas day. "Make sure dinner is ready for bang on seven o'clock. You know how the Master hates waiting for his food."

Anele's pace quickened. *So, what if they are there. Changed their mind about attending the party,* she self-argued. *They sure won't be up this early. They won't hear me entering the kitchen. They never do. But there is always a first time!*

The break of day began to stir with life: the cockerel continued to crow, brightly-plumed parrots swooped on sluggish insects, guinea fowl darted for cover, and toads croaked mating calls.

Ahead, Anele could see the alley of oak trees leading to the mansion. Like the enamel coating on the sinks in the old scullery, the house had seen better days—neglected after Lord Peter, Alan's father. The Greek columns surrounding the house were cracked, chipped in places, and badly in need of a coat of paint. The intricate wrought-iron balustrades on balconies were obscured by thick, dead ivy. The once magnificent plantation home looked positively ghostly in the morning mist.

From Lamella, Anele had learned of the manor's diabolical history. Saddened by this story, she had visited the slave building that now lay in ruins on the northern edge of the estate. Anele fled the place within minutes and later told Cook that she had heard the woeful, haunting cries of the dead—ghosts trapped within its walls of hell.

From that day on, Anele had vowed never again to set foot near the place.

* * *

Now, not unlike those wretched slaves, Anele's heart thumped against her chest as she waited under an oak tree. The house was in total darkness, but that didn't mean the childless couple weren't there. Anele pondered over a fact: If they had changed their minds about going to the party, her mistress would have driven to the shack and would have told Anele to prepare Christmas Day breakfast.

Stealthily she dashed down the alley, weaving around large sculptures at the end of the rows until she came to the garage. Pressing her face against a side windowpane, she made out the dark shape of a half-ton pickup. The spot where the family's car, a black Ford, was normally parked was empty. She let out a cautious sigh of relief. But her relief soon turned to doubt. Could one of them have stayed home? The couple was always at loggerheads.

Anele had often seen Alan storm out the front door, get in the car or truck, drive off, and be gone for days. She had seen Corrie do the same.

Nervous perspiration beaded Anele's forehead as she made her way around the house and slipped the heavy brass key in the lock.

Inside the kitchen, she moved an oblong rug concealing the trap door leading to an underground cellar, another forbidden area for servants.

In the cold, dungeon-like space, Anele wrestled with a heavy bolt. A loud creaking of its hinges the door opened and, stepping into the storage area, she gaped at the overstocked shelves extending from floor to ceiling. On the shelves were hundreds of canned jars: vegetables, jams, butter, pickles, relish, cornmeal, and an assortment of dried goods. Lady Corrie had carried on her mother-in-law's obsession to stockpile food. Anele wondered why white people hoarded stuff like squirrels but never used it up. The waste was wicked when so many black people went hungry.

The concrete flooring was icy cold on her bare feet as Anele sought out food to sustain her: a bag of cornmeal, dried milk powder, two cans of condensed milk, several jars of various jams, and a handful of deer jerky strips. She also managed to squeeze three glass bottles of imported English beer into an overflowing picnic basket. She couldn't wait to drink one of the whites-only beverages instead of *umncindo*—strong beer made from sourdough that was popular with the field workers. Once she was far from here, she'd toast her employers' bad health.

Satisfied with her selection, Anele was about to leave the dungeon when she spotted the scurrying grey mouse. Instinctively, she reached for the broom by the door, and then her heart softened, and she withheld the blow. "Help yourself, little creature," she said to the rodent, its tiny, beady black eyes flashing with fear. A smile creased Anele's lips as she watched the mouse disappear through a tiny hole in the floorboards. "Eat whatever you like before someone finds you," she whispered on her way up the cellar ladder.

Glad to be out of the dingy hole, Anele set the heavy basket down on the floor, closed the trapdoor, and ensured the rug didn't appear to be disturbed. She happened to glance over to the double window above the sink, and her eyelids shot up. *I couldn't have been that long down there,* she thought. With the fingers of bright sunlight already poking though the ivory net drapes, it was her cue to get going, and quickly.

Though it wasn't unusual to be in the kitchen before the girls, Anele wanted to be long gone before they arrived. She couldn't bear to see them break down when they learned of her intention to get the hell out of this place and never come back. She was just about to leave the place where she'd slaved for the better part of her life when a thought crossed her mind.

In the scullery, Anele rummaged through the ironing basket and removed a bias-cut full-length flared navy skirt and a white crepe blouse belonging to Lady Corrie. Anele stripped and put on the outfit. A smug smile on her face, she scrunched her uniform into a ball, returned to the kitchen area, and flung it into the scraps bin along with her white work shoes. Staring at the bin, she shook a fist: "Never again," she vowed, "will I eat leftover white food or wear a stupid uniform! Nor will anyone ever again speak down to me!"

Bitterness rising like bile, Anele went to the fridge, removed the fresh turkey covered with thick, fatty bacon and placed it on the butcher's block. Then from under the kitchen sink, she retrieved a dark blue box containing DDT—insecticide. Her fingers pummeled a handful of dry powder into the stuffing. If it didn't kill them, it would at least keep them in the lavatory for days. That thought amused Anele immensely.

Cackling like someone crazed, she was now ready to leave the

awful residence that had been—a place to work—a place to live—
and a place to die. But no more.

A handful of notes and change from the copper teapot stuffed in
her skirt pocket, Anele tossed the kitchen door key into the nearby
thorny shrubbery, lifted the heavy basket onto her head, and in
perfect balance, set off.

The best route to take, she reckoned, was through the overgrown
bush rather than the more risky back road leading from the estate.
Without travel documents signed by Lord Alan, Anele could face
scrutiny by the white police officers who often patrolled these roads
leading to the Valley of a Thousand Hills. God knows what would
happen if they searched her and found the wad of bills in her
pocket. No black person ever earned that kind of money, not even
for years of labor. Oh, there were times when Anele had been
tempted to dip her hand into the grocery money just to hang onto
her precious sewing machine…

It didn't matter now.

Walking the path wary as an alley cat, Anele followed the trail
that led past the old slave ruins. Holding the basket with one hand,
she used her free hand to hack through the thick foliage with the
stolen butcher's cleaver.

Humming an African tune that Lamella had taught her about
freedom from white oppression, Anele chopped away and began a
steep uphill climb. She was happy to feel the warm sun on her back
and to look up and see the sky suffused with vibrant colors like
those found on an artist's palette. It was an awesome feeling for a
servant who had spent her days cooped up indoors.

Further along the trail, Anele noticed several creatures enjoying
the sunshine: green salamanders basking, a harmless garden snake
wiggling out of its dead skin while a small red and black feathered
bird swooped down on a grasshopper. Anele also delighted in hearing a songbird's joyous trebles.

As the climb steepened, a sharp twinge from Anele's lumbar

region overshadowed her contentedness. Although she was used to climbing stairs all day, she certainly wasn't used to walking uphill with an additional weight on her head. *If Namandla is willing to help me,* she entreated, *I'll make it back home safely and get good medicine for my aches and pains.*

A grimace crossed her mouth as the climb steepened. To distract her mind from the pain, especially the cramping of leg muscles, she thought of her father.

Was he still alive? Had he missed her? What did he look like now?

The more she tried to conjure her father's image, the more her heart ached. There wasn't a day she hadn't missed him, Tswanas village where she was born, and her loved ones. But how was she going to break the news of the twins' demise? It was something she would have to face if her father *was* still alive. But for now, she hoped that she was heading in the right direction. Then she remembered the boy who had dragged her to the manor house all those years ago.

"Up there—" Kelingo had pointed in the direction of the Valley of a Thousand Hills "—and a good ways beyond—that's where the Kingdom of Zululand is, the beating heart of Africa. Never… *never* forget your true roots, young Anele of the Tswanas tribe. It will help you to survive through the dark days to come—"

Chapter 4

The late afternoon sun, warm and soft as a whisper, fell upon Anele's weary body. She had walked nonstop since sunrise and fortunately had not encountered any police patrols, but had been given the "look-over" by a Bantu woman (not from the Hallworthy estate) who had stared at Anele's outfit.

Yes. The expensive European clothing *was* a dead giveaway.

She hurriedly undressed and wrapped the floral fabric intended for the manor drapes around her body. Her colorful makeshift outfit knotted above her breasts made Anele feel, inside and out, more like the African she was, and had forgotten how to be, until now.

With Lady Corrie's outfit tucked in the food basket, Anele plodded onward. But the lack of sleep, growling hunger pains, thirst, and excessive heat took a toll on her. Could she risk stopping yet?

As far as the eye could see, there was nothing but miles of red soil, fields of daisies, clusters of large-leafed fig trees, and in the distance, an outcrop. Would this be far enough away from Hallworthy soil to feel a hundred percent safe, or should she carry on until nightfall? Should she make her way to that outcrop, rest in its shadows for a while, eat, and drink a beer, then move on? Or maybe she should find a native village and pay them for a good night's sleep?

Anele decided to walk on until she dropped.

After a mile or so, in the distance, Anele could just make out what looked like the thatched roof of a traditional Zulu homestead. At last, she could rest and even share her food with the residents.

While taking a quick bathroom break, she happened to look back down the winding trail, and what she saw brought a deep frown. What *was* that swirling mass down below? Could it be a funneling sandstorm, common in these summer months? A prickly feeling ran down the back of her neck. She strained her eyes. Then, she froze. Without a doubt, the shapes of galloping horses were definitely heading her way.

Her inner voice shouted: *Run, woman! Run!* But her body was mired in imaginary quicksand.

Anele's mind raced, leapt, and darted like a scared jackrabbit. Was someone tracking her? Was it the police? Was it Alan? Had he been at home all along and seen her leaving the grounds? No. He definitely would have chased after her. Then, who were these horseback riders? As far as she knew, no blacks owned horses in these parts...

Adrenalin spurring her into action, Anele lifted the basket of provisions, and with both hands gripping the weight, she ran barefoot over an empty cornfield toward the traditional Zulu hut. Would the occupants take pity on her? To Anele's dismay, the home was empty—abandoned. Just as well, she reasoned—much too obvious a place to hide, although she'd enjoyed its familiarity.

Eyes darting from side to side she searched for another place. Would that outcrop she had seen earlier hide her? She made a beeline for the rocky formation.

Panting like a dog, Anele reached the base of the outcrop and looked up. Was that a cave opening half way up? How would she get up there?

Gripping the rock ledges, she climbed up to the entrance and then made a disgruntled click of her tongue. How on earth was she going to get through the tight-knit cleft? A slim child would have no problem. But size or time wasn't on Anele's side. She had little choice.

Shoving the basket in as far as it would go, Anele undid the knot of her clothing, threw the makeshift garment inside, and, taking a deep breath, slithered in.

She wished she hadn't.

The overpowering odor of animal feces assailed her nostrils with such force she could have fainted. Her thoughts were no better: *I hope whatever creatures made this disgusting stench aren't waiting for me.*

Regardless of the bad odor, the refuge was a godsend. From this higher level, Anele had the advantage above the trail. And the density of the dried bracken sticking up from a lower ledge would hopefully make her hiding place difficult to detect.

Crouched, her heart pounding and arms locked in a nervous embrace, she waited.

Suddenly, a horse neighed directly above her. Anele shrunk back against the cave's rough wall as the top of her hideout began reverberating with horses' hooves. The color drained from her face, and the hair on her neck stood upright like pig's bristles. There was no mistaking that malevolent tone of voice—Lord Alan. He would certainly show no mercy. He would shoot her, just as he had her sisters.

A backhanded gesture from the sour-faced Alan brought the other riders to a halt. His voice boomed, "The rotten bitch is here somewhere. I'm going to find her. And when I do, I'll break her neck, so help me God."

Insides trembling, Anele was scared to breathe.

The next voice was also as unmistakable.

"Why are we searching out here in bush land?" Lady Corrie asked. "Wouldn't it make more sense to check out the Durban docks?"

"Jesus, woman! The tracker has found her footprints leading up here—"

"I'm telling you," Corrie cut in. "We should search the docks, not here."

"Don't be so stupid," Alan said, gruffly. "Woman, are you deaf?" He exhaled loudly. "Why the hell did you come along just to stick your nose where it doesn't belong? My affairs are not yours!"

"Oh yes they are!" she countered angrily. "I've had to put up with your nonsense for years. And my dear, I wouldn't want to miss out on the fun. It seems it's the only pleasure I get seeing you insane like this."

"Shut up, Corrie!" Alan hissed. "You feeble-minded excuse for a woman."

Their eyes locked like horns for the longest moment.

In her mind's eye, Anele could see the stubborn jut of Lady Corrie's jaw and lips drawn tight with anger. From the sharpness of his tone, Anele could also well imagine the ugly contortions anger had etched on Lord Alan's handsome features. Why, Anele wondered, and even though she couldn't stand the woman, had she put up with Alan's despicable behavior for so long?

Corrie had her own thoughts on this matter. She knew why she had sold herself to this devil, and if she were able, would gladly sell her soul again to be free of him.

* * *

Afraid that her only daughter would never find a beau, Beatrice van de Hoof, Corrie's mother, was thrilled with relief when the eighteen-year-old Hallworthy boy began courting her unattractive daughter. Corrie's father was not as enthusiastic. He was sure it was necessity, not love, that fueled Alan's interest. It was common knowledge the Hallworthy Estate was in financial crisis due to past gambling losses. If Corrie's ample dowry served as bait to hook his daughter a suitable husband and spare the shame of spinsterhood, then so be it.

Alan's scheming mother, Lady Ethel, had plenty of "dirt" on her son, enough to put him behind bars for a long time, and used this to her advantage to save the estate. Alan was livid. When his father, Lord Peter Hallworthy, intervened between mother and son and begged his son to be reasonable, Alan reluctantly agreed to marry the heiress. He was very fond of his father, but not his overbearing mother, so Alan was devastated when shortly after shaking his father's hand in loyal commitment to honor the deal, the penniless Lord Peter died of congestive heart failure.

A year later, Alan would keep his promise to his father but vowed that the marriage would be in name only. No man who was a man would willingly sleep with Corrie van de Hoof without being blind drunk.

Like Roquefort cheese, Alan and Corrie's mutual hatred was well aged by time and circumstance. It reeked of their foul tempers and sadistic temperaments. Alan could not easily cut their legal shackles. Corrie, on the other hand, had insisted on joint ownership of the estate, contingent upon settling considerable restoration costs. There would be no divorce, she'd said.

* * *

Now, in the desolation of the valley's wilderness, sitting high on his black Arabian horse, the trigger-happy Lord Alan would have liked to have also shot his abominable wife. Her high-pitched voice, calling him a bastard, broke his murderous thoughts.

Leading her mare closer to him, and out of earshot of the workers awaiting further instruction, Corrie was on a roll. "Only yesterday, I saw you chasing after that young field worker…" She bit her lip from saying: *You know, dear, another child, hardly out of puberty, you put in the family way.*

Alan swatted a fly and laughed. His dry cackle was humorless as a crow. "Yeah, I know the one," he bragged. "She shot off like a race horse, didn't she?"

"So don't tell me that the bitch you kept in the cottage can't run like the Bantu girl," Corrie huffed. "And why is this plaything so important?"

Alan's face flushed dark red. "Shut your mouth, Corrie," he spat. "Or I'll shut it for you."

"Why are you taking your anger out at me?" she whined. "*I* didn't leave the door open for your precious Italian *thing* to escape."

"She's not Italian. She is Sicilian."

Corrie made a clucking agitated sound with her tongue. "It's the same thing, isn't it?"

Below them, Anele's lips moved silently: *Thank the gods. I'm not the one they're looking for.* She hoped with all her heart that the young girl, known as Maria, was long gone, heading homeward like herself.

Alan leaned across and roughly grabbed the bridle of Corrie's horse, pulling her closer. Corrie wrinkled her nose. Her husband stunk of whisky.

"If my so-called wife took better care of my needs—" Alan's upper lip curled derisively. "—I wouldn't need to go elsewhere, would I? Woman, you're nothing but a cold fish. The only time I can stand you in my bed is when I'm drunk. If my mother were still alive, I'd kill her for making me marry you. Get out of my sight; go home. Let me get on with what has to be done." He raised a fist. "I know who helped Maria escape. It had to be Anele. As God is my witness, she will vanish from the face of the earth when I get back. And I'll just have to find myself another plaything, because as sure as there is a hell, I won't be coming near you!"

Stung by his loud, heartless words for all to hear, Corrie gasped and clutched at her throat. Molten anger now flooded her veins. How dare he speak to her in that despicable manner! Whatever glimmer of affection she might have nourished died like the last rays of the sun. She'd had enough. It had gone on way too long. This evil monster had a sick appetite for young girls. Some were little more than children. Disgusting!

Gloatingly, in the knowledge of her power, she said, "Husband dear, as you normally never set foot in the kitchen I can tell you that Anele has run away… along with my grocery money. To crown that, we won't be having a turkey dinner later on. Maekela and Isona can't boil an egg, let alone prepare our Christmas meal. And I'm damned if I'm going to start cooking for you!"

At the stunned look on Alan's face, Corrie laughed the high contralto of a flute's trills. "I spoke to *your* bastard child, Maekela. She saw Anele get up well before dawn. It seems Anele told her to go back to sleep."

"*What?*"

"My dear, do I have to spell it out for you?"

"Why didn't you tell me this earlier, before we set off?"

"Because all you were interested in was finding Maria."

Alan exhaled so sharply it lifted the hair of the horse's mane. He just stared straight ahead.

Still crouched behind the ledge, fear seemed to have sprouted roots to Anele's feet. She could not move and could not breathe.

Corrie was having difficulty breathing also. The partying all night, the long ride back from the new police chief's home, and the horse ride out here had worn her out. All she wanted to do was to go home and relax. Have a few more martinis, smoke cigarettes; open presents and eat an alternative meal—one she'd have to make. The girls had no culinary skills and were only fit for cleaning. The thought of not having a traditional meal waiting riled her. She decided to break the icy tension. "Alan, I could kill Anele with my bare hands… the ungrateful bloody *wog* thief! It's too late to prepare something for us, so we will have to eat out."

Alan patted the horse's flank and replied through tight jaws, "Not if I get to *her* first. If I find the fat black bitch, I'll put a bullet between her eyes. So help me God, I will."

It was not an idle threat. Corrie had seen firsthand what happened to people who'd crossed paths with her husband. She, too, was afraid of him at times. This was one of them. In a pacifying tone, she said, "My dear, why don't we concentrate on finding Maria… and before she blabs to whoever will take her seriously. You could end up in jail. No, good lord, no. I wouldn't want that to happen!" she ended glibly.

"Who on God's earth is going to believe anything that crazy bitch says?" Alan jeered. "I'm a Hallworthy, for God's sake. I practically own the Port of Durban, the police and judges, and well over a thousand *golliwogs!*"

Wisely, Corrie remained silent. It was pointless now to argue. As though punctuating his anger, white knives of lightening split the sky, followed by drum rolls of thunder. Corrie's spooked horse reared, and she was sent flying from the saddle.

Dusting the dirt off her riding pants, Corrie moaned, "For Christ sake, Alan! Let's go home. There's a really bad storm coming. And there's always tomorrow."

Alan rotated in the saddle and spoke to his workers. "Turn around. Follow me."

As one, he, Corrie, and the black trackers turned and galloped homeward.

* * *

The sound of their retreating hooves was music to Anele's ears. She was safe… at least, for now. Time to celebrate.

She rummaged through the picnic basket and retrieved a bottle of beer. The frothy drink trickled down her throat like nectar from the gods. Within seconds, she was light-headed. She slouched to take a long overdue sleep. She almost started to doze—

Something seized her arm with the grip of a bird of prey's talons. Anele drew in her breath and tried to scream, but there came only the rasp of shocked terror as a sibilant hiss pierced the tomblike quiet. "*Ees* okay, Big Mama. No worry, the *bastardo… ees* gone."

There was certainly no mistaking *this* foreign-accented voice. Anele had taken enough food trays to the guest cottage to know her well. Had Maria been there all along? Why hadn't she said something?

Anele fumbled in the dark and snatched Maria's arm.

"You make me hurt!" the girl shrieked.

Anele dragged her to the opening. They crawled out onto the ledge.

Without saying a word, Anele stared into the pain-haunted face of the pregnant fourteen-year-old white girl. Anele's heart went out to her. By the look of her dirt-covered pink dress, an outfit she had sewn for her, Maria had been traveling for some time. The girl's arms and legs were beyond filthy.

"Let me go," Maria screamed, trying to pry Anele's fingers from her forearm.

"No! You nearly scared me to death!"

"I no mean scare you, Big Mama."

"Well, you did! My heart almost jumped out of my chest!"

"I no mean—"

Anele cut her off. "Maria, I set you free *yesterday*. You should be long gone by now. I showed you which way to go to the docks, not to the Valley of a Thousand Hills."

Maria clutched at Anele's waist. "I run fast from *di diaula* (white devil in Sicilian dialect), Big Mama. He tried to kill my babies and me. The *bastardo*, he beat me bad. I scared, not know way to big ship to take me home to Sicilia. Then I see *diaula* on big horse. I run. I hide in hole here."

"You've been here the whole time!"

Bottom lip quivering, Maria nodded. "Yes, Big Mama. I think I'm lost in big land until I see you coming up the hill. I not know you run away like Maria. In my heart, I know you sad like me, no? You too run like me from the *diaula*, no?"

Anele sighed deeply. She knew little about the girl's background, but she could recall the day she met her. As though it was only yesterday, Anele's memory went back to that spring day, when

Maria arrived at Hallworthy Manor.

That encounter would turn out to be unforgettable.

Chapter 5

On that fateful spring day, Anele was outside hanging laundry when the shabbily dressed foursome arrived at the back door—a stunning teenager, flanked by a thin man of about forty, a short woman of similar age, and a handsome dark-haired young man.

Anele couldn't take her eyes off the dark, olive-skinned girl. She was the most beautiful white girl she had ever seen. Her waist-length black hair, glistening like polished ebony, was as thick as a horse's mane, and the unadorned cotton dress matched perfectly her emerald eyes.

The older man spoke first, "Signóra, where is the *proprietario* of this plantation? We need work."

Anele did not recognize the accent. *Ah, these foreigners,* she thought, *would be better off starving to death than coming here to work. The girl was far too lovely. The Master would devour her faster than a fox in a henhouse.* The expression on her face spoke volumes. "Take your pretty daughter and go quickly," she cautioned. "There is no work here for you. The refinery owner isn't hiring anyone at the moment."

Before the man could respond, there came a fast-approaching clatter of hooves. All heads turned as the rider came to a halt.

Anele's heart skipped a beat at the barely concealed lust lighting Alan's eyes as they took in Maria's developing body. "Are you looking for work?" he asked, his eyes remaining on Maria.

Cesare Girrdazzello nodded eagerly. "Si. Si. Raphaela, my wife," he said, pulling the petite woman beside him, "is hard worker. My son Paolo," he pointed, "he strong boy also. We work hard for you, Signóre." He made no mention of his daughter also working hard.

"Are you Spaniards?" Alan asked.

"No, Signóre. We are from Sicily."

"You're a long way from home. What brings you here? Or shouldn't I ask?"

"We have bad times from the war," Cesare answered. "Need to make new start in new land."

Without a second glance at Cesare, Alan nudged his steed closer to Maria. "You're such a pretty girl. What's your name?"

Maria shrank behind Cesare.

"She not talk, Signóre," he said. "She has how you say—" Cesare tapped at his head "—brain sickness... *ees* no good in the head. But this no stop her working hard."

"What a shame," Alan said, in a voice that would melt butter. "I'm sure I'll be able to find her something to do. Now are you and your family prepared to work for food and lodging only?"

Cesare frowned and scratched his chin. "Work for *no* money, Signóre?"

"Yes," Alan said icily. "That's exactly what I mean. If you don't like the idea, you can try to find work elsewhere. But I assure you, not too many white folk are hiring refugees, especially the illegal kind—" he paused long enough for Cesare and his son to exchange worried glances, "—which most probably you are. You get my drift?"

Concerned that the owner would change his mind, Paolo, who understood English well but didn't let on earlier, stepped forward and said, "It *ees* okay, Signóre. Food and a place to sleep will be fine."

As the family grouped and conversed in their own tongue, Alan got hold of Anele's arm, and pulling her to face him, he whispered, "Take the girl to the guest cottage. Put her to work. Give her some cleaning cloths. See that she scrubs the place from top to bottom. I'll take her parents and brother over to the stables. They can stay there for the time being, until I've fixed up the place."

It was one place Anele dreaded. She knew every inch of that hellhole and tried to get out of going there. "But Master Alan, how will I get through to her having a sick brain and all?"

"She's not blind! Show her what to do, stupid!"

Later that night, locked in the cottage, Maria would weep in fear and pain, little knowing that so many other girls before her had shared the same fate—rape.

* * *

The next morning, Alan, sporting a deep scratch on his cheek and a smirk on his lips handed his cook a key to the cottage and ordered her to take Maria a breakfast tray. Anele was sickened to her stomach, and yearned to remove with the butcher's knife she held in her hand and plunge it into Satan's sidekick. But simply bobbed her head in agreement.

Anele placed the tray containing a bowl of porridge, a slice of marmalade toast, and glass of milk down, removed the key from her pocket, and unlocked the heavy oak door. Her heart was almost wrenched out of her chest when she saw the half-naked Maria restrained with leather strapping to the brass bedposts.

Sighing deeply, Anele sat on the bed and untied her restraints without saying a word. Even if Maria spoke English, no words could ever soothe what had been done to her. Wide-eyed with fear, Maria's sharp fingernails sunk into Anele's neck and into the scalding wound, still tender after all these years. Wincing in pain, she grabbed Maria's arms, pinning them to her sides. "Why did you do that? I'm not your enemy, you stupid girl!" Anele snapped. "I'm the only friend you'll ever have here."

She released the struggling girl, picked up the food tray from the floor, and sat beside her on the bed. She tried to hand-feed her lukewarm porridge. The petrified girl jerked her head away, teeth clenched.

As silently as she had entered the room, Anele left, locking the door behind her.

Back in the manor kitchen, she tried not to think about Maria, but the white girl's pain-filled eyes haunted her. Anele nearly jumped out of her skin when she heard a loud knock. Looking out of the window, she saw Raphaela, standing on a tree stump in order to reach the glass pane. The woman made her request understandable by hand gestures that she wanted to see Maria. Anele raised her hand in a "wait-there" sign.

Outside, she took hold of Raphaela's arm. "Come with me, "Anele said, "I'll take you."

Instead of taking the woman to the guest cottage, Anele led her to the front entrance of the manor. There, she knocked sharply, smiled at Raphaela, then dashed away and hid behind a pillar near the doorway. Afraid to be seen, she waited to hear who came to the door.

"What the bloody hell do you want?" Alan demanded. "Shouldn't you be working?

Raphaela blurted out her request in Sicilian dialect.

Alan laughed. "Good Lord, woman! I haven't got a clue what you are saying. You better learn English fast, because I'm sure as hell not going to learn to speak Sicilian."

"Maria… Maria, need look her. Look her now!" Raphaela stressed, doing her best to get her message across.

Alan's eyes narrowed. "You can't come in contact with your daughter, not at the moment. I noticed some sores on her legs, so I got my doctor to check her. She is contagious. Do you understand what I'm saying? *Contagious!* She has a bad blood infection. I can't have her working alongside you or my other field workers in this condition. You can see her when she is well. And I'm warning you—"

Anele could envision his wagging finger and frown.

"—don't go near the cottage," Alan warned. "Alfred, my overseer, has instructions to shoot."

Anele could not hear a response from Raphaela. Perhaps she did not understand him, or perhaps she understood only too well.

After the front door slammed shut, Anele shot back to her workplace.

By the next day, she learned from a field worker that the Girrdazzello family had simply vanished from the estate without a word to anyone. It was a mystery. But Anele had to wonder: Had Alan silenced them for good? She was even more mystified at Maria's reaction when Anele broke the news in words and hand gestures about their sudden disappearance. Maria's face lit up, then pointing to the door, she said, "You no lock. Me run, okay, Big Mama."

Anele lowered her head. "Oh, child, if only I could. But *he* would hold me responsible and probably shoot me if I let you go."

* * *

Now, the heavily pregnant Maria was here with her—two sad runaways. If Alan found them together, without a doubt, he'd blow off *both* their heads. Anele hurt for the pitiful expectant mother. Her matted hair was a bird's nest. Her lovely face and eyes were blackened and swollen from cruel punches.

Then, Anele's eyes widened in shock. "The gods of good Zulu hearts, help me!"

"What is it, Big Mama?"

"Maria, can't you feel it?" She pointed. "—that's blood I see trickling down your legs! Does your belly hurt?" She counted on her fingers. "If my memory serves me well, you're in your final month."

Maria remained silent. She seemed not to comprehend what was happening to her. Or did she?

Anele let out an exasperated sigh. "I was able to deliver my own baby years ago, but I'm not sure if I'll be capable delivering yours... No. I will have to find a birthing woman. There has to be someone living around here—"

Maria's face scrunched in pain.

"Do you have hurt in your belly, Maria?"

Maria still didn't reply.

Anele squeezed the girl's hand tenderly. "Don't worry child. I'm going to get help."

Maria grabbed Anele's hand and kissed it. "Big Mama, you nice lady, but you please no go back to bad sugar place. You no worry for me... no *bambinos*... babies no more."

Anele clucked her tongue. "Of course, I'm worried. You and your baby may die if I don't get help. And no, I'm definitely not going back to the *sugar place*."

"No, me no die... me *libero*—how you say? Yes, me *free!*"

Anele rubbed her forehead. How on earth could she get through to this girl?

"Yes, yes, you're free, Maria. I know that."

Puffing out her cheeks, Anele was going to ask her to lie down so that she could check the position of the baby's head when Maria grabbed Anele's hand. She placed it on her swollen abdomen. "See, black Mama I *libero,* free. No more *demonio* babies. No *diaula sangue*. The devils blood no more in me."

Anele scowled. "Missy Maria Girrdazzello, I've no idea what you're rambling on about, but you need to be lying down, not standing up. It may help the blood loss."

Angrily, Maria countered, "My name is Maria Picasso Genovese. No say Girrdazzello name. Not my real *familiare*. Those bad people bring me here to this country."

"Now what on earth are you gabbling about, Maria?"

"Paolo steal me from Papa and Mama in Sicilia…" As though to blot out the memory, she covered her face with her hands.

Anele wanted to wrap her arms around this wretched girl, but was more concerned about possible internal bleeding, the baby's safe delivery into the world, than the girl's heart woes.

"Maria. How long has your blood flowed?"

"I don't know!"

"Lie down, so I can check you."

"No."

Maria began to sob.

Like the kitchen servant, Maria had experienced more sorrow than any heart should hold. A long and tortuous road had brought her from her home nestled in the shadows of Mount Etna in Sicily to the dark shores of Africa.

Maria Teresa Picasso Genovese was her real name. She was the only daughter of Sofia Maria Picasso, a Spanish-born socialite, and Don Alberto Vincenzo Genovese, a wealthy landowner and a reigning Mafia boss.

"Paolo steal me for my Papa for big money," Maria cried. "My Papa no pay the boy. Paolo then sell me to German man. After war, I go with American soldier to "lost war place" (Salvation Army) camp. I no know my name. Paolo, he see me there. He scared. He tell his mama and papa. They bring me here to dark land by boat. Bad people the Girrdazzellos. I remember… I remember—"

Maria's sobbing rose into the humid evening air.

"Please don't cry anymore," Anele crooned, using the hem of her floral outfit to dab the girl's cheeks. "I'm so sorry to hear that you have had so much hurt in your young life, but we have to deal with the now. Listen to me, Maria. First babies don't always come out that quick. If I can't find a birthing woman, I'll come straight back and help you myself."

Picking her teeth with the tip of a mud-caked fingernail, Maria pretended not to have heard her.

Anele stared at the girl's nails. "Maria, how did your nails get so filthy?"

"Me no say."

Did she mean she wouldn't, or couldn't, say? Anele wondered. "If you like, you can change out of that filthy dress. I've a blouse in my basket for you to put on. I also have some food. Are you hungry?"

Maria's eyes were vacant, her mouth mute.

Anele worried at leaving her alone in the approaching darkness, but what else could she do? "I'm setting off now, Maria. And with a little luck I'll have the birthing woman with me when I return."

"I say again! No need birth woman."

"Yes, you do! What if something goes wrong? The baby could be stuck."

"I tell you last time, Big Mama, the babies ees *morto*... they are dead!"

"Your baby, *not babies*, is going to pop out before the full moon shines tonight."

"Too late... babies have gone," laughed Maria. "Me no die... babies die. I make sure."

Uneasiness swelled in the pit of Anele's stomach. Something wasn't right...

It crossed her mind to continue homeward, just leave the befuddled white girl with her pregnant belly no bigger than a brussels sprout, let her birth her baby alone. But Anele knew she'd never be able to live with herself if she abandoned this helpless girl. Maria was dangerously thin. Would her baby even be born alive?

Anele tilted Maria's face upward to meet her eyes. "Maria, I've changed my mind. I've decided not to leave you here alone. But I'm going to need your help. Does the pain come one after the other?"

"No say."

In an eating gesture—fingers to her mouth Anele asked, "Are you hungry, Maria?"

"Me no want eat, Big Mama." Maria made a sucking noise with

her lips. "Me want drink. Me very thirsty."

"Would you like some sweet, condensed milk? I stole it from the *bas-e-tar-do's* house."

Maria's face lit up like a moonbeam. She loved Anele's pronunciation of the Italian word for bastard. "No. Want water. And Big Mama, pain I tell you *ees* gone for good."

"No, it's not gone for good. The pain is going to get much worse."

Maria shook her head and smirked.

Anele sighed. "Okay, Maria. Here's what I'm going to do. I think I saw a rainwater barrel near an abandoned homestead. I'll go get enough for you to drink and to wash the baby when it comes out."

Maria pulled a funny face.

"You cheeky monkey! I bet you understand everything I say… am I right?" Anele gestured. "Come along, girl."

Reluctantly, Maria followed Anele deeper into the cavity. There, Anele spread Corrie's skirt onto the ground and handed Maria the woman's blouse. "Take off your dirty dress," Anele said. "Then I want you to sit down…" she pointed to the clothing item, then ended, "I'm going to go for water. I won't be long."

Holding the empty beer bottle, Anele set off. She had a supply of dried milk, and one can of condensed milk, in case Maria had no breast milk. In her emaciated state, weighing less than one hundred pounds, it seemed unlikely Maria could produce a drop.

Thankful to hundreds of fireflies flashing their lanterns in the diminishing light, Anele retraced her steps to the hut and water source. As she was scooping the discolored water into the bottle, she heard a peculiar sound. She tilted her head to the side. It was like a kitten's mewing. The sound became louder. Now it struck a note resembling a faint human cry.

No. It couldn't be.

Anele carried on with her task.

But a loud rustling followed by a thin wail made her stop. *That is no animal…!*

A scruffy wild dog, crouching beside a pile of cornhusks, suddenly sprung to all fours and bared her razor-sharp teeth. Anele dropped her eyes and backed away.

Taking this as a sign of submission, the dog sat back on her haunches and returned its attention to the mound. Anele's taunt muscles relaxed. It was only doing what any mother would do: protecting her young.

"It's okay, little mother dog," she said in a soft comforting voice. "I'm going. But you should have found a better place to have a litter than out in the open field."

Whistling to show the dog that she was not afraid, Anele walked on. Then, again, she heard a faint human cry.

It couldn't be…!

Cautiously, avoiding sudden movements, she put down the bottle, picked up two large stones, and retraced her steps.

The dog was pawing at something.

Anele's blood turned cold, then adrenalin rushed through her veins like hot lava. She screamed, "*Go. Get gone. Shoo. Go away!*"

Throwing with all her might, the first stone struck the animal between the eyes. The hungry critter yelped but was not about to leave. Snarling, it stood its ground. The next rock broke open the skin on its scalp. Yelping in pain, the bitch shot off into the bushes.

Anele darted to the spot, looked down, and gasped in horror. She dropped to her knees and lifted the tiny form from its intended grave. A rush of tears clouding her vision, Anele did not see the other baby, a layer of pawed dirt mantling her corpse.

Wiping the dog drool from the child's ashen face, she cried, "Namandla, Great God, have mercy."

There was no mistaking the parents of this abandoned infant.

Maria's green eyes stared up at her.

Tiny tufts of flaxen blonde hair identified her father: Alan Hall-worthy.

Barely breathing, the baby snuggled in the warmth and security of Anele's arms—the first she had known since birth. Heart beating so fast, Anele thought it was going to pop right out of her chest; she pulled a long strand of horse grass and tied the baby's mangled umbilical cord. Then she nestled the cold child between her breasts.

Anele raced back to the shelter. At the entrance she called, "Maria. Come out here *now!*"

No response.

"Maria. I know you're in there," Anele yelled. "How could you do such a terrible thing? Your baby is alive!"

There was only silence.

Holding tightly onto Maria's baby, Anele, angrier than a wounded wasp, wiggled through the gap and into the cave.

Empty.

Not only was Maria gone, so was the makeshift bedding and the money Anele had stuffed into the blouse pocket. Maria's earlier words now made sense: "I'm free. The devil's blood is no longer in me."

When she'd given birth, Anele could only guess.

Why couldn't Maria have told her?

Anele didn't have the luxury of time to ponder the situation. The baby was as still as death.

She laid her ear against the infant's tiny ribcage and held her breath. At first, she heard nothing. Then Anele's heart jumped with joy. There was a faint heartbeat.

A fierce urgency possessed her being, and not wanting to rely on Namandla, who had turned a deaf ear over the years, she beseeched the dark side of African culture—the Guardian of the Underworld. "Great oNgewele, with your powers make this child live, even though she is *umlungu,* the pale color of the ones I hate. But she didn't ask to be born, or left to die in such a horrible way…" Anele's angry tears fell onto the baby's tear-stained little face. There was one more deity to try: "Please, God of the white people, let her live."

Suddenly, the baby girl took a gulp of air and curled her tiny pink finger around Anele's.

It was a miracle. *Who* had answered her plea was another question? Only time would tell.

Anele cradled the baby, kissed her cool forehead, and whispered tenderly, "It looks like I'm your mother now. Grow strong for your *Umama*. So fight as hard as you can, little one. We both have a lot of living to do."

Another miracle occurred.

Astonishingly, from Anele's nipples, a milky substance had begun to flow. She coaxed the newborn to her breast, and the baby suckled greedily.

Life couldn't have been sweeter for Anele.

Mantled in a single garment of fate at that moment, Anele felt blessed. No more will the void in her womb cry out to be filled with her own baby. With the lovely trill of a songbird, Anele's song floated up to the heavens:

"*Great Spirits of the white people and of black skins, I thank you for the channel of peace, love, and forgiveness. From the ugly darkness, you have shown me the light of joy. I will forever sing your praises.*"

If Anele could have peered into the murky waters of the future, she might not have prayed so fervently for the gods to spare this foundling, who would be *Shiya*—the forsaken one.

Chapter 6

On this cloudless late December morning in Zululand, the Tswanas tribe went about their business, tending to crops and small gardens, milking the cows, and performing other mundane daily chores. They were blissfully unaware that before the sun was level with the western horizon, their lives would be turned upside down.

Down at the kraal's wooden gate, a tall, stooped old man paused to retie the homespun blanket that had slipped off his waist, exposing his nakedness. He clucked his tongue and retied his cover. He was the village chieftain, a man of tradition and culture but intolerant of the endless prattle of women, boisterous children, and the incessant barking of the village hunting dogs.

Chief Naboto Dingane, a respected tribal leader, daily left the compound to enjoy his customary afternoon nap away from their hustle and bustle. Molded by the harsh elements, his leathery face scrunched like a deflating ball as he sucked in his cheeks. As his crooked fingers fumbled to undo the gate's rope latch, he griped, "Why are things not made easier for the old?"

Freed of the gate, and leaving it ajar, Naboto headed for his favorite resting place not far away.

Forlornly in the distance stood a solitary baobab and according to African myth, the tree was accidentally planted upside down, accounting for the odd shape of its branches. This ancient giant was known to the locals as the "dead rat tree," named after the ovoid, rodent-shaped hairy fruit it bore. The old man and the tree had long known each other. He revered this tree, as he had climbed it in his youth, shared passionate moments under it, and marked diagonal lines after the birth and deaths of each of his children.

The chieftain leaned his gaunt frame against the thick trunk and stroked the thick-stemmed greyish bark. "*Ingundane abafileyo,*" he greeted his friend. "I've come to take my rest with you."

As Naboto ran his gnarled fingers over the long line of previously made incisions, a look of sadness crossed his wizen face. Then exhaling loudly, he turned his back on his calendar of memories and, removing the blanket from his waist, spread it over a carpet of brown crinkly leaves and arid soil.

Comfortable under the tree's leafy canopy, he shut his wrinkled eyelids, and within seconds loud snoring escaped from his throat. Oblivious to the approaching evening shadows, Naboto slept longer than normal until he was rudely awakened by a shrill voice: "Chief Naboto. Chief Naboto. Wake up!"

Naboto's body jerked to alertness. He squinted, trying to focus on the ponderous bulky shadow holding a blazing reed torch. He recognized her. "What is it, Vimbela? Why have you come to my private place?"

"Chief, I h-have just c-come from the-the village," stammered Vimbela, trying to catch her breath. "Granny Matudia said to find you here."

"Cannot a man have some peace? Tell me your message, brainless girl."

"It's past the time of crows," she yelled. "The night is as black as their feathers. You better listen to me."

"You don't have to scream like that. I'm not deaf."

"Yes, you are!"

"I'm not going to argue with you, girl."

"I don't care, old Chief. I've an urgent message for you!"

"Well, what is it?"

"Anele, your daughter, is coming."

Naboto slapped the side of his head in disbelief. "Brainless girl, it cannot be her."

"Wrong. Wrong. Wrong," Vimbela blustered in a singsong voice. "Matudia is a wise-woman. She knows where people are without seeing them. She says that Anele does not walk with the dead, and that *you*, who is supposed to be a gifted man with the spiritual insight of the Ancient Spirits, already know of this. Your daughter is alive. Come, old man, and see for yourself."

Naboto rose. "*Indulo injonga,*" he muttered, telling his old bones "don't let me down."

Vimbela lowered the torch and started to giggle.

"Now what is it, girl?"

She pointed at his drooping genitals, one testicle hanging lower than the other.

It brought a toothless smile from him. "Child, you have the innocence of a baby. Now pass me my blanket. We must make haste."

Wrenched so abruptly from his dream world, his shaky legs could not match Vimbela's pace. It took some effort to keep up with the lively girl, so he gripped her arm to slow her feet. Naboto's ankle adornments—pod-beads containing seeds—rattled and clinked rhythmically as a backdrop to Vimbela's cheerful tune. He recalled that Anele loved this particular song and sang it often as a child. After a few more verses, the jingle no longer triggered happy memories but a very disturbing one. It ushered him back to the day when all three of his daughters, the last of his children, went missing eighteen years ago.

* * *

On that day, the sun rose gleaming like a polished gold coin. Mercy—one of many meal-makers, and the most dictatorial, waited by the campfire hands on voluminous hips. She made a guttural sound of impatience. Where was the wood to start a fire for breakfast? The twins had let her down with the needed firewood. Where was the water to boil the mealie-meal? *This* task was allotted to Anele and two other girls. And where was she?

Rubbing sleep from their eyes, and tummies rumbling with hunger, the children were the first to arrive at Mercy's side. She sent one little girl to Naboto's hut.

She soon exited. "Thaka, Zhana, and Anele are not there," the child informed Mercy. "Only the chief sleeps."

Mercy stomped into Naboto's hut. He was woken by her loud complaint. "How am I supposed to get food ready if your daughters don't do as they are told? When I see them, I'm going to take a stick to their behinds."

As the day turned to night, a perplexed Naboto summoned the *Imikhuba*—the local witchdoctor—to help solve the mystery.

The revered soothsayer arrived within minutes. He squatted beside the chieftain in his hut, and with a stick etched secret African symbols into the dirt floor. Then he lifted his goats-horn filled with magic stones and, with a swoop of his hand, threw the contents onto the dirt. Eyes squinting, he studied the stones methodically then said, "Your daughters are indeed gone from Tswanas. They left before the sun rose."

"Why? Where are they? Please, tell me more?" Naboto urged.

The witchdoctor wrung his hands. "The magic stones bring bad tidings. Are you sure you want to know the truth?"

"Yes, Great One."

"Your twin daughters are in the Invisible Kingdom of Souls, shot by a white man's steel bullets. And your last child that you have named "Enough" is enslaved. The whites own her now."

Naboto didn't want to believe it.

After the witchdoctor was gone, the chieftain buried his head in his hands and wept.

* * *

The skeletal fingers of Tswanas' campfire smoke wafted up Naboto's nostrils as they approached the kraal, snapping him out of his reveries. Eyes stinging from unshed tears, he entered with Vimbela's help at the gate. At once, she left him behind and rushed through the compound shouting delightedly, "See, I told you I'd find the old chief in the dark. He is not a happy man."

Naboto shook his head. This girl could make a mountain shake with her yelling. He was hardly through the gate when a throng of women and children surrounded him. Some older women in the crowd, who had known Anele as a child, began whooping and hollering jubilantly. It was way too much for the old man's ears. "Be still!" he commanded. "Calmness brings harmony to our souls, not the wild chatter of monkeys. Go about your business. Leave me with mine."

His mind racing with elation, he lowered his old body into a bamboo chair outside his hut. Question after question flooded his mind:

Is it really Anele? Why had she never tried to get word to him in all these years? What did she look like now? Would he recognize her? Was she in good or frail health? Was she married? Did she have children with her—?

The chief's thoughts were interrupted by one of his many relatives. Natongo handed Naboto a clay jug filled to the brim with strong beer and said, "For your heart to sing with joy."

Naboto's first cousin dragged a tree stump closer and sat. The pair chatted, the topic naturally on Anele. Before the questions had answers, a sharp-eyed boy's voice, loud with triumph, shouted, "Chief, *she* is here! I can see her. Your daughter comes!"

The pack of village hunting dogs sprinted to the gate. Barking ferociously, they thronged around Anele. Unafraid, she shooed them away.

She pushed her way through the crowd of villagers that threatened to squash her by their attempts to welcome her. Anele didn't recognize one face. Had she been gone that long?

In the twilight, the village where she had spent the first nine years of her life now seemed unfamiliar. She had even sought help along the way to locate it, so unfamiliar the entire area had become. She looked into the faces of her people and asked in English, "Is my father, Chief Naboto, still here?"

She was answered by blank stares.

Anele clicked her tongue at her stupidity. This time she asked in the language they understood. Vimbela touched Anele's arm. "Oh yes. Come, I will take you to him."

Babbling excitedly, Vimbela linked arms with Anele and led her through the compound toward Naboto's hut at the far end. As they neared, Anele's heart fluttered with love to be home again and to see her father rising from a chair, arms outstretched. Her inner voice rejoiced. *Thank the Great Spirit! He is still alive!*

She handed the basket containing the sleeping baby to Vimbela and rushed to him. "Father, it brings me great joy to find you alive."

"Anele, Anele, Anele," Naboto repeated, holding her with such remarkable strength she could hardly breathe. When he finally released her, and before Anele could say a word, Naboto addressed the gawking crowd. "Fetch drinking water and bring a bowl of *isinambathi* (pumpkin cooked with mealie-meal, a porridge-like gruel) for my daughter—"

Anele's weary legs finally gave way, and she hit the dirt.

* * *

It had been a long perilous journey, about 289 miles, mostly through wilderness fraught with hungry critters, leopards, lions, jackals, and other feral hounds all wanting an easy meal. The smell of baby was delectable to their noses. Often, Anele had wielded the butcher's cleaver like a warrior, daring her attackers. But it wasn't the creatures of the wild that bothered her most; it was the tribal folk she encountered along the way. They, at first, had been friendly, until they noticed the *unana*—white baby—strapped to her bosom. Questions from one curious woman were flung at Anele:

"What are you doing with a white infant so far from the white townships?"

"Are you blind?" Anele retorted. "Can't you see my baby's dark skin?"

"Since when do Zulu women give birth to blonde-haired babies with green eyes?"

"When they are raped by a white man!" Anele had wanted to shout at her. After that unpleasant encounter, she had avoided settlements along the way.

* * *

At the chieftain's request, two old men carried an unconscious Anele into his hut. An amber glow from pig-oil-filled lanterns cast eerie shadows against the oval walls. To aid his dimming eyesight, Naboto lit a third, larger lamp and placed in on the ground next to his bed. He then squatted before his daughter, his eyes examining her disfigured face and neck.

Anele came around. Her vision focused on the person staring down at her.

"Did I faint, *Ubaba?*"

Naboto beamed with pride. "Yes, daughter. And it is good to be called 'father' again. There is no doubt you are the daughter of Tuttia. Her special eyes shine through you. But I'm shocked to see you have the wrinkled face of an ancient one. According to my markings on the sacred tree, you have seen only twenty-seven summers. Daughter, what has happened to you? Why do you bear such terrible scars?"

A knife of grief twisted deep inside Anele. How could she tell her father about what had happened to her sisters, or the loss of her child, or most of all, finding Shiya? Would he order her and the baby to leave Tswanas like Lamella, the former Hallworthy cook had predicted? Anele sighed. She doubted that his hatred of the white people had diminished with time. Now she had brought into his home a white man's infant.

Naboto broke into her thoughts. "Daughter, you may have my *ndlunkulu* until a new hut can be built for you."

"No, Father, don't give up your hut for me. We can share it like when I was a child. I can sleep on the floor."

"Anele, you'll do as you are told. I'll sleep in Natongo's hut. He has two empty beds since his wives died."

For an instant, the past collided with the present, and her surroundings whirled in her mind. Where was she? Blinking rapidly, it took but a second to realize that not only had she made it home safely, she had returned to a time she'd thought was forever gone, back to taking orders from her father. Oh, how she had missed him and his no-nonsense ways. She wanted him to know this. "Father, my heart is glad to see you again. I have missed you so much."

"But why, did *you* leave with Thaka and Zhana? Why?"

Shiya's sharp wail within the closed picnic basket raised Naboto's thin eyebrows nearly to his gray hairline. He burst into delighted laughter. "I'm a happy man. You have brought home a grandson, yes?" Without waiting for her reply, he hobbled toward the doorway. "My daughter returns with my grandchild," he loudly announced to his people milling about outside. "We must celebrate! Bring more beer to my hut."

Anele quickly rose from the bed, rushed over, and clasped her father's arm. "Please, Father, no celebration, not yet. I'm too tired for that. And I bring to you a granddaughter, not a grandson."

"Girl... boy... it doesn't matter. You bring home a child, who has my royal bloodline."

Anele sighed. "Please father, I need for you to ask a nursing mother to come quickly, as I have no flow of milk."

"Does your husband follow? Do you have other children... where are they?"

Questions. Questions. Questions.

It was too much and too soon.

"Father, I'll answer anything you wish to know later, but first my baby must be fed."

"Go and fetch a nursing mother to my hut," Naboto ordered a little girl standing in the doorway gawking at Anele. After shooing other onlookers from peeking inside his home, he sat in his chair outside the door like a sentinel and finished his beer.

Inside, Shiya's tiny chest heaved between wails. Somehow Anele had to muster up the energy to care for the baby. "Hush, my precious, little miracle baby," Anele crooned, holding Shiya tightly against her chest. "Milk is coming."

As though Anele had uttered a magic mantra, the crying stopped, and Shiya drifted back to sleep. Anele gazed lovingly at her newfound child whose lips twitched and eyeballs rolled in innocent dreams. Touched by this tiny infant's will to survive against the odds, Anele wondered how long she had lain in her cornhusk grave, her umbilical skin ripped and bleeding. Anele could only guess. Had it not been for her meager breast milk, and the small supply of powdered milk, the child would have surely died.

While she waited for a wet nurse, Anele speculated what it would feel like for the black nannies that permanently took care of white children. Did they come to love them as their own? Did the white children love their nannies equally?

They must have, Anele reckoned, because their own mothers were too busy enjoying their social freedom to be bothered with the physical and emotional rearing of their children.

A proud radiance flushed Anele's face for rescuing Shiya from the jaws of the African wild dog. It didn't matter if the baby was Zulu or not. She would love Shiya and raise her as though she had been born from her own body. The deep feeling of loss for her own child, taken from her, gripped her still like a pain in her heart.

The melancholy vanished when a wholesome girl with enlarged

breasts entered the hut, a warm smile lifting her full lips. "Welcome home, daughter of Chief Naboto. My name is Umia. Like you, I have just given birth. I drink the milk of the goat to make sure my breasts are full. You should try it. It will help your own milk flow."

This constructive advice given, Umia sat cross-legged on the dirt floor and stretched forth her arms to receive the baby. Anele handed her the swaddled infant. The happy-to-help look vanished in an instant. Wide-eyed, Umia stared at Shiya, and then the nursing-girl's blood-curdling scream shattered the musty air inside the hut.

Outside, a drunken Naboto slept through the mayhem.

Umia leapt to her feet, sending Shiya rolling across the floor like wind-blown sage. There followed a duet of Umia's horrified wails and the infant's outraged shrieks.

Anele bit hard on her tongue to hold back her own protests as her strong hands latched onto Umia before she could flee from the hut. One hand gripped firmly on the girl's arm, Anele bent and with her other hand swept up her infant. A quick look confirmed Shiya was unhurt.

Anele ordered, "Umia, you will feed her *now!*"

Arms crossed defiantly across her bosom, Umia gave Anele a look that could kill. The young girl glared stubbornly. "No. I will never let the lips of an *umlungu* suckle on my nipples."

"You'll do as you are told, or I'll strangle you."

Umia shook her head.

Anele tried a softer approach. "If you have a mother's heart, Umia, feed my baby. She is hungry."

Umia sighed. "Okay, I will do it, but only once." Then she sat down again.

Anele guided the baby's mouth to the girl's swollen breast, but pursed lips struggled to grasp the nipple, and Umia was not going to help. Anele was at her wits ends and past being nice.

Angrily, she squatted and squeezed Umia's nipple so firmly a spray of milk splashed onto the baby's face. Only then did her tiny mouth finally grip, and she sucked greedily. Umia looked away. Soon a healthy glow of pinkness spread over Shiya's naked body, and sparkling emerald eyes slowly closed.

"May the Great Spirit of all Zulus protect my good heart," Umia uttered. "This baby has the most frightening eyes I've ever seen." She reached for Anele's hand, clasped it, and begged, "Daughter of Chief Naboto, I've done what you asked, let me go now. I must feed my own child, a baby boy born just before you arrived."

Suddenly, Naboto entered.

Draped in leopard skin, feathers, bone ankle and neck adornments, and holding a long-handled *assegai,* he stood proudly in his regal outfit. Naboto claimed to be a descendant of a bygone Zulu king, Dingane, half-brother of King Chaka, who ruled the once vast dominion of the brave Zulu nation.

Unsteady on his feet, Naboto approached the trio. "By the power in me as Chieftain of Tswanas," he slurred, "I have come to evoke *Ukuvikeleleka,* the God of Protection, over the new life that carries my royal blood. The child must be safeguarded against harmful spirits."

Nobody said a word.

From a calfskin pouch strung around his thin neck, Naboto took out the fragments of his ancestor's bones and teeth, and placed them in symbolic order on the floor and then chanted the ancient rite. He finished the mantra and turned to Umia. "Hand me the child."

Umia thrust Shiya into Naboto's outstretched arms.

"We are all going to die," the distraught girl wailed. "The Fire-God is going to roast our village because of your stupid daughter! She is no better than the brainless one. I'm going to put hot beeswax on my breasts to kill the taste of the evil one. I wish Anele never came back. I wish she had stayed with the *umlungu.*"

Naboto's brow creased. "What troubles your brain so, young

mother? Your words sting like the venom of a snake."

"You'll find out yourself, blind old man."

Umia fled past him, exited the hut, and ran to the center of the compound shrilling. Her raucous commotion filtered into Naboto's hut, and Anele said to her father, "*Ubaba,* how dare she talk to you in this manner? You should take a stick to her bad mouth. I'd like you to get me another nursing mother for my child's next feed. I don't wish to see that silly girl again."

Naboto's attention was on the infant writhing under the blanket.

"Do not fret, little one, I'm not going to hurt you," he whispered, uncovering the child. His pupils grew large and droplets of saliva dribbled down his chin. He faced Anele. "You're no daughter of mine. No child of my loins would deceive me so. The blood of this baby does not run in my family. Nor is it the making of yours, Anele."

He tossed the wailing infant.

Anele screamed and caught the baby before the child landed on the floor. She hugged Shiya close to her breast, praying for another miracle. Could her father's heart ever soften toward the abandoned child? No, that was unlikely. She had almost forgotten how embittered he was against the whites.

Naboto continued to rant, "Madness has filled your head like the maggots of all dead flesh. Your lies have injured my heart, Anele. You are not the daughter of Tuttia, an honorable woman. She gave her life for your unworthy self…" He took a deep breath and swallowed a mouthful of spit. "And you have darkened her pure spirit. Worst of all, you have disgraced your own soul in possessing a child not of your birthright. Where is the white mother to this infant? Or have you stolen the blood of another?"

Anele remained silent. It would certainly trigger further retaliation if she spoke up. In his rage, there was no telling what he would do. She had seen this angry, out-of-control behavior regarding anything to do with the white people once too often as a child.

Naboto glared at his daughter, daring her to defy him. Then out of the blue, a look of sadness softened the old man's angry mask. "I've shed many tears for all my lost children, especially you, the "enough," last child born. Yes, I know what has happened to the twins. Thankfully, you never met their fate, and I ached for grandchildren to carry on our family blood. And what I am faced with an *umlungu* baby filled with the bad blood of whites."

In a blink, his anger resurfaced. "This child has no right in my village. And never will it as long as I have breath in my body."

He left the hut and shuffled past the campfire where most of the women were gathered. "None of you are allowed in my hut," he shouted at them. "Keep away. That is an order." Without a backward glance, he headed toward the gate.

"What has happened?" a young woman asked. "The Chief has the rage of a bull elephant."

Her eyes red from crying, Umia answered her, "I'll tell you why our chief has murder in his eyes…"

Throughout her tale of what she had seen and heard inside Naboto's hut, the village women gasped in shocked disbelief. The sound of incredulous hissing grew louder than the crackling fire's embers as Umia ended her story.

Words flew furiously as the women erupted in excited conversation.

"Are you *sure* it's a pure *umlungu* baby, Umia?" someone asked. "Anele could have been *taken,* perhaps forced to lie down with a white man—"

Not caring an owl's hoot about the Chief's warning, Umia snapped, "Go and see for yourself, if you don't believe me. The baby's skin is pink as a pig's, and her eyes are the color of green plant dye. Not one drop of good African blood is in that baby. It's pure *umlungu.*"

"Do you think Anele stole this child?" another quizzed.

"How else did she come by it?"

Mercy, who had known Anele as a child, didn't want to believe it.

"Merciful Great Ancestral Spirits of the Zulu people!" she uttered. "That's never heard of here. What's going to happen to us if the whites find out?"

Umia glanced furtively over her shoulder and whispered, "Not if we do something about it."

"What you do mean, Umia?"

"Anele and the baby must die."

Chapter 7

Down at the compound's exit, Naboto's already sizzling temper was stretched. Again, he could not get the rope latch on the gate to budge. Anger driving his clenched hands, he picked up a machete and sliced through the thickly entwined rope as if it were nothing more than soft butter.

A few yards out, Naboto disrobed and flung his royal attire on the ground.

Thankful for the full moon and starlit night, he was able to cross the field of sisal without stumbling. Up ahead, a rock formation resembling the outstretched wings of a gigantic bird loomed eerily. Naboto believed this particular outcrop was a gateway into the Spirit Realm. As he neared this sacred place, seemingly disembodied red glowing eyes studied his approach.

"Creatures of the night, I do not fear you," Naboto boasted in between breaths. "Find something tender to eat. This old body of mine will only give you bad indigestion."

He forced his steps onward until they breasted the summit.

Standing with his hands in the crook of his back he took a deep breath of cooling night air. After a brief respite, he raised his outstretched arms.

"Namandla, God of the Invisible Kingdom, your humble servant, Naboto Dingane of the Tswanas tribe calls upon you. I need the strength and wisdom from the *ibuthos,* warriors of old, who died fighting for our land. I want them to appear in my dreams and help me to fight a battle that will surely come. Without their guidance, the *umlungu* will kill all of us..." Naboto cleared his raspy throat. "Sadness and anger fills my old heart. I did not see in my dreams the terrible deed my last-born child has done. Why did she steal another's child? Is she without a womb to carry her own? But why, Great Spirits, did she take an *umlungu* baby? This not only is shameful, but is most foolish."

The stars twinkled coldly as he shifted from leg to leg awaiting a response of some sort. Moments passed that felt like hours.

"Ancient Spirits, I need a sign... an indication that my pleas to you do not go unheard—"

Something cold as a mountain brook brushed across his face. The old man's leathery features cracked into a broad, toothless smile.

"Beloved wife, Tuttia, I sense that you are close to my wretched old body. Good woman once on earth and now in spirit, my heart is full of shame and sorrow."

From spiritual experience, Naboto knew that the dead can influence the affairs of the living. But asking a woman's advice, dead or alive, was taboo. In case a male from his village had followed him, he whispered, "Wife, I need your wisdom to deal with the grave situation that our tribe must face. Please tell me what has to be done."

Silhouetted against the moonlight, Naboto lowered himself slowly onto a flat stone. Bony back resting against a boulder, he closed his eyes. His mind lifted with warm thoughts to that happy day, so long ago.

* * *

On that summer's morning, the Tswanas tribe had been busy preparing their chief's wedding to Tuttia Umdanuna, from the neighboring

Mtunzini village. Voices of jubilation filled the air. Hunters had returned with ample fresh kill of deer: impala and oryx. The older women made gallons of beer from the Marula fruit while children scattered wild flowers in the matrimonial circle drawn by the witch-doctor. The seventeen-summers-old groom noted that everyone was excited except his bride, Tuttia. Shy of her thirteenth birthday, she entered the matrimonial hut with the married women.

Chattering and buzzing around her like bees, they began preparing Tuttia in accordance with tribal rituals. The women noted that the girl's solemnity suited a funeral rather than her marriage. The bride-to-be pressed her hand across her aching heart. She was not joyous about joining other married women of the African bush.

While being rubbed down with sheep fat and oils, she stood still and silent as a tree stump until an elder began shaving *all* her body hair with the razor-sharp tip of a spear. Then she pulled back and cried out, "Why do you do this, old woman?"

"It's the Tswanas custom."

Wincing in discomfort, Tuttia yielded to their ministrations.

A crown of aromatic and colorful wild flowers was placed on the bride's head. It overpowered the foul odor of sheep fat emanating from her body. She was given a beaded straw skirt to put on, a carved animal bone and bead necklace, and hooped earrings to match. After a final critical inspection from the women, Tuttia was pronounced ready.

The Tswanas and Mtunzini guests surrounding the couple's nuptial circle burst into a frenzy of dancing as the groom was handed a mug by the local witchdoctor.

"Naboto of Royal blood, and Tuttia, daughter of Umdanuna and father unknown, drink the elixir of all life. On this your wedding night, new life will be certain."

Naboto took a sip and handed the drink to Tuttia. She downed the rest with one mighty swallow and gagged. "It is bitter and smells worse than any cow dung," she complained.

"You weren't supposed to drink it all!" the witchdoctor protested.

"It doesn't matter," Naboto said. "I don't need an elixir to prove I'm a man." He turned to face the crowd and pointed to a couple of Tswanas women. "Take my bride to my hut," he ordered. "Make sure she is properly prepared for the stallion of this village."

He thought this bravado would please his bride. Instead, Tuttia had a look of horror on her face as though she were being led like a lamb to slaughter.

The men folk partied until the beer ran out.

Sometime after midnight, Naboto staggered into his hut. The nimbus of yellow flame from the lamp exposed his naked flesh. Tuttia scooted to the top of the straw mattress.

"Wife, are you ready for the father of your children?"

"You smell worse than wild pig meat!" a muffled voice said under the blanket.

Laughing, Naboto fell upon the straw mattress and claimed his Mtunzini bride.

In the years that followed, Tuttia became a dutiful wife. She bore him eight children; the last—Anele—would take her life.

Tuttia died from birthing complications the day after her last delivery.

That same night, beneath a dusting of stars, his heart breaking, Naboto took the newborn to the sacred outcrop. Like his ancestors before him, he held her up.

"Namandla, I name this child Anele—*Enough*. Protect her, Great Spirit. Give her strength…" Naboto sighed in grief. "My beloved wife, Tuttia, I will forever see your image in her eyes. You are gone from me in flesh, but in spirit you will always remain within both our hearts."

* * *

Content with his memories, the aged chieftain slept until the early morning sunlight danced over his eyelids and woke him.

Groaning, he rose and rotated his stiff neck and stood motionless for a moment. Then his mind flooded with anguish: *What have you done Anele? These old bones were prepared for death, ready to join your mother, brothers, and twin sisters. How can I now leave this mortal plane a free man? Anele, Anele, Anele. You have to return the child to its rightful white tribe or you and I will surely die a horrible death. Our spirits will not fly free.*

The thought of not reuniting with his darling Tuttia and other children tore Naboto's heart from his chest. He bowed his head and let the tears fall.

As though heralded from out of nowhere, an eagle swooped down from the sky, its mighty wingspan stretching to within inches of Naboto's head. The bird made a deafening screech and then soared upward. The old man spread wide his crooked fingers and bent to pick up the tail feather that had landed near his feet. His heart quickened. This was the sacred sign he had been awaiting.

With renewed strength of purpose, Naboto hurried from the rock as fast as his legs allowed. Only a few feet from the entrance to the kraal, pain worse than the spears of a dozen enemies stabbed into his chest. He dropped to the ground. His dull eyes tried to focus on the sacred bird that had landed only a handbreadth away from his immobile body. With enormous effort, he lifted his head; its molten eyes were seemingly fusing with his own. It was telling him... it was telling him...

The revered creature of the African plains let out another loud screech as he circled Naboto's dead body and soared into the blood-red sunrise.

As was the mighty eagle, hordes of buzzards were summoned from the netherworld and tore ravenously into the still warm, lifeless flesh of the spiritual man who had been the Royal Chief Naboto Dingane.

Chapter 8

That same daybreak, ten-year-old Natu, Umia's youngest brother, snuck out of the kraal. He had an impish smile, knowing he needed permission to leave the compound that early.

A rusty spoon in his hand, Natu climbed over the gate. He wanted to dig for worms before the sun drove them deeper into their tunnels, or ant pupa from the many mounds dotted a couple of feet from the settlement.

Today, his brothers were going fishing at the river, and he wanted to join them. If he had juicy worms, Natu felt sure they would invite him to come along. This thought propelled his legs faster as he dashed toward an ant mound.

There, he was confronted by an enigmatic aardvark whose meal place Natu was invading. He clanked his spoon against the metal tin, and the hungry anteater made a hasty departure.

Natu rubbed his runny nose on his upper forearm, squatted, and began to dig at the base of the mound through the thick sand layer to reach the pupa. The soldier ants came out in droves and attacked his fingers. Bitten numerous times, the bites painful, Natu abandoned this quest and went in search of worms instead. A few feet away, he saw buzzards tucking into what he imagined was an animal carcass. Maybe the dead creature had maggots? Even better fishing bait.

The buzzards hit the sky as he approached. What he saw made him drop the spoon and tin and take off like a rocket.

The slapping of feet and his frantic cries alerted the villagers.

Out of breath, Natu flapped his arms as if trying to scatter the buzzards. He finally managed to get his words out. "The Chief lies dead outside the kraal. He has a big hole in his face and no eyeballs." Natu's body was shaking against his mother's hip.

"Are you sure, son?" Natu's father asked.

Trembling, Natu nodded.

"Come show me where this body lies."

Within minutes, they returned.

"Yes, our chief lies dead," Natu's father confirmed. He turned to his older sons. "Follow me."

The rapid high-pitched clicking of tongues and wailing of the tribeswomen brought Anele to the door. "What's happening? Who's died?"

Little Natu was the first to speak, "Your *Ubaba* has been eaten!"

"What!" Anele fiercely grabbed Natu's arm. "What did you say?"

The little boy cried out in pain, bringing his mother to his side.

"Let go of my child, Anele!" she insisted. "He tells no lie. Go and see for yourself. Your father is dead."

Anele clamped her hand over her mouth as the reed stretcher, lifted high and transported by Natu's sons, neared. "Put it down!" she screamed. "I want to see."

She pulled back the blanket covering Naboto's body. The scavengers of the African plains had not only plucked out his eyeballs and tongue, they had nearly stripped him of his flesh.

Her face frozen in shocked disbelief, Anele fell to her knees, raised her father's bloodied head, and cradled it to her bare bosom.

"Father you cannot be dead! No. No, this is not happening! You can't be gone, not so soon. I've been home less than a day! And there was so much I wanted to tell you about Thaka and Zhana. How brave they were. How I survived the dark days…"

She began to sob.

Vimbela strode through the crowd, pulled a face of repulsion, and then hunkered beside the distraught woman. In her simplistic way, she consoled Anele. "Your father was a *very* old man, as old as the stars. It was his time. Be happy for him. He's gone to a better place. Our ancestors will take care of him now."

The girl's words of comfort fell on deaf ears. Anele simply shook her father's limp shoulder. "Wake up, *Ubaba*."

Disbelief also written across his face, Natongo said, "It's a sad day for all, daughter of Naboto. Your father was a fine leader, and I'll miss my old friend. But the brainless girl is right. He's in a better place."

Anele began the high-pitched wailing ritual for the dead.

Granny Matudia shook her head, bent, and in a sympathetic gesture stroked Anele's tear-stained cheek. "My heart cries with you, child of Naboto, but you must let the burial women do their duty. It is custom to bury him before the setting of the sun."

Anele rubbed the tears from her eyes and nodded in agreement. She tried to get up, but her body remained glued to the dusty soil, weighted with sorrow. Vimbela noted her efforts and came to the rescue. Her powerful arms lifted the sobbing Anele and aided her back into Naboto's home. Inside, Anele freed herself, then flung her body to the ground and began pounding her fists into the dirt floor. "I've had more unhappiness than a heart can hold," she wailed. "This pain is too much to bear."

Her face expressionless, Vimbela went to the makeshift crib—a wood orange crate lined with calfskin—and lifted the sleeping baby.

To the prone Anele, the teenager said, "Sit up and hold your baby. Be strong for your *umlungu* child. She needs you now more than your dead father. Wailing and pounding fists will not bring back your dead *Ubaba*."

A solitary tear rolled down Anele's cheek and fell on Shiya's forehead.

"I love you with all my heart," Anele said, "but I can't be a mother to you at this moment. I must first grieve my loss."

She handed the baby back to Vimbela and slouched in the chair.

Heart heavy with regret, she wished she had followed her father to the sacred outcrop and begged forgiveness.

Outside, the rising sun was as intense as the accusations being flung by mostly the younger generation.

"If *she* hadn't come back, our leader would still be here."

"Yes. He was in fine health until she came."

"The shock of her stealing a white child is what's killed him."

"She is to blame for his sudden death."

One voice shrilled over the rest—Umia's. "The Chief is gone. Why don't we chase Anele and the white baby from our village? Or better still, let's do what we discussed last night, kill—"

Umia was cut short by a mighty shove from Granny Matudia. "Get on with your chores, you stupid girl. Who gives you the right to judge Chief Naboto's daughter! Go, or I'll take a stick to you!"

The previous evening, Matudia was not among the villagers who had welcomed Anele's return. She had taken to her bed with severe stomach cramps and diarrhea, blaming an undercooked meal of goat's liver and wild potato-like roots for her condition. During this illness, she had not taken kindly to people wandering in and out of her hut, gossiping about Anele and the white baby. Matudia had chosen to ignore their prattle until she was well enough to find out for herself. Now, she covered Naboto's desecrated face with his blanket. To the two elderly women wailing their tribal death cries, she ordered, "Burial women, you must now prepare our Chief for his journey to the afterlife."

To the oldest of Natu's brothers, Kumdi, she instructed, "Carry Chief Naboto to his hut, and place him on his bed."

Kumdi nodded.

The matriarch turned to young Natu, whose wide eyes were riveted on the covered body. "Go to the sacred cave in the hill, Twazli's home, and tell him to come quickly. His 'passing over' powers are needed."

Dust from racing feet flew everywhere as Natu and his three friends headed out the gate.

Meanwhile, Kumdi, a strapping teenager, lifted Naboto in his arms as if the old chief weighed nothing more than a handful of grain and carried him into the hut. He placed Naboto on the bed and glared contemptuously at Anele, then left.

Vimbela stood solemnly in silence as Anele stroked her father's cold forehead. She tenderly picked away blood-encrusted leaves sticking to his mangled flesh. Grief tugging at her heart, she whispered, "Father, my heart is like a swollen river. It overflows with loss. It was the hope of seeing you again that kept me from going crazy during my enslavement. The wisdom you gave me as a child— to look evil in the eye and conquer it—was how I survived those dark days. I'm sure you are watching over me with your all-knowing and all-seeing eyes, so my words of sorrow will not go unheard—"

Something caught her eye.

Her brows knitted as she removed the eagle's tail feather from her father's ankle bracelet. She had found a similar feather lying near Shiya's crib last night before going to bed. Was it a coincidence? Was there a symbolic meaning, finding two feathers?

Anele reached for the plume lying on a small handcrafted table, then tucked both feathers into a small lock of what was left of Naboto's knotty hair. "*Hamba kahle, Ubaba…* goodbye, my beloved father. May your spirit soar peacefully with the sacred eagles until the day we are all reunited in the Invisible Kingdom of Souls. Hug my mother, brothers, and especially Thaka and Zhana. Tell them I love and miss them dreadfully."

As she was placing a tender kiss on her father's cold lips, Matudia gently touched her shoulder. "Anele, daughter of our dead leader, the burial women have work to do. Leave the hut, so that they can begin."

"No. Not *now* Matudia. I want to spend more time with my father."

"This is your right, Anele. But maybe you have forgotten the bad flies that feed on the dead and then bring sickness to the living. This is why we must hurry to bury your father."

Her patience strained to the limit, Anele snapped, "*Get out,* Matudia. I will summon the burial women when I'm done speaking to my father."

With a look of displeasure, Matudia left. How dare the *umlungu* brainwashed woman speak to her like that? After all, she was the matriarch, the wise-woman, and a powerful soothsayer. Given the tragic circumstances, she'd forgive Anele this time, but would never allow her to shout at her again.

Vimbela wasn't happy either, and she made it known to Anele by giving her a contemptuous stare. To disrespect the wise-woman was bad. Vimbela loved Matudia, who had taken care of her since she was a child, and she felt sure that Anele was in for a tongue thrashing from the matriarch when this was over. Clucking her tongue, the teenager left the hut with the baby in her arms.

Anele gestured for the burial women waiting in the doorway to come in.

From the chair, she watched as the women removed items from their baskets.

Chanting a "passing over" litany, a freedom tune about the soul being rid of cumbersome "vessel" flesh, the women cleansed Naboto's body with boiled river water, plugged orifices with beeswax, and sealed his empty eye sockets and mouth with a resin-like mixture.

They dressed Naboto in his royal attire and then nodded at each other. They were done.

"Daughter of Naboto, your father's spirit is already in the Invisible Kingdom," the oldest women said. "His flesh is ready for the Sacred Worms."

A few at a time, the villagers entered to pay their chieftain homage but soon scrambled out when the centenarian witchdoctor's cane pushed back the door blanket. A bleating goat at his side, Twazli went to the bed. Anele pinched her skin on the back of her hand to make sure she wasn't dreaming. It had been a long time since she had encountered a witchdoctor, a highly respected and feared magician in African culture. She blinked several times. Yes. She was sure he was the same mystical man from her childhood—a man she had watched in awe perform a "miracle"—bringing back to life a calf that had been mauled nearly to death by a leopard.

Her heart skipped a beat. Could Twazli's supernatural powers work on her dead father? Immediately, Anele dismissed the thought. Sadly, she had to accept that her father was way past a miraculous resurrection.

Candlelight reflected the nightmarish figure.

At least seven feet in height, he had gangly limbs gnarled like the boughs of an ancient tree, and a white powdery substance plastered on his face accentuating his sunken red eyes. From enlarged earlobes dangled dried chicken feet.

An icy chill crept into Anele's veins. She smiled uncertainly, but he did not return the smile.

"I would like to be left alone with your father," the venerable man insisted.

Anele was taken by surprise. She wasn't expecting a boy's softness in his voice. If anything, she had expected his vocal cords would be croaky like a toad. She made a hasty exit.

A half hour passed before the witchdoctor reappeared and

beckoned Anele.

Away from the curious onlookers, his remarkably strong hands closed firmly around her fingers. She felt a tingling, almost electric sensation.

"I have spoken to your father's earthbound spirit," he said. "He warns you to return the *umlungu* child to its own people before it's too late. The sacred eagle messenger told him of the consequences in keeping a white child here." Twazli bushy eyebrows furrowed. "Daughter of Naboto, many here would gladly hand you a child born of their ripe bodies, just to mend your emptiness. You cannot keep what is not your blood!"

Pulling away, she made brazen eye contact. "If you are as truly gifted as you claim, then you will know the circumstances of how I came upon this child. Her mother is probably dead by now."

Twazli's demonic eyes bored into hers. "Yes, I do. I am blessed with the insight of the Ancients," he stated, snappily. "I know the *lungu*—little white person—is a *Shiya,* a forsaken one. But she does not belong among our people. She is to be raised by her own blood. You must return her to the man who sired her."

"I can't do that. The man is evil."

"I know that, lost daughter of Naboto. But many will die by this white man's hand if you don't heed my warning."

"You are wrong. No one is going to die. Master Alan doesn't know of this place. Nor does he know his offspring lives."

"You're a good hearted woman in saving this child's life. But, in doing so, you have forever condemned her pure spirit and physical body to a life of untold sorrow and pain. You should have left her for the jackal dog."

Anele gasped at his heartless remark. Then a shiver of fear ran down her spine, which prompted her to reach for his bony hand. "Please, Great Man with All-Seeing Eyes, explain what you mean by this."

He yanked his hand away and waved it over her head, as if in benediction.

"Heed my warning. Leave the child in the white township, or take her to the jungle for the beasts to devour. Either will be more merciful than what I have predicted. If you do not, your fate and hers will be by far worse than the sinking of a deadly serpent's razor-sharp fangs into your flesh."

His pet goat nudging his hand, Twazli turned his back on her and left the hut.

Anele cracked her knuckles. Had she forgotten how powerful this man was? Hadn't she been told as a child that his powers came from the underworld, a dark place where grotesque entities danced with flames of fire? The witchdoctor's dire predictions and the horrible thought of Shiya lying in a field somewhere ripped to shreds were too much for Anele's fragile state of mind. In tribal tradition, she threw back her head and keened her heartbreak, repeatedly slapping her chest like a gorilla, until she collapsed.

A few moments later, Anele opened her eyes. Her head swimming, she was confronted by Vimbela. "Get up, *Umama* Anele. The burial party is ready to take your father to the Sacred Hill."

Anele nodded.

Naboto's modest coffin was hoisted in the air by the strongest of the men. Along the way, the funeral entourage swigged beer, danced, and sang "happy tunes" as was their tradition.

At the burial ground, wolf spiders weaved gossamer threads, and canary-like birds flew from branch to branch warbling. Circling, high above, the Sacred Eagle soared.

Naboto's coffin, according to tradition, was lowered vertically into the six-foot hole facing north. Before the earth was replaced, Anele scattered a handful of tobacco leaves that had been soaked in Acacia tree oil, and her father's favorite clay pipe, on top of the coffin.

Granny Matudia flung baobab leaves from his favorite tree, and a few stones from the Sacred Rock.

Natongo dropped a corked jug of his best brew of *imfuka* to finalize his cousin's passing over. These gifts, a symbol of mortals, were to ease his transition into the world of spirits.

As the gravediggers commenced the fill-in, Matudia touched Anele's solemn face. "You shed no tears. This is good. Your father is smiling at you."

"Can you see him?"

"Of course. I'm a gifted woman."

"I wish my father knew how I regret not running away from the white man's place sooner."

"He knows that, child. Don't blame yourself for the evils of others."

From her heart, Anele spoke silently: "*I will always love you, Ubaba. One day, we will be together again.*"

Circular garlands woven from aromatic yellow wildflowers, similar to dandelions, were placed on the burial mound. Then the village men took turns urinating around the grave's perimeter. The deceptive flowers were extremely poisonous, and the urine a territorial marker to prevent creatures from digging up the body.

Naboto lay in the heart of this small mountain where he had once played as a boy. A few yards from him was Tuttia, his beloved wife. A decorated stone, faded by many seasons, marked her resting place. Also on this hillside, cloaked by tall thorn bushes, was the unmarked grave of Vimbela's son.

Alone, Anele sat on the dirt beside her father's grave. She had so much to tell him, but mental fatigue got the better of her.

She buried her head in her folded arms and closed her eyes. Within seconds, she was fast asleep. The curtains of multicolored light flickered in transient patterns across the darkened sky. The loud haunting call of a wild creature snapped Anele awake.

Terrified, tripping over tree stumps and rocks repeatedly, she finally made it home. It was past midnight. Not a soul was to be seen around the kraal.

Anele found Vimbela breastfeeding Shiya.

"I was worried that you'd been eaten," Vimbela said.

"I'm here now, so no need to worry your pretty head. How is my baby doing?"

Playfully squeezing her breast, Vimbela laughed, "The way she guzzles, I'm going to run out of milk."

* * *

As the weeks passed, Anele's life was blissful, the rosiest it had been in a long while. Naboto's dowdy home was given a makeover. Wall to wall, the dirt floor was carpeted with braided reed-matting. A window had been cut into the mud on one side and covered with the drapery material Anele had stolen from the manor. A pinkish plant-dye colored the woven door blanket, and outside, around the renovated home, the wildflower seeds were sprouting. It was the rope-fashioned washing line that stirred the most interest.

Anele showed the women how to hang clothing with the carved wooden pegs she had made. They were delighted. No more leaving laundry on rocks to dry. The most pleased of all the village women was Mercy. Anele's culinary skills brought not only flavor: wild herbs were added to meals, but sweet desserts were made from dried Acacia leaves and honey.

Though accepted by the villagers, some men included, there was one person who shunned Anele.

Umia was as cool as a cucumber. "I don't like you, *umlungu*-loving woman. I'll never be your friend."

"That's fine, Umia. I don't need your friendship. I have plenty of friends." They avoided each other the best they could in the compound.

One peaceful morning, Anele and the villagers, except Umia, ate heartily on corn and mealie-meal patties drenched in honey that Anele had baked. Mercy smiled at Anele. "These are delicious. I'm glad to see that your appetite has returned. You've hardly eaten a morsel since coming here."

"It's a new day, dear Mercy. My father wouldn't want me to be sad, and I have made him a promise. On every full moon I will visit him and tell him news of his granddaughter."

Some frowned at her statement as if Anele was out of her mind. But no one said a word.

It had already been said. Or had it?

Only time would tell.

Chapter 9

Anele kept her promise. She traipsed up to the burial ground with Vimbela and Shiya. The garlands had long withered, but the tribal urination had kept the grave from being desecrated. Anele removed a sleepy Shiya from the comfort of Vimbela's blanket carrier and held the baby's drooping head over Naboto's grave.

"*Ubaba,* I wish to reintroduce you to Shiya, the forsaken one. She's not of my blood, but Father, she is the only child I'll ever have."

Anele lowered her head and silently told her father about the atrocities she had suffered. Aloud, she said, "But by now, I'm sure you already know this. Father, watch over Shiya as she grows into a fine Zulu maiden."

She removed Shiya from Vimbela's back, took her baby's hand, and firmly pushed it into the grave dirt. "My beloved *Ubaba,* Shiya greets you with the hand of pure love."

Shiya shrieked.

Vimbela rolled her eyes and protested, "Don't make her cry so. She's too little to know our customs. And anyway, she's *umlungu!*"

Anele puffed out her cheeks. "Vimbela, I know how much you love Shiya, but don't you ever question my actions again."

Vimbela pulled a rebellious face, bent, and snatched the wailing baby from Anele's grip.

"You can stay here all you want and talk to the dirt, *Umama* Anele, but I'm taking Shiya home."

Anele shrugged and let her march off with Shiya. What was the point in scolding the well-meaning, simple girl? Vimbela had the innocence of a child.

Her back up against the cairn, and determined not to fall asleep again like she had done before, Anele spent no less than an hour visiting with her family on Sacred Hill before heading home. Hardly through the kraal gate, she was confronted by Granny Matudia.

"Come with me," the matriarch said, latching onto Anele's arm. "Your presence is needed at the tribal meeting."

"Matudia, I'm exhausted from my long walk. Do you really need me?"

"Yes. There are those who are not happy with your father's successor."

"Who is it?"

"Kumdi."

"Umia's *brother!*"

"Yes. He's not fit to lead us. He thinks only of bedding girls rather than the welfare of our people."

Anele was lost for words, though her thoughts weren't lost. Would *her* opinion make a difference? No. She didn't think so.

"If my father has chosen this young man, he must have thought highly of him."

Matudia shook her head in disagreement. "I don't think your father was in his right mind when he selected this awful boy."

Anele delicately removed the old woman's latched hand and leaned against the wall of the cattle shed. Something told her Matudia was only beginning to get her point across.

"Kumdi has slyly taken married women to his bed. This doesn't sit well with me the eldest person in this village, who knows of these wrongs. If the husbands of these women learn this, blood will rightly flow."

Anele pulled a "whatever" face.

"Matudia, it won't be the first time married women cheat on their husbands. I blame the women for allowing Kumdi to bed them. Regardless of his sexual activities, the time has come for a spirited young leader like Kumdi to lead this tribe, although personally, I don't like him. With due respect, Matudia, I don't believe that anything I may say at this meeting will change the voting. I'm sure whoever takes my father's place will do a good job."

Muttering inaudibly, Matudia turned her back on Anele and headed toward the communal fire pit.

Anele went to her hut, put her tired feet up, and poured herself a generous beer.

* * *

As the full moon climbed in the heavens, villagers stopped what they were doing and gathered around the fire pit to attend the meeting. Sitting on upturned logs, elders waited for Kumdi to exit his family's hut.

Wearing a recently killed lion's pelt over his shoulder, Kumdi sidled up to the group, his two pregnant wives in tow. Young men, mostly teenagers, raised their spears and in unison voiced their approval: "Kumdi for our leader."

He smiled broadly, lifted his spear in the air, and declared, "I will honor this duty as newly appointed Chieftain of the Tswanas tribe. I will bring about change."

Nobody, especially the male presence, could have imagined what was to follow this oath.

Spurred by an earlier discussion about leadership, the women, who clearly outnumbered the males, joined hands and drew closer like stalking predators toward Kumdi.

Inches from his body, one elderly woman spoke up, "I don't like you, never have."

Veins in his neck pulsating, Kumdi thrust his spear within inches of the woman's heart. "Be quiet, or I'll spill your blood, old woman."

Retaliatory shouts filled the night air as the women made a circle around him.

"Come an inch closer and blood will spill," Kumdi threatened. Turning to the men who sat wide-eyed, he said, "Are you going to let your women disrespect me?"

Now the shouting came from the men.

A scuffle took place, a free for all.

Fathers, husbands, and brothers attacked their women with spears, fists, and rocks. The night air filled with helpless screams.

Flinging her sewing down, Anele rushed outside and was confronted by a young girl, no more than twelve, her cheek and nose bleeding profusely. She grabbed Anele's hand. "Help me, daughter of Chief Naboto. He is bad. He wants to kill us."

"Who did this to you, child?"

"I don't know," she replied honestly. The girl tugged at Anele's hand. "Come. See for yourself."

The scene around the campfire looked like a boxing ring with too many contestants, and Kumdi's voice outreached any other, "Men, kill your women, who dare lay a hand on your body."

Something in Anele snapped. She balled her fists and, with Alan Hallworthy's face frontmost, she picked up a rock, ran toward the fire pit, and hurled it into the flames, sending cinders shooting into the air like a firework display. The mayhem abruptly stopped. Now faces, some bloodied, stared at her.

"Have you *all* gone crazy?" Anele shouted.

Silence.

Kumdi straightened his lion's pelt and made eye contact with Anele. "Do not interfere in our business, *umlungu*-loving woman! You don't belong here. Return to the white man's world, and take the pale child with you. That is an order!"

Anele could feel her blood pressure rising. Temples throbbing, she rushed toward Kumdi and grabbed his neck in a fierce lock. She was physically strong, but despite her robust frame, she was no match against the muscular boy. He gripped her fingers bending them to breaking point. Anele cried out as the joint in an index finger snapped in two.

"I warn you, woman," Kumdi spat. "Don't ever lay a finger on me again!"

Anele lifted a burning piece of wood and advanced toward Kumdi. He inched away from the flame-wielding Anele. Cornering him, she hissed, "I carry the royal bloodline of the Dingane family. Don't ever lay a finger on me again! And, I have the rightful vote in the leadership of this—"

Like moths to a flame, the battered women swarmed around Anele. Their voices came one after the other.

"Anele is our true leader!"

"We want Anele to be our Chief,"

"She *is* of royal blood."

"Throw Kumdi out the village!"

"Cut him bad, and leave him to die in the jungle—"

The din coming from a metal object against a rock halted the sentence of the little girl who had begged Anele's help. All eyes turned to Granny Matudia.

"As matriarch of the tribe, I declare that Anele will rightfully succeed her father."

There were gasps from the men, but not Kumdi. His fists clenched, he countered, "Ancient woman, you cannot override tradition."

"Yes, I can. She has royal blood. You and the men will have to get used to it. Anele is the Chieftain of the Tswanas tribe. This meeting is—"

Vimbela pushed past Matudia and faced Anele.

"I tell the truth, words from my heart. *Umama* Anele, Kumdi is my half-brother. He is bad, like they say. He put the baby in my belly. He laughed at me when it died."

Anele put a hand over her mouth, looked at Vimbela, then over to Kumdi. He immediately reacted. "What lies you tell, crazy brainless girl."

"I no lie. You're a bad brother."

"I never touched your ugly body."

"Yes, you did."

Anele had heard enough.

She threw another rock with all her might, hitting the boy square in the forehead. Kumdi dropped to the ground.

Blood gushing from the head wound, he lay motionless.

Vimbela laughed and then waited to see if he would get up. When he didn't, she spat, "Kumdi, you are worse than a deadly snake. All those times you made me lie down with you and caused me terrible pain. I'm unfit for marriage now."

Kumdi's wives, who had not entered the earlier melee, glared at their sprawled husband, but neither said a word.

"I'm happy now, *Umama* Anele," Vimbela said. "He deserved a good beating. I go now to feed Shiya."

"I'm coming with you," Anele said, "I've nothing left to say or do to this awful boy."

Their backs turned, they didn't see him get up.

Removing a hunting knife from his hip strap, Kumdi dashed after them and lunged at Vimbela. The knife fell short. Anele swiftly knocked both the wielder and the weapon to the ground.

"Women of Tswanas, I need your help," she hollered. "Hold this snake called Kumdi while I teach him a lesson he will never forget."

The women happily obliged.

Under the weight of an obese woman, Kumdi was pinned down until his hands could be tied. Then the bombardment of stones came fast and furious.

The humiliated young man finally crawled to the safety of his family's hut. The rest of the men followed suit. There were too many women throwing rocks for their liking.

* * *

At midnight, Matudia initiated Anele with the blood of a newborn calf. As she smeared it on Anele's cheeks and arms, the matriarch declared, "Your father is proud of you. He visited me while you were having the confrontation with Kumdi. You will make a great Chieftain, he said. But, he has a warning: get rid of the white child, or you'll not see your twenty-eighth year of birth on this earth."

Anele shook her head. "Let's not think of doom. Tomorrow the sun will shine on all of us. For us women have rewritten tribal history."

Her head held high, Anele walked in victory to her hut.

* * *

The next day, after the falling out with Kumdi, the ear-splitting drums of thunder and lightning divided the dark early morning sky. Vimbela hid her head under a blanket, and Shiya shrieked. Anele rushed to the crib and consoled the shaking child. "Hush, little one. It's only a storm."

Nestled into her mother's breasts, Shiya drifted back to sleep, until torrential rainfall pounded the tin roof like a battalion of marching soldiers. It took a while for Anele to soothe her baby.

Unbeknown to the occupants in this hut, there was a worse storm on the horizon for mother and child.

Shortly after a breakfast of bread made from millet, Anele received a visitor—the little girl with the bloodied nose who had asked Anele's help. "Chief Anele, you have to watch yourself."

Anele frowned.

"Late last night," the girl said, "long after the ceremony, I overheard Umia telling Kumdi: 'I'll not rest in this body of mine until Anele and her *umlungu* child are dead.'"

"*Really!*" Anele exclaimed.

"Yes," the child responded. "Kumdi and Umia are going kill you and your baby and flee the village."

"Thank you for telling me this, child. Can you ask Umia and Kumdi to come to my hut?"

As usual, there was a flavor of poison in her voice as Umia protested her innocence with a straight face. "It's a lie."

Anele ended the animosity between them forever. "As Chief of the village, I'm ordering you and your brother to pack your belongings and leave Tswanas for good. You, and the likes of you, are no longer part of this tribe."

If looks could have killed, Anele would have been dead.

Unruffled, she resumed, "I have no objection to your parents or your younger brothers staying here. Make sure they know this."

Brother and sister pulled faces of contempt.

"You'll regret coming back," Kumdi said. "I'll make sure of it."

"You don't frighten me, *little* boy. *Go!* Before I have you chased out."

Standing like a gladiator, hand on his knife sheaf, Kumdi threatened, "You haven't heard the last of me. I'll seek Twazli's underworld powers to destroy you, stupid *umlungu*-loving woman!"

The evicted pair stormed out.

Anele and the villagers would not see the last of the humiliated wannabe leader. His return would bring shocking consequences. He would play a part in the nightmare of all nightmares, and the Tswanas tribe would never be the same again.

Chapter 10

During the weeks that followed Kumdi and Umia's departure, Anele's strong leadership helped her tribe to grow with the times: men and women now worked side by side planting sugar cane, millet, yams, tobacco, and profitable commodities on the open market. With the monetary return, Anele wanted to improve her village by having homesteads built to house large families, and corrugated roofing on the cattle sheds to protect the animals during the monsoon weather. Even build a schoolhouse. Yes, Anele reasoned, she *could* bring about these improvements.

* * *

Five summers and winters passed.

Anele's power had grown in leaps and bounds. There were no more naked villagers. Fashioned from the finest woven cloth and hand-sewn by Anele, women wore colorful skirts, halter-tops, and cotton undergarments. For the men, young and old, green plant-dyed pants and short-sleeve shirts. And a small schoolhouse had been erected at the far end of the newly fenced kraal. The delighted children wore school uniforms: white blouse and navy-blue pleated skirts. Finally, the kids attended school.

Sister Babavana, a black nun from a missionary in neighboring

Swaziland, whom Anele had met at the marketplace, volunteered her scholastic skills.

What did Anele feel about religion being taught in the classroom?

As long as the parents didn't object, Anele hadn't seen a problem. But she still had a sour taste in her mouth regarding the priest, Father Batuzi, who had, she believed, "stolen" her child and had "married" Nyasha against the teaching of the Catholic Church. However, Anele let it go but had stressed that the children of Tswanas also be taught cultural history of the many brave Zulu warriors and their battle for freedom.

Unfortunately, the nun couldn't keep that promise.

Four months after starting her post, Sister Babavana ended up in a bloody battle of her own.

While on vacation in her hometown, there was an uprising by two rival factions. She was raped and stabbed to death. The schoolhouse now stood empty. The children were heartbroken.

Unable to find a replacement, Anele took over the classroom, telling them stories about their heritage. Once more, villagers were in awe of their leader until a credulous incident changed their hearts.

* * *

On a hot Sunday afternoon in November 1950, Anele, Vimbela, and five-year-old Shiya joined the women on their daily trip to the river inlet to wash clothing and collect water for cooking.

Anele's heart brimmed with a mother's love at the sight of her adorable, angel-faced daughter boisterously frolicking in the murky waters with the other children.

Slapping the water, she shrieked in fun. Shiya's curly blonde hair was glistening with water droplets, and her once fair baby skin now shone in a dark suntan that blended well with the skin tones of the other kids. She had grown quite tall, a genetic Hallworthy trait.

For some unknown reason, Anele's thoughts switched suddenly

to another man. In a way, she regretted not trying to make peace with the scorned Kumdi. His parting words, shouted for all to hear, still haunted her:

"What if Anele's child *is* stolen from a white woman? I'll get lots of money if I say where she hides it."

Anele shrugged. Surely, they were only idle words of injured pride, or she would have known about it by now.

Shortly after the brother and sister's departure, word had returned: Umia had sought refuge in neighboring Mtunzini. Kumdi had not joined her. His whereabouts were unknown.

Anele dismissed all thoughts of Kumdi, Umia, and the evil Alan. It was too splendid a day to dwell on worthless men. But she did have a fondness for another male—Tekenya, a fifty-year-old goat herder, who in the early days of her arrival had pledged his love for her. Anele had been flattered but not ready to commit to marriage, so Tekenya had agreed to wait.

Humming a lively tune, Anele attended to her washing and only looked up when she heard Vimbela's high-pitched squealing.

As tadpoles darted between her legs, the eighteen-year-old yelled excitedly, "Look *Umama* Anele, I've caught a fish," she said, gripping the tail of a small, silver fish.

Anele smiled fondly at the girl whose mind was not much older than her Shiya's.

She laughed. "Catch lots more, Vimbela. They will make a good feast."

Anele adored this unfortunate girl born with mongolism, a common infliction of interbreeding in these parts of Africa. No man was ever again going to take advantage of Vimbela's innocence, not if Anele could help it. From Granny Matudia, Anele had learned that the gentle sweet girl, then barely twelve, had given birth to a malformed, blind baby boy with an enormous head and twisted limbs. Mercifully, the infant had lived only a few minutes.

For hours, Vimbela had clung pitifully to his limp body. In the end, the infant had to be removed by force and for days after, the heartbroken Vimbela had slept beside her baby's hillside grave. She had refused to come down until Matudia showed up the night of Anele's return home. "You are the only brave child that fears no creature of the night," the matriarch had said. "That is why I need you to go quickly to Naboto's "rat tree" and tell him…"

* * *

From the moment Vimbela breastfed Shiya, the simple girl had become devoted to her "shared" baby. That strong bond was to manifest itself this very day.

Laundry done, Anele was ready to leave. "Shiya, time to go now, Mother has lots to do—"

Her teeth clenched against an outcry. Gripped in fear, Anele couldn't believe her eyes—nor could the other washing women, nor the wide-eyed children standing frozen like statues beside Shiya. Loud gasps rose above the river's flow as some pointed at the child.

Gripped in Shiya's hand was one of Africa's most aggressive and feared snakes—a black mamba. Highly toxic venom in its hollow hypodermic fangs usually delivered a slow death.

Grinning mischievously, Shiya said, "Look, *Umama*, "I've got a big stick."

It seemed an eternity before Anele could retrieve her vocal chords. "*Shiya*, put it down," she ordered in enforced calmness. "Stay very still and don't move. It is not a *stick!* It's a bad snake. Please, my child, listen very carefully to your Mother—" She took a deep breath, fighting the panicky words that would terrify her child. "Precious little girl, drop the stick and stand very still."

Shiya tossed the snake high, caught it on the way down, and then draped it scarf-fashion around her neck. She squealed in enjoyment at this new game. The snake didn't seem to mind a bit. Its forked tongue flickered at the child's face. Then, as if fed up, uncoiled, and slithered into the shallow water, disappearing under mossy vegetation.

A snake-bitten superstitious woman shouted, "These harmful snakes have killed many with their poison. Why not *her?*" She pointed a shaky finger. "Does an evil *umlungu* spirit from their underworld possess her?"

"Maybe she *is* an evil spirit send by the White God," another ventured.

"I don't think so," another disputed. "I think this child is a gift from our God to protect us from harmful snakes."

Ignoring the irrational prattling, Anele waded into the river, grabbed Shiya's arm, and yanked her onto the muddy bank. "You are a bad girl," she admonished. "Next time I tell you to do something, listen to me or I will beat you."

Shiya's bottom lip trembled. "I am not a bad girl," she pouted. "The stick snake is my friend. He was happy to play with me. He told me he would not bite."

The rambling of a child was one thing, but disobedience was another.

Forcefully, Anele gripped Shiya's shoulders. "If you *ever* disobey me again, you'll be in for a spanking. Do you understand, Shiya?"

Vimbela hurried to the riverbank. "*Umama* Anele, she is a little child. How is she to know about the nasty creatures that can harm us if you don't tell her? You should not make her cry so."

"Vimbela, you are *not* her mother," Anele responded coldly. "Please do not tell me *how* to raise my child."

Her bottom lip drooping worse than Shiya's, Vimbela countered, "You're a bad *Umama*. I no like you no more."

"Yes, bad *Mother,*" Shiya repeated.

Anele chose not to respond to either of them. Instead, she took Shiya's hand, and together they crossed the river, back to where Anele had left her washed laundry. She placed the basket on her head, gave Shiya a "follow-me" look and, with long strides, Anele headed back to the kraal.

Shiya's legs raced to keep up. "*Umama,* wait for me."

Anele's mind was preoccupied. In her heart, she agreed with Vimbela. How could little Shiya know about the dangers that lurked around them, especially the Big Five: elephant, rhino, buffalo, lion, and leopard? *Had* she been too harsh?

Sighing, Anele sat the laundry down and waited for Shiya to catch up.

Lifting the out-of-breath child onto a tree stump, Anele squatted beside her. Patiently, she informed her daughter about the dangerous wildlife, the other poisonous snakes, tsetse flies that carry a sleeping sickness, and dangerous spiders, especially the Black Widow that had poisoned her blood shortly before she had run away with the twins.

"There are many, many creepy-crawlies of the bush that can harm not only little children like you, but *Umama* as well," Anele informed her daughter. "So we have to be careful at all times. Do you understand what I'm saying, child?"

Bewilderment wrinkling Shiya's nose, she darted her eyes everywhere but at Anele. Nothing could convince her. Hadn't the snake played with her? But to be on the safe side, not to rile her mother further, Shiya nodded.

As the trio entered the compound, Granny Matudia hurried to Anele's side.

"The young ones ran from the river to tell me of the snake. Is it true?"

Anele nodded. But she was in no mood to discuss the incident further, until a group of mostly elderly men, and her father's cousin, Natongo, surrounded her.

Shoulders stiff, Natongo's voice was hard with authority. "I speak for our people. The magic stones must be read by Twazli. Only *he,* a gifted man, can assure us why the serpent of a slow death has spared this child. Many lives have been lost to snakes. So, we all ask, is she a good spirit or a bad spirit?"

The man standing next to Natongo pointed a finger at Shiya. "She's an *Idimoni*—an evil spirit all right, hiding in a white child's body. Yes, the *Imikhuba* will know, for sure."

Fear draining her face of color, Shiya tugged at her mother's skirt. "I don't want the witchdoctor to come. He scares me."

Anele's heart melted. "It's okay, little one. There's nothing to be afraid of. As Chieftain of the village, I'm not going to allow it."

Matudia shook her head in disagreement. "This time, you have little choice, daughter of Naboto. It has always been our custom to call the *Imikhuba* when we need answers to troubling unexplained happenings. And this, I must agree, is definitely one of them."

"Do what you have to do, Matudia," Anele huffed. "But I won't let the witchdoctor in my home. If he has to read the stones, then he will do them outside."

Shiya and Vimbela in tow, Anele walked away, heading for the washing line outside her home. As if she hadn't a care in the world, she turned to Vimbela.

"I'll hang the clothes and you take Shiya inside. It's time for her nap."

Within minutes, Vimbela was back by her side. "*Umama* Anele, come quick. Shiya is shaking real bad. She looks sick."

Anele dashed into her hut. Had the snake bitten Shiya after all? Anele examined her.

Satisfied that there were no fang marks, Anele rocked Shiya on her lap and sang a song: "*A little baby I named Shiya, freed my soul from the village of hate. She came into my life and healed my troubled mind and childless body. At each tender smile my heart now rejoices with so much love for you.*"

Shiya's pale face broke into a wide smile. She hugged her mother, and drifted into sleep.

The sun climbed another hour higher in the sky.

Without announcement, the witchdoctor, followed by Natongo and Tekenya the goat herder, entered Anele's house.

Carrying a tree branch and other mysterious items of ritual, the uninvited guests avoided eye contact. Vimbela squealed in fright and burrowed her head under a blanket.

With the memory of the witchdoctor's visit five years ago still fresh in her mind, Anele stared impassively at him. Unexpectedly, a strangling fear such as she'd never felt before gripped her throat so tightly she could barely swallow. Could this overwhelming feeling have something to do with Twazli's previous warning?

Tread carefully, Anele. Don't provoke him this time, a voice inside her cautioned. But aloud, she suggested, "Let's go outside witchdoctor. You can read your stones there. I don't want Shiya to wake and see you."

Twazli glared at her. "The child of *umlungu* blood will not hear or see me. I have seen to that."

"What do you mean? If you've harmed—"

"Silence!" he roared. "You speak when I tell you. I'm here at the request of the elders. The casting of the Ancient Stones of my forefathers will not alter what I have already predicted—"

"I *never* asked you to change our future. Nor did I ask you to come here. Shiya is *not* an evil spirit, and your stones will prove this."

Twazli sat cross-legged. With the overgrown nail of his right index finger, he traced a circle in the dirt, then gestured for the tree branch and placed it across the circle.

Anele's eyebrows arched when the ancient man took out his long shriveled penis and urinated on the bark. Then chanting the ancient rites for truth, Twazli threw a magic stone, pink in color, onto the floor. Should it roll out of the urine-sealed ring, trouble would befall the person. It fell within the circle. He threw another stone. It too, fell safely. He threw a third. It bounced out of the ring and rolled across the room. The witchdoctor let out a squeal that sounded more animal than human.

"What do you see, honorable *Imikhuba?* Tell us now," Natongo eagerly questioned.

"I see the fires of the damned spirits consume this child, the one who has been named Shiya. The vengeful breath of the Dark One will deliver a white messenger…" Twazli inhaled sharply as if his eyes were deceiving him. "And the Dark One will also send one of us, a black traitor. Blood will flow from wounds in their heads, holes not made by spears but round balls that fly from fire."

Feigning nonchalance, Anele forced a chuckle. Her lack of respect brought Natongo face to face. He poked a gnarled finger into her upper arm. "Your father must be crying. You have brought the anger of *Ikloba,* the Dark One, not just on yourself and the white child, but all Tswanas people."

"I've long left this nonsense behind," Anele stated, moving away from him.

"Stupid daughter of a great and noble man," Natongo spat. "You may mock the words of the great *Imikhuba,* but it's our right to have the child tested."

No one took any notice of Vimbela sneaking out. She had witnessed this very man bring a dead goat back to life, make a crippled man walk, and cause other unexplainable events.

Anele clenched her jaw. "Get out now, or I will throw hot pig oil on all of you—"

Picking up the oil lamp, she swung it back and forth like a pendulum. The men stood their ground. A mere woman would not take this moment from them.

Natongo placed a trio of bongo drums between his knees and began tapping from drum to drum, the warrior's beat. As the rhythm increased, Twazli's painted face twisted in a wry grin. "This is a man's domain," he seethed. "Women should have no say in it. I order that the child be taken to the Sacred Rock to spend the night. If she is not a bad seed come to lure our people into the dark cave of no return, no harm will come to her."

"You are *insane!*" Anele shouted. "To leave Shiya on the rock for the night is madness. Hungry wild creatures will eat her, you dung-for-brains man."

"The Ancients will close the mouths of beasts if the child is pure, but if she is not—"

Anele was relieved to see Granny Matudia enter. She looked pleadingly into the old woman's eyes. "You have to stop this insanity. He wants Shiya to go to the Rock. Stay there the whole night."

"Anele, Vimbela tells me that you are brainless, like her. What did you expect? The snake incident would just go away! We are ancient people who respect the *Imikhuba's* judgment. It seems you are no longer one of us."

The matriarch's last words stung the worst.

Twazli smiled at Matudia and then made a loud guttural sound like a strangled goat. "Matudia, good sister of mine, your words are sound, but I've important work to do. Leave us."

Matudia made a hasty exit.

"Matudia, come back!" Anele called out. "I'm the Chief. You don't have to listen to him!"

Twazli's thin lips parted and erupted into braying laughter as though a demon within him exulted with gloating scorn. "No woman mocks the Great One. Unbeliever, be warned." He began mumbling incoherently.

Anele's skin started tingling as though a thousand ants were crawling over her flesh as she watched, spellbound.

Manifesting themselves at Twazli's feet were grotesque miniature beings with misshapen heads, fire-red eyes set in sunken sockets, and deformed hands and feet that were claw-like. He bent low to hear their high-pitched squeaky communiqué. He nodded in agreement, then, in a mocking tone, he relayed their statements. "My friends from the underworld tell me that I look weak in their eyes for the disrespectful words of a woman who dares taunt me. They confirm that the forsaken one is indeed a reincarnated bad seed. No serpent power can protect her in this life or the afterlife. They will welcome her should she die this night on the Sacred Rock."

Hot fury flowed over Anele and swept away her prickles of fear. Ignoring the ungodly eyes staring up at her, she adopted a warrior's stance of defiance, slapped her chest several times, and spat into Twazli's face.

Natongo and Tekenya gasped in horror. Anele had broken a sacred tribal rule. Spitting in any form was taboo, they told her, not just at the witchdoctor, but at young or old, male or female. She had evoked the highest insult. She could face death by stoning—a Tswanas custom.

Anele's inner voice reasoned: *That was part of the old ways. Surely not today...*

"Anele must be punished," the witchdoctor demanded.

"Yes, I agree, she must be stoned," Tekenya said.

Anele was flabbergasted. Was this cold flat voice coming from the same person who had fervently pledged to love and protect her? Only yesterday, he had begged her to marry him.

Full of disgust, Anele gave him the evil eye, and then turned to the witchdoctor.

"I ask you not to harm me or my child. At first light, I will take Shiya *and* Vimbela and leave Tswanas for good. If we are gone, there will be no cause for fear. But I'll say this: I wish I'd never come back to the village of my birth—" Lord Nigel's words spilled into her mouth, "—to be among savages who have no hearts."

The witchdoctor smirked, and then with a wave of his hand, the impious entities vanished into thin air. Twazli's eyes, deep and dark as fathomless pools, locked on Anele.

"Your running days are over, Anele of Tswanas. Before the sun dances over the Sacred Burial Hill, your fate will be set. Nothing you can say or do now will affect that outcome. You should have listened to me, brainless daughter of a good man."

He turned his back on her and headed for the doorway. Natongo left with him. Tekenya stayed behind. In a whisper, he said, "Anele, I didn't mean what I said."

"Oh yes, you did!" Anele replied. "Now get out, before I throw you out myself."

His chin nearly touching his chest, Tekenya exited.

An eerie silence now surrounded Anele's home, inside and out, until Vimbela rushed in. "*Umama* Anele. I listen by the window. I fear the *Imikhuba's* words."

Anele stroked the trembling girl's cheek. "Everything is going to be all right. You're coming with me and Shiya. We leave in the morning. We'll go to Mtunzini, where my mother Tuttia and my grandmother were born. We will be welcome there."

"But how will we take care of ourselves, *Umama* Anele?"

"Don't worry. You can mind Shiya while I work the fields."

"What about Umia, Shiya's first wet-nursing girl? She lives there. She hates you and Shiya. She told me so. She might take a knife to your heart."

"No, she won't. The Mtunzini women couldn't stand Umia's ugly ways, and they have chased her and her children from their village."

"But Anele, what if—"

"That's enough, Vimbela. I've lots of things to do before we leave: preparing food for our journey, packing clean clothes, and retrieving the money I've hidden near my father's favorite tree. Why don't you take a nap? You will need your strength to help me with Shiya. The rainy season is upon us, and it could be dangerous to cross the mountain rocks on foot to Mtunzini."

Pouting, Vimbela got into the bed and snuggled next to Shiya.

That night, Anele slept fitfully.

Chapter 11

Well before daybreak, and guided by a waning moon, Vimbela, piggybacking Shiya, walked quietly beside Anele on the way to the kraal gate. Behind them, the tribe was sleeping. Suddenly in the distance, a loud rumbling noise could be heard, stopping them in their tracks.

Vimbela frowned. "What *is* it that makes the ground shake so badly?"

"I've no idea. But I don't like the sound of it."

Peering over Vimbela's shoulder, Shiya muttered, "Maybe lots of elephants run away from the jungle?"

It took a split second for Anele to realize what it might be. *No!* How could it have gotten through the narrow single-track and rocky mountain pass up to the village?

When blinding lights stabbed the darkness, Vimbela dove behind a pile of firewood stacked against the fence, Shiya's face striking against her backbone. A trickle of blood from her bitten top lip dribbled down the child's chin, but she seemed to know that she should not cry out.

The camouflaged vehicle barreled through the fence, snapping it as if it were matchsticks. There wasn't enough daylight for Anele to make out the faces in the vehicle or the four horsemen following.

Anele quickly jumped behind the firewood to join Vimbela and Shiya.

Hunkering next to them, Anele's mind scrambled for answers. Who are they? Could it be game wardens? What did they want? Had one of the villagers been poaching in the nearby national game reserve?

The Jeep careened through patches of garden, knocking over a large cauldron hanging in the fire pit before screeching to a halt. Tails tucked in, dogs yelped and slunk behind buildings. Startled villagers, illuminated in the Jeep's headlights, peered from doorways. Most had never seen this or any other mode of modern transport. Perplexed, they watched silently as the four uniformed white men dismounted and stood in a line, revolvers at the ready, awaiting orders. Then all eyes turned to the tall man with a rifle slung over his right shoulder alighting from the vehicle.

From the rear of the Jeep, another man appeared, a lanky shabbily dressed black man with a floppy hat obscuring his features.

The tall man roared in Zulu at him, "Where are Anele and the kid?"

The man's raucous demand froze Anele's bones. She clamped a hand over her mouth. She knew that razor-sharp voice only too well. How did he find her? Zululand was a vast area, over ten thousand square miles. *And kid!* How could Alan Hallworthy possibly know of Maria's child?

Alan aimed his weapon at the person nearest to him—a fifteen-year-old boy. "Speak up *kaffir,* or you're a dead duck."

The whites of his eyes as large as a moon, just like the day he had found the dead chief, Natu was speechless.

Alan beckoned to the black man wearing the floppy hat to come forward. "Get the bitch. You said you knew which hut she was in."

"Yes, *baas,* right away, *baas.* I know exactly which hut Anele and the child sleep in."

Anele's betrayer's voice floated on the wind. It could not be? But it *was*—him—*Kumdi!* How many pieces of silver, she wondered, was her Judas paid for his treachery?

Granny Matudia, her nightgown trailing the dirt, rushed up to the scorned wannabe leader. No one stopped her.

She grabbed Kumdi's khaki shirtsleeve. Nearly ripping the garment off his body, the ancient woman growled, "What brings you here with the enemy of our people? You are a piece of dung to do this!"

Kumdi tossed his head haughtily, "It's none of your business old woman. Let go of me, or I'll get him to shoot you."

Noses almost touching, Matudia spat, "You ungrateful dung-for-brains boy, I made sure you and your sister left the settlement with full bellies. Now my kindness is repaid by your leading the *umlungu* to us." Adrenalin pumping through her veins, she balled a fist and knocked Kumdi off his feet with one blow to his chest. Alan and his entourage watched in amusement and amazement at this old woman's amazing strength and tenacity.

Laughter dancing with the first rays of sunlight echoed throughout the settlement.

Springing to his feet, a shame-faced Kumdi shoved Matudia so hard she fell backward, hitting her head against the hard dirt. She groaned. Two women rushed to the matriarch and helped her to her feet. Although dazed, she wasn't badly hurt.

Dusting the dirt off his shorts, Kumdi faced off. "Don't you dare touch me ever again, old woman!" he bellowed smirking with satisfaction. "You know Anele has stolen a child!"

"Next time, you won't get up," Matudia hissed shaking her fist. "You've betrayed your own kind. Twazli's Dark Ones will come for your miserable black soul."

"Enough of this mumbo-jumbo crap," Alan growled in English. "Kumdi, go and get them *now!*"

Followed by two of the deputies, handguns raised, he entered Anele's house. Within seconds they exited, shaking their heads.

"There's no one in here, *baas*." Kumdi announced.

"They're hiding somewhere," Alan snorted. "Search all the homes."

Secreted behind the woodpile, Anele whispered in Vimbela's ear, "Please don't ask any questions. We are in terrible danger. Listen to me carefully. Take Shiya and run like the wind to my father's dead rat tree. Can you remember the way?"

Teeth chattering in fear, Vimbela nodded.

"Climb as high as you can. Stay there with Shiya until I come for you both."

"*Umama,* why do we—?"

"Be silent Shiya, if you know what's good for you. You'll be all right if you listen to me. Go with Vimbela, and I'll come shortly, I promise."

Shiya didn't utter another word, but her terrified eyes spoke volumes.

Anele kissed the girls on their cheeks and said, "Hurry, please go now."

Shaking like a bush in the grip of a savannah storm, Vimbela climbed over the mangled fence, and fled.

While waiting until they were out of sight, Anele had a premonition. She tilted her chin and sniffed the air. What was that smell? Yes. It definitely was the rich aroma of her father's tobacco. Was he here with her? She closed her eyes. "*Ubaba,* I can't see you, but I feel you are here with me. Please whisper in my ear and tell me what to do."

* * *

An incandescent sun rose in the sky, bathing the former Hallworthy servant in a soft blue light.

Head high, spiritual courage from her father shrouding her body, Anele walked toward the unwelcome intruders. "I am here,

Master Alan."

Alan spun around to face her and in a fluid movement swung his rifle, the butt hitting Anele on the head with a tremendous blow. She flew backward onto the dirt.

With a finger, Alan flicked off scalp flesh from his weapon and stared down at her. "Where is my child? Don't look so dumb. You know damn well what I'm talking about."

Anele feigned innocence. "Master Alan, I do not know what you mean. What child?"

The rifle's wooden stock slammed down again, and a fountain of blood spurted from her nose. "Don't act smart with me, you black bitch," Alan hissed. "You know damn well what I'm talking about. Where is my child? I know she is here somewhere…"

His snarling voice was a blur.

Praying to die before he learned of Shiya's whereabouts, Anele murmured, "Spirits of the Underworld end my life now."

Straddling her like a game trophy Alan scoffed, "Did you think I wouldn't find you?"

She tried to speak, but no sound escaped.

He nudged her mouth with the cold steel muzzle. "Has the cat got your tongue, black bitch? You want to *know* how I found out about you and my kid? Well. I'm going to tell you—"

"Sorry to interrupt you Lord Hallworthy," a police officer said. "Would you like us to continue searching?"

"Yes. Search every inch of the godforsaken place."

Alan refocused his attention on Anele.

"Maria, you know, the Sicilian bitch you freed, and hoped I'd never find, told me she'd given birth to twins." Alan tapped a finger against his chin. "Now, let me think, could it be someone I know, who helped the *wop* deliver? She couldn't have done it all by herself! Maybe it was a black bitch named Anele who killed one baby and stole the other?"

Anele's silent voice screamed: "*Maria didn't give birth to twins!*

She couldn't have! Great God in the Spirit World, in my haste to save Shiya perhaps I didn't see the other baby? Had the twin fallen deeper into the compost pit?"

She tried to sit up, but Alan's boot pressed down like a massive concrete block on her ribcage. At that moment, she would have sold her soul to Twazli's creatures for a gun to shoot him dead, so Shiya would forever remain safe from his evil ways. In Anele's tortured mind, to Alan, age didn't matter, and Shiya would probably become another of his victims.

Many clouds had darkened Anele's life, but this was the worst. Utter helplessness tore apart her heart: *I tried, dear God of the white people, I tried to protect Shiya.*

Anele struggled to rise.

"Don't dare move. I'm not finished," Alan snapped. "After Maria gave birth, you took the healthy child and ran away with it, didn't you? How do I know this? Ah! I can see by the look on your face that you're dying to know. Am I right?"

Anele's hate-filled eyes glared back at her former slave-master as he continued, "Maria thought she could get away from me. Wrong! I found the whore not far from my house, bleeding like a butchered pig. I'd have left her to rot if it wasn't for her telling me about my children. If it wasn't for Maria's psychiatrist in the state mental hospital, where I put her, I would have dismissed her crazy story—"

"*Bastard*—"

A rib bone caved in under Alan's boot pressure. Anele grimaced in agony.

He resumed as if nothing had happened. "At first, I didn't believe any of it, because Maria is nuttier than a fruitcake. It was a cleaner at the hospital—" He gestured to Kumdi to come forward. "—it was this man who verified Maria's crazy story."

The moment was Kumdi's. Like a demented lunatic, he grinned.

The other nutcase, Alan, didn't break a smile. He shouted in

English for all to hear. "Where is the *white* child? One of you better bring her to me, or I'll pick you off like flies."

Not understanding, the tribe stared at him.

The rifle's blast lifted the matriarch off her feet and, blood gushing from the chest wound, Granny Matudia was dead before her body thudded onto the ground.

Paralyzed with fear, no one made a move or said a word except Anele. "Please don't kill any more of my people, Master Alan," she begged. "They are innocent bush people, and they don't understand English. I've no idea why Kumdi would make up such lies. There's no white child here."

The next shot Alan fired nicked the side of Anele's earlobe. "You are a lying runaway bitch. For the last time, where—"

Loud gasps directed his eyes in an easterly direction.

Leaping like a gazelle over obstacles, Shiya raced toward them, a wiggling green snake clasped in her hand. She sprinted past Alan and the other intruders as if they weren't there and, releasing the deadly green mamba onto the earth, hunched and stroked her mother's battered face.

"*Umama,* did the *umlungu* man hurt you? Do you want me to get the *Imikhuba?* The witchdoctor will destroy bad men."

Pain forgotten, Anele wrapped her arms around her precious child.

Alan's face showed no sign of jollity.

He bent to study his child. He was amazed how much she resembled him. She was tall, towering over most children her age. She had his blonde hair but not his blue eyes. Hers were green, reflecting Maria's Sicilian heritage. Shiya's nose and mouth were finely chiseled like those of his mother, Lady Ethel. Yes, she belonged to him all right, but she would never be a *true* Hallworthy. No, definitely not. But, she would be his, in more ways than one.

As if reading this depraved man's mind, Anele pulled Shiya closer and whispered in her ear, "Run, child, run. This man is going to eat you like a crocodile."

Shiya pulled a comical face. "He's not *ingwenya,* silly *Umama.* He's not a crocodile, he is a white man."

Alan assumed what had been whispered to the child and smirked. His patience strained, he snatched Shiya from Anele, threw her over his shoulder, and marched to the Jeep. She struggled violently to free herself, crying out, "*Vulela umlungu…* bad white man, let go of me."

A backhand across her little face sent her into a flood of tears and tore Anele's heart from her chest.

A wailing Shiya was flung into the passenger seat. In a pitiful voice she begged, "*Umama,* get up and save me."

Badly injured, all Anele could do was beseech the Underworld: "*Watch over this special child. Make this child strong with your spiritual serpent powers, for she will need them against this evil man. He will show her no mercy—*"

A loud boom halted her prayers.

In a tidal wave of willpower, Anele forced herself into an upright position. She couldn't see Shiya in the Jeep. "Oh, no," she groaned. "The *bastardo* has killed her."

She fell back against the hard earth and wept. Then a voice startled her, and she looked up. Through her tear-filled eyes, she could just make out the shape of a stooped man standing over her.

"Shiya isn't dead, Anele," Twazli grunted. "But you will wish she was. I tried to warn you."

Anele puffed out her cheeks. "Twazli, I hope your flesh rots in the fires of the white-man's hell."

A second dark shape loomed over her.

"It's true, Anele," her suitor reaffirmed. "Your *Shiya* sits in the chair of the tin cart. I want you to know that I shouldn't have listened to the mouths of others. My heart now tells me otherwise. Will you forgive me?"

Anele closed her eyes against the sight of him. There was nothing in her heart to forgive. Tekenya had betrayed her when he asked for her to be stoned.

The contrite suitor knelt and stroked Anele's battered head.

"You should have married me when I asked. I would have taken you and the child far from here, to Basutoland, where I was born. The *umlungu* would never have found you there—"

He was pushed aside by a white policeman.

"Out of the way, *kaffir,* or you're next!"

Too weak to resist, Tekenya stepped aside and watched Anele being hogtied, dragged across the dirt, and thrown into the back of the Jeep. She landed on the body of Kumdi, dead eyes gaping at the sky. A single gunshot wound to the back of his neck, execution style, marked his end. Anele felt no anger toward Kumdi, only pity. "I forgive you, Kumdi," she murmured. "Fly free and seek out my father. He will guide you into the Invisible Kingdom of Spirits."

Alan stuck his head out the window and addressed an officer, "Thanks for your help. I couldn't have done it without you."

"It's been a pleasure to have been of assistance, Lord Hallworthy. And thank *you* for your most generous *donation*. If you ever need our help again, please don't hesitate to call my contact number in Nairobi."

Through his rear-view mirror, Alan, a wry grin escaping his lips, watched the ex-cons and mercenaries disguised as police officers mount and ride away. He chuckled. He had pulled off the perfect charade. He knew from experience, the tribe would just mourn their dead and simply resume their bush ways. There would be no outside investigation into what had happened this day.

The Jeep, transporting its unwilling passengers, sped from the kraal in a fog of red dust riding over thorn bushes as if they were merely clumps of tall grass.

High above, hidden under the canopy of baobab leaves, Vimbela clung to a broad bough. When the flap at the back of the Jeep flew open, exposing Anele and Kumdi, the terrified woman scrambled down and raced after the Jeep, coughing and choking in the dust of the vehicle's wake. "*Umama,* where are you going?" she screamed. "Come back. It isn't my fault. I did what you told me. Shiya wouldn't listen. She climbed down the dead rat tree and ran. I couldn't catch her. She has the legs of a cheetah—"

Vimbela tripped over a tree stump, and her temple struck against a jagged root, knocking her unconscious.

As the Jeep sped away, a petrified Shiya, held in a vice-like grip on Alan's lap, cried out, "*Umama,* Shiya wants you…"

Alan dug his fingernails into her tender flesh. "That black bitch is not your mother. Do you understand? And you can forget that *kaffir* name. From now on, your name is…" Alan scratched his chin's stubble. "Little Shit! Or better still, Little *Wop* Shit!"

There came a fire in the child's tear-swollen eyes. The grizzly in her stood up and attacked. "The witchdoctor is going to kill you for hurting me and my *Umama.* The *Imikhuba* can make his body invisible, you know. He'll cut your throat, and you'll die just like the cattle at slaughter time. Then the cook will boil your bones, and we'll eat you."

Alan's chest shook with laughter. But his mirth turned to fury when Shiya sunk her teeth into his leg and her small hands beat against her captor's arms and chest. A bunch of keys gripped in Alan's hand hit her head hard, and she screamed out, "One day, *umlungu,* I roast you alive for hurting me and my Umama."

Chapter 12

The afternoon sun bleached the earth as the Jeep, carrying its hostages, drove past the infamous Hallworthy guest cottage and came to a halt at the edge of a sugar cane field.

Alan opened the driver's door and got out to stretch his legs, leaving the fast asleep child bundled in a blanket under the passenger seat. He strolled to the rear of the vehicle and lifted the flap. "Jesus!" he cried, swatting the swarm of horse flies that flew out of the back. Kumdi's decomposing body was shrouded in these flesh-eating pests. Next to him, huddled in a corner, they were also attacking Anele.

Alan dragged out the lifeless body of Kumdi and left him lying on the dirt.

"You are next, black bitch. But I'm going to wait for the police to arrive to take you to where you belong… in jail."

He returned to the passenger side, lifted the now wide-awake Shiya, tucked her under his arm, and began walking. A few yards down the pathway, he lost his grip on her. Shiya rolled out of the blanket and hit the dirt. In a flash, he grabbed her by the neck and squeezed. Gasping for air, she tugged at his hand, loosened a finger, and bit hard into his palm flesh. He let go.

"You little bastard!" he howled.

Feet churning even before they hit the ground, Shiya ran into the dense crop. On and on she fled, ignoring sharp-edged leafstalks that sliced her feet like spears. Finally, lungs heaving, sweat streaking her dust-caked cheeks, she crouched in the thickest part of the foliage. She cocked her head. What was that *whooshing* sound? Her imagination conjured up a leopard, a lion, and a crocodile's tail. Terrified, she tucked her head between her knees. When the pocketknife nicked the back of her ear, she shrieked in pain.

"Did you think you could get away from me?" Alan mocked. Brutally, he yanked Shiya up by her left arm, ripping her elbow out of its socket. Pain like hot knives stabbing ran up and down her arm.

Alan dragged his silent daughter into a clearing.

Her ear bleeding, elbow throbbing, and legs and face scratched, she bore the pain remarkably well for a child of her age. It was as if she knew her cries of pain would only antagonize this cruel man further.

Waiting for them on a grassy bank was a black girl wearing an outgrown and faded maid's uniform. The kitchen servant stared at her master and then down at the dark-looking child with emerald eyes. What on earth was going on? Who was this child?

All Maekela had been told was that she was to meet her employer here at the clearing at three o'clock sharp. She had been waiting for over an hour.

"Take this child straight to my house," Alan instructed his servant. "Clean her up, and I'll be there later. And, Maekela, if she gets away, I'll murder *you!*"

Her insides trembling, Maekela nodded.

Shiya stared at the young black woman. Her eyes were as blue as the sky. Momentarily, her pain forgotten, she was captivated by Maekela's sparkling eyes, her mind switched gears. But the opportunity to flee again was thwarted. Maekela's vice-like grip sent a shooting pain up her injured arm. Her eyes rolled backward, but she didn't cry out. What Shiya's little brain couldn't understand was that this was a *black* person, and the blacks she had known and loved were kind and not hurtful.

Her small feet raced to keep up with Maekela's long strides.

Deep in thought, the Hallworthy servant wondered who the girl's mother was. As far as she knew, there were no green-eyed fieldworkers, housemaids, or foreigners on the property. But there was no doubt—this child had *white* blood. But whose?

With her free hand, Shiya tugged at Maekela's skirt. "My name is Shiya, and I'm nearly six summers old. What's your name?"

"Be quiet," Maekela answered in Zulu. "I can't think. This is all too much for me. I'm just a simple girl."

"What's a simple girl?"

"Shut up and let me do my job!"

"Let me go, *simple* girl. I have to find my *Umama.*"

"Do you want a beating?"

"No."

"Then be quiet!"

As the Hallworthy mansion came into view, Maekela stopped to take a breather and inadvertently slackened her hold. Shiya was off like a rocket down the manor's pathway with Maekela hot on her heels.

Dozing in a garden chair outside the kitchen door, a gray-haired woman was woken by Maekela's high-pitched shouting, "Child, stop. Get here *now!*" Shiya darted around the deckchair, but her clumsy pursuer tripped over the woman's outstretched legs, and Maekela did a nosedive. Shiya broke into a fit of laughter, but not for long. Maekela got up and snatched Shiya, and now her grip was like a steel vice.

Lamella's poor eyesight, the result of encroaching cataracts, followed the pair heading for the back door. "Maekela, where have you been? The table linens need to be..." Lamella eyes narrowed.

"Stop when I'm talking to you… and where do you think you're going with that child?"

"I'm taking her into the house."

"Maekela, you of all people know black children are forbidden inside."

Maekela huffed, then held tighter onto Shiya, cutting off the flow of blood to her disjointed arm. In reaction to the agonizing pain, Shiya bit hard into her escort's hand, drawing blood. Maekela cried out, "Why am I the one that has to deal with this wildcat child? My sister never gets orders from Master Alan."

"You're the oldest Maekela. Anyway, Isona is my eyes when *you* are not around," Lamella countered. "And she is a better shopper at the market than you are."

"Let me go, you nasty black *mamba!*" Shiya spat.

Lamella shook her head. "Why do you hold a black child like a chicken's neck?"

"Didn't you see it? The *white* kid bit me."

The aging cook frowned and her lips parted, but nothing was said.

"She deserves a beating," Maekela stated. "And I'll tell you again, Lamella, this is not a *black* child. She belongs to the master just like I do. And if she gets away from me again, he will kill me… that's what he said. I have to clean her. And I am doing just that."

But not only was the senior's eyesight poor, so was her hearing.

Clucking and scratching her head under her headscarf, trying to remember a moment dimmed with time, it suddenly came to her: the long-ago incident with young Anele.

"Black child bathed in my clean kitchen? *Never again!* Maekela, take her to the irrigation pump. Clean her there if you must!"

Exasperated, Maekela exhaled loudly. "Your old eyes deceive you, Lamella. Take another look at the child you think is one of us."

Cook's large hands gripping her aching back, she bent until she reached Shiya's eye level and checked the child over. "What nonsense do you speak, Maekela? The child is as black as you and I."

"You need glasses, old cook."

Shiya's head swung back and forth like a pendulum between the arguing females, then she reached for Lamella's prune-wrinkled hand. "Please, old lady, tell her to let me go. I have to find my *Umama*, Anele. Bad *umlungu* men took her away from Tswanas…"

Lamella's eyes went round as dinner plates. Shiya's eyes searched hers. "You know my *Umama*, old lady?"

Invoking the gods for protection, Lamella's mouth opened and snapped shut. She recoiled from Shiya as if the child had leprosy.

At the sound of approaching footsteps, Shiya turned to see a chubby white woman entering the kitchen. She cringed at the sight of the first white woman she had ever seen. Was she going to hurt her like the *umlungu* man?

Sausage-shaped fingers on her wide hips, Lady Corrie glared at the filthy child. Then she barked in a language strange to Shiya's ears. But her tone and hand gestures were clear. "How dare you bring this *thing* into my home! Take her to the old washhouse…"

She was an ugly white woman, Shiya observed, who would for sure frighten frogs. Indeed, her own heart was pounding as the voluminous woman waddled from the kitchen. As young as she was, she knew this woman was not to be messed with.

As soon her mistress' shoes faded from hearing, Maekela let out a sigh of relief. Now safely out of earshot, she mocked Corrie's instructions in singsong:

"*Maekela, make sure you check her for lice and fleas. Douse her with paraffin oil outside if you do find any nasty creatures. Scrub her well, cut her disgusting hair, and burn her clothes. I'll be back in an hour to see that you have done what I've told you to do.*"

Defiantly, she took Shiya into the indoor scullery. There she removed the child's only item of clothing—a pair of cotton-woven panties—lifted her into the deep enamel sink, ran the cold water, and proceeded to cut off her blonde curls with a pair of scissors. Shiya uttered not a murmur, nor did Maekela. Then she began scrubbing Shiya's tender flesh with a hard-bristled brush.

The child's chilling screams brought Lamella rushing in. Maekela pointed to Shiya's elbow, swollen to the size of a cricket ball, then handed the sobbing child to Lamella's waiting arms. Cook carried her into the main kitchen area and sat down with her on the rocker. For a small child who had lost everything she loved, snuggling onto the cook's large lap was blissful.

Chewing on toothless gums, Lamella lovingly looked down at her. The cook's voice was kind. "Old Lamella is going to make you better, child." She lifted the hem of her apron and said, "Dry your eyes, little one."

Her own eyes glistening with sorrow, Maekela stared at the child.

"Maekela go into the pantry and bring me an orange," Lamella instructed.

Thinking that at last she was going to get something to eat, Shiya wrapped her arms around the cook's neck and kissed her cheek. "I like you, old lady."

Lamella laughed. "And I like you too, Missy,"

When Maekela returned with a huge orange, Shiya's eyes lit up. She was hungry. She tried to snatch it from Maekela's hand, but Lamella got the fruit first. "You can have it in a minute. But first, I need you to do something for me."

Shiya raised her sore arm as instructed.

Cook placed the orange under the child's armpit, lowered her arm, and in a wink of an eye snapped the dislocated elbow back in place. Shiya passed out.

She awoke to being rocked gently. Arm still throbbing painfully, Shiya cried, "Old lady, make the pain go away."

"Hush now, child," Lamella said. "It's going to hurt for some time, but it *will* get better, I promise you. Would you like the orange now?"

Shiya tore ferociously into the juicy fruit, devouring the skin and pips. Lamella laughed and waited until she'd finished. "Child, I know who you really are. While you were *sleeping*, Mistress Corrie came back and explained why you are here."

At Shiya's blank look, Lamella shrugged. "For whatever reason Anele took you to her home, you will have to, from this day on, forget all about her. I know you are only little, but it's best you never mention her name again. She's been taken to Montclair prison, a very bad place. Nobody gets out of there alive, do they Maekela?"

Glumly, Maekela nodded.

"I also knew your *real* mother," Lamella continued. "Maria was such a pretty child, just like you. I know this because Master Alan brought her back here shortly after she nearly starved to death in the bush, so he told me—"

At the sound of high-heels reentering the kitchen, Corrie's presence sent Shiya diving for cover under Lamella's apron. Against the cook's warm belly, she listened to Corrie's harsh voice rising and falling like a storm-whipped tide. Then came silence.

The coast clear, Lamella lifted her apron. "You can come out now, child. The witch is gone. I can't keep calling you 'child.' What name do you go by?"

"My *Umama* calls me Shiya."

"Anele chose well. It's the perfect name for you. Now, I have to tell you something, and I don't know how much of it you will understand. But you will have to realize that *you* are a white Missy. You must put behind you the life you have led with Anele in the bush, because—" Lamella took a deep breath, "—because little Shiya, it's never going to be the same for you, ever again. You will have to live in a white's world. You will then learn to hate the skin color of the ones who have raised you. But like us, your heart will burn with hatred for those who treat us like animals—"

* * *

Shiya would come to learn that unhappiness had no color in a country that judged peoples' worthiness by their skin tone. Of course, she didn't know if she were white, yellow, or green. Nor did she know that her skin resembled Middle-Easterners, even with Alan's blonde hair and Maria's green eyes. In years to come, her mixed-blood heritage from her Sicilian mother and British father would classify her as "colored" by the Afrikaner National Party when South Africa was given its independence from Great Britain.

* * *

When the next person entered the kitchen, Lamella clambered to her feet, dropping Shiya from her lap. The look on Alan Hallworthy's face as he stood in the doorway sent Shiya fleeing into the scullery and scrambling under the sink. Like a mouse, she flattened her body and crawled into a hole that was no bigger than a mailbox slit. Alan's voice boomed into her hidey-hole. "Come out, you little shit, or I'll skin your hide."

To the servants' bowed heads, he ordered, "Don't you say a word in *kaffir* language! The bitch *will* learn to speak the Queen's English. I don't ever want you talking to her in Zulu. Is that clear?"

Chins nearly touching their breasts, the women nodded.

Alan turned to Maekela. "I haven't got time to deal with this. Get that little shit out and take her to the mistress. She's waiting in the sitting room."

He marched away.

"Please, come out," Maekela pleaded in Zulu. "Life is bad enough here without you causing the devil in that man to appear."

"Is the bad *umlungu* gone?" Shiya asked.

"Yes."

Covered in cobwebs, she crawled out.

Maekela wrapped a kitchen towel around Shiya's body and gently led her upstairs into a place Shiya could never have imagined existed. Mouth agape, she stared at the trappings of the white world where strange furniture and even walls were covered in cloth more splendid than the witchdoctor's ceremonial robe. Objects shining golden as the sun and white as the moon adorned the room. Her eyes finally came to rest on the mistress sitting in a chair large enough to seat her entire family.

Corrie motioned for the servant to bring Shiya over to her.

Maekela placed a shaking Shiya on the floor in front of Lady Corrie, who bent and grabbed her swollen arm. Shiya howled like a banshee.

Clasping hands over her ears, Corrie shouted, "*Shut up!*"

Shiya continued to make her discomfort known.

What started as a mutter rose to a shout from Corrie, "If you don't shut up, I'll break your bloody neck."

Maekela rushed to the child and with lips partly closed begged her to be silent in Zulu.

Like the scrubbing brush, Corrie's angry words tore into Shiya. "You're not going to come between my husband and I, ever. Do you hear me? He wants you around, but I don't. I'm not able to bear his children, but I'll be damned if I'll raise his bastard kid. I'm going to make sure you leave here, sent as far away as possible. Your real mother is a whore and insane. I hope she rots to death in the mental asylum, and Anele… well, I certainly don't wish her well." Corrie stared into Shiya's tear-filled eyes. "God only knows what is in *your* blood!"

Shiya could not comprehend Maekela's translated version, nor did she wish to hear another word. She clasped *her* hands over her ears and remained silent, fear rendering her mute. Many years would pass before she uttered another word to a white person; not a sound would escape her lips through some of the worst ordeals a child could suffer.

* * *

Renamed Lynette by Corrie, Shiya kept the heinous events that she endured at Hallworthy Manor, and later, at the convent for "colored"

children, and after the convent, the mental institution, locked in
the attic of her mind for most of her life. There it stayed until she
decided to record her life story for *her* only child, a daughter named
Brianna.

So, in 1998, more than anything, and for the very last time,
Lynette would exorcise the ghosts from her past—tell the shocking
truth of an incredible life and her unshakable will to survive.

But she would not find deliverance that easily.

Part Two
Lynette Hallworthy-Martinez

Chapter 13

British Columbia, Canada, February 13, 1998

Lynette Hallworthy-Martinez gave a tremulous sigh and, with the tip of her fingers, brushed away the tears falling down her pale cheeks. *How,* she wondered, *can I bear this?*

Eyes that usually sparkled with the hue of faceted emeralds stared dully out the cabin window at the heavy snowfall, grim and gray. The nasty weather locking in the tender shoots of spring bulbs didn't help the emotional roller coaster she was on.

I don't want to—I cannot!—go through this, not now…

This latest mind-boggler was the proverbial straw that broke the camel's back, although it felt more like a ton of bricks.

Fate had decreed her life would be a terrible struggle, but her stubborn tenacity had always outplayed the most insurmountable odds. As a newborn, she'd been discarded like a half-eaten mango, but through sheer grit and force of will, she'd not only beaten Fate's hand, she had gone on to become an enormously wealthy and powerful woman, a far cry from her humble beginnings. Even when her beloved husband, Lionel Martinez, had died a few months ago, she had not allowed herself to wallow in grief. She had survived that loss, as she had all of life's afflictions. But this time Fate had finally dealt her a hopeless hand.

She buried her face in the palms of her hands and anguished to a god whom she was not sure she believed in:

Why me God? Haven't I suffered enough emotional and physical bloodshed? Haven't I had more than my fair share of "hell on earth"? I could have stayed burrowed in that foxhole of hatred and bitterness, but oh, no, not me. I chose to fight. She looked upward and yelled, "What do you *want* from me? Why are *you* doing this to me?"

Cancer.

That frightful six-letter word spelled a grim fate for the fifty-three-year-old.

She was more than stunned, considering she hadn't needed to see a doctor in over twenty years. She had only gone to get a prescription from him—to relieve her worse-than-migraine headaches of late.

She had urged her to undergo a brain scan.

Reluctantly, she drove to Kelowna Hospital, and the results from the MRI floored her. They revealed the advanced cancerous tumor growing quickly at the base of her brain—surgery would be risky without damaging the surrounding brain, she was later told.

Now, not only was the cancer destroying her brain tissue, it had mercilessly fast-forwarded her body's clock. Before receiving this bombshell diagnosis, she loved life—felt youthful inside and out—until today.

The slim, five-foot-nine woman, who was a Meryl Streep look-alike, hadn't a gray thread in her blonde, shoulder-length hair. Her sun-bronzed complexion, smooth as a baby's bottom, was the result of a skilled cosmetic surgeon a year ago. Not an age spot, wrinkle, sagging jowl, drooping eyelid, or unwanted moustache was to be seen.

She had never run from a good fight, and with all her might she'd tackle this foe, too. And without undergoing chemotherapy or taking the high-dosed steroids offered her. But what sent icicles dripping down her back was that cancer did not observe a fair set of rules. The good, the bad, and the ugly; young and old, male and female, black, yellow, brown, and white—there was no negotiating. One could rail and rant at it, plead to it and pray about it, but the outcome seemed a whim of Fate, a toss of the dice.

Some lived. Others died.

Many suffered so greatly that they longed for death. Others suffered greatly but still longed to live.

She exhaled loudly. She'd never been a quitter, and she wouldn't be one now. She'd not be an easy notch on the belt of this heartless condition. But she would not give up—lie down—accept defeat. She'd keep swinging to the last gasp...

But Lynette Hallworthy-Martinez had to admit: for the first time in a long while, she was truly scared. She wasn't ready to die. Not yet. She had unfinished business.

From infancy, she had exhibited a stubborn will to stay alive—to get through life not as a victim of circumstance but as a winner. Not only had she fought, not only had she survived—she had triumphed!

At fifteen, she had escaped from a mental institution. She had vowed she would never be caught and forced to return to the asylum where she had been placed against her will. She also vowed that she would never become a dependent psychiatric patient, a hardened prostitute, or a drug addict. The volcano of psychological odds had predicted she would succumb to every one of those conditions. Instead, she had outwitted them all. Oh, yes, she *had* played life like the famous Monopoly board game, always landing on the right squares, and had never been dealt a "go directly to jail" card. Her survival strategy had been simple:

Do not dwell on the past. Do not dream of the future. Stay focused on the here and now.

Until now.

Lynette turned away from the window and reached for the

cordless telephone on the breakfast bar. She knew she would be bequeathing unto her daughter a can of worms, but truthfulness was her entitlement. Lynette felt that she could no longer avoid exposure. Finally, she would share with her only child the bombshell "tell-all." It was a truth Brianna had long beseeched her to divulge.

Now she could only hope that when her daughter peered into that can, Brianna would see with her heart and not only her eyes.

Lynette pressed number one on the speed dial.

When the disembodied voicemail message prompted her, she sighed with resignation and then, in a tone so soft, almost a whisper, she spoke, "Brianna, I'd like you to come out here as soon as you can. I want you to know that I'm so sorry I've let you down… not being a very good mother to you, but I love you dearly, my darling daughter, always have. If you cannot come to my home in time, I'll see you in heaven… if I'm let in…"

With the phone still clutched in her hand, she stood unmoving, for a very long time just staring at a small cassette recorder she always kept by the phone. She did not see the instrument, because reeling before her eyes were memories projected onto a screen that would transport her back in time to the tragic childhood she'd so long ago survived and escaped.

Lynette's taped confession would forever change her daughter's life—and what remained of her own.

Chapter 14

On high beam, the halogen headlights of the blue Nissan Pathfinder punched holes into the dank fog ushering in the 1998 Valentine's Day. For the young woman driving on the slippery, snow-laden highway in the British Columbia interior, this day would bring anything but romantic expectations.

In a "ten-to-two" position, Brianna Elizabeth McTavish's hands gripped the steering wheel with such intensity that the skin stretched over her white knuckles. The fifth-year law student found it hard to concentrate. Worry lines etched on the aging face of the twenty-three-year-old. The lids above her velvet black eyes were heavy with fatigue.

The breathtaking scenery of winter whizzed by without a glance. She could think only of the unnerving message left on her voice-mail at 4:00 P.M. yesterday afternoon. In a small voice, almost child-like, her mother had ended her message with a cryptic *"See you in heaven…"*

Icy chills had crept down Brianna's spine after she heard the message. Concerned, she immediately called her mother back only to hear a recording: "Please leave your number and a brief message, and I'll get back to you. Thanks."

Brianna had spoken quickly, "For goodness sake, Mom! Answer your damn phone! Look, I'm really sorry. I didn't mean to be so rude the last time we spoke."

No response.

Brianna tried humor, "Mom, if you don't pick up, I'm going to come out there and kick your butt."

No response.

Finally, Brianna's emotionally grounded character exploded. She thumped her fist on the kitchen counter. "Damn you, Mother! I have an important presentation to prepare for. I could do without this damn melodrama."

Silence.

Brianna flipped shut her cell phone. Why was her mother giving her the cold shoulder?

Stone-faced, she glanced up at the wall clock: 10:00 P.M. It was late, but if she hurried she could make the nine-hour trip, spend the weekend, sort this out, and get back in time for Monday's classroom appearance.

In minutes she'd packed an overnight bag and was halfway to the underground parking of the high-rise when she had a sudden thought: *Forgetting something?*

"Roberto!" she gasped.

Her boyfriend, a first year ER resident, was on a night out with his friends. He immediately answered his cell. "Drive safely, Sweetpea. Give me a call when you get there. Love you."

"I love you too, Honeybun. I'm so sorry about missing our Valentine's date, but I'll make it up to you when I get back."

* * *

On the last leg of her journey down the mountainous highway, Brianna's thoughts were as gloomy as the dismal weather. Was her insensitive reaction the sole cause of her mother ignoring her return calls? Or was it due to their previous telephone conversation a week ago? It had not ended well.

"Hi, Mom. Sorry I haven't called for a few weeks, but I've been up to my neck in papers and presentations. How are you?"

"Fine."

"You don't sound fine. Are you mad at me?"

"No."

Something wasn't right. "What's up, Mom?"

"Nothing's up."

"I know you, Mom. Tell me."

"It's not something I want to talk about, okay!"

A long, grueling exam preparation overruled Brianna's usual patience. "Oh, that's typical!" she snapped. "Just like *you* to keep secrets."

"W*hat* do you mean by that?"

"You're the most secretive person I've ever met. Come to think of it, I don't know anything about you, your past, or what you *really* did for a living. I'm not stupid, Mother. I know you're hiding things from me."

"I suggest that you come out of your courtroom mode and stop this Gestapo-type interrogating so we can talk more civilly. My past is none of your business."

A lifetime of simmering curiosity and resentment about her mother's younger years boiled into indignant, wounded anger. "You've been lying to me all my life," she said, abrasively. "Who *are* you? Who's my father? Why won't you tell me the truth about any-thing?"

"I'm your *Mother*. And you are my heart—my soul—my every-thing—and if you want to have a future with me by your side... what am I saying? There is no future..." Lynette's voice faded.

"What did you say, Mom?"

Brianna heard a long sigh. Then came the soft reply, "I'm sorry Brianna. I'm very tired. I'm going to hang up now before we both say something we will regret."

"Here we go again, always ducking out. You're not going to

answer my questions, are you?"

"What questions?"

Brianna exhaled loudly through her nose. "Who *are* you, Mom?"

"Mata *f-in* Hari—"

A click, then silence.

Once again, Lynette had escaped her daughter's probing.

Brianna could have kicked herself. Revealing her long pent-up anger had only antagonized her mother and caused her to draw back into her shell. With serious trust issues marring their relationship, she had tried to coax from her mother the missing pieces of the jigsaw that was her life. Lynette had remained tight-lipped. Brianna couldn't even begin to guess at the reasons for her ongoing secrecy. As a top law student, she could "read" people, but not her mother! It was like trying to get blood from a stone. The pair had always been incompatible.

* * *

Traveling down the Coquihalla highway, Brianna, upset over their recent blowup and mysterious phone message, silently vowed: *By hook or by crook, I'm going to get the long-overdue answers—even if it means strangling her.*

Though in four-wheel drive, Brianna's vehicle barely made it to her mother's isolated log cabin. No lights glowed through the windows. Morning's cold, grey light had not yet intruded upon the still pitch. Snowdrifts mounted the surrounding evergreens, bending low their branches, and piled high against the cabin's sides.

This doesn't look good, Brianna thought, pulling into the familiar driveway. According to her mom, a local guy ploughed daily when the snowfall was this heavy.

A deep frown knotting her brow, she brought the Nissan to a stop outside the garage door. It was wide open, and the silver truck her mother drove was missing, and there were no fresh wheel ruts. Maybe, Brianna wondered, it's in for repair? *It's brand new, Dumbo!*

Maybe she's gone shopping? At seven in the morning!

She rummaged through her shoulder bag. Where was her spare key? Not finding it, she turned the doorknob and was surprised when the door opened. This was most unlike her mother, a super-safety freak. Lynette always kept her cabin, nestled in the quiet serenity of the Arrow Lakes Valley, bolted like a fortress day and night.

The worried woman flung open the door. "*Mom?*"

Silence.

Her mother was not an early riser, but *oh please,* she implored whatever divinities might be listening, *let her be all right!*

Brianna hurried for the bedroom still wearing her snow boots.

"Wakey, wakey, Mom. Surprise!" she forced in a singsong rhythm as her slender fingers fumbled for the light switch in the darkened room. Blinking at the sudden brightness, her tall frame went rigid.

On the unmade bed was a mountain of clothing stuffed into dry-cleaning bags: blouses, slacks, and winter sweaters. Shoeboxes were stacked high. Handbags and bulbous plastic bags littered the king-size mattress. It was as if her mother intended to have a garage sale. Brianna spotted the note in capital letters taped to a shoebox: BRIANNA. PLEASE SEE THAT ALL THIS GOES TO CHARITY.

"What the hell's going on here!"

The laces of her boots flapping, Brianna darted from room to room in the upper section of the two-story cabin.

Empty.

She flew downstairs to the basement.

Empty.

Where was her mother?

A shiver creeping along her spine, she headed back upstairs to the kitchen and flopped heavily down on a leather-padded stool at the breakfast bar. She needed to think—get her trained mind in gear.

For that, she needed strong coffee. Also, she was starved. She hadn't eaten a thing since taking off from Vancouver the night before.

Though her thoughts were in turmoil, the large tin of Arabian coffee in her hand triggered a whimsical memory that prompted an involuntary smile.

"Mom," she had asked. "Why do you always stick to this awfully strong brand?"

"Because, my dear," Lynette had answered. "It's dark and mystical, like me."

* * *

With the coffee perking, Brianna looked up at the thick, Douglas-fir log beams bracing the ceiling. Sure, her mother was mysterious. But having said that, she was also a fascinating person and a likeable character, loved by everyone who crossed her path. Her mother also was a prankster with a wicked sense of humor. She loved to tell "clean and some dirty" jokes and delighted in pulling April Fools' Day capers on unsuspecting victims.

Brianna looked around the large kitchen—every item neatly in place. She suspected her mother's organized home bordered on a compulsive disorder. She tackled and mastered life's every challenge with the precision of a military strategist. Even her culinary skills were exceptional. She could concoct a meal fit for a king in little or no time at all. And she was not a woman who would run from trouble. She met it head on.

So where was she?

Surely, their disagreeable phone call would not have caused her mother to run away. And anyway, it wasn't the first time they'd not seen eye to eye; they were too much alike—stubborn and strong willed.

Brianna ran her fingers through her uncombed hair. Should she file a missing person's report? She shrugged it off—much too soon to jump to conclusions. What should she do? Perhaps drive around the small village in the hope of spotting her mother's truck? Could she have stayed at a friend's house? No. Her mother had never mentioned that degree of closeness to anyone in the hamlet. Indeed, after Lionel's accidental death—a fall from a roof, six months ago—a grief-stricken Lynette had become reclusive and rarely ventured from her cabin, except for necessary supplies.

Her mother's fairy-tale romance and sudden marriage to Lionel fifteen years ago had upset the then eight-year-old Brianna. It mattered not a fig that her single mother had devoted herself entirely to raising her.

On the day of their wedding, Brianna had rushed to her bedroom, slamming the door behind her. She threw herself on the bed and thumped her pillow. Into the feathers she had blurted, "I wish you were dead."

The tempestuous child had remained unforgiving: "I'm mad as hell! How could you, Mom! He's ten years younger than you are! All my friends at school are going to make fun of me."

Tears welling in her eyes, Lynette had responded, "Oh, Sweetpea, for the first time in a very long while, my empty heart is filled with the purest of love. And if you can't see it, and can't find it in your selfish heart to accept my happiness… then I'm sorry."

"Fine. If that's the way you feel, I'll go and live with my *real* father. Just tell me where he is! I know the bald-faced lie you told me about him being dead is bull!"

Lynette's green eyes had dulled with painful memories.

"Your father doesn't know you exist, and Brianna, I haven't the heart to tell him. For many reasons best left unsaid, he mustn't ever know. But you don't have to look far for a decent parental heart. It's right under your nose. The man I married is your *father* now. Be happy you have this wonderful, kind, and loving man in your life, as much as I do."

She had tried her best to console her daughter. "I wish I had a magic wand to erase the past and put things right, but I can't. There has been too much water under the bridge. The identity of your father is a secret that must remain untold."

"I hate you! I'm going to run away if you don't tell me!"

Despite her daughter's frequent badgering, Lynette had remained silent about her natural father.

As the years passed, Brianna finally accepted her mother's partner into her life, and Lionel turned out to be the best father any young girl could ever have. He doted on her. Drove her everywhere she needed to go and spoiled her rotten. Often, he gave her spending money behind Lynette's back, even though her mother's disciplinary philosophy was: You have to earn your own money to appreciate how hard it is to make it.

Brianna became the envy of her classmates, who thought the muscular Hispanic man was a drop-dead gorgeous hunk. On Graduation Day, one of her teachers made a remark, "If I didn't know better, I would say that you were his offspring! You two look so alike. And he's not that young... he could be your biological father—"

Brianna's reflection was cut short by the ringing of Lynette's phone. She waited for the ID display: BRITISH AIRWAYS. The caller's voice talking to the answering machine was cheerful: "Good morning, Mrs. Martinez. This is Cheryl Lacey at British Airways. Please call me regarding your flight to South Africa—"

Brianna grabbed the receiver and intercepted the call. "Hi. This is Brianna Martinez. When did my mother book this flight?"

"I'm sorry. I can't give out personal information."

"For God's sake, I'm her daughter, not some stranger. And I'm also a lawyer," she lied.

"I'm sorry. It's against policy to give out flight information without the traveler's permission."

"Can you at least let me know where in South Africa she intended to go?"

"Like I said, we can't—"

Brianna ended the call.

She slumped in a chair and stared into the steamy depths of her coffee mug. Why would her mother go anywhere without telling her, especially to South Africa? She recalled an earlier discussion, not long ago:

"Roberto and I are thinking about flying to South Africa. Go on a safari, soak up the sun, and try scuba diving. Why don't you come with us? It will do you good to get away. Pappy is gone, Mother. He wouldn't want you to spend the rest of your life grieving, now would he?"

Lynette's face had tightened. "You two go, but you will never get me to go to that beastly place."

"What makes you say that, Mom, if you've never been there . . . you haven't been there have you?"

Typically, Lynette avoided the conversation.

* * *

Brianna went to her mother's basement office and checked through desk drawers for flight notes, or a credit card statement, or *anything* that would help explain her sudden disappearance. Nothing.

Brianna called various airports in British Columbia. Nothing.

She phoned local hospitals. Nothing.

A call to the police crossed her mind, but it was way too soon to get that panicked.

Too weary to think, Brianna went to the spare bedroom to lie down, hoping that after her nap, her mother would arrive safe and sound.

As she was removing her boots, she spotted a brown leather brief-case propped against the night table. She dumped its contents on the bed.

"*Holy mackerel!*"

Several banded wads of crisp one-hundred-dollar U.S. bills— fifty thousand dollars in total—stared back up at her. She turned her attention to the velvet drawstring bag and opened it. The gravity of this discovery finally hit home:

"*Oh-migod!*"

Dumbfounded, Brianna stared at the jewelry: a Rolex, several gem-encrusted rings, a black pearl necklace, gold bracelets, gold and silver earrings and brooches—adornments Brianna had never seen. She took little notice of the plastic folders containing legal documents, or the hand-held microcassette recorder and boxed tapes, and put her hands over her eyes to make sure she wasn't dreaming. Nine hours on slippery roads could play tricks on a brain. Then bells started ringing:

"*I want you to come to my home.*"

Not yet in panic mode, Brianna picked up one of the plastic folders and noticed the blue envelope bearing no name. She slit the envelope with a fingernail and pulled out the letter dated: *Wednesday, February 13, 1998*. Brianna's mind reeled: *Yesterday!*

For the longest moment, she stared at the handwriting. Her mother's usual confident hand had formed the shaky letters of a little girl:

My precious daughter,
If you are reading this, you must have received my message asking you to come urgently. I didn't want it to be this way. I wanted so much to patch up our differences in person. I don't blame you for being angry. I'd have probably responded the same way if I were in your shoes. God knows, I never wanted to hurt you, Brianna. I've loved you from the day you were born. You are my pride and joy, the love of my life. You are a charming, intelligent, and witty human being. Thank goodness, you are emotionally grounded, not like your neurotic mother who definitely has a few screws loose. Gosh, I don't know where to start. This is the hardest letter I've ever had to write. You know I'm not an impulsive creature, but awful news has forced me into action. You see, my darling, I recently learned I have an inoperable brain tumor, which will most definitely bring about memory loss sooner than later. My brain is dying, and my memory cells will become fickle, unable to rejuvenate new

growth. It's not only from aging, it's a bitter curse, maybe karmic debt—who knows? You don't know this, but I enrolled in medical school years ago at the age of nineteen. That tells you something! I did three years and gave it up because the sight of blood made me faint. Some doctor, right! After being diagnosed with gliomas cancer, I, as a private patient, was given the "royal" treatment. Didn't have to wait long in waiting rooms, had the best specialist at my disposal, and I was able to obtain copies of my MRI scans. The absolute horror of this "malfunction" not only has dumbfounded me, but frightened and numbed me. I didn't know how to tell you. At this moment in time, I know my brain cannot function without my voice—so I'm going to spill what's left of my memory banks before the well is completely dry. Oh, honey, I never want to see the day when I don't recognize you, share birthdays, your marriage one day, or hold my grandchildren. I have so much to do before this blasted lump robs me of everything and everyone I hold dear in my heart. At first, I thought maybe it wasn't a bad thing to fade into oblivion, forget some ghastly memories, of awful times in my youth that made me into a fighter, a survivor. I suppose if I hadn't suffered, I wouldn't be who I am today… a bloody tough cookie. Wrong! That was how I felt before I got my bad news. Now, inside, I feel like the Pillsbury doughboy. Brianna, my past has a dark side that I never wanted to share with you, or anyone. It was too terrible, too ugly, and I did not want to soil your pure spirit with such knowledge. The tapes I left you will explain everything, especially the reason why I'm now so passionately driven to return to the land of my birth—to search out the Zulu woman who saved my life. I never intended to air my dirty laundry on those tapes. Before I was diagnosed, which is probably "cosmic" payback, they were to remain a secret, one I listened to occasionally to remind myself of my origins and how blessed I was in my new life. But my ongoing secrecy has only served to invoke your continuing anger and suspicions. So, as precious time slips away from me, perhaps the hour has come for you to meet the mother you never knew. I hope you'll find it in your heart not to hate, but to forgive me. Before I forget, please get in touch with airport security at Vancouver airport to reclaim my vehicle.

"Vancouver!" Brianna exclaimed, scrunching the letter to her chest. Had they passed like ships in the night on the Coquihalla Highway? That thought struck her like a sledgehammer.

She read the last page of the letter.

I left written instructions and my signed authorization on the driver's seat. If you have any trouble getting the truck, which you now own, call Mike Rodriguez, my lawyer. His contact numbers are on my office Rolodex. Mike has the Power of Attorney to deal with my affairs in my absence. I've also sent him a couriered parcel, containing items he needs to handle. Brianna, it's in your best interest to contact him. He is a wonderful human being, a trustworthy soul, and he has my permission to tell you everything you want to know about the remarkable "man" whose blood you carry. I know this won't mean much to you at this moment, but I loved your father with all my heart. I would have gladly given my life for him, but then he went and left me... the swine! But in one way it's okay, because in death, I'll be closer to my beloved Lionel forever.

As the brain specialist couldn't give me a time line... you know, when my memory loss will start and shut me down, I'm going to do all the things I should have done years ago. Once you give up hope, what do you really have left? Do I have a lot of catching up to do! Yes. Mostly, I'm hoping to find my foster mother, and, with a little luck, trace the whereabouts of my biological mother as well. That's if they are both still alive. I'm sure you're thinking. "What the heck is she going on about? She told me her parents were dead." I hope you will forgive this deception. My heart is heavy with sorrow as I say goodbye to you in this letter. I would have given everything I own to have hugged you before I left. I'll try to call you when I get there. But don't expect me home anytime soon, if ever. While I still have breath in my body and a mind that

functions, I'll love and miss you. Be strong. You have finally met your
mother, my precious daughter. Now I must search for, and hopefully
find, my own.

> *Love from SHIYA—that's my real name.*

Now in panic mode, Brianna put her hands over her mouth and rocked back and forth. Her young shoulders weren't prepared to carry this heaviness. What should she do? Call Mike? She had often heard his name mentioned but had never met her mother's personal attorney. As far as Brianna knew, he resided somewhere in the States. Now she couldn't wait to meet him and ask him long-over-due questions about her parents.

Though also anxious to listen to the cassette tapes, but with a pounding headache and stomach groaning for food, she knew if she didn't eat a little something she'd be in a far worse state.

Feeling light-headed, she headed back upstairs.

She opened the refrigerator.

Stacked full, there was enough food to feed an army. She shook her head. Why her mother kept so much food for one person was mind-boggling. Then she spotted the capitalized note stuck to a pizza box: BRIANNA, PLEASE TAKE SOME OF THIS FOOD AND FREEZER STUFF BACK WITH YOU TO VANCOU-VER. DUMP THE REST IN THE COMPOST FOR HUNGRY CRITTERS. UNPLUG THE FRIDGE AND FREEZER. THANKS.

Juggling a microwave-warmed small veggie pizza, a can of soda, and the recorder and tapes, Brianna returned to the family room. Setting everything on the walnut coffee table, she sank into the black leather loveseat, then bit into the pizza and forced herself to chew. It tasted like sawdust, but she needed the energy to think.

Slipping the tape marked AFRICA (1) into the recorder, she turned up the volume and pressed PLAY.

Lynette's British lilt was clear as a bell:

Brianna, I assume by now you have read my letter explaining that the only way I will ever find peace is by returning to the land of my birth, South Africa.

Brianna's eyebrows arched. Her mother had told her she'd been born in London, England.

What I have recorded is the unvarnished truth. You see, I never told anyone about my life in South Africa. I wanted to forget. But every now and then, diabolical images haunt me with nightmares. I would have thrown in the towel years ago if not for you and my amazing husband, Lionel. When I learned about this tumor, I wanted to crawl into a hole and never come out. But I know I must finally face my past so this chapter of my life will be closed with dignity, not regret. Brianna, I'd like you to listen to an incredible journey. Although it has bled my soul, heart, and mind of happiness, I want you to learn why my having been abandoned by my Sicilian migrant mother and the events that followed rendered me incapable of being a good mother to you. You have wanted to know who I am. Now you can. But I fear you will wish you didn't. Well, here goes. I believe I was born sometime in December 1945. The only person who knows for sure is Anele Dingane, my foster mother. Apparently, she found me as a newborn, near to death, buried alive under cornhusks.

Is this is for real! A voice inside Brianna shouted.

I don't know why my biological mother discarded me like a dirty rag, but I intend to find her and get the answer to this and other missing pages of my early life. The black woman who found me named me Shiya, an African word meaning, *forsaken one.*

Brianna listened intently as her mother stepped back in time, and with the remarkable clear eye of childhood, described her happy years in Tswanas Kraal up to the time of their abduction. Brianna barely breathed as Lynette's soft-spoken narration continued:

> I'm surprised I can think so clearly, but then, I've always been possessed by uncanny powers of vision. Whether my eyes are opened or closed, it is as if he is standing before me now—Lord Alan Hallworthy, the wealthy South African landowner who is my biological father. He was an evil man who lacked any sense of humanity, morality, or kindness. Alan learned from Kumdi, a wannabe Zulu leader, that a *white* child was living in Tswanas. Alan put two and two together. Anele and I were badly beaten, tied up, and taken away separately. I wiggled free from Alan's grasp. He was foaming at the mouth like a rabid animal. All I had left of the mother I loved was a shred of colorful material, clenched in my hand, that I was able to get before he bundled me up like a meat parcel under the car seat. I will never forget Anele's eyes, wild like a trapped animal. Something told my child's heart that I'd never see my precious mother again, so I clung to that strip of cloth as if my life depended on it. I have it to this day. It is sealed in my gold locket, the same piece you wanted and I wouldn't let you have. I'm wearing it as I record this.

Brianna nodded. She remembered well that antique locket. Lynette had always refused to part with it. Now, she knew why. She swallowed against the lump rising in her throat and concentrated on what her mother was saying:

>Brianna, when I look back… No, I don't have to *look*
>back. I am already there—

The tape whirred to a stop and began automatically rewinding.
"Damn!"

Chapter 15

Tape marked number (2) whirred into action. This time, Lynette's voice was not as clear. Brianna turned up the volume to MAX.

> Brianna, I must warn you that what I have to tell you is very graphic. If you don't wish to hear it, destroy this tape.

Brianna wondered what could be worse than what she'd already heard? Her poor mother ripped from the arms of Anele, elbow wrenched from its socket, and to be so horribly treated not only by Lady Corrie but her own father.

The Bastards! Oh, how I'd love to have the Hallworthys squirming in the witness stand—

Her angry thoughts were halted by the phone ringing. UNKNOWN NAME: UNKNOWN CALLER: flashed on the screen's caller ID.

With excited expectancy, she answered, "Is that you, Mom?"

"I must have the wrong number," a male voice said, and disconnected.

Brianna grunted in disappointment and stared blankly at the

wall as though its plain surface would yield answers to her questions. Nothing could have prepared her this "tell-all." She had no clue that it was going to get far worse, without solutions.

> If you are listening, Brianna, the story you are about to hear is a true account of my life. According to some shrinks, five-year-old brains aren't capable of storing too much information. Well, I can prove that theory wrong. I remember everything, like it was yesterday. You see, my scumbag father stole my soul, and it took me a very long time to reclaim it. I would have succumbed to a lot worse than childhood neurosis if it were not for my pent-up anger in the foxhole of hatred I lived in for too many years to count. My bitterness, a coping mechanism I believe, became my crutch from going insane.

Brianna remembered little about her own early childhood but never doubted for a minute that the woman who could memorize directory phone numbers could remember hers. Brianna was all ears, but she would wish she weren't.

> My elbow injury seemed insignificant to the unbearable pain in my heart. I longed for Anele... the Tswanas village... the river I played in, and even the mealie-meal, a porridge like mixture, that bloated my stomach and always gave me terrible gas. We kids used to have farting competitions. Guess who won that game!

Brianna's eyebrows arched. The heart-wrenching story was horrible, but her mother's throaty chuckle at the end of "guess who" tore at her heart. Lynette continued:

> You're probably wondering how I can find something

funny about all this, but without laughter I couldn't have survived. In my child's mind, I intuited that I'd never return to the African bush and the natives I viewed as my people. How right I was. At sunset, the same day I arrived on the Hallworthy estate, Alan marched me off by the scruff of my neck to an old cottage that had once been used for overflowing guests. He hurled me like a rag doll onto the urine stained, coil-spring mattress of a bed and told me in English and then Zulu that he'd chop me up if I tried to escape. I was a small child, but smart. I vowed that escaping was the first thing I'd do after he'd gone. Somehow, I was going to find a way out of that putrid-smelling cottage.

After Alan slid the outside bolts into place, I waited, listening for the sound of his retreating footsteps, then examined the filthy room. The only other piece of furniture, apart from the brass bed, was an old dust-covered Victorian dresser lacking a bottom drawer. Opposite the dresser was a barred porthole-sized window. Could I slide my skinny body through the bars? I sure was going to give it a try. I took off the clothing Corrie made me wear: a long vest, which would have better fitted a ten-year-old. I had no worries about my hair snagging on the rusty iron bars… my shaven head was bald as a newborn mouse.

A push at a time, I dragged the bed to the window and, boy, did that take some doing. The bloody thing was like pushing a ten-ton elephant, but somehow I did it. Then I climbed up onto the bedrail. I had to brush away the thick cobwebs draping the sash-window. I then rubbed as much spit as I could muster onto my skin and began pushing the bottom half of the window up. It budged not an inch. I clambered onto the windowsill to push the top half. It wouldn't budge, either. I realized that I needed both arms to hold the sides of the frame to have a better go at it. But one was still very swollen, useless from the elbow being wrenched out of its socket. I was so frustrated; I could have chewed through the wood like a rat. I jumped down and went to the door. Maybe I'd have better luck, but it was solid and immovable as a tree trunk. I remember thumping the door with my good fist and went to the bed feeling defeated. Folded at its end was a moth-eaten blanket. Although the room was stifling hot and airless, I wrapped the blanket around my body. It felt comforting and smelled earthy, like the bedcover Anele had made me in Tswanas. Exhausted, I fell into a deep sleep.

Perhaps an hour or so after, I was awakened to the sound of creaking bolts. It was my cue to bolt. I flew off the bed and hid behind the door, ready to run. That was a waste of mental energy, because Maekela was faster than me. Her fingers latched onto my ear like a mosquito. "No you don't, Missy. I'll get skinned alive if you get away."

I struggled but, of course, I was no match. With her apron, she tied my good arm to the bedrail then sat down beside me. "Little child, it hurts me to tie you up, and I'd like nothing more than to let you go, run free, like Anele did for your real mother. But I have a child not much older than you, and the master will take his anger out on me *and* my son." Her lovely blue eyes looked into mine. "Like old Lamella, I knew Anele Dingane well. I used to work with her in the kitchen. I missed her so much when she ran away. I still miss her dreadfully. Anele was a brave and loving woman for saving you."

At the mention of Anele, I burst into tears. Maekela untied my restraint and cradled me in her arms. "Don't cry, little child. Pray to the white God and ask him to help you."

She began crooning a tune I'd heard Anele sing many times about freedom. It was a lovely few moments that we shared until Lamella arrived, huffing and puffing as if she'd just finished a marathon. She came over to the bed and examined my arm. "Lynette, how is this ever going to mend if you undo my good work?"

"My name is Shiya. My name is *Shiya*," I stressed.

"I know, child. But if the Mistress says your name is Lynette, then Lynette it is!"

I let out a shriek when she tried to lift my sore arm. Though it had throbbed for some time, I didn't know it was out of the socket again. Had climbing the window done it? Or had Alan caused this injury again when he threw me onto the bed? While Maekela left the room to empty the pee bucket, Lamella got to work. She did her "orange" surgery and snapped the socket into place. I cried but didn't faint this time. My nurse pulled a metal tin from her apron pocket and opened it and smeared the "God's knows what," some type of greasy ointment on my inflamed elbow. Tearing a strip of material from the bottom of her skirt, she bound my arm.

I had electively chosen never to speak a word to a *white* person, but I knew it was safe to converse with my *own* people. Remember, I didn't know I was *white!* I asked Lamella what was to become of me. When I saw the "oh, God, I can't tell you" look on her face, I naturally continued to probe. "Why am I kept here like a caged leopard? Why does that *umlungu* man hate me? And the *umlungu* woman said she doesn't want me here on her land?" I saw tears in her dull eyes. "It's not for me to understand the workings of the white people's minds," she said. Intuition told me she was keeping something

dreadful from me, but I had no clue what it was. I was to
find out only too soon. They told me they had to get back
in time to serve dinner for seven o'clock or hell would
break loose. Cook hugged and kissed me goodbye and
told me that she'd see me in the morning, bring me breakfast, and check on my arm. Maybe it was her tenderness
toward me, or maybe I saw a substitute mother in Lamella,
I don't know. But I didn't try to escape again from the
cottage or sneak past these kindly women who took care
of my simple needs. They were my family now.

In hindsight, I wish I had run as fast as my legs could
carry me away from that foul cottage that would destroy
my childhood innocence. The long lonely days, weeks,
and months with nothing to do but wait for Lamella and
Maekela's daily visits were driving me crazy. I longed to
be in the sun, to see the creatures of the wild… swim in
the river… and climb trees. But most of all, I longed for
my mother. How was she? Did the people in the prison
treat her well? Was someone like Maekela or Lamella taking care of her needs?

Not long after my arm had completely healed, Maekela
brought me my evening meal. I could see she'd been crying. Was something wrong, I asked? Her own answer was
painful. I wouldn't see Lamella any more. She had died
in her sleep. And this time it was for real, not the lie Corrie had once told Anele. I learned much later that Corrie's
best friend needed a cook, so Corrie had simply shipped
Lamella off to her friend and only brought her cook back
to the manor when Anele ran away. I recall grabbing
Maekela's hand and begging her not to die also. The
thought of Lamella being dead was bad enough, but this
kind woman with blue eyes leaving me as well tore my
young heart into shreds. She wasn't going anywhere,

Maekela promised me. As long as Master Alan and Mistress Corrie wanted her to feed me, she would be there every day.

Maekela sat on the bed like she normally did, but poured her heart out to me as though I were an adult. She told me that she hated working for the whites, but she needed her job to help support her son, a year younger than me, born a year after Anele left. At the time, I wasn't wise to the awful life black women endured because of racial hatred, and I tried to understand her plight. "I had to give my baby to a field worker to look after because I couldn't," Maekela said.

"Why?" I asked.

"Because Mistress Corrie threatened to have my child sent to an orphanage. Servants are not allowed to have or even raise their children while they are in service. So I gave my son to Rose, a migrant Bantu field worker, to raise. In return, I give her all my wages. That's why I put up with the awfulness. But I do see my son on my afternoons off. He thinks I'm just his big sister... It's better that way."

"Where is his father?" I asked.

"We never speak of him."

"Why not?"

"Because he is an evil man, possessed by an evil spirit."

"The *Imikhuba* can make your son's father vanish if you want."

Maekela laughed, then became serious. "You've a lot to learn, child. I hope and pray you never have to suffer this evil." We spoke about many things that day. Not all doom and gloom. I told her about my happy life at Tswanas and my love of snakes and other creatures. She pulled a face when I mentioned snakes. She told me how her own mother, a Hallworthy field worker, had died from an unknown disease and how Anele became their substitute parent, saving Isona and herself from being placed in an orphanage. We parted that day with love in our hearts for each other. She filled the huge gap in my sorry life. But could she save me from an orphanage? And how long would Maekela remain my "substitute" mother?

Days later, I stood at the window searching the pathway below. I had no real conception of time, but two sunrises and sunsets had passed. Where was she? Had she died, too? I hoped not. Who would take her place? Her sister Isona? I prayed it wasn't Corrie. Four sunsets went by. No food, no water, and the stinking toilet bucket was full. I knew that I had to do something, or I would starve to death.

With no bad arm holding me back, I managed to get the top half of the window open. But I could not squeeze through the bars. I had put on weight, and the fear of being permanently stuck in between these rusty dividers sent me to my bed, dejected. I fell asleep, cold, lonely, hungry, and I prayed to Namandla, Anele's Zulu God, to let me die.

Sometime during the blackness of night, I heard heavy footsteps. "Maekela. Maekela," I shouted and rushed to the door. The door was flung open, and a flashlight blinded me. Then a strong hand grabbed my neck. Alan smelled as if he'd fallen into a vat of beer.

He flung me on the bed…"

A gut feeling told Brianna that she was about to hear something horrific. She closed her eyes and heard Lynette's articulated voice change into a childlike, frightened voice:

What happened that night never leaves my mind. I was raped…

"Oh-migod!"

Brianna threw up in her hand and raced to the bathroom, leaving the tape playing.

"You sick *bastard!* She was a *child!*" she shouted between stomach spasms, her head hung over the basin. As awful as she felt, how could she or anyone else truly feel the pain her mother and others endured without actually experiencing what it was like to be a victim of sexual abuse?

She washed her hands and face and went back to the room. Her fingers felt like ice, almost numb, as she rewound the tape. The horrendous narrative was hard to listen to without feeling totally paralyzed.

Her mother's sobs seemed endless, and then she said:

Through blurred, pain-filled vision, I saw the shape of a woman and the long object in her hand. I saw it rise and fall and heard the thud. Corrie stepped over Alan like the piece of dung he was and came to my side. Never had I expected such softness or feel her hot tears mingling with mine. "Oh, dear God in heaven! What has he done to you?" she murmured, and lifted me into her arms. Then came the veil of pitch darkness.

I awoke in an unfamiliar bed to find Corrie and a black man standing by my side. I knew nothing about molestation, rape, or any of the other heinous deeds committed against children, but I did know whatever Alan had done to me, Corrie was going to ensure no one ever found out. Why else would she get a *black* doctor to attend to me? Later, I learned Alan had used a hunting knife to cut my—

Brianna hurriedly pressed PAUSE.

After downing a generous shot of brandy, she stared at the tape recorder as if it was possessed. With the awful rape scene recurring repeatedly in her mind, she cried silently: *Oh, Mom, I thought I was your best friend. You could have told me about the pain you carried and so bravely locked inside your heart.*

Her heart breaking, she didn't want to hear what came next but knew she must.

> I watched as Corrie spoke quietly to the black man. He turned, bent, gently stroked my new hair growth and, in Zulu, he introduced himself. "My name is Doctor Mubani. How are you feeling? Do you have any pain?" I shook my head. "Miss Corrie wants you to know how sorry she is for the terrible thing done to you. As soon as you are able to walk, she is going to arrange for someone like myself to take you to an orphanage, a new home, where you'll be taken good care of. She begs you never to breathe a word to the nuns of what has happened here. Can you promise her that? Keep it a secret?"
>
> I don't suppose I understood the gravity of what had happened to me, or why I was asked to keep it quiet, and simply nodded. I looked away as he placed fresh gauze on my stitched privates. He then gave me an injection… an antibiotic, maybe. Who knows?
>
> The day my vaginal and rectal sutures were removed, Dr. Mubani whisked me away from Hallworthy Manor and handed me over to a smiling white nun in a traditional penguin suit. I wasn't to know that the Angel of Mercy Convent was for half-caste orphans known as "colored."
>
> Some years back, I hired a private investigator. At my expense, he went to South Africa and tracked down that

black doctor. Oh, the retired doctor was very willing to tell the investigator about that day in Corrie's house and the day he had to take me to the convent. The physician asked the private eye to relay a message to me. He had not been able to rid his mind of the part he had no choice but to play. He wanted my forgiveness. What for? He was a victim like me. Doctor Mubani died a year later. In his memory, Baragwaneth Children's Hospital now has two newly built wings to house the overflow of AIDS-infected children. I donated the money anonymously.

Brianna's thoughts felt like fishing weights, but one thing was for sure: her mother was the most soft-hearted person she'd ever known. Lynette had donated vast sums of money to many worthy charities—tons of tinned goods to food banks—meal vouchers and luxury blankets for the homeless—and if someone came to the door with a sob story, Lynette was there for them. And when it came to neglected animals, there was no limit…

Brianna's nice thoughts were overruled with a tragic one.

She couldn't push the picture of an emaciated little girl with stubby golden hair, whose green eyes were wide with terror and her small mouth crying out for help, out of her mind.

"Mom, please call, so I can tell you how much I love you," Brianna cried.

But Lynette was gone from her, and she had only her disembodied voice.

Chapter 16

Riveted to her seat, Brianna reactivated the recorder and concentrated on the continuing narration:

At the convent, I underwent a barrage of clinical tests: to determine if I was autistic… severely retarded… truly mute… There was no doubt I was a traumatized child, but *not* mentally challenged was their conclusion. But they couldn't get around the "mute" question. I believe it was out of loyalty for taking care of me in those awful days after the rape that I continued with the façade… "Speak no evil. See no evil. Hear no evil."

The best part about Corrie's nurturing guilt after the rape was the lollipops, chocolate cake, ice cream, and a potpourri of foodstuffs a child of the African bush never knew existed. In my young heart, I felt I owed her my life, and the only way I could keep our secret was to remain closeted in silence. That charade would be my downfall. The Angel of Mercy Convent viewed me as an aberration. I was denied education, for I was merely a blighted thing of the Devil who had no use or ability for learning, so said Mother Superior. I won't go into lengthy details about my convent years, but what I can tell you is that the memories still hurt like hell.

There is no such thing as "God's angelic servants." Devil's aids, more like it! But the white priest definitely was the Devil incarnate. The dirty bugger would lift up his hammock and flash his penis at whoever had the misfortune to cross his path. He only did it to me once. I never set foot in his chapel again. How did I get away with that? I peed on the bench, ripped up a prayer book, hit the priest in his groin, and nearly set the church on fire by tipping over candles. This "ungodly" behavior only fortified the nuns' belief that I most definitely was possessed by the Devil.

Although her mother's story was heart wrenching, Brianna's lips could not help but lift in a partial smile.

However, nothing can compare to the daunting experience of learning to read and write as an adult. It is an experience I wouldn't wish on my worst enemy.

Brianna frowned. Did she hear right? *Adult!* She rewound tape. There was no mistake. Just thought of her well-read mother being denied an education was unimaginable.

This convent housed some older orphans, mostly pregnant teenagers. I was the only child. What I saw there was nothing more than a cattle market—young mothers— some willingly—some reluctantly—handing over their babies. Many of those poor girls didn't have much choice. I believe that tax investigators finally shut down the convent not long after I left, thank goodness. Those so-called

"Angels of Mercy" were running an adoption racket for profit, with clients mostly from overseas. I don't want to knock every convent, just that particular one. Some of the nuns were definitely sadistic. I took an awful amount of beatings, even had a chunk of hair ripped from my head for stealing a slice of bread from the kitchen. I think I was eight or so at the time. Yet, those miserable years locked away from the outside world were paradise compared to my next place of imprisonment.

Shortly before my tenth birthday, to my horror, I recognized the tall man, flanked by two uniformed white men and being shown the way by Mother Superior. The sight of Alan Hallworthy sent me scrabbling up a large sycamore fig tree. Up on the highest bough, I wet myself and was sorry it didn't land on him. "Lynette, come down this instant," bellowed the nun. Oh, how I hated that name. Inside I was *Shiya* and would be 'til the day I died. "No, no, no…" I yelled. The strong voice that emulated from an unused voice box took me by surprise as much as it did the people below. Alan and Mother Superior's mouths fell open as if catching flies. She bellowed for a helper. When I saw the African gardener begin to climb up after me, I freaked out: "I'll throw myself out of this tree if you come any closer," I said to him in Zulu. How the hell was I to know he only spoke Swahili? He continued upward, and I wrapped my legs and arms around the branch like a boa constrictor. The gardener would have to cut off my locked limbs before I'd let go. Standing near the trunk below, Alan shouted, "Go ahead, jump and save me a bloody headache, you crazy *wop!*"

I had played deaf and mute for some time, but I was neither and had learned well *this* man's language. What should I do? What *could* I do? Fight the gardener or fall from the tree and live? Come down and die all over again? When the gardener reached the bough below me and extended his hand, what choice did I have? I climbed down.

Alan shot me a look of contempt, whispered something to one of the uniformed men, and then left the scene. Was I glad to see the back of him! I thought he had come to take me back to the cottage and abuse me all over again. What I didn't know was that Alan Hallworthy was my biological father. As such, he had the legal right to commit me to an asylum. His motive? To shut me up for good! Who would believe the accusations of a crazy person! According to the court records obtained by the same investigator, I was unfit for society—to remain incarcerated for the rest of my natural life…

That's how it was in those days.

Skoemansdaal Asylum was a state-run institution, not far from Pretoria, the capital of South Africa, and I can assure you it was a sane person's worst nightmare. I'd had more than my fair share of horrors, but this place, which had once housed prisoners of war, beat the lot. The day I arrived at the steel gates of the sanatorium, it looked like it should have belonged to the "Adams Family" movie set. But I couldn't believe the most spectacular display of flowerbeds and well-kept lawns, green as my eyes. I remember gawking at what I saw next: an enormous three-tier fountain with its cascading waters. However, it would hold no awe for me in the days, months, and years to come, because we *loonies* hardly ever got to walk in the gardens. And if we were given this *privilege,* one wouldn't know if the sun was shining or not or if the fountain flowed. This was because the daily dose of potent tranquilizer drugs kept most of us in a constant zombie state, and some almost catatonic. I outwitted the pill-givers by hiding the tablets under my tongue and then spitting them down the toilet. Then came the acting game… *"Look nurse, I'm spaced out. I can't harm a fly. So, please, please take my on a walkabout."*

Anyway, back to what happened the day I arrived at the madhouse. The matron refused to register me. She argued that the institution housed only insane "white" adults, and was no place for a "colored" ten-year-old kid, crazy or not. She also pointed out that they didn't have trained staff to deal with kids. After several frantic telephone calls, the problem was resolved by a paid-off white judge. I was forcibly taken to the top floor and restrained to a metal cot, the only one in the attic. I was given nothing to eat or drink, and during the night, I wet the bed. The next morning, I was moved to the second floor and locked in a large room with eight women ranging from twenty to ninety. I was the only child ever to be admitted to Skoemansdaal.

Years passed with not a ray of hope of ever getting out of that dreadful place. Not only was I attacked by loony inmates, I was sexually abused by the male and female staff members. There was one staffer who took sadistic pleasure in stubbing out lit cigarettes on my skin.

Brianna nearly choked on her saliva. She had seen the tiny pink welts on her mother's upper chest and curious had asked, "How did you get those, Mom?"

"From a bad bout of chickenpox," had been her mother's glib reply.

Lynette's narration of events resumed:

My silent prayers for liberation from this hellhole came

when an angel arrived at Skoemansdaal. Doctor Cecelia Harcourt. She was the newly appointed psychiatrist and the first female doctor ever to take up this position. I will never forget the look on her face when I was ushered into her examination room. "Lord Above! She's a *child*," she said. "What's *she* doing here? How old is she?"

"Fifteen, we think," the matron said, handing over my file to the doctor.

Cecelia's brows arched. "What you mean you *think?*"

"She doesn't have a legal birth certificate." In those days, production of a birth certificate was not mandatory as it is today. According to convent records, which I'm sure were falsified by Mother Superior, I was registered as illegitimate. A terrible stigma in those days, too.

Cecelia never said a word as the matron offered further information, but the doctor's body language spoke volumes. She shuffled in her seat more times than I did.

Finally, the doctor closed my file, looked at me, her eyes brimming with compassion, and told the matron and the male nurse that had accompanied me to leave her office. The matron protested, saying that I could possibly be dangerous. She couldn't vouch for the doctor's safety. "Rubbish," Cecelia said in her strong Yorkshire accent, got up from her chair, and shooed them out. "You can wait outside. I'll let you know when I finished."

The staff nowhere in sight, she bombarded me with questions. "Lynette, do you know *where* you are? Do you know *why* you were put away? Do you know your real age? How did you get vaginal and rectal tearing?" She shook her head when I didn't answer.

"I don't know if you will truly grasp what I have to say, but I'm enraged that a young *white* girl has spent nearly five years in this adult facility."

I had drawn deep within myself to cocoon my mind and body from a world that inflicted upon me terrible pain. But I wasn't insane. As a matter of fact, I was sharper than a butcher's cleaver. And of course I knew the motive behind Alan's haste to have me committed. I was growing up fast and could spill the beans. His intent was as evil as the man himself. But there was something about the kindness in this woman's voice and eyes—tenderness I hadn't known in years—that broke that long, long silence.

In between glasses of water for my tongue that seemed dead, out flew words, tumbling over each over, everything that had been bottled up for years. As the doctor listened to the trauma I had endured, I, for the first time, felt freed from the wretched guilt trip as if what had happened to me had been all my fault. Now, I had someone else would help me carry the heavy load. Swearing that she would never let anything ever happen to me again, she hugged me and said she'd be back tomorrow to see me, even though it wasn't her official "shrink" day.

That night, I cried myself to sleep—only this time they were tears of happiness.

Someone cared about me. She was going to save me. She was my Angel of Mercy.

The next day, in Cecelia's office, I met her cousin. Fifty-year-old Roland Giles Harcourt was a British Consular, stationed in Johannesburg. Cecelia explained that she had broken medical ethics by telling him about my case, but it was the only way she would be able to get his help. Giles took up the conversation.

He had sought advice from a Supreme Court judge, a friend of his, about my situation, and this learned person promised to look into the matter. A week later,

Roland returned with Cecelia. It seemed the Court judge's phone call to Alan's lawyer paved the way to my freedom. Alan disowned me, and the South African court released me from Skoemansdaal to my new legal guardians. I was ecstatic to be the ward of Roland and Cecelia Harcourt. Although I was terrified of all men in general, I was not afraid of him. Cecelia informed me that I would have to live at his apartment, not hers, until she found an alternative arrangement, as she had accepted a new posting back in England. Of course, Roland was against this living arrangement. It was not "proper" to have a very attractive young woman living with him in his flat, he complained, but as I had nowhere else to go, he finally relented.

In gratitude, I cleaned his apartment and made sure that he had a decent dinner to come home to, which incidentally was hilarious. The poor man never once complained about the burnt offerings I set before him. To cut a long story short, I felt myself falling for this much older man, who was the kindest, most caring person I had ever known. A love affair with a minor was the farthest thing from his mind. But I didn't want to lose the only man I could possibly love.

On my sixteenth birthday, Roland took me to dinner at a fancy restaurant. After the delicious lobster meal, Roland excused himself to go to the bathroom. As soon as he left the table, I sneakily drank the rest of his red wine. Oh, I remember it well. It was my very first taste of alcohol, and my carefree brain loved the intoxicated feeling. Roland chastised me when he found not only his glass empty, but the wine bottle too, but I didn't care. I'm surprised I didn't pass out. I was so unsteady on my feet that Roland had to carry me to the car.

Back at his apartment, the warm fuzzy feeling I was experiencing made me feel all grown up and stirred a part of my body I never knew existed. For the first time in my life, I wanted a man to love me in this way. Knowing what a gentleman Roland was, an old-fashioned man in the warmest meaning of the word, he would never have laid a finger on me if I hadn't instigated matters.

Shamelessly, I asked Roland to help me undress. The look on his face was priceless: "Good Lord, no!" he cried. But I persisted, and one thing led to another. Unfortunately, my adolescent fantasy turned to outright terror when he tried to make love to me. I screamed my head off. He understood. After that, I stayed away from wine, and neither of us allowed our thoughts to build romantic castles in the air. However, we became inseparable, much to the distain of his fellow diplomats. Poor Roland came home one night saying that, due to our living arrangements, they had made him out to look like a pedophile.

"We can get married," was my simple solution. Oh, the foolish mind of a romantic girl! I had no birth certificate—parental permission was needed to marry under the age of twenty-one, and besides, I was still legally his ward. I believe it was about this time that, confronted with such stark facts, Roland started having second thoughts. He snapped at me for the slightest thing, and his hot passion turned into cold hostility. I was young, not stupid! It was time to part company.

Where could I go? Johannesburg might as well have been in the Himalayas. I didn't know my way around, could not read the street signs with certainty. But my Maker had granted me attributes that would make me a survivor: a photographic memory and the craftiness of a professional thief. Brianna, I had no other options. I stole a blank British passport from Roland's office, as well as a Home Office seal, a passport camera, and a large pile of cash from his home safe. I had watched him open it, and my amazing memory chip had the combination.

Later, when Roland left the apartment to buy groceries, I packed a small suitcase and hightailed it out of there. I caught a train to Durban, feeling it was best not to be seen in Johannesburg. I doubted Roland would report me; if anything, he likely would be relieved. He had come under scrutiny by the Home Office and probably would have lost his job.

Did he really love me? No! Did I love him? No! School-girl's crush, that's all.

With the stolen items and the clothes on my back, I arrived in Durban. My mind was set. I knew it was more than risky, but I asked for the directions to Hallworthy Refinery, as it now was called.

Under the cloak of darkness, I snuck in to the servant's quarters and prayed it was Maekela who returned that night. It was! She and her sister Isona were overjoyed to see me, although my new appearance—already five-foot-nine, and cosmetics that made me look much older, and long, platinum-dyed hair that flowed to my waist—took some adapting.

We hugged and kissed like long-lost siblings. I brought them up to scratch. Gasps echoed in that dingy shack. As to helping me—yes, all they could. I gave Maekela some money and told her what needed to be done. But I was concerned about Alan. Maekela told me that he didn't come to the shack anymore to order them to do his bid-ding at the cottage. His sights were on new, younger refin-ery workers, both white and black, and also he was away on business. I breathed a sigh of relief. But Maekela warned, "Don't wander outside during the day, in case you are seen by a curious field worker."

In short, the money I gave Maekela, which she handed over to a black policeman, paid for my forged paperwork. I became a twenty-one-year-old British citizen named Lynette Smith, an identity stolen from Durban Births and Deaths registry. The real Miss. Lynette Smith, a nanny from Yorkshire, died three weeks before I handed over the blank passport for doctoring. My intentions were to fly to Great Britain and make a new start. Before I could do that, however, I had some unfinished business in this land that held so many awful memories.

As we speak, Lord Alan Hallworthy rots in jail. I put him there. You see, I had the incriminating evidence—a personal journal belonging to Corrie. But I'll explain about that later.

Thankfully, I had more than enough money to buy the one-way ticket to London, pay for hotel accommodation, food, and running expenses for the time being. When I arrived in Great Britain, December 1962, I was shocked. It was the first time I'd seen snow. The white stuff mesmerized me, but now I detest the winter months.

I found a cheap hotel and had another shock: registering. I made up a story about hurting my wrist, and the helpful desk clerk filled in the details. That embarrassing incident made me determined to get an education.

At the Adult Learning School in London, I concocted a story: I was an orphan, raised by missionaries in North Africa who were deceased, and I needed an English education, not Swahili.

Working in a strip joint as a glass washer (the only employment I could find without too many questions asked) and going to school during the day was hard, but

I graduated high school with honors in two years. Unbelievable—you bet! Gifted, or perhaps cursed, for I rarely forgot anything, and some things are best forgotten, I surprised more than a few learned personnel. After a vocational exam, I was informed by the examiner that I could pick any educational field I wanted. I chose medicine.

At nineteen, I entered medical school, and after three years, I gave it up. Can you imagine a doctor who can't stand the sight of blood? So I enrolled in a pharmaceutical science course and worked for a pharmaceutical company in my spare time as a formulator. That career didn't work out, either. What I really wanted to do for a career, and how to go about it, was a problem. Whom could I trust to set my lifelong ambition in motion? *Peter Graham McTavish!*"

Brianna smiled. She was glad that she had kept his name and not changed it to Martinez as her mother had wanted to do.

The day I gave my notice to quit chemistry classes and my job, he nearly ran me over in the university car park. He jumped out of his Bentley. "Are you alright? What an idiot! I should have checked my mirror before I backed out. Do you need to go to the hospital?" Assuring him I was fine, he helped me up, collected the scattered contents of my handbag, and offered to take me to a hospital just to be sure. But I argued, "A stiff drink will do the trick." Need I say more? Alcohol and I are not the best of friends. But this time, I didn't scream my head off.

Peter was a forty-year-old wealthy landowner in Scotland who had partnerships in several pharmaceutical firms and had never married. I towered over him, but it didn't matter; he made up for it in charisma. As did I, he loved animals, and so we hit it off. I not only found a wonderful boyfriend, I found a shrewd businessperson whose shady character and dealings made mine look like a saint's. I never did tell him the real truth, only what I thought would prevent him from prying.

In August 1970, at my real age (twenty-five), I agreed to move into Peter's house, "Fairfield," on the Isle of Skye. It had a lot of history, that farmhouse. Allegedly, it was the very same house where Flora MacDonald gave shelter, and her love, to Bonnie Prince Charlie. It could be folklore for all I know. But leaving behind the horrors of South Africa and starting anew in Scotland brought me magical times.

In the months following my moving in with Peter, for reasons I'll discuss later, I refused to marry him. He wasn't upset, nor were his well-to-do parents, but there was always a coolness, and I don't think they approved of me. However, a year later, I caved in and agreed to became Mr. and Mrs. McTavish in name only—"

Brianna pressed the STOP button. She wanted to reflect if just for a moment. Serene, picture-postcard scenes now flooded her mind. Not long ago, she had stumbled upon some photographs and had asked her mother, "Mom, these are beautiful. When were they taken?"

"That's Fairfield House were you were born. We lived there for the first few years of your life."

"Really!"

"Who is the man in the picture? Is he my father?"

"No, he is not. Put those blasted pictures away. I don't wish to see them, and I don't want to talk about it."

Sighing, Brianna reactivated the tape.

I loved my new home in Scotland but soon became fed up with Peter's endless dinner parties, stuffy men, and their boring wives. Also, there were lonely times when my so-called husband went on long business trips overseas, or that's what he liked to call them. That's when I decided to put my original plan into effect. In order to do that, I had to return to school, yet again! This time, I enrolled in law school, wanting to specialize in Immigration. At Glasgow University, I used my married name and not the numerous fake ones used in the past to get me into various educational facilities. In four years, I passed my exams with flying colors, of course!"

Brianna's eyelids shut as if sleep had overpowered them. She had always believed her mother was a free-lance journalist and had accepted this lie without question when her mother left for days on end. "A good story has come up," she would say. "Need to make money, sweetheart, so I'll see you in a week or so."

Brianna recalled the many times she'd been left with the live-in nanny… and, lonely for her mother, had cried all night. A tumultuous mixture of sadness and anger pounding at her heart, Brianna continued to listen.

I began advertising my legal services in an overseas newspaper. It didn't take long before my private mailbox in Glasgow was full of requests for assistance, mainly from people who had problems with their visas or landing applications. Using our home as a legal base, I began filing them through the proper appeals channels. I was very successful with most of the applications. Peter was upset, to say the least: "My dear, I fear this may bring undesirable people to the house. You must stop immediately." Shameless, I lashed back with the only thing I knew would shut him up—blackmail—a secret I had honored in our early days together: "If you don't let me live my life as I want to, I will tell your parents, friends, and your business associates that you are a faggot."

I know this is hard to believe, but we only ever made love that once, the day he had knocked me over onto my backside in the car park. He regretted making love to a woman. He told me the truth, and I told him a truth of my own: I hated sex, so we'll get along fine. Even now, I regret that demeaning outburst calling him a queer. He was such a gentle, kind soul, so good to me and to you too, when you were born. I knew I had hurt him, but he never uttered a word in his defense.

The next day, he went out and rented office space in a good part of Glasgow. The five-story red-bricked building housed other lawyers, medical specialists, and shipping agents. I had the top floor all to myself. After fitting out my spacious office, I hired a legal secretary and began work. I loved my job, and I saw very little of Peter over the next few months. He traveled a lot and, now, so did I.

Then, one day, I received a registered letter from Germany that intrigued me. It seemed that Gerda Düsseldorf had applied several times to enter England to visit her English boyfriend but was consistently being denied. Being a hopeless romantic, I traveled to Frankfurt to see what I could do for her. Apart from my eye color, I was surprised to note how much alike we looked, and we were about the same age—twenty-seven.

I met up with Gerda in an open-air café. Immediately, I warmed to the bubbly blonde woman. Gerda handed me the "no-way-are-we-going-to-let-you-enter-Britain" rejection document. I explained that I would need some quiet time to go over it. She gave me a phone number to call once I was done. In the quiet of my hotel room, I pored over a rather large pile of paperwork and learned that she was a registered prostitute, but this didn't seem a sufficient or legal reason for denial. Something told me it was far worse. I placed an international call and spoke to a friend of Peter's who worked for Interpol. It turned out that they had plenty on her.

In the 1960s, Gerda had been registered as a Nazi sympathizer after being arrested at a swastika-wielding demonstration outside a university. I didn't want to buck the immigration system, but the British, especially bureaucrats, weren't forgiving. And the German wars had left many with embittered hearts.

Over dinner, I asked Gerda what had happened at the demonstration. In her naiveté, she said she'd been brainwashed by a boyfriend of the time. She agreed that her stupidity had left her marked in the pages of history, like the rest of her country. Now she was paying a hefty price for a long-ago teenage love. But nothing she said appeased the strict British immigration rules.

I left an optimistic Gerda at the airport. I'd do everything I could for her, I said. Her chances were slim to none, but I didn't tell her that. Upon returning to England, I filed an Appeal Application. As expected, Gerda was denied entry. That same evening, I discussed her case with Peter. He, too, had no love for the Germans. He begged me to drop the case. I argued, why should the government hold Gerda solely accountable for the long-ago demonstrations when others with worse records had slipped through the British net of red tape?

I didn't sleep a wink that night. How could I help this poor woman? Part of me wants to believe my reason was one of pure sympathy; in truth, I suspect it was my young daredevil attitude goading me on. Let's beat the British at their own game. I wasn't patriotic like Peter. My adopted homeland was just a temporary stopover on my way to as yet undecided new horizons. So, I hatched a very dangerous plan. I was willing to take the risk for a woman, whose only motive to enter Britain was for love, not politics! Something in me changed after that struggle to help another person. I connected to her pain in a strange sort of way. You see, I had been trying to deal with my own internal pain and not doing too good of job of it at that time in my life. Oh, yes, I had everything in the world to make me happy, but I still hadn't dealt with the shame that comes with molestation, although I stopped slamming doors after I met Peter.

I arranged to meet Gerda in a different German city. I didn't want anyone from her hometown to see us together. It was on a sunny Friday morning in June that I booked into a Berlin hotel and waited. As instructed in my registered letter, Gerda arrived wearing a maid's uniform to blend in with hotel staff. Over a glass of wine in my hotel suite, I explained the plan I had hatched for her. I could tell she was nervous about it, but then so was I. I had a lot more to lose than she. We went into the bathroom. I dyed her mousey blonde hair a lighter tone to match my own. Then Gerda put on the clothing I'd worn on entering the hotel. Being large breasted, she had a problem buttoning up my suit jacket, but with an extra tug, I managed to fasten it. A pair of dark sunglasses hid her Germanic blue eyes. I was thrilled with the makeover. You couldn't tell us apart. Gerda was ready.

I gave her the airline tickets, my credit card, and passport. We hugged goodbye.

She left the hotel bound for London. Never once did I feel afraid that she might stay in Britain and leave me stranded in Germany. However, if the disguise backfired, then that was another ballgame. She would have to face the consequences alone as arranged. She would have to admit theft by saying that a cousin who worked at the hotel had stolen my passport.

My heart flew with Gerda on that late evening flight. With a "DO NOT DISTURB" notice hanging on the doorknob, I spent a boring weekend, watching awful German television and munching on the various food packets Gerda had brought me. Peter was in Mexico. I had told my secretary and the household staff back in Scotland that I was off to Egypt to see a client.

At last, around midnight, came three short knocks—our signal—on my hotel door. Gerda rushed into the room, her face radiant. The reunion had gone well with her lover. Of course, Gerda never told him how she managed to get into Britain, and Tom never pushed the matter. They were just happy to be together. I've not mentioned that the love of her life was an invalid, paralyzed from the waist down from a motorbike accident. The couple paid me handsomely for their stolen time together.

After a year-long fruitless battle to get Gerda a permanent residence status, I decided to take matters into my own hands and do what was right. I smuggled her into Britain once more. She finally married her sweetheart, and they live on a farm in Yorkshire. For obvious reasons, I never went to their wedding. I severed all ties. This was best, we both agreed. Because of her, I found my true calling.

I was sick of the legal bureaucratic red tape that

prevented some desperate good people from entering the country. The immigration system treated them as if they were lepers. Those poor souls—families torn apart, political dissidents, people denied refugee status, women fleeing abusive husbands, and so on. They didn't and wouldn't have had a hope in hell if I hadn't helped them. Oh, I'm sure you must be squirming in your seat, Brianna, knowing now that your mother is a felon, that I've broken the law more times than you've had hot dinners."

Brianna was more than numb. Her mother was the last person she would ever have suspected of criminal actions. She'd always been one who went "by the book." Or so Brianna had been led to believe.

The law student was all ears.

Well, I suppose I can say it's all in my past, but then I would be lying. The profits from my smuggling days have given me more money than I could spend in a lifetime, and now it is yours. I had the bulk of the money transferred into your name. I've only kept what I will need. The account details are in the briefcase..."

Brianna hurriedly pressed STOP.

"How could you, mother!" *Your cloak-and-dagger activities risked not only your life, but mine as well!* She paced the room, practically bouncing with indignation, anger, and self-pity. How could she return to law with a clear conscience? She wanted to take the tapes, burn them... but somehow she couldn't bring herself to. Reluctantly, her finger trembling, Brianna pressed PLAY.

Oh, I found my calling all right and loved every minute of it. I ran Operation Grassroots, as I'd aptly named it, until a few years ago. I never personally met my clients, Irish forger, or helpers. Personal contact was taboo. Pseudonyms, pay phones, and out-of-the-way mailboxes ran my undercover operation. That is, until my best "coyote" got himself caught. As I didn't trust another soul and had already committed to a "run," I decided to take on the risk myself. I'm sure you've watched many movies about Spanish-speaking "guides"… runners between borders. I became, I believe, the first *"gringa"* coyote. It was during this particular job that I met your father for the first time. You always wanted to know who your father was, and now you will—"

The recorder whirred, stopped, and began rewinding.

"I don't friggin' believe it!" Brianna shouted at the inanimate object in her hand. She reached for tape number (3).

Chapter 17

Brianna held the recorder a few inches from her ear. She didn't want to miss one word of this astounding revelation—one that she had waited a long time to hear.

In the summer of 1974, under a stormy sky, my plane touched down in Guatemala City. This was a short flight from Mexico City, but it had been a much longer journey the day before from Scotland to Mexico. At the passport and customs desk I faced a stern officer. As a cow masticates cud in slow motion, the officer chewed his gum. "What is the purpose of your visit, Señorita Edwards?"

"Tourism," I replied, without blinking. Under tanned eyelids, the man's beady eyes examined my fake British passport then ogled my skin-baring, almost indecent, skimpy outfit: an extra-short, white miniskirt, matching sleeveless top, stiletto sandals, and the large straw sunhat perched on top of my Farah Fawcett wig, one of many in my arsenal of disguises. Did I pass for a tourist? You bet. I had on more makeup than a streetwalker, and in my carry-on luggage I had made sure to pack a pile of tourist brochures, colorful shorts, skimpy tops, several bikinis, and suntan oil—not that I needed it. Born with a natural suntan was a bonus.

My passport tucked back into my bucket-shaped handbag, I headed for the exit. In the ARRIVALS area, I had to smile. Standing behind the guardrail was a chauffeur in an immaculately pressed, green uniform holding up a cardboard sign that read: SEÑOR. L. ANDREWS. We were both smiling as he led me to a black sedan with tinted windows, engine running and parked in a NO WAITING zone. A typical Hispanic man with greased hair tied in a ponytail slouched on the back seat.

"*Señorita* Edwards," Carlos Miguel Rodriguez announced to his employer with a grin.

"*Bienvenido.* Welcome to Guatemala," Juan Dominguez greeted. "I hope you had a good flight? Please, get in." Somewhat hesitantly, I slid in next to him.

Extending my hand, I said in eloquent English, "I'm Lynette. We spoke on the phone."

With his sloppy wet kiss on the palm of my hand and beady brown eyes fastened onto my chest, it gave me an opportunity to quickly check him out. I guessed him to be in his late forties.

"You're not what I expected, Señorita."

"What were you expecting—a man?" she laughed.

"Si."

"I know my voice is a little husky, but did I really sound like a man on the phone?"

"No. You are a very beautiful woman."

"Well, thank you, Señor Dominguez. And please call me Lyn." After the formal introduction and a little small talk, he came to the purpose of our meeting. "Did you bring the money, *Leeen?*"

I tried hard not to snigger at the way he had pronounced my name. I tapped my luggage and said, "Of course! But before I hand over a penny, have you sorted out his release? Do you have his passport ready?"

"No. My contact is waiting for my call. And no, I don't have what you want, not on me. It's at my villa. Not far from here."

Uneasiness ran through my veins. Was it a setup? Was I about to be mugged?

"Señor, it was agreed over the phone that our business would be conducted in a public place... like this airport."

"*Leeen,* I'm a government official. It is better we're not seen together. We can drive to my villa and do business in private. Then Carlos can drive you back to the airport, okay?"

Something caught my eye—a tattoo—peaking from under his crisp cotton short-sleeved shirt. I felt a shiver of fear. "*Oh, shit!*" was what I wanted to say but instead said, "It looks like I don't have much choice. But let me tell you that if I don't make a phone call to my boss in a couple of hours, all hell will break loose. Do you understand?"

His throaty laugh sounded like the rattle of an insane person. "There is no need to be afraid. Nothing is going to happen to you. I am a man of my word." He patted my hand and added, "Please relax and enjoy the ride."

I wanted to throw up. Juan was not only a corrupt immigration official—he was clearly Mafia. The underscored marijuana leafed tattoo—a symbol of the Mafia organization—was etched on his upper arm. If something were to go horribly wrong, I thought, nobody would find my body in this godforsaken third-world country. Back in London, England, a few months earlier, I'd thought long and hard about accepting this particular assignment. Most of the "courier" jobs I'd done in the past had been risky, but I learned Mexico and Central American dealings were much more dangerous. Being relatively young and enjoying the "spoils" of my job—lots of money—I chose not to heed the warning.

Traveling to his villa, I sat rigid on the back seat. I found it hard to concentrate on Juan's chitchat, especially the personal questions: "Are you married?"

"No."

"Do you have a boyfriend?"

"No."

"How old are you?"

"Old enough!"

"How long have you been doing this?"

"Too long is the answer to your question."

"Why do you take such risks?"

"Naturally, for the money, Señor."

I was relieved when Carlos announced that we had arrived at Juan's villa. The massive wrought-iron gates were hurriedly opened by a uniformed security man. Impressive rows of bougainvillea shaded the driveway leading up to his home. It was somewhat amusing to see a salmon pink adobe-styled house—an odd color, I thought, for a burly Mafia man. Inside, a large wall-mounted mirror reflected an array of vibrant local art hanging on every available wall space. He ushered me into an adjacent room cluttered with modern furniture and tropical plants. The walls were painted the same shade as the outside. I realized that only a woman could have chosen this decor. I hadn't noted a wedding ring. "Your wife has excellent taste."

"Yes, she *did* have. But sadly, she died a year ago."

Not wishing to pry into his affairs I simply said, "Oh, I'm sorry to hear that."

Juan's sudden impulse took me by surprise. He flung his arms around me and gave me a bear hug. It seemed an eternity before he let go. "*Mi casa es tú casa, Leeen,*" he gushed. "Make yourself comfortable. I'll get Magdalena to make lunch. Do you like seafood?"

I hadn't seen a female presence when we entered, and assumed that he was referring to a housekeeper. "Juan, I love seafood. But truly, I'm not really hungry. I had a huge breakfast this morning. I would like something to drink though."

"Would you like coffee, tea, or tequila?" What I would have liked was red wine, but when in Rome… I downed the tequila in one gulp. The tensional headache I'd had all morning vanished. I was feeling quite relaxed, not to mention a little bit tipsy. I often humored friends at a bar by saying, "Two strong drinks and I'll be anybody's."

Sunk into the plush pink and grey floral sofa, I took note of the many intricately carved horse statues in various poses on pedestals. "I see that you love horses, Juan?"

"Yes. A passion I've had since a boy. I own several thoroughbreds. Do you like horses?"

"I love them."

"That makes two of us," he smiled warmly. "I can show you my horses if you want?"

"I'd love to, Juan, but my time is limited here. I think we should get down to business."

I dumped the contents of my luggage onto the tiled floor and then slit open the extra plastic coating under the material lining. I removed the money hidden beneath.

"Twenty thousand U.S. dollars as agreed." Juan thumbed through one bundle of crisp thousand-dollar bills.

"It's all there," I confirmed.

"You must love this man very much, *Leeen*."

"Good Lord, no! I've never met him. I told you on the phone that I'm *only* the go-between... a courier," I responded glibly. "When can Julio Sandoval be released?"

"About an hour after I make the call, then my driver will take you to a safe place where you can meet."

"That's not a good idea. A return phone call from him will be enough."

"*Leeen*, I'm curious. If you've never met your coyote—"

I butted in, "He has a code—a password."

"And what code is that?"

"I'm not a 'dumb' blonde, Juan!"

"I apologize."

"Apology accepted. Now please make the phone call."

Unaware that I was fluent in Spanish, he spoke uninhibitedly during his phone conversation. Returning to sit next to me on the couch, he said matter-of-factly, "It's done. My contact at the prison will get him to ring here as soon as possible."

"That's great. Can I have the passport?"

I watched as Juan removed a large painting exposing a wall safe. He handed over the blank Guatemalan passport. I'd hardly tucked it into the secret compartment of my luggage when the phone rang. I spoke to Julio—my coyote—who, as I said, had unfortunately had been caught at the Mexican-American border a couple of weeks ago and was immediately deported back to Guatemala.

He had languished in jail until I could get him out. His "client," an El Salvadorian teenager, had somehow managed to escape. The boy's sister, a legal immigrant of the U.S., had coughed up five thousand U.S. dollars to get her brother into the States. The money order was cashed in England. Then one thousand of it was sent, via Western Union, to Julio. Now that "retainer" money was gone—"liberated" by an unscrupulous American border guard. Before embarking on the perilous journey, Julio had told the boy that if anything went drastically wrong and they became separated, the young man was to use the two hundred dollars hidden in his shoe, return to El Salvador, and await further instructions.

During Julio's brief stay in the American detention camp, he was able to contact Guadalupe, the boy's sister, who was living in San Francisco. Julio gave her my London-based number. The operation to reunite brother and sister had gone horribly wrong; even more so when I learned that Julio was no longer fit to do another "run" for the boy. The severe beating he'd received in the jail from a deranged inmate had resulted in serious lacerations to his face and a fractured thighbone. This awful event left my mind scrabbling. I'd have to do the job myself. No. That was out the question. A fractured thighbone would be the least of my concerns if I were caught. The thought made me shudder. An idea crossed my mind: Why don't I just pay another coyote to smuggle the boy through the tunnel—a drug smugglers' passageway that snaked its way from Tijuana, Mexico, to San Diego.

I decided I couldn't risk getting an unknown person involved. Then I had wondered, *Could I trust the someone in the Guatemalan Mafia?* I wasn't sure, but it seemed I had little choice.

So now, I looked at Juan, closing the safe, and said in his own language, "I need your help."

His mouth fell open. My fluent Spanish must have blown him away, but he agreed to help me—for a price of course. Was I willing to pay? Why not? I thought it wasn't *that* big a sacrifice.

Long after his moaning ended, I lay naked in his muscular arms…

"Eeewww!…" Brianna didn't really want to hear about her mother's sexual escapades and wanted her mother to get to what she really was wanting to her—the identity of her father.

Brianna began gnawing a thumbnail.

Juan was sated. For me, it had started with a get-it-over attitude—count the mosaic tiles on the ceiling and then get on with rescuing the poor boy waiting at the El Salvadorian border. To my surprise, I enjoyed myself. I've never been highly sexed, probably a psychological blockage that I, at that time, thought I'd probably wear for the rest of my life. In the past, ghastly sexual abuse memories always sent me screaming to the nearest bathroom to throw up. That's why my life with Peter was perfect. We had the best platonic relationship. And I loved him dearly in my own special way. Because he drank like a fish, he died from liver failure when you were three, Brianna. But enough of that, I can't think of Peter McTavish without feeling sad.

A contented Juan laid his head on my chest and devised a plan. He knew someone, he said, a high-ranking government official in El Salvador who owed him a favor. Juan would get him to locate the boy, take him to a place where Carlos, Juan's driver, could pick him up, and then return with him to the villa. But, Juan added, it was up to me to get him across the U.S. border. I had promised myself that I would never mix business with pleasure, but I found myself warming to Juan. He was not only a worthy partner in crime and lover, he turned out to be an excellent chef. Ravenous, he served me a large puffy omelet filled with every seafood delight you could imagine, topped with fresh garden herbs and hot rum. It was delicious. After the meal, we took a shower together, taking turns in washing each other's backs. Then the romantic interlude came to an abrupt end.

"*Leeen,* I'm a devout Catholic. I'm going to evening Mass. My darling, would you like to join me?" I could have swallowed the soap!

"Hell, no! I haven't set foot in a church since I was a kid, and I don't intend to change that for anyone."

"Ah, come on," he pleaded. "The church is over a hundred years old. You will be very impressed."

"No. The Catholic faith and I don't see eye to eye."

"Why?"

"It's a long story, Juan. I don't want to get into it."

"I promised my wife that I would go to church every Sunday."

"Oh, that's *nice!*" That definitely squashed the intimacy.

I got out, wondering how this tough Mafiosi could be such a softie at heart. "I won't be long, *Leeen,*" he informed me. "In the meantime, if you like, you can take a swim. No one will disturb you."

What was the point in taking a swim in chlorinated water after my shower? But what else was I to do while he was in church? The earlier rainstorm had passed, and glorious sunshine awaited me outside. Wearing a red-and-white polka-dot bikini, I followed Juan, dapperly dressed in a black suit and tie, to the piano-shaped pool. I couldn't believe how the sun was blazing hot at 5:00 P.M.

Sitting with my legs dangling in the warm waters of the tiled pool, I counted myself lucky. I had come a long way from my humble beginnings in Africa. Now, I could afford anything I desired. Apart from the Scottish house I shared with Peter, I owned a cozy two-bedroom sixth-floor apartment overlooking the River Thames—now sold. I drove a Rolls Royce, had a wardrobe full of good clothes, and ate at the finest restaurants. Mostly, I loved the English races, hobnobbing with the rich and famous in the horse business. Unthinking, I once used the name Hallworthy when I introduced myself. The horse trainer smiled. "Are you related to the famous Hallworthy family of South Africa, by any chance?"

"Yes." It wasn't a lie, but I let those who asked believe that I had inherited a vast sum of money from the Hall-worthy Estate. Nothing was farther from the truth. From an early age in my miserable childhood, I had mustered up a strategy born of the need to survive—*willpower,* an inner strength that flowed from an ocean of sorrow. But thanks to a highly intelligent brain—I'm not bragging, this is just a fact of life, such as being born with blue or green eyes—as I've told you, Brianna, I found a way to escape from that godforsaken place that trapped my body and soul. I not only survived, I fought back. I refused to be a victim. I would be a winner and kept self-pity at bay by helping other poor souls—people who were desperate and unable to provide for their families in their country of birth, victims unable to get past the red tape of immi-gration bureaucrats, to finally be able to migrate to another country and earn a decent living. The El

Salvadorian boy was one of them.

Working long hours in peanut fields, he earned literally "peanuts." Unable to support his elderly parents and younger siblings, the teenager had turned to his sister for help. It had taken over a year to raise the smuggling money. No, there was no way I could abandon this boy. Three days later, he finally arrived at the villa. I stared in amazement at the nearly nineteen-year-old. I'd seen many exceptionally good-looking Latinos, but this boy was more than handsome—he was drop-dead gorgeous. His ebony eyes glistened like the black pearls I wore. His long, curly hair, as thick as a horse's mane, hung loosely on his broad shoulders. With a doe-like flutter of his extremely long eyelashes he greeted me, "*Hola.*"

"*Hola,* Leonel (Lionel) Martinez. I am Lynette. You'll soon be with your sister, I promise…"

Brianna gasped so loud she nearly choked on her saliva. *Her stepfather!* Yet another falsehood! Her mother had told her that she had met Lionel on a trip to the United Kingdom. She twisted a strand of her hair in anxious expectation as her mother's voice droned on:

Lionel's warm hug had been very gratifying. But it was his look of gentle sadness that made me want to cry. The time had now come to say goodbye to my host. "Be careful, *Cariño,*" Juan warned. "May God go with you and the boy."

"Thanks for everything, Juan. I don't know what I would have done without your help."

He grinned mischievously. "You can repay me by coming back to visit."

"One day, Juan."

"Call me when you're safely across, okay?"

Although our relationship had been very brief, I was going to miss him, but I did not intend to ever return to Guatemala. Sunshine was turning to dusk as I drove the top-of-the-line rental black Mercedes through the American checkpoint without incident. A couple of miles clear, I let Lionel out of the trunk, gave him a Pepsi and, like excited children playing a game of tag, we pinched each other and danced on the road's hard shoulder.

"*Gracias,* my special *gringa* coyote," he said, flinging his arms around me.

"You are most welcome, my special Latino. Now I think we'd better go and find a phone booth, call your sister, and tell her that we will be arriving by plane as soon as I can book a flight."

What he did next nearly knocked me off my feet. He kissed me full on the mouth and said, "I love you, *gringa.*"

I turned scarlet.

All the way to San Francisco, he held my hand tightly. I hate to think what the first-class flight attendant thought. Thankfully, I still looked too young to pass as his mother. But it wasn't that maternal thought that caused a guttural noise of self-disgust from my mouth. Whatever are you thinking! I asked myself. He's only a boy! But this boy was more mature than any I'd ever known. We had a real connection, intense chemistry, as though our meeting was meant to be—that we were soul mates... Brianna, I'm talking about your *biological* Pappy, the man I married...

Brianna nearly fell off the couch. She hugged herself and shouted, "No. No. No!" *It can't be true!* There was no way he was her natural father… She clasped a hand over her mouth, her mind shrilling: *Oh, migod!*

Her index finger shaking, she turned up the volume.

> I'm sure you are reeling with shock. Yes, the man you hated for a while *is* your biological father. I wanted so many times to tell him, and to tell you, but couldn't. You see, I thought our marriage wouldn't last and then *both* of us, Brianna, would be heartbroken. Oh, I can imagine what's going through your head. What about Juan? You slept with him Mother! But I made Juan wear a condom, and I can assure you, it didn't break. As you well know, your father went and died on me. I wasn't supposed to outlive him. You know, I even considered joining my soul mate by an overdose. And I could not do that, either. I had *you* to think of. Well, now you're all grown up and will be, I'm positive of this, a successful lawyer, and I'll be joining the only man I've loved from the day we met. But before I end this recording, there is one more confession I have to make—

Click. The tape ran out.

Brianna buried her head in the sofa's scatter cushions and wept uncontrollably. Some moments later, chest heaving, she snatched a handful of tissues and wiped her nose and eyes. If only she had known. If she had, she would have treated Lionel better. A new flood of tears rolled down her cheeks. *I can't go and tell my father that I'm sorry and love him, because my friggin' mother took his ashes to El Salvador. God knows where my poor father's remains are scattered. Maybe Mike will know?* Rage dammed her tears. The thought of the mother she loved above all else keeping this secret was intolerable. She could not stop the words spewing from her mouth, "*Mommie dearest!* You are already dead to me!"

Her attention was drawn to the ornate humidor sitting on the coffee table.

"Why not?"

As the ghostly fingers of cigar tobacco swirled above her head, she wanted to run from her mother's home and never look back, but she couldn't. The nonsmoker coughed, stubbed out the Cuban cigar, and, with a look that could kill, she inserted the last tape.

Her mother's voice now seemed coldly indifferent.

It happened less than a year after I gave birth to you. Peter told me there was a black woman at the door, wanting to speak to me. I was surprised, as there weren't too many around the Isle of Skye. I took her into my office and closed the door. The woman rubbed her hands nervously. "My name is Marina," she said in an accent I immediately recognized. Her South African lilt was undeniable. "Gerda Düsseldorf gave me your address. "

"I don't know anyone by that name," I replied evasively.

"Madam, immigration is looking for my daughter and me. If they find us, we will be deported back to South Africa. My daughter and I hate the place like poison."

I asked her to explain. Marina told me that they'd been hiding in Manchester with a friend, who just happened to be my old German pal, Gerda. Of course, I had great sympathy for the poor woman's plight, but I had to make sure she wasn't a "plant." Undercover immigration spies were as good at their jobs as I was. Naturally, I grilled her. The personal details she relayed about Gerda could only have come from the source. I was in two minds to call Gerda but thought better of it. Having determined Marina wasn't a plant, I loosened up, and we talked about our similar lives in South Africa. Her daughter in

Manchester was the result of a brutal rape by three white police officers. I agreed to help without further question. This time, I didn't want money for my services. I had unfinished business of my own in that country. With Marina's help, there was a chance I could at last bury the nightmares of my youth.

Three weeks passed. My Irish forger did a fantastic job on our new British passports.

Marina and I were all set to return to South Africa. She wasn't happy about returning but knew she must. I wasn't going to help her if she didn't return the favor. As you were too young to be left, I got a qualified baby nurse to take care of you and gave some excuse to Peter. He didn't even seem to mind that I was rarely home nowadays. Perhaps he was even relieved. I suspect his new boyfriend was jealous of the woman who took precedence over him, and a rather uncomfortable triangle was developing.

On the long flight to Durban, I told Marina about my life in the African bush and what Alan had done to Anele and me. She wasn't surprised. She had seen the horrors fist hand. But she was shocked when I explained how I was going to avenge the wrongdoings. I thought she was going to back out; thank goodness, she didn't. With a vendetta-ridden heart I asked Marina to find a young black prostitute who was HIV positive. I hadn't specified age, so I wasn't shocked when I learned Naomi was shy of her thirteenth birthday. It happens all the time in most Third World countries, not just in Africa.

Poverty is the diabolical crime, not prostitution. The promise of costly antiviral medicine, food, and shelter induced this poor young girl to participate in my plan.

Brianna, what I'm about to tell you is worse than a

horror movie, so if you don't wish to hear this next bit, fast-forward the tape.

Part of Brianna wanted to hurl the tape in the trash bin, but then what could be worse than what she had already been subjected to? Lynette continued:

Naomi dressed in the revealing new clothing I bought her. She would go to Hallworthy Manor and ask to speak personally to Alan, whom I knew still resided there. She'd tell him that she desperately needed work and would do anything for it. She would entice him with her prostitute ways and arrange to have sex with him. The plan was for another paid helper to take photos and catch the bastard in the act. Then I would anonymously blackmail him. I had read in a South African newspaper that Alan had become the new Mayor of Durban. My intention was to mail—secretly, of course—the evidential lurid photo-graphs to a black-owned newspaper in Durban.

However, my plan backfired. The Polaroid photos I received mailed my own soul into hell. The camera cap-tured Naomi, her neck broken, lying naked in the hay—

Finally, Brianna lost it. She flung the recorder across the room glaring at it as if it had come from the bowels of hell and used every swear word known to man. Then, eyes still red and face pale as parchment, she retrieved it and continued listening, even though she didn't want to.

At Heathrow Airport, I mailed the incriminating tape to the district attorney's office in South Africa and waited in Scotland for news. Subsequently, I heard from Marina, whose cousin had sent her an article from a prominent

South African newspaper. Alan Hallworthy had pleaded insanity at his trial for the murder of Naomi. He was sentenced to a mental facility for the criminally insane for the rest of his natural life. Antiviral medications for full-blown AIDS prolonged his life. Yes, the bastard got what he deserved, and I got my revenge... but I'll never forget the price another soul paid for it. I know it doesn't appease what I did, but I had Naomi's body, with the consent of her family, reburied on the Sacred Burial Hill near the Tswanas village. I plan to visit her.

At my request, Marina periodically returns to South Africa to take money to Naomi's family; most of them are infected with the virus. I pay for doctor checkups and medicine. Shipments of drugs are heading to South Africa as I speak. I know my millions won't bring back Naomi, but by God, while I still have breath in my body, I'm going to spend every penny to make things right. From some people's perspectives, I'm guilty. On the other hand, I'm considered a hero by many. I'm not trying to justify my misconduct, Brianna. What I'm trying to say is that I have a good heart that honestly tried to do good things. My intentions have always been free of guile and innocent of malice; I have only tried to help people who are desperate and have no recourse. I was a victim of a brutal crime, but there was no support and guidance. I was on my own. So, I'm going home to die. It will be of my own free will. Before I do that, I'm going to try to make a difference in the lives of my African people, yes, *my* people! In my heart, I've always been one of them. Don't hate me, my darling daughter. Please, love me for who I am...

On hearing Lynette's last words, Brianna, her eyes vacant, stared at the ceiling. After what seemed an eternity, she got up off the couch, went over to the fireplace, and stacked it with kindling. She then struck a long barbeque match and lit the wood shavings. Soon, the odor of burning cassette tapes filled the downstairs room.

She returned to the bedroom and placed the money and jewelry into the briefcase. She slid the damper on the fire on low, locked the front door, and climbed in her car. All she could think of now was Roberto. Before leaving, she had made a call to him, "Roberto, it's me."

"Are you okay? You sound upset."

"Upset isn't the word. I'm on my way home."

"How's your Mom?"

"I don't wish to talk about her!"

"Drive safely, Sweetpea. Can't wait to see you and give you a big sloppy kiss."

Brianna "escaped" from Lynette's driveway.

Chapter 18

The Indian Ocean sparkled like sapphire gems as the British Airways Airbus descended from clear-blue sunny skies. It made a smooth landing at Durban International Airport. The pilot informed passengers it was five o'clock local time on this fine February evening. Lynette adjusted her wristwatch and prepared to disembark from first class.

Wearing a pair of white Capri-length pants, pale-blue tie-back top, and open-toed sandals, she made her way through to customs.

"What is the purpose of your visit?" the customs officer asked.

"I'm here on a little business and lots of pleasure," she responded with half a smile.

Silently, he stamped her "authentic" British passport and waved her through.

In the ARRIVALS LOUNGE was an elderly black man, the hardship of life written across his leathery forehead. He ambled toward her. "Are you Mrs. Martinez?"

"Yes, I am."

"Welcome to South Africa. My name is Kelingo, Mister Durval's driver. He asked me to tell you that he is sorry he is not able to meet you but will see you later at the hotel. Follow me, please. I'll drive you to the Hotel Edward."

"How far is it from here?"

"Thirty-five miles, Mrs. Martinez, but I'll have you there in no time."

As Kelingo loaded her luggage into the trunk of the four-door black Audi, Lynette sneaked a sideways peek at him. His back was bent, and his face was wrinkled and brown as a walnut. "Milk-bottle" glasses had slid to the end of a stubby broad nose.

He looks as old as the hills. He shouldn't be driving at his age—

The pain caused her to cry out, "Oh, not now!"

"Are you alright, Mrs. Martinez?"

"Yes, I'm fine," she lied.

The sudden onset of a blinding migraine had distracted her thoughts about Kelingo's motoring skills, but not her distress. Severe headaches, double vision, dizziness, and trouble concentrating were to name of few symptoms of the brain cancer. Despite her declining health, she coped and was determined to see her objective through, regardless.

She dry-swallowed two prescription capsules, something she had become quite good at, but she would have preferred to lie down, bury her head under a pillow, and sleep until the blasted headache subsided.

When the medication kicked in, she was more able to focus and, much to her surprise, Kelingo was a good driver. He handled the car well as he drove along the scenic route, Durban's Golden Mile, where the hotel was located.

She peered out the window at the Indian Ocean flanked by subtropical beaches of pristine golden sand and sighed. This breathtaking country held too much sorrow for her to appreciate its natural beauty. She both passionately hated and loved it, this land that was her birthplace.

Kelingo adjusted his rear-view mirror to make eye contact. "I hope you don't mind me asking, but is this your first visit to South Africa, Mrs. Martinez?"

"No, Kelingo. I know this country pretty well."

Kelingo's eyes searched hers for an explanation, and she quickly diverted his curiosity. "How long have you worked for Mr. Durval?"

"Nearly fifteen years, Mrs. Martinez."

She just had to ask, "I hope you won't be offended, but aren't you just a wee bit too old to still be working... and driving a car?"

A broad smile crossed the old man's lips. "There's still a lot of life left in my old bones. There is no welfare state here, Mrs. Martinez, so I have to work. I'm a grandfather of twenty grandchildren who always need extra money for this and that."

Lynette felt a twinge of admiration for this man who should have long ago retired. "You said you worked fifteen years for him. What did you do before that?"

"As a child, I was a..." he took a deep breath. The word that came to mind was "slave," but Kelingo thought better of it. After all, she was a *white* woman! "...from the age of six onward, I worked cutting sugar cane, then I got a job in a sugar refinery packing raw sugar into sacks. While I was at this factory, I met my present boss. He is the legal advisor to Lady Corrie Hallworthy, who owns the refinery."

Lynette sucked in her breath noisily.

Kelingo's challenging eyes met hers. "Do you know the Hallworthys?" he asked cagily.

Lynette turned away from his intense stare. "Not really," she replied convincingly. But her heart and thoughts raced like an Olympic sprinter, forcing her to take rhythmic breaths.

Yes, yes, yes! A boy named Kelingo rescued Anele from the jaws of death, Maekela had told her.

Was this old driver Anele's savior?

The coincidence was too much to ignore. "Many years ago, a

young fieldworker saved the life of a little bush girl named Anele Dingane—"

She was nearly flung from her seat as the Audi came to a screeching halt on the shoulder. Kelingo looked like he had seen a ghost. A black person can't turn white, but so drained of color, his features had turned a pale greenish hue. "How do you know of this?" he asked in a shaky voice.

"Are you the one who saved her?"

"Yes."

Lynette could have done handsprings. She hurriedly got out of the car and seated herself opposite Kelingo. They talked for what seemed hours. Neither could believe this was a complete coincidence. Whoever or whatever had pulled these cosmic strings had another shocker for Lynette.

"Anele Dingane *is* alive, Mrs. Martinez."

"Dear God in heaven! Do you know where she is?"

"Yes. She's back home in Tswanas."

Lynette was blown away. "How do you know that for sure?"

"I saw her there."

"Explain?"

"Some years back I returned home to Mtunzini, which is far from Anele's home, to visit my younger sisters, only to find they had moved from our village to Tswanas Kraal. You can imagine my surprise when I found Anele there. Of course, she was no longer the little girl I had marched off to the manor house. Also, it was no secret that she had been jailed at Montclair prison. I can't remember the whole story, but it had something to do with her stealing money and a white child..." Kelingo paused long enough to take a long look at Lynette. "...you wouldn't be that child, would you?"

"Yes, Kelingo. I'm *that* child."

"Great Spirit of the black people, protect my heart from failure. I was told Anele's *Shiya* was dead."

"Well, you were misinformed. As you can see, dear Kelingo, I'm very much alive and kicking at this moment. I'd love to continue this conversation, but please get me to the hotel. I have to phone my daughter. And then after that, hopefully, we can work out a plan to go home to Tswanas. Perhaps you can come by the hotel in the morning?"

Kelingo nodded.

The car came to a considerably smoother halt outside the Hotel Edward.

Kelingo's clasp of her hand as she exited the car was warm and tender. Lynette gave him a hug then pressed a couple of hundred-dollar bills into his hand and thanked him, "*Ngiyabonga,* Kelingo. You're a hero in my eyes."

"This is too much," he said staring at the folded notes.

"Not too much for a loving grandfather. Buy your grandchildren something nice from me. And if you have any trouble exchanging the American currency, let me know, and I'll exchange them at the hotel."

"I don't know what to say—"

Metal nametag glinting in the sunlight, the bellhop stood ready to pounce on her luggage. "Welcome to the Hotel Edward," the black boy beamed.

While the bellhop put her luggage on a cart, Lynette touched Kelingo's sleeve. "Goodbye, for now. And thank you for everything."

"It's been my pleasure, Shiya of Tswanas," he replied in Zulu.

Lynette's smile was as wide as the Nile.

She watched the Audi drive away then followed the bellhop past the miniature palms in enormous clay pots flanked by Greek pillars, and looked up at the 1911 art deco façade as she walked through the dark wood glass paneled doors into the cool air-conditioned foyer. She headed for the reception desk. "My name is Mrs. Lynette Martinez. I believe I have a suite reservation made by a Mr. Bryan Durval?"

"Good evening, Mrs. Martinez. Welcome to Durban and the Hotel Edward," the white desk manager greeted her. "Mr. Durval insisted that we provide you with our premier accommodation. We hope you will enjoy the presidential suite. It is a sea-facing on the seventh floor, with magnificent views of the Indian Ocean."

The suite was indeed up to five-star standards. The four air-conditioned rooms were decorated in pastel colors with dark wood furniture and coordinated rich floral fabric. In the main bedroom sat a king-sized bed adorned with the best of linens; exquisite Italian crystal bedside lamps sat on carved tables, and a huge TV screen dominated one wall. In the en suite bathroom were an enormous whirlpool tub, a separate shower cubicle, and vanity mirrors running down the length of one wall. In the lounge, a bouquet of flowers accompanied by an enormous basket of fruit, and a bottle of champagne, compliments of the hotel, graced a dark walnut bar cabinet filled with miniature alcohol drinks, bottled water, and fruit juice. Lynette was more than satisfied with Bryan's hotel selection.

Clutching his generous tip, a happy bellhop closed the door behind him.

She hardly had time to remove her footwear when the phone rang. "Hello. Lynette Martinez speaking."

"Good evening, Mrs. Martinez. Bryan Durval here. I'm sorry I couldn't pick you up at the airport. Got caught up in business."

"Don't worry about it. I got here just fine, thank you."

"Would it be too inconvenient if I popped over in, say, an hour and a half?"

"Sure. That's fine by me. Looking forward to meeting you."

Lynette browsed through the Brasserie Restaurant a la carte menu, and the seafood specialty section caught her eye. She lifted the telephone. "Hello. This is Mrs. Martinez in the presidential suite. I would like to order the *Agnolotti Cinesi* (fresh pasta squares stuffed with oysters, shallots, and ginger) and a bottle of your finest red wine to be sent up to my suite, please."

She hardly touched the food but managed to drink two full glasses of wine, then went to the bathroom, refreshed her makeup, brushed her long hair, and changed into a lace-accented floral skirt and cotton-spandex halter-top. Italian leather sling-back sandals complimented her outfit. She awaited her guest with her heart playing hopscotch.

* * *

In his late 30s, Bryan Durval was a physically imposing figure. Standing well over six feet, his chiseled features were softened by sun-bleached hair and gentle aqua-green eyes. He was casually dressed in a khaki shirt, shorts, and brown leather sandals. The lawyer was not what Lynette had expected.

His father, whom she had met with Peter McTavish at St. Andrews Golf Club in Scotland, was extremely short, almost dwarf-like. His son, on the contrary, was strikingly handsome. Instantly, Lynette felt his strong sexual magnetism drawing her to him, but it was soon thwarted by a chastising internal voice: *Hussy! Lionel is hardly cold. You are here on business, not to get romantically involved! And quit drinking alcohol!*

Shaking her hand firmly, Bryan smiled. "Pleased to meet you, Mrs. Martinez."

"Likewise, but let's dispense with the formalities. Call me Lynette, but not Lyn. I dislike abbreviations. May I offer you a glass of red wine, or would you prefer a cold beer?"

"No wine or beer for me, thank you. But I won't say no to a glass of water."

She handed him a bottle of Perrier and a glass tinkling with ice cubes.

"Bryan, how long have you been in practice?"

"Fifteen years."

"Does your father still work?"

"No. He's retired. I informed you of this when we spoke on the phone."

"You did! Boy, is my memory getting rusty! Then I'm bloody well stuck with you," she laughed.

Bryan smiled. "How may I be of assistance?"

He's a smooth one, Lynette thought as she reached for her handbag and removed a notebook. "I have itemized my instructions. But before we get down to business, I hope that I don't have to remind you of attorney-client privilege."

"Of course not."

"Good. So I can tell you now that I was born here in South Africa. I left the country when I was a teenager."

"Really! You have a strong British accent. I thought that you were definitely English when we spoke on the phone."

Lynette didn't feel the need to explain. Or to tell him that English was, in fact, her second language. "Before I discuss the list I've given you, I want you to know what prompted it—a wake-up call, so to speak. You see, I have a tumor on the left side of my brain and have chosen not to undergo surgery, and while I'm of sound mind, I have things to do, and quickly. There will come a time when I won't know my arse from my elbow, and that's where you come in."

Bryan tried not to show his surprise. Her coarseness didn't befit the articulate and classy woman facing him. She also was very attractive. Before his mind and good manners stomped on his tongue, he'd lavished her with a compliment. "I hope you won't mind me saying this, but you are darn good-looking for your age."

Lynette felt her face growing hot. "Well, thank you. But adding the suffix 'your age' doesn't make a woman feel youthful!"

Encouraged by her informality, he leaned forward and asked roguishly, "Well, how old *are* you, then?"

"I'm fifty-three going on twelve."

Bryan chortled, and then channeled his wayward thoughts back on track. "Now, how can I help you?"

Lynette reopened her notebook. "I'd like to address the first item on my list: Lord Alan Percival Hallworthy."

Bryan's eyebrows knitted.

Lynette noted his frown and smiled. "Yes, I do mean Alan Hallworthy, the plantation owner and former mayor."

"Oh, I'm afraid that would be a conflict of interest," Bryan stated. "I handle the affairs of Corrie Hallworthy, his wife. And you should be aware of this fact. If my memory serves me well, you stated on the phone that you were an immigration attorney."

"Oh, don't preach the law to me. Do you want to know why I deliberately picked your family practice for my needs?"

His blonde eyebrows lifted.

"I don't know so much about you," Lynette said, "but I know your father is as crooked as a pretzel."

Visibly shocked, Bryan glared at Lynette. Holding his angry gaze, she continued, "Oh don't look so surprised. Don't tell me you didn't know all about the theft. How your father amassed a fortune, is able to own homes here and in the Caribbean and pay for a Lear Jet and an expensive yacht. They certainly aren't from a lawyer's salary. Your father made his fortune from cooking the Hallworthy books. He made a tidy sum swindling money from the refinery—"

"Bullcrap!" Bryan erupted. "I'm not going to sit here and listen to this!" He snatched his briefcase and marched toward the door. "I'm out of here, you crazy woman," he uttered without turning his back.

"I think you'd better sit back down, Bryan. I have to show you something."

With a curiosity scowl, he turned around and faced her.

Lynette retrieved several folded ledger sheets from the back of the notebook, walked over to Bryan, and handed them to him. In the back of her mind she was thinking, "It's like sending a thief to catch a thief! Come to think of it, wasn't there a movie with the same name, Cary Grant and Grace Kelly? Well, if it's good enough for

Hollywood, the same plot will work for me."

Flipping through documents, Bryan's golden tan faded. "How did you get these?"

"How I got them is irrelevant. What's relevant is your pledge to work for me now."

"If I do just that, how do I know that the information you have on my father is not going to go any further than this room?"

"You don't! But I will tell you this… once you have carried out my wishes, I will hand over the entire ledger."

Lynette knew that she couldn't have held the lawyers to ransom if not for Maekela.

On her last trip to South Africa, Lynette had contacted the Hallworthy servant. She not only had stolen the ledger, she also managed to get Corrie's handwritten personal journals, which Lynette had brought with her.

Shoulders rounded in defeat, Bryan said, "Okay. What is it you want me to do?"

"Let's sit down."

Sat opposite him, Lynette took a deep before saying, "Firstly, I have to tell you that Alan is my biological father."

"I don't recall seeing any Hallworthy children listed in *WHO'S WHO*."

"You're not likely to find me in any book. I'm not even going to bother to have a DNA test done. I *know* who's my father! Would you like to hear the shocking truth?"

Now beyond surprise, Bryan bobbed his head.

Omitting only the graphic sexual details, Lynette went back in time. Bryan's face was so florid, he looked as if he were about to have a coronary.

"Are you okay, Bryan? Do you want something to drink?"

"I think I'll have that glass of wine now."

He drank the red wine like soda pop, then leaned forward, eyes meeting and holding hers. "I followed Alan's trial closely. The man got what he deserved. There isn't a person in Durban who wasn't glad to see him locked up. Everyone in these parts knows that the man is pure evil. He hasn't a remorseful bone in his body, and he strangled that girl as if she were an unwanted kitten. How many other people has he murdered and gotten away with? So, in God's name, why would you want to see him walk free?"

Lynette sighed deeply. She couldn't get Naomi's pretty face from her mind. Fighting back tears, she confessed, "You see, Bryan, *I'm* responsible for Alan taking Naomi's life. If I hadn't been so bitter and twisted, she'd be alive today. Or maybe not. She was HIV positive when I hired her to go to the Hallworthy refinery and subsequently infect Alan. I wish I could take it all back, but I can't. The deed is done, so to speak. But more than anything, I curse the new drug Kaletra, which I believe is an antiviral vaccine that's keeping my father alive."

Tears stung in her eyes. "When I learned of my brain tumor, I had to ask myself: What is my life worth? Absolutely nothing compared to the deliberate taking of another's. What I did was wrong. I'm no better than that bastard who sits rotting away in the mental hospital. He should have died years ago, but somehow his symptoms didn't show up until many years later. But then, you know the saying: *The Devil looks after his own.* And Lord knows how many victims have succumbed to AIDS, but not him. I hate him like poison, but my moral compass has to be set back on track. I have to undo the wrong I've done, or I'll never see the gardens of eternity. I'm not a religious person, but I do believe in hell. You may not agree with me, but it is my wish that you enter my signed admission of guilt into court."

Bryan shook his head. He was used to dealing with a mixed bag of criminals, including the insane, but this woman beat the lot. Such a classy person, he would never have believed it of her. A part of him wanted to vindicate her control over him, and yet he was filled with genuine sympathy. He looked at the woman who had bared her soul, knowing that Alan Hallworthy was behind bars because of his own sick actions, not hers.

"Why on earth would you wish to spend the rest of your life in prison?"

"I owe it to Naomi. But I need some time before you put the wheels in motion."

* * *

Two hours had passed.

What had occurred during this time was unbelievable.

Lying together on the bed and wrapped in a lover's embrace, they told each other secrets that they would not have told a priest. Then, Bryan's lips found hers… And time stood still.

Later, with daylight sneaking through the bedroom window, Lynette removed his draped arm from around her waist and gently nudged him. He opened his eyes, pulled her close, and murmured, "I wish we had met under different circumstances."

"You mean you don't *hate* me?"

"Of course not. You did what you had to do. And by God, it worked. But on a serious note—" He winked. "—as your lawyer, I advise you to drop it. Alan's deviant behavior far exceeds your, or anyone else's, capacity to forgive."

Lynette nodded in agreement. "You're right. Nothing will bring back Naomi."

Dressed and ready to leave for work, Bryan handed Lynette his business card. "I've written my private number on the back. I'm not in court today, so I can be here in minutes. I'll see you later on either way. We can sit down and work out a way for you to see Anele."

"I feel like such a witch for treating you the way I did."

"Ah, don't worry your pretty head over it. It's forgotten."

Left alone with her thoughts, Lynette's inner voice spoke out again: *You didn't come here to have an affair. And what's with this cradle snatching!*

She took a shower and, wrapped in the towel, ordered breakfast. Lovemaking had made her ravenous. While waiting for her meal, she picked up a magazine and flipped through the pages. Her eyes came to rest on the glossy photograph of an Italian beauty advertising a "Never Fail Makeup" product. The model's seductive smile sent a message like a missile to Lynette's brain: *Brianna.*

She grabbed the bedside phone and dialed out. A sleepy voice answered at the other end, and Lynette heard him say, "Bri, there's a woman on the phone who sounds like the Queen."

Brianna snapped awake and literally snatched the phone from Roberto's hand.

"Mom, where are you?"

"I'm in—"

Brianna cut her off, "How could you just leave like that? I listened to your tapes, and I'm very angry. You could have told me yourself. To find out all this stuff is beyond words."

Lynette sighed. But what did she expect!

Brianna wasn't going to let her mother speak. "Mom. Come home, *please*. I'm devastated by all this. We need to talk."

"I can't."

"Yes, you can!"

"I thought I made it clear why I needed to come here to South Africa."

"Then give me the number there, so I can at least call and see if you are okay."

"I'm staying at a hotel, but not for long."

Angry and worried to the point of despair, Brianna shouted, "For crying out loud, Mom, I thought I'd always have stability, a safe place with you in my life, but I guess I never saw how truly selfish you are."

Lynette could only imagine how her daughter felt, but her irate tirade hit Lynette hard. Coolly, she responded, "Brianna I'm suffering enough without *you* in my life. And your attitude isn't helping matters. Stand on your own two feet now, and don't look back—"

The line went dead.

There was nothing Lynette could do. It was too late to turn back the clock, but not what she had to do now.

She dressed quickly.

The ankle-length black skirt, cream print blouse with shoulder buttons, and flat black shoes made her look matronly. That's how she wanted to appear for this clandestine assignment.

She ordered a taxi and waited outside for it.

The East Indian cabdriver opened the back door of his taxi, returned to the driver's seat, and asked, "Where to, Lady?"

"I'd like you to take me to Pinetown Mental Hospital."

"It's quite a ways from here and will be expensive."

"Just take me there, *please*. This is a wait-and-return, so you'll make good money."

After an hour and a half drive in total silence, the cabdriver pulled up in front of a four-story grey-stone building with barred windows. On the lawn were a number of disabled patients. Some sat in wheelchairs, and some, accompanied by nurses in red capes, strolled in the gardens.

At the admittance desk, Lynette wrinkled her nose at the overbearing smell of disinfectant. It was almost unbreathable. This was her last time, she hoped, ever to walk into a medical facility of any sort.

Bifocals perched on her thin nose, the black attendant looked up. "Can I help you?"

Heart pounding, Lynette replied, "A close friend of mine asked me to check up on her uncle, whom I believe is a patient here. I'd like to see him to pass on her message."

"What is the name of your friend's uncle?"

"Alan Percival Hallworthy."

The nurse peered over the top of her glasses. "Mr. Hallworthy, to my knowledge, doesn't have any relatives abroad. I don't know if your friend is aware of this, but he is under court order in solitary confinement, and the only visitor he is allowed is his wife. She visits him every day at three. I can telephone Mrs. Hallworthy and tell her that you are here."

An icy shiver raced down Lynette's spine, and then her nerves gave way. "I can't do this," she muttered as she walked briskly away from the desk, heading for the exit doors. The attendant rounded her desk and chased after her. Grabbing Lynette's arm, she said, "You seem dreadfully upset. Am I right in assuming that you gave me a tall story? You know Mr. Hallworthy personally, am I right?"

Lynette blurted, "Yes, I *do* know him. He is my father."

The nurse stared in disbelief. "That's hard for me to swallow, but I have to ask myself, why else would you make up such a pathetic story? Okay, come with me before the lunch staff come on duty. I'll let you see him—unofficially, of course."

They came to a door marked 144A.

Taking a chain-attached key from her waistband, the nurse opened the steel door.

There, sitting on a cot, his eyes cast to the floor, was a wizen old man wearing a urine-stained, pale blue hospital gown. Saliva dribbled down his chin. He didn't look up.

Lynette's nerves gave way again. She wanted to flee from the pathetic character who was her father. She nearly jumped out her skin when the nurse touched her arm. "Remember, you only have a few minutes… or I'll be in hot water! And no bodily contact. He's HIV positive." To the inmate she shouted, "Hey Alan, you have a visitor." When he didn't look up, she said to Lynette, "He's as deaf as a doornail, the old fart! You'll have to shout if you want him to hear you."

Hatred locked in her heart, just barely contained beneath the surface of consciousness, yet pity threatening to intrude upon her lifelong rage, Lynette wondered how she ever could have contemplated forgiveness. It was beyond all human reasoning.

Alan's gaze remained focused on the floor.

Every bone in her body cringed when the cell door closed behind her. She wanted to scream: *Let me out!* But reasoning stepped in: *What the heck! I've nothing to lose.*

She bent at her waist to come face to face with her father and verbally went for his jugular, "You sick son of a bitch! You should have died years ago. But then, the devil *does* look after his own, doesn't he, you decaying bastard? Look at me, you evil shit!"

Slowly, Alan lifted his head.

"Do you know who I am?" she bristled. "You should. I'm your daughter… You know the one you raped when I was a child. And I promised you that one day I'd get you, and I did. I set you up… sent the incriminating Naomi tape that put you here! Why don't you die and go straight to hell where you belong?"

Instead of feeling relief from expressing her long pent-up rage, she felt ashamed for venting herself on a helpless old man who didn't know who she was. But the venom oozing from her heart soon resurfaced. She slapped hard his sunken cheek. In a flash, Alan's bony frame lunged forward and with surprising strength gripped his daughter around the neck. His stranglehold pinned her to the wall. Lynette managed to kick over a small metal table alerting the staff. Two burly male nurses entered and restrained Alan.

Livid finger marks bruising her neck, she fled to the waiting taxi. She wept all the way back.

In the safety of the hotel room, a visibly shaken Lynette examined the raised marks on her neck. They were nothing in comparison to the welts she had clinging to her bitter heart. Now, she'd rather die first then ever let this evil monster go free.

Later that day, when Bryan arrived with Kelingo, Lynette was thrilled to see them both, but especially the old man. She had hardly closed the door behind them when Bryan said, "I must tell you that things have changed since you last lived here. The pendulum in South Africa has swung, and now we have discrimination in reverse.

To be white is a great disadvantage in the African bush, so I don't recommend going to Tswanas Kraal."

"You're right," she agreed half-heartedly. "I don't suppose things have changed much.

Apartheid is still alive in some black hearts, not just here in Africa but in the world in general.

But after the entire white race crippled the true people of this country, can you really blame them for wanting to retaliate? Personally, I could kill a few white folk myself."

Discomfort written on his face, Kelingo looked down.

"I'm just trying to protect you," Bryan said.

"Protect me! If I'm killed, the money runs out, doesn't it, Bryan?"

He winced. "That was uncalled for. What I'm trying to say is—"

Lynette simply turned her back on Bryan and to Kelingo, who was looking even more ill, she said, "Kelingo, how would you like to earn ten times the money you make with Mr. Durval?"

Shifting from one leg to another, Kelingo remained silent. Bryan saved his driver's embarrassment. "I'm certain that Kelingo would love to escort you to Tswanas. I'm quite prepared to forego his services for a while to help you on this assignment. I know how important it is to you."

Lynette gently touched her lawyer's arm. "Forgive me for being so darn rude. I seem to be making a habit of it lately."

"It's okay. I've had worse flung at me."

"When can Kelingo and I leave?"

"As soon as I can make the necessary travel arrangements," Bryan replied in an exasperated tone.

"Great! Thanks."

Lynette handed Bryan an eighty-thousand-dollar Euro check to cover the expenses of hiring a helicopter pilot to fly them to Kwa-Zulu—"the place of the Zulus." The funds would also cover

Kelingo's wages, Bryan's fees, and the purchase of various supplies Lynette wished to take with her.

After the men left, her veins throbbed with excitement. She danced around the room. "*Umama,* I'm coming home at long last."

Happiness bouncing throughout her body, she went to the liquor cabinet, took out a miniature brandy, poured the contents into a glass, and toasted, "Here's to the final chapter of this story. To all of Anele's ancestors, if you are listening, I thank you for guiding me home. Bless you all."

Chapter 19

The morning couldn't have come fast enough. Lynette had hardly slept a wink, and now her stomach was jittery with excitement. She took a quick shower, packed her bags, making sure that her photo album containing pictures of Brianna and Lionel were within easy reach, and was about to leave the room when her scatterbrained memory gave her a nudge.

She lifted the telephone receiver and dialed the international number. The phone line at the other end rang and rang, then the voicemail cut in: "Hi, this is Brianna and Roberto. We are not here to take your call…"

Disappointed, Lynette waited for the customary beep: "Brianna, I was hoping to speak to you, but never mind. I want you to know that I'm truly sorry I let you down, but I have some good news. I've found Anele, and I'll be leaving today for the African bush. Before I leave, I'm going to buy a cell phone, but I'm not sure it will work out there. I want you to know that I love you with all the love in the world. When this journey is over, I just want to join my beloved husband, and your father. I know he's waiting for me in the Invisible Kingdom of Souls, and I don't want to make him wait too long. Take care my special child. See you in heaven."

Lynette hung up and then rang the hotel desk for her luggage to be brought down.

In the foyer, a poker-faced helicopter pilot awaited her. "I'm Captain Johannes de Klerk."

Lynette extended her hand in greeting, but his hand wasn't forthcoming. "Follow me, Mrs. Martinez."

They stepped outside into the start of a glorious sunny day. There wasn't a cloud in sight.

It was a short car ride to Durban's executive airstrip, but airborne, it seemed forever in the hot, sticky air until they landed on a dirt patch not far from Chief Naboto's resting tree. The giant leaves on the baobab tree whipped back and forth like a ping-pong ball as the blades of the canary yellow chartered helicopter rotated. Lynette was more than happy to be on dry land. She had never mentioned this to anyone, but she was afraid of flying.

She thanked the pilot, who had hardly spoken a word to her and not one to Kelingo since leaving the hotel foyer, then reminded him, "See you back here in a month, okay, Captain. And here's a little something extra for you," she said, handing him an envelope.

Johannes forced a smile and counted the RANDS. He was surprised to find nearly as much money as Bryan had paid him. *Bonus!* He thought, and tucked the money into the top pocket of his taupe-colored shirt. At first, he'd been hesitant about this trip—too dangerous to land his operator-owned chopper in unknown territory. That snake in the grass, Bryan, had been persuasive: "Look man, the woman is loaded. She is willing to pay plenty. Take it. You need the cash. You have another baby on the way. Here's a map of the region, and I've highlighted a suitable place to land."

Johannes was glad to rid himself of the English woman—too la-dee-da for his liking—but even more of the old black person sitting behind her. He'd been inappropriately familiar with her. Johannes made eye contact with Lynette. "I'm curious, lady. Why would a *white* woman—" he emphasized the word, "—want to come out to this place?"

Obviously, Bryan had paid him but had not given an explanation for her journey.

Lynette resisted the temptation to give him a verbal smack. This was the beginning of her new life, ushered in on a fine February midmorning with such a racist boor?

Head held low, Lynette scrambled out of the cockpit into the eddies of swirling dust. Kelingo followed.

Away from the whirling blades, Lynette waited for the pilot to unload the cargo—several boxes—items for the village that Bryan had purchased from her list.

Johannes didn't budge from his seat. Lynette was momentarily perplexed.

Choking on a mouthful of reddish dust, she climbed back up and rapped her knuckles against the window. Johannes opened it a fraction and glared at her. "What do you want, Lady?"

"I'd like my money back," Lynette bellowed above the din.

He sneered. "Hell, no!"

"I have just paid you extra, well over the airfare, to help unload!"

"You are crazy! I'm not lifting a finger to help a *kaffir*-loving woman. You had better get the stuff out, or I'm taking off with it."

Lynette blew a gasket. "You rotten dirtbag! I'm never going to use your services again."

His lips curled into a smirk. "You had better hurry. My time is precious."

After the backbreaking unloading, Lynette gave Johannes the finger and received one back.

"Your days on this planet will be numbered," he bellowed before lifting off.

Lynette paid no heed to his threat, but his parting words would one day come back to haunt her.

Safely away from the chopper, she brushed dust from her white jeans, wondering why she'd chosen to wear white when khaki would have been far more appropriate.

Dusting his own pants, Kelingo sidled up to Lynette. "I'm sorry for the way that awful man treated you. I hope you understand that it's not my place to get in between the arguments of white people."

Lynette wrapped an arm around Kelingo's shoulders. "Good Lord, there's no need for you to apologize." She could see by his look that her apology wasn't enough.

"When Nelson Mandela was appointed our President and apartheid abolished, I was a very, very happy man. I hoped that things would get better between our races. Sadly, hatred in the hearts of both black and white still festers. That's the way it is. It will never change."

"I don't believe it ever will," Lynette agreed. "Even though I lived continents away, I tried to keep up with the news over here in South Africa. But I believe that it's not the old apartheid ways that cripples this country now, it's your people... black people who are fighting and murdering each other."

"That's a fact," Kelingo sighed.

"Enough about this distasteful subject, Kelingo. Let's get what we can carry and come back for the rest of it later. I can't wait to see Anele." She felt like pinching herself. She couldn't believe that she was actually stepping back in time, to where she had spent the first years of her life. Unable to contain her emotions, she did a hop and a skip. "Whoopee! I'm home at last!"

Kelingo's old eyes smiled. He too, was happy to be in his homeland.

"How much further do we have to go," Lynette asked.

"It's not that far now."

"These darn shoes are killing me." She bent, removed the

expensive sandals, and flung them to the side of the dirt pathway. Whoever found them was welcome to them.

Kelingo stared after the discarded footwear. "It's not wise to go barefoot here," he cautioned, retrieving them and tucking them into his waistband. "—unless you have leathery old feet like mine that nothing can penetrate," he laughed. "— and there are lots of poisonous thorns, centipedes, and fire ants that would be happy to bite into your soft feet."

Lynette grinned. "The buggers won't like the taste of my blood. My feet will just have to get leathery like yours."

She skipped along the pathway like a sprightly teenager until a stabbing pain halted her. "Oww! What the—!" She looked down at her foot. Thorn barbs.

Without an "I told you so," Kelingo's experienced fingers plucked the thorns, then he handed her the sandals.

Wearing the footwear, she sprinted down a well-trodden path. Her green eyes dancing with joy, at last she saw the tops of thatched roofs. A childhood memory flashed: She remembered the spanking Anele gave her for climbing over the kraal gate when she was about four years old: "Shiya! You won't be able to sit down for a week if you do that again. There are dangers out there that a little child knows nothing about!"

Is this where I truly left my heart? She thought after reflection faded.

Her presence at the gate sent the village dogs into a barking frenzy. Teeth bared and saliva pooling on jowls, they rushed at the fence. Unafraid, Lynette fumbled with the rope hitch. No one from the inside came to her aid. She looked back. Kelingo was nowhere in sight. Had he stopped to relieve himself? Impatience overriding logic, and with unladylike composure, she clambered to the top of the wooden-slatted fence, lost her balance, and landed flat on her backside into a fresh cowpat. Spattered with manure, Lynette was at first mortified and then laughed to the point of tears.

Kelingo had had no problem undoing the latch. He clapped a hand over his mouth to muffle his giggles. Lynette scowled playfully. "Please feel free to laugh your head off, Kelingo. I should have waited for you, shouldn't I?"

Still smiling, he offered his hand. "Here, let me help you up."

He pulled her to her feet.

Wiping her dirty hands on the sides of her jeans, Lynette muttered, "Oh, this is a fine way to see my family."

By now, many of the villagers—mostly women—had surrounded Lynette and Kelingo. Some had curious frowns. Kids pointed fingers, sniggering. And a stocky elderly woman pushed her way through. "Brother Kelingo, my heart sings with your presence!"

Lynette couldn't stand the suspense a moment longer. "Kelingo, my Zulu is rusty. I haven't a clue what she's saying. But please tell your people why I'm here, and take me to Anele."

To the gawking crowd of about twenty, Kelingo announced, "This is Mrs. Lynette Martinez. She has come all the way from America see her mother, Anele."

Frowns of disbelief appeared, mostly on the elderly.

Kelingo continued, "Some of you older people may remember the white child who lived here for five years—" he paused for a second then hit them with the revelation. "—before she and Anele were stolen by the white man."

The loudest intake of breath came from a large-breasted woman, brows creased like tram tracks. She elbowed her way to the front line, bent, and with remarkable strength lifted Lynette up. "I didn't recognize you," she murmured against Lynette's cheek. "We have both grown old." Lynette stared into the bright blue eyes sparkling with sunlit emotion. "Oh, my God! Is it really you, Maekela?"

"Yes, dear friend."

"Is Isona here too?"

"No. She is with our loved ones in the Invisible Kingdom. She died in childbirth. She taking care of the children we lost to disease, and my only child, a son. He was killed in a diamond mine explosion."

"I'm so sorry to hear that. But darling Maekela, please take me to my mother," pleaded a tearful Lynette. "I can't wait another moment."

Before Maekela could answer, a tall old woman stepped between them, blue eyes also twinkling in the sunlight. "I've heard so much about the white baby my mother rescued. I'm thrilled to know you, my younger sister."

Now it was Lynette's turn to stare. "I'm sorry. Should I know you? I don't remember Anele having another child when I was here."

"No, I was born before you were found in the corn pit in the Valley of a Thousand Hills. I was raised in Kenya by Father Batuzi and his wife Nyasha. My name is Insikazi, which means 'fawn' in English."

The penny dropped.

"Oh, my goodness, I can't believe it! Maekela told me that a child had been taken from Anele when she was a teenager! How did *you* find your mother?"

"It's a long story, and I'd love to share it with you. We'll have time to do this because I'm sorry to tell you... you happen to arrive on the day that *Umama* visits the grave of her father, my grandfather, who once was chieftain of this village."

"Show me the way to the burial place," Lynette urged. "I must see her. It just can't wait—" she suddenly remembered her appearance and laughed. "Good Lord! I can't let my mother see me like this! Is there somewhere I can wash and change? I don't want Mother to think a cow with diarrhea has come to visit with her!"

Insikazi translated for the gawking crowd. Laughter rang out. Then the tribe dispersed as if it were an everyday occurrence having a *umlungu* visitor among them.

"By the time I get water fetched from the river for you to wash,"

Insikazi said, "our Mother will be on her way back. Vimbela always brings her back before the sunsets. That will give you plenty of time to get ready."

"That name sounds familiar."

"Vimbela was your wet nurse, Shiya."

Lynette's smile stretched ear to ear. It was wonderful to hear her real name spoken again. Kelingo interrupted her happy thoughts. "Mrs. Martinez, do you need me for anything?"

"No, Kelingo. I'll be just fine."

"Before some animal gets to the food boxes, I'm going with the boys to collect them."

"Kelingo, no more Mrs. Martinez. Out here my name is Shiya... my true name. From now on, the awful English name given to me is no more while I live here. I want you to call me Shiya, okay?"

"I'm not accustomed to calling white people by their first name, but if you insist, Shiya is a good African name."

Her heart flooded with appreciation and love for this ancient man who had so willingly assisted her. And she found it delightful the way he pronounced her name—*Shee-i-ya*.

But what Lynette couldn't see in the soft brown eyes that smiled back at her without apparent guile was the hard glint of intended betrayal.

"Kelingo, when you bring back the boxes, you'll find one marked with a large 'C.' Open it and hand out the treats for the children. I don't suppose these poor kids have ever seen candy bars."

Kelingo's eyebrows rose to his hairline. "*All* of them!"

Lynette laughed. "No silly! Just give each of them a lollipop for now."

"A pleasure," Kelingo said. "I can't thank you enough for your tender heart toward our people."

She placed a hand on his shoulder. "You don't need to thank me, Kelingo. It is you whom I should be thanking."

Kelingo bowed at the waist. "It has been an honor; I know you will understand this: In the white man's world, I was half a man, but here, I am a whole man. I don't want to return to the legal firm, but it doesn't look like Mr. Durval will let me out of my work contract. I only have one year left."

"Maybe I'll be able to work something out with Bryan to make that possible."

Lynette watched Kelingo head for the gate with a bevy of boys close behind.

* * *

Anele's natural daughter handed a pail to a girl. "Go quick to the river, fill it, and bring it to my hut. Go fast, Leticia." To Lynette she said, "Come, I'll take you to my hut and you can undress there. When the girl gets back, you can wash."

The two women strolled leisurely toward the cluster of a dozen or more grass-thatched huts at the far end of the compound.

Underneath the dung spatter on Lynette's cheeks was a healthy glow. Her illness was furthest from her mind. All she needed was Anele to complete her happiness.

Insikazi pointed to two huts at the end of the mud-walled assemblage. "That one is mine, and the big one to the right is Anele's. Do you remember it?"

"Not really."

She had lived alone in her hut, Insikazi told Shiya, since her husband was snatched by a crocodile in the river four years ago. Shiya shuddered, and her thoughts diverted to the girl who had gone to fetch water. *I hope to God a crocodile doesn't snatch her.*

Lynette was pleasantly surprised when she stepped into the hut.

Although the woman's living quarters were no bigger than a broom closet, and windowless, the well-pounded soil was shiny and immaculately clean. In the center of the hut was a raised single bed covered in a colorful patchwork quilt. Small tree stumps served as nightstands on which sat clay oil lamps. Intoxicating aromas wafted up Lynette's nostrils. "What *is* that glorious smell?"

"Oh, that is the oil from the black ironwood trees. I sprinkle it in between the floor stones to stop the pests, spiders, ants, and dog fleas from getting to my bed and eating me alive!"

Lynette giggled.

Insikazi made tea from crushed red leaves, and they chatted, happily. Lynette did not want to appear rude and resisted the urge to rush the pleasantries. At last, just when her impatience was about to burst, Insikazi told her of Anele. "Our mother is frail in body from being so long in jail, and eyesight is poor, but her mind is sharper than the claw of an eagle. This you will find out—"

They were interrupted by a visitor who introduced herself: "My name is Sister Bertha. I'm the schoolteacher. I was down at the river, and word soon got to me of your arrival."

"Nice to make your acquaintance."

Lynette's eyes took in her beauty, her almost purple-black skin and eyes twinkling like onyx. She did not have typical Zulu features: a rounded face, broad flattened nose, long neck, or high forehead. Instead, they were the opposite. "You're not from these parts, are you Sister Bertha?"

"No, I'm not. I'm Nigerian. I was born in a village very similar to this."

"What brought you all this way?"

"Not long after you and Anele left Tswanas, I volunteered to take the previous Sister's teaching position. But that's enough about me. I'm dying to hear all about you. Can I ask you how long you intend staying here?"

"For the rest of what remains of my life."

Sister Bertha frowned. Had she heard right? But it would be too impolite to question further, and she instead spoke of the progress her students were making. Lynette found herself warming to the friendly schoolteacher. Yes, she finally decided, she appeared open minded enough to be trusted.

"Insikazi, I would like to talk to Sister Bertha in private," Lynette said. "I hope you don't mind."

Outside, she took hold of the nun's hand. "Sister, I'll let you into a little secret that I hope you will keep for now. The reason I'm here is that I have a tumor growing on my brain that will shorten my life. So, you see, I've come home to reclaim my foster mother and my lost childhood before I have no memory of them."

"I'm so sorry to hear about that," Sister's dark eyes moistened. "I hope we become close friends. I'd like to make your stay here a happy one. And let me assure you, your secret is safe with me."

"Thanks, Sister. I'm looking forward to having some wonderful chats with you…" Lynette happened to glance down at Bertha's feet. Her patched oxford-style black shoes had trod more miles than could be expected of them.

"I've got something for you. Wait here a moment." She dashed inside, retrieved her sandals, the pair she had arrived with, and handed them to Bertha. "You look about the same size as me, so I'd like you to have these."

"Oh, th-ank you," the nun stammered, clutching the footwear to her chest. Her eyes shone with gratitude. Then she dug deep into her tunic pocket, removed a small silver crucifix, and handed it to Lynette. "And I'd like you to have this."

Lynette stared at the gift. "I sorry, but I don't want it. Don't try to put your belief on me! I've had more than my fill of Catholicism."

"I didn't mean—"

"I didn't mean to be ungrateful. Do your good work for these people, but please, leave me out."

Sister smiled in a way that told Lynette this holy woman would not give up trying to convert her.

You're going to have to wait until hell freezes over!

What Lynette didn't know was that those very sandals would find their way back to her own feet yet one more time.

* * *

Lynette felt perfectly at home. It was as though she'd never left this village of her youth, had never come to live in relative luxury. All thoughts of her previous life—creature comforts and the bane of her pending brain condition, and even the loved ones she'd left behind—vanished from her mind as though by the wave of a sorcerer's wand. This day was second in importance in her life only to the birth of her daughter, Brianna. And today, she would meet the woman who had saved her from an awful death and become the only mother she had ever known.

The washing water arrived.

Lynette removed her soiled clothing and washed her entire body with the lukewarm, muddy-looking river water. Then she donned the native attire provided by Insikazi—a gold and green colored cotton full-length caftan, a headscarf of the same material, large metal-beaded hoop earrings, and Cleopatra-styled necklace. She felt like an African princess. Insikazi beamed her approval. "You are, once more, one of us now, Shiya of Tswanas. Let's go and see the woman you love."

"I do hope no one has told her that I'm here."

"Don't fret. I warned the whole village to remain silent."

Insikazi at her side, nervousness—and not a little fear—kneading her stomach like lumps of dough, she began walking toward Anele's hut. Would she recognize her? Would she love her just the same as she had continued to love her?

* * *

The one Lynette had waited an eternity to find was lying on her side, facing the mud-thatched wall. Anele was asleep. Lynette was beyond thrilled to see her mother. Her heart thumped so noisily she feared it would startle Anele awake.

Quietly, barely breathing, she crept to the bed and knelt. The form that housed her foster mother was so terribly thin as to be skeletal. Her backbone protruded through skin stretched tight over limbs that once walked and ran and jumped, and over a shrunken skull whose eyes once flashed with mischief, or anger, or tenderness, shriveled lips that once stretched a pout or laughter. Tenderly, Lynette touched Anele's arm and said in broken Zulu, "*Umama*. It's me. *Your* Shiya."

Bones creaked as Anele turned over. "Who is it? She asked in a croaky voice. "I smell a strange scent, not of our village."

Lynette couldn't wait for a translation. She enfolded Anele's bony face into her hands and gently kissed her on both cheeks. Startled, hands that were more bone than flesh pushed Lynette away. Then eyes dim with cataracts stared long and hard. Finally, her fingers traced Lynette's face. "Namandla! Great God of the Zulus, is it really you, my precious Shiya?"

Tears coursing down her cheeks, Lynette murmured, "Yes, my darling *Umama*. Your Shiya has returned home for good."

Lynette took the fragile form into her arms and rocked her gently. "I love you, *Umama*."

"I love you too, my *Shiya*."

Quietly, Insikazi slipped outside, leaving mother and daughter to share with each other their many lost years. But while their tears of joy intermingled on their cheeks, before the night's darkness fled, there would be tears of despair.

For what Lynette thought she had at long last found would instead be irretrievably lost.

Chapter 20

Lynette and her newfound foster mother drew apart from their tight embrace when a portly white haired woman with sagging jowls entered the hut and plopped herself down beside them on the bed. The old woman patted Lynette's cheek. "You won't remember me, white lady, because you were so little when I was last in your life, but I'm happy to see that my milk has given you strong, tall bones."

Again, Lynette's knowledge of Zulu was tested. The visitor had spoken so fast, Lynette didn't have a clue what had been said, nor did she know the person who had sat down beside her was Vimbela, now much older in body but not in mind.

Anele translated, and suddenly it became clear to Lynette. She remembered the day she was yanked up a baobab tree and then fleeing from Vimbela back to the kraal.

"Darling Vimbela, how could I ever forget you?"

Her sentiment was translated.

Vimbela was animated, flaying her arms, and jumping up and down. Then her shoulders sagged and the smile was erased. "I cried lots of tears the day you didn't listen to me and were taken by the *umlungu* man—"

Anele interrupted, "That's enough, Vimbela. I don't think Shiya needs reminding of that awful time."

"Yes, *Umama* Anele, I say no more words. I just came to see my baby, who is a big old woman now."

Vimbela's childish spirit brought a rush of pity to Lynette's heart. "I want to thank you, Aunty Vimbela. Your milk did indeed make my bones strong."

Like the cat that got the cream, Vimbela grinned, but her smile dried instantly when Anele told her to leave the hut. "Shiya and I have many more things to talk about. You may come back later, if you wish."

Lips pouting, she argued, "But *Umama* Anele, I want to stay with my baby. Don't want to go to bed."

Anele shot her a disapproving look.

Muttering under her breath, Vimbela left.

The cloak of night descended quickly around mother and step-daughter lying side by side on the narrow bed. Wrapped in each other's arms, too excited to sleep, they talked nonstop for hours.

Not a single day had passed without her Shiya in her thoughts, Anele had confided. Then she revealed how she had lost her natural daughter to a priest, Father Batuzi, and his so-called *wife,* and finally, many years later, how she and Insikazi were reunited.

"The Nigerian priest was not the religious soul he made out to be. Insikazi was deathly afraid of her adopted father's volatile temperament. At age fifteen, she ran away from him and hitched rides from black travelers and ended up in Durban. There she got a cleaning job in an accountant's office. About a month into her employment, her white boss accused her of stealing money from his office drawer. Of course, Insikazi swore her innocence. He promised to keep his mouth shut if she would have sex with him. She refused. His sexual advances spurned, he called the police. The white magistrate handed down a ten-year sentence. Insikazi's incarceration took place at Montclair jail—the very same prison I was in. Then one day in the courtyard, I saw a girl with bright blue eyes—eyes I could never forget. Alan's eyes have never left my tormented soul. Could it be my daughter? Or could it just be another of Alan's offspring? You can just imagine my shock when I learned the truth. We clung to each other. As I was in another section of the jail, I begged for a transfer to Insikazi's block, but, of course, this was denied."

Anele's soft-spoken voice hardened with anger. "I was willing to do anything to be with my own flesh, but it wasn't to be. We caught moments in the courtyard, but it would be many years until we could finally share a life together. After Nelson Mandela came to power, I thank the Great Spirits for this man, we were both released. I would have died before ever seeing Tswanas again if it hadn't been for the strength of my daughter. It took us many long, tiring days to reach here. But we made it, and I have her to thank for the long life in these old bones that come from my father's side." A toothless smile creased her lips. "I'm doing quite well for an eighty-year-old woman, don't you think? We blacks don't stress about everyday things, like white folk… that's our secret to long life."

Lynette didn't comment. Anele bowed her head and began to cry.

"What's the matter, *Umama?*"

"Child, I wish it could be washed away."

"Wash what away?"

"I wasn't expecting to ever see you again."

A little voice warned Lynette she wasn't going to like what Anele had to say. Curiosity killed the cat however, and Lynette persisted. "You can tell me, I'm past hurting."

After a deep labored breath, Anele began, "When you were a baby, our first schoolteacher, Sister Babavana, and I became very good friends. She would come by my hut each day after school ended. We would chat and drink tea. Although she had heard about you from village gossip, she was curious to learn the real facts directly from me. I told her how I found you, but one day, when Sister returned from a holiday, I was happy to see her, but she avoided me, which is hard to do in an enclosed compound. When I finally demanded to know what was wrong, all she said was that I had lied to her. She went to the tapestry bag that she always carried to and from the village and handed me a crumpled newspaper. I informed her that I couldn't read, so she read the article to me—it was about the skeletal remains of a newborn baby girl found not far from the Hallworthy property line. I didn't think anything of it until she came to the part about the baby being white and not black, as was first assumed. The newspaper showed a map of where the child was found. I knew the area well. It was the same place where I found you."

Lynette frowned then let out a deafening cry. "Oh my God!" she cried breathing into the palms of her hands. "There were *two* of us! Maria gave birth to *twins!*"

Anele clasped her hands over her ears as Lynette let out another loud cry.

Insikazi rushed in. "What is it that makes you howl like a hurt dog, Shiya? *Umama* looks scared half to death."

Lynette's eyes were vacant, lost in a forest of pain.

Anele hands latched onto Lynette's face. "Look at me, Shiya. I swear on my father's spirit, you were the only one I found under the pile of corn husks."

Her tongue numb with shock, Lynette could not find any words.

Anele shook her head then turned to Insikazi. "Make us strong tea; use the leaves I collected from the red-bush. We both could do with it."

"I need a bloody drink, and I don't mean tea!" Lynette griped.

"Would you like some beer?" Insikazi asked.

"Yes, that will do."

Silence hung in the hut until a large pitcher of beer appeared.

Lynette pulled a face as she drained a mug of the vile tasting alcohol—anything to wash away the horror—to knock herself out—to hopefully wake up to a new day—the past totally erased from her memory.

It wasn't going to happen.

* * *

Collapsed in an unconscious heap, Lynette was unaware of the strong arms of the young man lifting off the floor and placing her limp body on Anele's bed. An hour or so later, when she came to, her sodden brain tried furtively to bring her to earth. Were the voices she was hearing coming from inside or outside of her head? Through blurred vision, she discerned two grey shapes moving toward her and cringed against the wall.

"It's alright, Shiya. Don't be scared," Anele reassured her. "This is Sliman, a Tswanas witchdoctor."

Lynette regretted bolting upright.

For an instant, the room spun like a top, and she feared losing her stomach contents. Then it hit home. "Why in the world do I need a witchdoctor!" she protested. "I got drunk on that awfully strong beer, that's all. And if my childhood memory serves me well, the *last* person I wish to see is Twazli!"

Anele's laughter pealed like a church bell. "Shiya, it would be a miracle if Twazli stood here. He would be over a hundred and fifty. Sliman is Twazli's youngest son. And he speaks English."

Lynette sighed. "No disrespect, young man, but I've long left my childhood. Boogie men are no longer part of my belief system."

Anele clucked her tongue. "Child, you are going to need this medicine man if you wish the cancer cells to leave your brain."

Bertha!

Had she been there, Lynette would have slapped the incipient do-gooder nun for breaking her promise. She had to wonder how Sliman had slipped through the nun's fingers. Had she tried to convert him and failed?

"Mumbo-jumbo is going to cure cancer!" she said, looking Sliman in the eye, lips curling disdainfully.

Sliman smiled complacently. "You'll never know, Shiya, if you do not put your faith in a medicine that has been practiced since dinosaurs roamed the earth."

That brought a huge smile. "Okay, on that note you win," she laughed. "I'll try anything to be rid of these bloody awful headaches."

Illuminated in the warm glow of candlelight, Sliman bared no resemblance to Twazli, the nightmarish ghoul she remembered. Unlike him, his son had forsaken his predecessor's garb of a goat's pelt, white face paint, and dried chicken feet for earrings. Instead, he was well-attired in a beige shirt and shorts. Cocoa-bean brown eyes and teeth the envy of any toothpaste commercial were set in a mahogany face whose features were not demonic and terrifying, but benign and reassuring. This spiritual lad Lynette decided wouldn't hurt a fly.

At his gesture, she squatted opposite him. He smiled at her, and she felt a warmth spreading throughout her body. Interesting, she thought. Am I bewitched already? *Don't even think about it!*

"I'd like you to place your hands in mine," Sliman directed. "I want to sense your spiritual color."

Immediately, she experienced a tingling sensation in her captive hands, and it was electric. The sensation spread progressively. Her muscles tightened, and she found she was unable to move. Strangely, she felt no fear. Then she was floating. Weighing less than a dandelion seed on a gentle summer breeze, she drifted toward Sliman. Were his eyes, she wondered vaguely, growing in size? They became two huge dark orbs, drawing, sucking her in until she became fixed in their center. Now traumatic scenes from her life became a disjointed collage, the product of some mad artist's brush, and then an undulating light appeared in the distance. Her mind floated toward it like a moth to a candle. Never one to easily relinquish self-control,

Lynette had sworn never to be hypnotized for any reason, so now she fought hard to regain control of her own will—

She jerked to full consciousness. Her head swiveled, fuzzy images coming into focus. She objected, "Sliman, it is bloody wrong to control another's will. No one has the right to dominate my mind. I don't want to be 'put under.' Please don't ever try it again."

Sliman had a calm personality and softly replied, "It is the Gardeners of All Life who have chosen to shut down your brain by giving you the cancerous mass, not me. They feel that the vessel they bequeathed unto you has been disrespected—blighted—with internal rage for too many years. Your receptacle overflows with hatred and unforgiveness, Shiya. To drink in the light, you must first spit out these demons. They are more than your spirit can bear. Let go of them, Shiya of Tswanas. I know it is not easy to forgive, but you must—if... if you wish to remain mortal. The tumor that grows in your brain is a spiritual forewarning. Ignore your demons of hatred and unforgiveness, and you will succumb to them for eternity. If it comes as any solace—" Sliman allowed himself the hint of a smile. "—you are not entirely to blame. Tainted blood flowing through your body comes from white evil that sired you."

"Well, that comes as no surprise."

"Shiya, my all-seeing stones will help you fight your battle with the demons of darkness."

He placed several objects on the floor in front of them. They appeared to be three small, rounded stones composed of a crystalline material. One appeared to be an off-white color, another the blackness of ebony, and the third a smoky grey.

Beside the stones, Sliman placed a small soft-brown leather bag, a long drawstring at its end. "Through these spiritual stones, I am able to see a chain of many lives. None of your past lives have been good ones. Badness from ancient worlds has followed you through many reincarnations. Your inner self is fighting to erase that badness so it can be admitted into the Kingdom of Pure Souls."

Uh-huh, Lynette thought. She prided herself on being open minded, but this seemed entirely too far-fetched. But she would hear him out.

The seer continued, "The whitish stone is for light, the black is for darkness, and grey, their battleground. All of us contain these three elements, and they are constantly at war. You are to place the stones in the bag I have provided, and at all times keep it by you. Do not let another touch them, or the power of the stones will inflict their fury upon you."

Yeah, right!

"I will prepare some herbal medicine to put in Rooibos, reddish tea leaves from a shrub that is indigenous to our mountains, which will turn your good cells into cancer-fighting warriors." He got to his feet. "I must go now. But I would like to leave with you an Eastern saying: Do not let the sun set on your wrath... on this or any other night... for it will be your undoing, Shiya of the Tswa-nas."

Sliman spoke quickly in Zulu to Anele, bid Lynette good night, and then exited the hut.

"What harm can it do?" she thought and, as instructed, she picked up the stones one by one, then strung the pouch around her neck, undressed, and slid into bed beside Anele.

Lying back to back, almost instantly Lynette fell into an exhausted sleep.

Chapter 21

The next morning, fingers of sunlight were filtering through the door curtain. Lynette opened her eyes. Anele was not beside her. Maybe she'd gone to the toilet, a crudely built latrine at the perimeter of the village. Just the place, Lynette realized with some urgency she also needed. So, grabbing a handful of tissues from her handbag, she dashed outside the hut. Some children's sniggering made her aware she was as bare as a peeled banana! Ah, too late, she thought. I'm sure I'm not the first naked woman they have seen—then again, maybe I'm the first *white* butt-naked one!

The lavatory was unoccupied and stunk to high heaven.

She squatted over the hole, pinched her nose, and swatted the ever-present blowflies with the other hand. There had to be a way to improve this unsanitary place. She didn't know much about septic fields or tanks, but she could ask where the nearest town was to get building plans to have a proper toilet installed. If this plan failed, she could ask Bryan, who had promised to come and see her in about a month.

Without a care in the world, she strolled back to the hut, waving at the villagers, and at the same time keeping an eye out for Anele. She was nowhere in sight.

Back in the hut, Lynette opened her suitcase and removed clean underwear, a pair of khaki shorts, and a plain white T-Shirt. She'd have given anything for a long soak in a tub, a soft robe, and a pair of slippers but made do with baby-wipes to wash her perspiration-drenched body. She'd hardly gotten the zipper in her shorts fastened when Sliman entered, silent as a shadow. She'd have to get used to no one knocking.

"Did you sleep well?" he asked.

"Like a log. And for the first time in ages, I haven't woken up with a headache. Even though I kicked up a stink about hypnotism, it sure has done the job. I'm more than grateful. Thanks, Sliman."

A smile of satisfaction curving his full lips, he handed her an earthenware bowl decorated with obscure symbols. "I want you to drink this," he said. "Today, you start your treatment."

Lynette stared at Sliman and then the bowl. What was in it was another question. She took the bowl from his hand and stepped outside with it. Sniffing and peering at the vessel's reddish-colored liquid, she pulled a face. Insoluble particles floated on the top of the concoction. "This looks like embalming fluid made up of scarab beetles!"

Sliman's infectious laughter sounded like a braying donkey. "It is an ancient herbal tea," he explained. "Its secret properties will start your healing process."

This is utter madness, she thought, starting to hand back the bowl. Then she stopped: what if this ancient remedy really works? She was reminded of the stepchild in the Madagascan proverb: If he doesn't wash his hands, he is dirty; if he does, he is wasting the water. Was she indeed wasting what precious little time she had left by not being with Brianna? Or would this vile-looking nectar be her unlikely healer? Her will to survive pulled back the cup and, pinching her nose, she downed the potion. Licking her lips, she turned to Sliman and said, "It's not that bad, actually. It tastes just like honey… lovely and sweet."

Sliman gave her an "I-told-you-so" smile. "I'll give you a supply of the dry fermented leaves. You must first boil water, steep the leaves for half an hour, and then wait until it goes cold. You are to drink a full cup when you rise, at noontime, and at sunset."

"How much do I owe you?"

He sniggered. "You owe me nothing. In my father's day, you would have had to buy ten head of cattle, or sleep in his bed and—"

"Ugh! I'd go into a coma before I'd do that!"

"And I wouldn't take you to my bed," Sliman laughed. "You are way too skinny for me!"

* * *

In the passing days, Lynette began to feel she was actually breaking free of the hate chains that had nearly destroyed her body, mind, and soul. Her linguistic abilities in Zulu were also improving, and she assisted in the various tasks to support village life such as planting seeds and picking root vegetables.

During the day, she lived for the moment. But in the dead of night, Brianna's face haunted her. She missed her daughter dreadfully. Having no contact whatsoever hurt the most, as the cell phone she had bought in Durban proved useless. So, under the shade of Naboto's baobab tree, with Sliman at her side, she wrote her daughter a long letter that was almost a mini novel, telling her of life in Tswanas and how happy she was now. She mentioned Sliman's medicine and magic stones and that they seemed to be helping her. But she omitted that the young witchdoctor and herself were sharing special moments away from the kraal. Although nothing improper between them had arisen, she did not want to sully their warm friendship with even a hint of suspicion.

They held hands and yakked about everything: poetry, literature, Lynette's love of classical music, and her referral to modern-day music as "muck."

* * *

Two months flew by with no sign of the helicopter. This suited old Kelingo, not having to work out his signed contract duties with Bryan, but it did not suit Lynette.

Why hadn't her lawyer turned up as promised? Had he changed his mind? Had she gummed up the works by sleeping with him? Had she been strung along by the smooth-talking Bryan?

Another month passed, and her letters to Brianna piled up.

Although Brianna was never far from her mind, Lynette's days were never lonely. The five women—she, Anele, Insikazi, Vimbela, and Maekela—were one, big happy family. Anele taught Lynette how to weave cotton for general clothing and school uniforms and to sew hides. Insikazi taught her how to milk the goats. Maekela taught her how to play the equivalent of a card game with numbered stones. And Vimbela taught her how to weave baskets and make bead jewelry.

Time slipped by, and her patchwork quilt of sights, sounds, smells, and colors, sewn together with a generous thread of words, led to the healthiest she had ever been. It was as if the brain cancer never existed. Then, on the last day of June, there came the sound of an aircraft flying over Tswanas. She ran to the landing area and was thrilled to see the familiar yellow chopper, but not the face of Captain Johannes. Smugly, he said, "Look lady, I don't ask questions. I don't know why Bryan didn't come himself. He just paid me to bring the supplies I have in the back."

She bit her tongue from saying, "For your information, you arrogant SOB, *I* pay *you!*" But to do so would only fritter energy. "Did Bryan send a message or letter?"

"No."

"Did he tell you when he might be coming out here?"

"No."

"Can you wait while I run back to the kraal and get some letters for mailing?"

"No."

If she'd had a baseball bat she would have swung it.

Village helpers had hardly gotten the last box onto the ground when Johannes lifted off.

Growling like a pit bull, she spat after him, "Damn you, Johannes, you're an asshole—and so's Bryan!"

How was she now going to retrieve her personal belongings from Bryan, given to him for safekeeping? He had her passport, bankbooks, checkbook, credit cards, and at least fifty thousand in U.S. cash and fifty thousand in other currencies. What was she going to do? How could she provide necessities for the villagers? Thinking he would come at least once a month, she'd brought little cash with her.

She stomped back to the kraal and ranted her concerns to Anele. Her response was not what Lynette expected.

"Shiya, I hope you won't take this wrong, but we got by fine before you came with the fancy foodstuffs. We are simple people. We survive by our own means. It won't bother me if I never see white indulgences again."

Lynette exhaled loudly. "Why didn't you tell me this before?"

"I didn't want to hurt your feelings. I may be old and set in my ways, but I'm not senile. I know how much it meant to you to pamper us simple folk. But once you start spoiling my people especially the children, they won't accept you for who you truly are... a kind-hearted person. No. They see you now as a supplier of fine things, that's all. And I know you have a soft spot for the white lawyer, but I'll bet anything he's a bad apple. Remember child, not everything is what it seems." Stung by this, a visibly upset Lynette left the hut.

She walked hatless and shoeless for what must have been miles in the hot sun, unmindful of the mosquitoes biting at her bare sweating arms and legs. Had her usually keen lawyer's mind been blinded by infatuation?

It came as a shocking realization that she was not invincible to a charlatan's charms. How could she have been so trusting… so stupid…?

Now, she had to find another way to help the Tswanas people live a better life.

Fortune would smile upon her and present a solution to this problem.

Chapter 22

It was the start of August—springtime in South Africa. The season brought a profusion of color and a hive of activity—bees swarmed around the nectar-laden flowers of the wild bougainvillea, dark-red aloe flowers, and the intense yellow flowers hanging from ends of laburnum branches. On this fine spring afternoon, returning from a brief vacation in Nairobi, Sister Bertha was accompanied by a young black priest, Father Samuel Ungobo. They entered Anele's hut. Lynette was delighted to learn Samuel was a qualified pilot who had landed the borrowed two-seater, twin-engine aircraft three miles from the village. The priest and nun had walked the rest of the way.

She couldn't wait to put her plan to him.

Without hesitation, Father Samuel agreed.

* * *

Five days later, upon landing at a private Nairobi airstrip, Father Samuel drove Lynette in his dilapidated Volvo truck to the nearest International Bank.

Wearing a two-piece beige suit and Bertha's "gifted" Italian sandals, hair pulled back in a ponytail at the nape of her neck, Lynette walked into the colonial-designed building. Bank tellers and customers stopped what they were doing and stared at her as if she were an apparition. Not too many white customers frequented this part of Nairobi.

"I'd like to speak to the bank manger," Lynette said to a desk clerk nearest the door.

"Certainly, Madam."

She watched the clerk disappear into a side room. Within seconds, a burly man attired in black pants, black tie, and crisp white shirt emerged and walked over to Lynette. "How can I be of assistance to you?" he asked.

"I'd like to withdraw money from my Swiss bank account, but I don't have my bank book with me."

He frowned. "Do you know the telephone number of the branch in Switzerland?"

"Yes."

"Then come with me. You can make the call from my office."

After providing personal details necessary for security reasons, Lynette was able to transfer one million dollars U.S. into her new account at the Nairobi Bank of Commerce. And the delighted bank manager waived the cost of the phone call.

She came out of the bank smiling. She would after all live to enjoy her fortune, but at a price. How she would love to talk to Brianna, to share her abundance of good news, bring her up to date. She could, of course, ask Father Samuel to drive her to Nairobi International Airport. Then she could do some ocean hopping—fly to Canada, see Brianna, and then fly back... Oh, she'd do absolutely anything, *anything,* to be with her daughter, to hold her in her arms and tell her how much she loved and had missed her, and to convince her she was only trying to protect her from the painful truth...

For an instant, the thought buoyed her spirits. Just as quickly, though, they sank. She'd so hurt her daughter with deceptions that it seemed certain that she wouldn't get a good reception. She felt tears sting her eyes and shrugged. Perhaps it was best to let sleeping dogs lie—at least for a while.

In a chilling twist of fate, Lynette's emotional pull to be with her daughter would get a chance to be tested.

But there was one person she must talk to at all cost.

* * *

As though expecting her call, Bryan answered his cell phone on the first ring…

Lynette attacked him like a pit bull, leaving the lawyer little opportunity to defend himself. She spoke her mind, then, shaking with rage, slammed down the receiver in the public telephone booth. She would go back to Tswanas and forget she'd ever met him.

The return trip home was a nightmare.

A thunderstorm's gale-force wind buffeted Father Samuel's over-loaded ancient aircraft, bouncing it like a rubber ball all over the sky. Teeth clenched tight, not a paper bag in sight, Lynette worried she might lose her lunch—a large portion of fish and chips eaten at the airport cafeteria. Thanking the gods, Samuel's excellent navigational skills guided his laden craft through the storm, and he landed safely. She gave a huge sigh and wanted to kiss the ground.

Back in Tswanas, Lynette was surprised to be handed a package Johannes de Klerk had dropped off only hours earlier. Bryan had not mentioned this during their heated telephone conversation, but of course she had given him little chance to say anything.

His stiffly worded communication began:

Lynette,
I'm returning your personal belongings. I also enclose a detailed account of the quarter of a million-dollar retainer fee. I've honored my side of your scurrilous request, and I hope you will keep your promise to destroy the "you-know-what." Don't expect to see me again.

Yours faithfully,
BRYAN

* * *

In the days following his letter, Lynette barely thought of it, because she was too busy getting on with life in the wilderness. When not in Sister Bertha's classroom, the children surrounded the newcomer like moths to flame. They delighted in her reading them stories from popular children's books she'd purchased in Nairobi. She became their "sweetie giver" and played games with the children but refused to swim with the kids in the river. And she became a comforter for adolescent girls who poured their hearts out to her. Most evenings, the oil lamps and candlesticks close by, she read historical accounts of the Anglo-Zulu war of 1879 to Anele.

"My father fought in that war, Shiya," Anele said. "He was shot twice and survived. But one of my uncles didn't make it home."

"I'm sorry to hear that."

* * *

Lynette continued to bask in the love of her adopted mother but had become concerned by her declining health. Anele could hardly get out of bed. She was also incontinent and sometimes refused to eat anything.

One morning, Anele latched onto Lynette's arm. "Would you take me to the sacred rock? I want to go when the first stars are out."

At night? Lynette's head screamed.

For all the love she had for her mother, this was a no-no. She was terrified of bumping into a hungry leopard or other deadly creatures the village children delighted in telling her about. So far, she had encountered none, although she had heard their hunting cries, which always sent the pack of village dogs into frenzied barking of their own.

Now goosebumps marched along her arms. "Why do you have to go at night, *Umama?* Can't it wait until daylight?"

"No, it can't." Anele's chin jutted. "Night is the best time to see the crystal bowl with diamond pinpoints of light which are the souls of our ancestors."

"Ah," she cooed, "You put that so beautifully, Anele."

"So, you'll take me tonight?"

"Why not," she replied nonchalantly, rubbing at the goose bumps.

But the *worst* scenario hadn't shown itself yet.

An oil lamp lighting the way, they walked hand in hand to the sacred rock resembling a large bird. They stopped frequently to allow Anele to catch her breath and to readjust the wooden crutch under her armpit. Just before they reached the rock, Lynette saw red glowing eyes—a large cat. The hairs on her neck and arms stood up. Then bravado took over, and she yelled, "Be gone, creature of the night. You won't like either of our flesh, for it's tough like turtle shell and just as nasty tasting."

The "telling off" brought a chuckle from Anele. It was something her father would have said.

They waited until the creature, probably a leopard, slunk into dense shrub, and they continued on their way.

The women stood side by side atop the spiritual rock, aromatic scent like no other mantling them. Many sought out this sacred place, confided secrets, begged for mercy, and waited for their loved ones to pay them a visit from the netherworld. Anele raised her arms upward toward the heavens as if trying to snag a star. "Namandla, I thank you for bringing my Shiya back to me. I want you to take good care of her now, because I'm ready to join my family in your invisible kingdom."

Lynette grabbed her mother's shoulders. "No, you are not leaving me yet, *Umama*," she pleaded.

"Ah child, it's time for me to go... leave this mortal place. Namandla, the Great maker, has sent me a message. Shiya, can you see them?"

"What do you see?" she asked tearfully.

"Look all around you," Anele said lowering the lamp. "See, the stonecrop plants, miniature orchids, have flowered. I can smell them. They have not done this since you were a child. This is truly a spiritual sign." Her hands groped over the jutting rocks then picked and handed the delicate white flower to Lynette. Gently, she stroked the velvet-like petals.

"It's the sign I have been waiting for," Anele said. "The spirits have come to take me to heaven."

"Please, don't say that, *Umama*. I couldn't bear the thought of losing you so soon."

In barely a whisper, Anele replied, "My beloved Shiya, it is not that I don't love you, but please try to understand that I'm eager to join my father, mother, my siblings, my best friend Lamella who took care of me as a child, and I'd like to see Isona, who died giving birth to Alan's umpteenth child."

Sorrow welled within Lynette like a wash of brine. She could not bear the thought of Anele, the only mother she had ever known, who had been lost to her for so long. But deep down, she knew that it was only a matter of time, and that time would come soon.

"God of Africa," she prayed softly. "Please don't let my mother die, not just yet. I haven't been given much time to get to know her again. But if this isn't to be… I want you to do something for me. When you open your arms to take her, I want you to take me, too. I want to be with my mother and *my* loved ones, especially my beloved husband, Lionel, for all eternity…" A little voice in her head interrupted her prayers—reminding her that selfishness was not a virtue.

She hugged Anele and whispered in her ear, "If that is your wish, *Umama,* then I have no choice but to let you go. God forbid I should be the one to hold you back."

"Don't worry, my child, I'll be watching over you. And when I'm gone, I do not want you to cry. I want you to go home to your daughter. She is the one whose love will make you strong in mind, not Sliman's tea leaves. Will you promise me this, Shiya?"

"I promise."

Clutching the little flower, Lynette trekked in silence back to the kraal. She could not prevent Anele's passing, but she was so thankful to have made the choice to return to South Africa when she did. The times spent with her were the happiest she'd known.

Lynette climbed into bed and snuggled next to her mother—watching every minute—listening—making sure she was still breathing. Finally, her drooping eyelids closed, and Lynette fell sound asleep.

The next morning, the sound of loud snoring was music to her ears. Her precious mother was still with her, and she thanked the Zulu god for hearing her prayer.

While Anele slept on, Lynette lit the single-burner propane stove—another requisite from Nairobi—and set about making a pot of a tea. When she saw movement under the blanket, she called out, "I'm making your special Indian tea, *Umama*. Would you like some chocolate biscuits to go with it?"

Anele's muffled voice replied, "No, child, tea will do fine."

While waiting for the water to boil, Lynette sat on a chair and began singing a Johnny Mathis song: "*Let your heart remember...*" Halfway through the chorus, her mouth went as dry as parched soil. For no apparent reason, she began shivering uncontrollably as a foreboding sensation flooded her body like a tidal wave, then was gone.

What did this mean?

Was this the day Anele would leave her?

Was Brianna okay?

Had the tumor cells in her brain regrouped? Ready to do battle—shut her down for good?

Forcing herself to remain calm, she cocked her head and frowned. Strange, she thought. I can't hear the hustle and bustle of the villagers going about their daily chores. She was about to investigate when she heard the dogs barking.

"The damn dogs only bark like that when a stranger comes," Anele remarked. "Or if they spot a leopard."

"I'll go and see what's happening," Lynette said.

She couldn't believe her eyes as she made her way to the gate.

The horses were being made skittish by the snarling dogs so that the riders were none too pleased about entering the enclosure. Kelingo dismounted his brown roan, reins in hand, and undid the gate hitch for his boss, Bryan, to enter.

"Hello, Kelingo," she greeted. "I was sorry to learn when I got back from Nairobi that you had returned with Captain Johannes to Durban." Then she confronted Bryan. "What brings *you* here? I don't take kindly to 'white' people," she added, mordantly. "And neither do *my* family."

"I had no choice but to come out here," he replied, his voice cool. "There are important matters that couldn't wait. I don't suppose that too many of these people surrounding us speak English, so I'll come straight to the point. My father received a telephone call from Judge Kubrick, a friend and colleague of his. It seems your unauthorized visit to see Alan Hallworthy at the State Mental Institution has caused a serious problem."

Her face impassive, Lynette waited for him to finish.

"Corrie Hallworthy is demanding an enquiry. It was in the news."

"What's in the news?"

"Of course, you couldn't possibly know, being stuck out here. Well, Alan Hallworthy tried to commit suicide. Corrie learned from her husband that your visit prompted his action. She blames you for his desperate state of mind."

"I wish he *had* killed himself," Lynette responded contemptuously.

Bryan's eyes sought hers. "The new District Attorney is close friends with Judge Kubrick and my father. He has broken the law by repeating their conversation to me, but he is my father and is very concerned about my welfare."

"Oh, I think he should be more worried about the stuff I have on *him!* But I leave that alone for now. Anyway, there's no real proof that I was there."

"Oh, yes, there is," Brian replied. "The reception nurse, and the male orderly, and the taxi driver have given sworn statements. With that proof, Corrie has hired the best there is in lawyers. Only yesterday, a top prosecutor handed the affidavits over to the DA's office."

"Why are *you* so bothered about all of this? You didn't go to the institution, *I* did. They are after me, not you!"

"That's where you are wrong, which surprises me. I booked the hotel room, remember? And it won't take long for Corrie's legal team to find that out—"

"Shit! You might have been followed out here."

"That should be the least of your concerns. To put your mind at rest… it's highly unlikely. I'm not stupid. I had a bush pilot drop me off on the outskirts of the game reserve, then I traveled by a safari tourist truck to the border, where a prearranged horse was waiting for me."

Unconvinced, Lynette inhaled deeply. "I really don't see what all the fuss is about. I simply visited my own father, that's all."

"You, of all people, should know about unauthorized visits without the court's permission," Bryan countered. "Alan is a convicted inmate, not just a patient. You, personally, are being held accountable for his suicide attempt."

Exasperated, Lynette ran her hand through her uncombed hair. "So, counselor, where do we go from here?"

"Since I wasn't present when you decided to break the rules," he said coldly, "I can add nothing to the enquiry. If Judge Kubrick summons me to court, I will be in a very difficult situation. On the one hand, I'm bound to honor my original attorney-client privilege. As you full well know, I would be disbarred for withholding knowledge of your whereabouts. Surely, you can see my predicament?"

"Bullshit! No judge is going to hold you in contempt if you simply say that you have no idea where I am. This is an open-and-shut matter. It's simple… no Lynette Martinez… no court case."

"I cannot in all conscience lie under oath."

"Well, what can I say, Bryan? I'm sure the cleared check will prove beyond any reasonable doubt that the retainer for your legal services was, in fact, not deposited into your law firm account but into your personal savings account outside South Africa! How do I know that? Because I also have friends in high places, dumb cluck!"

Bryan was visibly squirming in his riding boots. Lynette was about to make him squirm even more. "You are just going to have to brazen it out, aren't you? Otherwise, this hostile client-from-hell will turn tail."

Open-mouthed and speechless, Bryan glared at her, turned his back, and mounted his horse to leave.

"Let me put it this way," Lynette yelled. "I not only can have your father prosecuted for stealing money, but I can put *you* in *his* shoes. Oh, don't look so surprised," she added as Bryan's blonde eyebrows rose. "I know exactly how much you've squandered from my retainer fees. You were foolish enough to send me a *detailed* expenditure account. I think you were hoping that my tumor would rob me from finding out about the false claims you've made. Some of the items you have claimed as expenses didn't happen, did they Bryan?"

"I resent—"

She cut him off. "I have an idea, and if you want to keep your sorry ass out of jail, then this is what must be done."

Lynette outlined her plan. It was brilliant, and daring, and dangerous. A pasty-faced Bryan listened in abject silence, eyes rounded and unblinking, not twitching a muscle. He might have been a mannequin aboard his mount. When Lynette finished, he exploded into life. "Are you *fucking* crazy? I'll never pull it off!"

"Yes, you will. You are one of the most cunning men that I've ever met. I hope you enjoy Switzerland, Bryan. Pack some warm clothing. It's friggin' cold this time of the year!"

When the horse's hooves were out of hearing, Lynette sought the seclusion of Anele's hut. She could have kicked herself for her utter stupidity of going to see Alan. Whatever was she thinking! But she had no qualms about coercing Bryan to criminal deception. If everything went according to plan, no one would end up facing a judge. And there was no doubt in her mind that her good friend, Gerda Düsseldorf, would help without hesitation or question. It was a brilliant rabbit she'd pulled out of her hat at the last minute. But in the doing, she'd made an enemy of the worst kind.

Would Bryan betray her?

Time would tell.

* * *

Across many oceans, Gerda, as instructed by Bryan, booked the next flight to South Africa. From an airport payphone in Durban, she contacted him on his private line. An hour later, they met at a bar in a dingy part of town, and there Bryan handed the decoy Lynette's passport, a platinum credit card, and a cosmetics bag bulging with Swiss francs to cover expenses.

Traveling on separate flights, Bryan and Gerda re-met at a prearranged hotel in Switzerland. There, she returned Lynette's documents and gave Bryan the canceled airline ticket she had used to enter Switzerland, then asked him to give Lynette her love, and flew back to Britain using her own identity. With proof of Lynette's departure from South Africa to Switzerland, Bryan was home free, and so was his "client from hell." However, this client was not going to leave everything to providence. Lynette had an ace up her sleeve—a card she would play should the plan fail to throw Corrie Hallworthy's bloodhounds off her trail.

From under Anele's bed, Lynette pulled out her suitcase. Beneath a section of lining, she removed the journal belonging to Corrie Hallworthy, in which the woman had written every sordid detail that had occurred to Lynette while she had been held captive at the cottage. Corrie's diary's notes left not a single felonious stone unturned. Page after page, her notes held the sequence of tragic and horrifying events, not only about Lynette, but Anele, her twin sisters, Thaka and Zhana, and Maekela and Isona, and many other nameless girls who had suffered at the hands of their tormentors, past and present. Now, they would serve to incriminate not only Lord Alan Hallworthy, but Lady Corrie as well, should the need arise.

Upon receiving this stolen journal many years ago, it had torn Lynette's heart to relive the past, but the handwritten entries enabled her to record, in detail, her childhood trauma to Brianna.

Lynette glared at the journal resting in her lap. "Revenge is sweet, sayeth Shiya." She had vowed all those years ago that the Hallworthys would not go unpunished. But she would have to wait for the outcome of her "Switzerland" plot. Soon… soon, it will be all over, she thought. *The door to my ugly past will be firmly closed.*

Entering the hut, Anele was accompanied by Insikazi.

"How did the meeting go with your lawyer?" Anele asked.

"Not well, *Umama.* I'll tell you about it later, but first—"

"What do you have there?" Insikazi interrupted. "A new storybook?"

"No. This is no storybook. This is Corrie Hallworthy's one-way ticket to hell."

Anele heaved a loud sigh. "Leave us, Insikazi. I wish to speak to Shiya, privately."

Sitting together on the bed, Lynette read Anele a few entries. It was too much for the old lady. She put her hands over her ears and burst into tears. "Oh my dear Shiya," she cried over and over. "We've both been treated so wickedly…"

They clung to each other and wept, their tears a salve on a tragic past.

Chapter 23

Bryan returned to Tswanas. He seemed a lot less tense, Lynette noticed, even a little friendly when he gave her the good news. Gerda had been more than happy to have been of help, he reported, and the plan had gone well. The district attorney's office had dropped the case.

Although relieved it was over, Lynette felt a nudging of guilt. Kindly, she touched Bryan's hand. "I want you to know that I don't feel particularly happy about the precarious position in which I placed you and Gerda. I'm relieved you're both safe. Of course, it's best we never see each other again."

"I definitely agree." Bryan said, remounting his horse. "I promise you that I will never betray your whereabouts to any party, should any query arise in the future."

"Thanks, Bryan. No hard feelings, okay?"

"Yeah, none taken Mrs. *Martinez.*" He gave a mock salute, grinned and, like a scene in a Hollywood western, rode off into the sunset.

He didn't fool Lynette. She knew by the way he had emphasized her married name, he hated her guts. She was, after all, the woman who had tried to destroy him, his father, and his family's good name. A man like Bryan would not be forgiving. No, he would seek revenge, and she would be wise to watch her back…

But for now, it was over, and Lynette rushed into the hut to tell Anele. "My name and passport details will be in every airport computer from here to Timbuktu, *Umama*. And until I can get a replacement, a forged one, I will have to stay here. In one way, it is a good thing, as I don't want to give my daughter false hopes."

"Your absence will make her grow into a strong woman," Anele said. "Children shouldn't be pampered and protected by their parents. It's up to them to learn to walk a good path. If they don't, well, we mothers cannot be held responsible for their actions."

"Gosh! You are one wise old owl." Lynette playfully pinched Anele's sunken cheek.

Later on, candlelight shadows making eerie shapes on the mud walls, Anele enjoyed their evening meal: a bowl of stewed wild rabbit and mealie-meal pancakes. Lynette hardly touched hers. Her stomach, for some unknown reason, was in knots. Why, she hadn't a clue. She should be without a care, but the odd feeling she'd had some days ago rushed at her, setting her insides to shuddering.

"Why aren't you eating?" Anele asked. "Is your belly upset?"

"The food smells wonderful, but I just don't feel hungry."

"You're not still worried about the lawyer man?"

"No. I don't know what it is." She got up from the chair. "I think I'll make my red-bush tea. Maybe it'll give me an appetite."

After drinking her tea, she announced, "I think it's time for my beauty sleep."

"Mine, too," Anele laughed.

Lynette gave her mother their nightly cuddle. Normally, Anele have would let out a happy, contented sigh, but tonight she stiffened her back and sat upright. "Shiya," she said in a very soft tone. "All of a sudden, a very strange feeling is flowing through my blood. I keep seeing the stonecrop flowers opening up before my eyes. I sense, dear daughter, that my time has come to leave this earth."

Lynette sighed and held the old woman tightly, as though shel-
tering her with her arms would stop her from leaving. "No,
Umama," she cried. "Please don't go."

"Child, don't be scared," Anele whispered comfortingly. "We will
rise together into the tranquility of the Invisible Kingdom where
souls are free of cumbersome grey-flesh vessels. Our loved ones are
waiting for us. We will never be parted again."

"*Umama,* I know your body is tired and your soul wishes to
depart, but please don't leave me yet. Stay one more night, okay?"

Anele did not reply.

Dreading not hearing Anele's raspy breath, Lynette forced her
brain to be alert. She didn't want to miss a nanosecond of being
with her beloved mother, but her eyelids had other plans. They
grew heavy as tombstones and closed the doors to her well-meaning
intentions. Sleepily, she kissed Anele goodnight.

It would be one of Lynette's last actions.

Neither heard the plaintive whining of village dogs. Nor did they
see the two men wearing camouflaged canvas jackets, hoods pulled
down low, stealthily enter the hut. With panther-like grace, they
moved like shadows in the night past the spluttering beeswax candles sitting on the orange crate. They crept toward the bed. Captain
Johannes aimed the nine-millimeter handgun, complete with
silencer, and cold-bloodedly shot Anele and Lynette at point-blank
range. Then he and his black accomplice fled into the pitch of
night.

Breathing shallow, growing shallower, Lynette, a bullet lodged in
her cranium, was barely alive.

Outside, a buffeting wind began pummeling the trees and brush
surrounding the village. It swept through the compound and
entered Anele's hut. Its powerful breath lingered briefly over Lynette,
then Ugwele, the sacred wind god of Africa, soared toward the dark
heavens, carrying the precious soul of Anele.

Chapter 24

A full moon hung low on that tragic night.

In the home next to Anele's, an aging man groaned. His internal plumbing desperate for relief, he stepped outside to relieve himself. He noticed strange shapes lying outside Anele's hut and went to investigate. At the sight of the village dogs, white froth congealed around the rigid muzzles, Natu, who had discovered Chief Naboto's body all those years ago, scratched his head. He bent and touched the neck of the leader of the pack. The dog was warm to the touch but not breathing. What's going on here? He thought. He glanced over at the entrance. The door curtain was missing. It was laying in the dirt a few feet away.

Perplexed, he poked his head into Anele's hut. The candles were extinguished, and he could barely discern the motionless shapes on the bed.

"Anele. Shiya," he called.

He got no response.

Cautiously, he walked toward the bed, his bare feet stepping in something sticky. A finger to the nose told him it was blood.

He dashed into his own hut, lit an oil lamp, and rushed back. A terrible sight greeted Natu's eyes, and his hollering a second later awoke the village.

Insikazi screamed in horror as she stared at the blood-drenched heads of her mother and Lynette, who was teetering on the brink of death. Who could commit such a brutal crime on defenseless women? she questioned. What kind of monster would do this? Somebody had to be very angry to do this. Who was this killer?

It wasn't long before Anele's hut was crammed with people wanting to witness the grizzly scene.

Sliman rushed in and elbowed his way to the makeshift side table, where he grabbed a hand mirror. It fogged under Lynette's nose, but not that of Anele, who lay huddled next to Lynette in final sleep.

"Shiya's alive. She's alive," the witchdoctor repeated. "I need more light. Fetch more lamps and candles. Natu, get my medicine bag. Hurry!"

Natu raced to Sliman's hut.

Inside Anele's hut, women wailed.

Vimbela, in her simple innocence, leaned across and shook Anele's head. "Why do you not open your eyes, *Umama* Anele?"

Gently, Insikazi removed Vimbela's hand, stained crimson with blood. Confused, she looked up at Insikazi, who replied, "Because our *Umama* now sleeps with the dead, Vimbela."

Pounding her chest in grief, she fled from the hut, her sorrowful shrills shattering the darkness. "Fly free now, *Umama* Anele," she wept. "And my special baby, Shiya, please let the Ancient Spirit put his breath in your body. You must not die."

Shocked by the sight before her, Insikazi turned to Sliman. "Who could have done this terrible thing? Why would someone want to kill my mother and try to kill Shiya?"

"I don't know," Sliman replied. "But one thing I know for sure, the dogs were poisoned to get to the women."

"I am a light sleeper," Insikazi said. "I heard no dogs bark in the night."

"Ah! You wouldn't have. The killer knows the animals well. They do not fear him. He caused their mouths to close."

A boy, small enough to wriggle through the crowd, sidled up to Sliman. "I know who killed Anele and the white-faced woman."

"Explain, Zepsiweli."

"I saw Kelingo and the *umlungu* man, the one who comes in the big bird that falls from the sky—"

"*Kelingo!* You are full of nonsense, boy," Insikazi interrupted. "Why would he want to harm my mother or Shiya? He loved them—"

Natu rushed in with Sliman's bag, made from the hide of a baboon.

With the sharp point of a hunting knife, the witchdoctor tried to find out how far the bullet was lodged in the wound. Feeling no metal on metal, he withdrew the knife and filled the hole with a mixture of muddy-looking ointment and ground tree-aloe leaves. Then, with Natu holding up Lynette's head, Sliman bandaged it with long lengths of deer hide. Gently, they removed her from the blood-spattered bed and placed her body on the dirt floor. The coldness would slow down her heart rate, the witchdoctor explained to Natu.

Sliman sat beside Lynette, cut the bag from around her neck, and released the stones onto the dirt. Every one was a bright turquoise. *It's a great sign,* he thought. *Her spirit is not ready to fly away.*

Behind him, the debate continued.

"The boy speaks the truth, Sliman," an elderly woman said, patting the trembling boy's head. "Kelingo is a traitor. He pretended to love his people and the woman who saved him from the white man's work."

"He belongs to the Dark Spirit now," said another woman.

Sister Bertha pushed her way to the doctor's side and placed her hand over her heart. "God have mercy!" she cried, making the sign of the cross. "Zepsiweli," she said, taking the boy's hand, "Come with me. We will take the mule and go for help."

"Where are we going, Sister Bertha?" he asked.

"We will travel to the game reserve and find a white warden. Shiya is, after all, *white*, and—"

"Is that wise, Sister Bertha?" Natu interrupted. "We will be blamed for Shiya's attempted murder. She is a *white*—

"No, no! No one is going to accuse us. We didn't shoot her. We have no guns here."

"You are wrong, schoolteacher," Natu argued. "We, the people of Tswanas, might not have blasting weapons, but we will surely be marked for punishment."

Sister Bertha shook her head and sighed. No amount of reassurance would convince them otherwise. And a tiny voice niggled at her, maybe *they are right...*

"Come, Zepsiweli," she said. "We have sad business to attend to."

The Sister led the boy out of the hut.

Insikazi knelt beside her dead mother and whispered, "I know in my heart that you do not fly free. Please give me a sign that you remain earthbound."

As though granting her plea, an eagle's feather drifted into the hut and spiraled onto the foot of the bed. The heartbroken woman picked it up, held it over her heart, and murmured, "*Umama*, your killer has not taken your spirit, only the vessel that carried you on this earth." She leaned forward and placed the feather in her mother's blood-spattered hair. "I promise you this, *Umama*. I will hunt Kelingo, the snake he is, if it takes me the rest of my life. I will kill him with my bare hands. I swear it to you, my beloved mother."

Chapter 25

A retired crime reporter, Mandela Mandekana, happened to be touring the Umfolozi game reserve when Sister Bertha and the boy arrived at the game warden's post. Her shocking story was one he couldn't resist exposing.

The warden loaned him a Jeep, and with Sister Bertha in the passenger seat, he drove to Tswanas.

Standing behind the cordoned-off yellow crime scene tape, Winston positioned his video camera then cleared his throat. The veteran reporter began:

> Here, in Tswanas—a remote village in KwaZulu Natal, formerly Zululand—two people were reportedly victims of a brutal crime—shot execution style, sometime in the early hours of this morning. One of the victims, Anele Dingane—an eighty-year-old Tswanas tribeswoman—died at the scene. The second victim, Lynette Martinez—a visitor from Canada—is alive but in critical condition. In a race against the clock, she was airlifted by law enforcement's emergency response team of air medics and flown 200 km to Addington Hospital on the Victoria

Embankment in Durban. As you can see behind me (the reporter moved aside for viewers to see the activity going on), the man in charge of these brutal crimes is Detective Pieter Marquand, a renowned CSI from the Special Crimes Bureau in Durban. No one knows what really happened here. Neither the police nor I have been able to get information from the villagers. They are uncooperative. Their silence is unclear. Baffling questions remain. Who is Lynette Martinez? What was she doing so far out here in the desolate wilderness? Why were these women assassination targets? It will remain a mystery for now. For the BBC, I am Winston Mandekana, reporting live from Tswanas Kraal, KwaZulu Natal, South Africa.

Chapter 26

A continent and time zone change away, Brianna cuddled against Roberto's back. She'd gone to bed a happy woman.

Four hours earlier, over dinner in their favorite Chinese restaurant, he had proposed and presented her with a platinum, two-carat diamond ring.

"Will you marry me, Bri?"

"In a heartbeat."

Brianna's tears of joy had been mixed with sadness. She couldn't share this happiness with the only other person she loved dearly— her mother. At first, she had thought of traveling to South Africa to find her. Roberto squashed that idea: "It would be like searching for a needle in the proverbial haystack, Bri."

Now, she was moving forward with her life. What else could she do? And the meeting with the mysterious Miguel Carlos Rodriguez had solved many of her unanswered questions.

* * *

A weak February sun filtered through the lobby of the Denman Inn in downtown Vancouver. Waiting near the entrance doors, a brief-case clutched in one hand and the other tucked into the pocket of his grey pinstriped suit pants, Mike sighed and checked his wristwatch: 3:15 P.M. Brianna was fifteen minutes late.

In his early fifties, his salt-and-pepper hair was pulled back in a ponytail and rested on the starched collar of his immaculately pressed pale blue shirt. Almost nervously, he scanned every female face entering and leaving the hotel lobby, awaiting his first meeting with Lynette and Lionel's daughter. He had no clue what she looked like now. The last photograph Lynette had sent him was a high school photo, taken on the day Brianna graduated.

In the briefcase was a courier package containing Lynette's heart-wrenching goodbye letter. They had known each other since 1974. With her help, he had come a long way from working as a chauffeur. She had funded his law studies, and he had passed the bar with honors. All these years, he had kept in contact with her and thought he was her best friend. But why had she not confided in him? Why had she left the country without first calling him? Why—?

Mike's thoughts crashed to a full stop.

There was no doubt in his mind that the stunning young woman with windswept shoulder-length black hair, leather jacket, and chocolate-brown flared jeans, alighting from the mini-cab, was none other than Brianna. He walked briskly out the lobby door to greet her.

"You must be, Brianna? I'm Mike Rodriguez."

"Nice to meet you, at last," Brianna smiled, returning his firm handshake. "I'm so sorry for being late, but my car wouldn't start, and I had to order a cab. Let's go in. I'm dying for a coffee."

Sitting opposite each other in the hotel lounge, Brianna took in Mike's Guatemalan features: extremely dark skin tone, moon face, strong jawline, trimmed goatee, and chocolate-brown eyes. His Hispanic accent was sensual and reminded her of the Spanish film actor, Antonio Banderas. Mike, too, was regarding the slim woman with shimmering dark pupils, long black eyelashes, dark olive complexion, strong jawline, and glossy, bronze-color lipstick covering her full lips. Her singular flaw: her lovely hands, unadorned by fake nails, were bitten to the quick and red, as though dunked in rasp-berry juice. She didn't strike him as being a nervous person, but then her mother's vanishing act would be enough to cause anyone to bite their nails.

He had never understood Lynette's reasoning for not letting her daughter know about Lionel. In his opinion, it had been a heartless decision. Mike had gotten to know the gentle-mannered boy during the long drive back from the El Salvadorian border to Guatemala to meet up with Lynette. He had not been surprised to learn they, Lynette and Lionel, had found each other years later and married. But keeping the truth from her own daughter about her biological father was beyond his comprehension. Mike had chosen never to raise the matter when communicating with Lynette—something they did only by phone.

After small talk over coffee, he said to Brianna, "I have a return flight to Seattle this evening, so it's down to the unpleasant business at hand, I'm afraid."

Fingers laced so tightly her knuckles went white, Brianna watched Mike open his briefcase and place a legal-sized folder on the table.

"Your mother has instructed me to handle all her affairs and relevant issues relating to you." Taking a typical lawyer's stance, he added, "Do you have any objection to my acting on your behalf?"

"Why should I? She hasn't left me much option, has she?" Brianna's tone was cool. Her mother's shocking revelations had unhinged her feelings for Lynette—a mother she thought she knew. Did Mike know about the criminal admissions? Brianna harbored a suspicion that he wasn't entirely in the dark, but she had to ask, "Mike, how long have you known her?"

"I met your mother a long time ago. What I can tell you is that if it weren't for her, I would never have been able to attend law school in the States or have the private practice I have now."

"She was *that* generous?"

"Yes. And I'm only one of many your mother has helped. But I'll come to that later. I would like you to read these," Mike said, handing her some paperwork across the table. "And initial where I've indicated."

Brianna took her time checking over the documents that granted Mike the right to handle her mother's affairs, put her initials where he had marked, and handed the paperwork back to him.

"In your mother's letter to me, she deeply regrets leaving you at such short notice. She states that time is of the essence. May I assume you are now fully aware of her medical condition?"

"Yes."

"Your mother hopes her journey to the Republic of South Africa—" he paused, unsure, how much she knew. "Are you aware that your mother was born in Africa?"

"Yes."

"She also states in her letter that she had recorded certain information on tapes concerning past events. It's her wish that the tapes be handed over to me."

Brianna tossed her long hair. "Who's going to want them? The FBI, the CIA, the Mafia—?"

"This is not a matter to take lightly," Mike interjected. "In the wrong hands—" He shrugged and shook his head, the answer obvious.

"The tapes are legally mine." Brianna stated.

"Yes. I was only suggesting that we use caution in this regard." He was walking a tightrope. Just how much had Lynette recorded?

Had she revealed the smuggling operation?

Had she named names, his in particular?

No. Lynette was too smart to do anything that stupid. But he had to make sure. "Brianna, how many tapes did your mother record?"

"I can't remember... a few, maybe several!"

"Was I mentioned in the tapes?"

"Not really. At least I don't think so."

"Would you mind giving them to me?"

"I can't. I burned them. The stories she revealed were horrible. It made me sick to my stomach that she was subjected to and endured such atrocities. Why didn't she tell me… Trust me… ? She had such courage. Oh, if only I'd known…"

Still fishing, Mike asked, "Were the tapes *just* about her child-hood."

"Yes and no. My mother didn't leave anything to the imagina-tion."

"I'm sorry, Brianna. You may not wish to hear this at the moment—" He straightened his black and grey-striped tie. "In the event of your mother's death…"

Brianna's stomach lurched. "My mother's not dead, is she Mike?"

"Until I'm informed otherwise, your mother is still alive."

How, Brianna wondered, could she be so relieved to hear this but still be mad at her at the same time? If Lynette were here, she would hug her and *then* throttle her.

Mike came to the part that he was sure would shock Brianna. "You will inherit in excess of eleven million dollars U.S. when your mother dies."

"Holy catfish!" She could not have looked more shocked if she'd crammed all her fingers and toes into a live socket. Her mother had been frugal—bought a modest home in Canada and drove a plain truck—and to Brianna's knowledge had never once splashed money around, except for some appliance luxuries, and, of course, Brian-na's law studies. Most of the designer clothes her mother had left behind and rarely worn; she'd had them in her closet for as long as Brianna could recall. Seeing her faraway look Mike asked, "Are you okay?"

She shook her head to clear her thoughts. "Just a little flabber-gasted, that's all."

"In addition to the money you will inherit, there will be substantial sums from her investment accounts and all her personal possessions. Plus her home in Arrow Lakes Valley and the two houses she owns in Central America."

Brianna's eyebrows arched. "I didn't know Mom owned homes there. She never said anything about this on the tapes."

"She bought them for her husband's family."

"Ah, my father!"

"You know, then."

"Oh, yes. Did you know that Lionel was my father?"

"Yes. Again, I must stress that it was your mother's decision to keep your father a secret, not mine."

"I can't even go and say hello at his graveside. Mother went and had his body cremated then scattered the ashes. Is that correct?"

"Yes. I did that for her. I laid his ashes to rest in the river where he loved to play as a child, not far from the city of Santa Ana."

Fighting angry tears, Brianna burst out, "That makes me feel friggin' great!"

Mike squirmed in the chair wishing he were anywhere else but here in this uncomfortable situation. He had always been Lynette's puppet, but this time, she'd gone too far in leaving him to be the bearer of such difficult news and to having to deal with the aftermath.

"It wasn't a planned love affair, Brianna," he finally ventured. "It just happened."

"I know about that. It was on the tapes."

"Then may I tell you my side of it?"

"Go ahead."

"In the summer of 1974, when I collected your mother from Guatemala airport, she looked like a film star. She was tall, slim, and her long hair shone like spun gold. The exquisite color of emerald eyes melted me, as well as my boss, Juan. We were surprised at how well she spoke our language. She was so intelligent, and refreshing, and vivacious… absolutely delightful compared to the other foreigners that we encountered."

Brianna was tempted to let Mike know that her Spanish was just as good as her mother's, having taken it as a second language, but kept silent.

"Juan instructed me to drive to El Salvador and collect Lionel. This I did, not because Juan asked me, but for the most captivating woman I'd ever met. She risked her own life to rescue a young man whose life was about to be endangered by the political situation occurring there. In July 1969, El Salvador invaded Honduras and, fueled by the U.S. aid to the Salvadoran military, thousands of native teens were kidnapped by the soldiers and forced to enlist in the army."

"That's awful…" Brianna hesitated, thinking how much he must have admired her mother, and said, "Am I reading between the lines here? Did you like my mother more than you are going to admit?"

His cheeks reddened. "My dear, there wasn't a man in Guatemala who wouldn't have fallen for your mother. I'll tell you a little secret, seeing that you are reading between the lines. Yes. I've always had a soft spot in my heart for her but never have I told her so. Lionel would have challenged me to a duel!"

"Are you married, Mike?"

"Ah," he said, noticing Brianna's eyes directed on his ring finger. "I forgot to put my ring on after my shower this morning. Yes. I've been happily married for many years. I have two wonderful sons. Alejandro is twenty-one, and Ricardo is nineteen. And, if you like, it would be an honor if you could come and spend some time with me and family."

"I would like that, but there's something I desperately need an answer to. Why did my mother not tell Lionel about me?"

Mike sighed. "After your mother's departure from Guatemala and the U.S., she sent me, via Western Union, a large sum of money. She wanted me to cross into the States and personally hand the cash to Lionel's sister for his upkeep. Being illegal, Lynette knew it would be tough for him to find a job. I knew that she had more than a soft spot for the young man. Then one day, I had to tell her that Lionel was engaged to an American girl whose father owned the grocery store where he had managed to find work without too many questions being asked. I remember your mother sobbing on the phone. It broke my heart. Oh, she never stopped sending money, and she even insisted on paying for his wedding. Sadly, Lionel's teenage wife died in a head-on collision only ten days after they were married. It was by pure coincidence that your mother and Lionel met up in the States—"

"Can you bring me a large rum and coke," Brianna asked a waiter passing the table.

"Sure," he replied. "And for you, Sir?"

"Nothing, thank you. I'm okay with the coffee."

Continuing, Mike said, "Your mother was doing one of her 'courier' jobs, as she liked to call it, and bumped into Lionel in Los Angeles. That was that; they were never separated again until he died."

Tears welled in Brianna's eyes and spilled onto her cheeks. "Oh, she loved him more than she loved me."

"I doubt that. But if ever there was a true love story, this was the best."

"But why on God's earth didn't my mother tell him about me?"

"She was afraid of losing him. You see, even though Lionel was in love with your mother, and please forgive me for saying something so very personal, she wasn't highly sexed. So she let Lionel *wander,* if you know what I mean."

"Good Lord!"

"So you see, Brianna. Lynette's deep insecurity to hold onto the much younger man was what made your mother keep your birth a secret. If she had told him about you, she believed that Lionel would have hated her and left her for another woman."

Mike dug into his jacket pocket and handed Brianna an envelope. "This is the letter she was going to send to Lionel, via me, when she found out she was pregnant."

"How did you get it?"

"She gave it to me for safekeeping."

Written in Lynette's best handwriting, it was dated, 2nd April, 1975, the day after Brianna was born.

My darling, Lionel.

I will be lost forever in the memory of our time together. My soul is in sorrow, and my heart is in despair for a love that can never be. When the winds blow across the Scottish Highlands here in Great Britain, I will whisper your name in the hope that the wind god will carry it to your heart. Until we meet again in a world that has no mortal chains, I will see your eyes in our daughter. She is our love child who I will treasure with all the love in the world.

I will love you forever.

"L"

"May I keep this?" Brianna asked.

"Of course. I know it's not easy to do, but don't judge your mother too harshly. I know that she will contact you or me. Even without her permission, I think you should know about the great family you have on Lionel's side. I'm sure they would love to meet you."

Brianna shot off her chair and flung her arms around Mike's shoulders. "You're a great guy. Thank you."

Blushing, Mike rose quickly to his feet. "I have their addresses in my phonebook at home. Do you have e-mail?"

"Yes."

"Great."

Brianna wrote her email address on a paper napkin and handed it to Mike. In turn, he handed her his business card. "I'll e-mail their whereabouts as soon as I get back to Seattle."

"I've missed having family, Mike. You know it was hard growing up as an only child, but even worse not having grandparents, uncles, and aunts."

"Your paternal grandfather Jose Martinez, died some time ago, but your grandmother Rosaria is very much alive. She is a sweetheart. You and her are going to get on fine. And you have plenty of aunts. Rosaria gave birth to eight daughters, and every one of them is alive and kicking. Lionel was her only son."

"Wow!"

* * *

Back in the apartment she shared with Rob, an overwhelmed Brianna felt as if the world had stopped turning. The discovery that she would never again be genetically alone on this planet was something she could never have imagined. She couldn't wait for the day when she would look into the eyes of her grandmother and relatives and in them see her father once more.

She picked up a remote from the coffee table, activated the CD player, and danced to the rap tune playing. When the song was over, she flopped onto the loveseat and thought about Roberto. She couldn't wait to tell the man she loved her incredible news. But Brianna could not have known that her blissful newfound happiness would abruptly be ended the next day.

A bone-chilling long-distance phone call would send her into a downward spiral of hate, love, guilt, and revenge that would forever change her life.

Chapter 27

The sun shone like a golden coin over Africa, but it was not a bright spring morning for Brianna. Her tear-swollen eyelids were hidden under large sunglasses as she stepped onto South African soil for the first time. She had longed to visit this country: go on a safari, soak up the sun, go scuba diving in crystalline waters, and even give shark fishing a try, but now those dreams were furthest from her mind. Her thoughts dissipated when she saw a stocky man heading straight for her.

He removed his black fedora and asked, "Are you Brianna McTavish?"

"Yes, I'm Brianna."

"I'm Detective Pieter Marquand. We spoke on the phone." The police official's eyes turned to the man at Brianna's side. "And you are?"

"This is my fiancé, Roberto Caldrese. Whatever you have to tell me you can say in front of him."

With an approving nod, Marquand gestured with a wave of his hand. "Follow me, please. I have a car waiting outside. We can talk on the way to the hospital."

As the car swallowed up the miles, Brianna learned in more detail the circumstances of her mother's attempted murder and about the nun's long-distance mule trek to alert the park ranger who had then radioed for help. And in the detective's estimation, Lynette wouldn't be alive if it hadn't been for the intervention of a witchdoctor who had prevented the further blood loss.

"Any leads as to who might have done this?" Brianna asked. "I just want to know who and why."

"No, not yet, but I'm working on it."

"I hope you still have the death penalty here, because it's important that whoever did this pay the consequences of their actions. Personally, I'd like to see them hang from the gallows." Her state of mind: mixed emotions of rage, anxiousness, and sorrow gripped her heart. *If I had my way, I'd like to see the bastard hanging by his balls!*

Her punishment thoughts were curtailed when Marquand announced, "We're here now, at Addington Hospital. Take the elevator up to the top floor. Your mother is in a private ward of the ICU. I've already notified my deputy that you are on your way. If you need me, here's my number," he said, handing Brianna a card. "Give me a call when it is convenient to talk some more. I've a couple of things I want to go over with you."

Holding Roberto's hand, Brianna walked into the hospital. He felt it shaking. "It's going to be okay, Sweetpea. I'm here."

Brianna took several deep breaths, fighting back the tears. "Oh, God, I don't know how to feel," she whispered. "Part of me is still angry at Mom, and the other is breaking in half for her."

"I know, Sweetpea. But you can do it."

The uniformed officer asked them for ID then pushed open the swing doors leading into the ICU. A petite black nurse watched the pair approaching her. "Are you here to see Mrs. Martinez?"

"Yes. I'm her daughter."

"Come with me and I'll take you to her, and I'll inform her neurosurgeon, Doctor Cohen, that you are here."

In numbed horror, Brianna stared at the unrecognizable woman who was her mother, swathed in bandages. A life-support machine beeped, and intravenous plastic tubes gurgled into her nose, mouth, and arm. If Brianna hadn't known better, she would have thought her mother already in the first stage of rigor mortis.

Brianna felt helpless. Sobbing, no longer able to hold back her tears, she rushed over to the dying woman's bedside and cried out, "Oh, dear God! What have they done to you?" She held her mother's limp hand and kissed it. "I'm here now, Mom. Everything is going to be alright," she murmured. "Please don't die. I love you with all my heart. I have wonderful news. I'm going to get married, and you must be there at my wedding."

Roberto stood silently at her side. No words he could utter could dull the love of his life's sharp pain. He slipped quietly away in search of Lynette's neurosurgeon. At the nurse's station, he asked, "Is Mrs. Martinez's doctor on his way?"

The nurse looked up from her paperwork and pointed. "He's here now."

Roberto headed toward the short man with a stethoscope draped around his neck. He introduced himself as a fellow physician and enquired after Lynette's condition. The surgeon's voice was soft with compassion. "It's touch and go at the moment. The next forty-eight hours are critical," he stated, handing over Lynette's medical chart.

Roberto read his commentaries and noted that the air ambulance paramedics had had to defibrillate her and that she had undergone emergency surgery to remove two bullets lodged in the base of her brain. Her head had been shaved, the scalp peeled back, skull bone sawed, and the circular piece of bone removed—rather like taking the top off a boiled egg—enabling Dr. Cohen to remove the bullets. Miraculously, both projectiles had lodged in a fibrous mass, Lynette's tumor. This, too, according to the surgery notes, had been removed. Roberto placed the medical notes on the counter and commented to Dr. Cohen, "It's a miracle she's still alive."

"Yes, I agree. Ironically, it was the tumor that ultimately saved her life."

They chatted about the differences in medical practices in South Africa and Canada. Thanking the surgeon for allowing him to check the records, Roberto returned to Brianna.

He saw the lowered bed rail and found his fiancé, arms wrapped around her mother, lying next to her. Brianna's tear-wet face and tightly gripped bed sheet in her hand brought a lump of pity to his throat. "You okay, Sweetpea?"

"No, I'm not."

Roberto pulled a chair nearer to the bed, took rosary beads from his pants pocket, and silently began the ancient prayer: *Hail Mary full of Grace...*

Brianna could just imagine what her mother would say to this: "Don't bother praying for me. I don't believe in that crap! And I'm beyond redemption!"

A nurse entered, scattering Brianna's thoughts, and shooed her off the bed. She replaced her sandals and rocked her body back and forth, not taking her eyes off the nurse or her mother.

Checking her patient's vital signs, the nurse smiled at Brianna, "I'm told that talking helps when a loved one is in a coma. I remember one patient whose loved one sang to her every day for nearly two months. When she finally awoke, she said to her son. "For Pete's sake, no more! You can't sing to save *your* life, let alone mine!"

That funny story prompted a smile, the first since arriving in South Africa. "Well, nurse, I can't sing, either. And even if I could, my mother hates my taste in music. She calls it "muck." And when she wakes up she'd most probably... like that guy's mother... give me an earful."

The nurse glanced at Roberto, his fingers thumbing through the rosary beads. "That will also help," she added, and left the room.

A caucasian woman holding a clipboard passed the black nurse at the doorway. She strode purposefully toward Brianna. "Good afternoon. I'm Mrs. Kloof, the hospital administrator. I'm told that you are her daughter?"

"Yes."

"I would like some personal information, please," she said, pen at ready.

"I thought Detective Marquand had already done that."

"Yes, he has given me her passport details, but what I need is her medical information. Would you happen to know her doctor's name in Canada? What surgeries she's had? Allergies, infections, inoculations, etc.?"

"As far as I'm aware, my mother never had a day's illness until she was diagnosed with a tumor on her brain. I don't even know the name of her doctor. But it won't be hard to find. She lived in a rural area called Arrow Lake Valley in British Columbia, Canada. I'm sure you can find the names of doctors there through the Internet."

Jotting down the information the administer continued, "No childhood ailments?"

"Not that I know of."

"There is some severe vaginal scarring and long-healed bone fractures. Do you know how they came about?"

"I've no idea," Brianna answered glibly.

The woman's next question was to be expected. "Who is going to pay for her private care?"

"My mother's lawyer is on his way here to South Africa. He will sort it out. This hospital does not have to worry about not being paid. My mother could most probably buy the place."

The poker-faced administrator left the room.

"Gee, Bri. You put that nicely," Roberto said a ring of laughter in his voice.

The couple held hands and gazed out at the sea from the high-rise hospital building.

* * *

Day turned into night.

Roberto encouraged Brianna to return to the hotel. It had been a long flight for both of them, and he thought she needed to rest. She shook her head. "What if Mom died while I'm gone? I'd never forgive myself. No, I'm staying put. You go, Roberto. Ask someone at the nursing station to call you a cab. Go to the hotel, and if all goes well here, I'll join you later."

"Are you sure, Sweetpea? I don't want to leave you, but I could eat a horse and go back for the rider, then sleep for a year!"

Brianna laughed. "Off you go for that *delicious* meal. I'll catch you later."

"Would you like me to ask if there's a cafeteria here? I could go and get you a snack of some sort."

"Honeybun, I'm not hungry. Go now. I love you."

"I love you, too."

When alone, Brianna placed her warm hand against her mother's cold cheek. With a steely resolve, she whispered close to her mother's ear. "Mom, I'll find whoever did this to you and make them pay. I promise you that. I want you to know that you are my hero. I love you so much and can't bear the thought of never seeing you smile, hearing your laughter, or see your beautiful green eyes sparkling with life. Mom—"

For an instant, she thought she saw a facial tick, an eyelid flicker, and joy leaped into her heart. She studied her mother's face, looking, waiting...

Lynette remained still and silent.

Past midnight, jetlag overtaking her tired body and mind, Brianna climbed into bed next to her mother. Within seconds, she was asleep, but not for long. In a sleepy dream fog, she tried to visualize the face of her mother's assassin. Was he white? Was he African? Was he—

"I'm sorry, but you'll have to get out of this bed," the nurse said to a jolted-awake Brianna. "It's against hospital rules for a visitor to get into bed with a patient."

"We have to turn Mrs. Martinez and change her dressings," the second RN said. "You can wait outside, and we'll let you know when we are done."

"Do you have a spare cot to put in my mother's room? I don't want to leave her."

"No. That's against hospital rules."

"This would never happen in Canada," Brianna mumbled. She kissed Lynette on the forehead and whispered her goodbyes. "Mom, I'm going to the hotel. I'll be back in a little while. Hang in there. I love you, and don't forget that."

Outside, she inhaled deeply of the cooling night air and then got into the taxi. "To the Edward Hotel, please."

In the dark hotel bedroom, she found Roberto snoring softly and spotted the note propped against the bedside lamp:

> Wake me up when you get back. Love you lots, my brave
> girl. Your teddy bear, Honeybun, Rob. XXXXX

Brianna smiled, quietly undressed, and climbed into bed beside him. Roberto was so flat out that he didn't feel her warm naked body pressed against his back. She sighed. She wanted the "touchy-feely" magic he was so good at. Sex would distract her mind from the hospital scene and what could lie ahead.

But it wasn't going to happen.

As soon as her head touched the soft pillow, she too was out flat. Neither of them heard the phone ringing in the other room but did hear the loud knocking the next morning.

"It's eight o'clock," Brianna said after a quick glance at the clock. *Who could it be? Oh, God. I hope it's not bad news.*

She hurriedly grabbed a white toweling robe from the bathroom and rushed to the door while Roberto slipped into the shower.

Detective Marquand looked unforgivingly chipper for the hour. He noted her makeup-streaked face and tousled hair and apologized, "I'm sorry to disturb you at this hour, but we need to talk."

"It's alright. Come in," Brianna said, gesturing for him to take a seat. "Give me a moment, please. I just want to make a quick call to the hospital to see how my mother is doing."

She slipped into the bedroom to use the phone.

"No change, I'm afraid," the duty nurse informed her.

"I'll be there as soon as possible."

Making her way back to the detective, she caught a glimpse of herself in a decorative wall mirror. *Oh, my god! I'm a mess!* She did a quick hand-comb through her tangled locks and straightened her robe. "I'm sorry to have kept you waiting, Detective."

"How is your mother?"

"Stable, but no change."

They sat opposite each other. Brianna couldn't help but notice his smug expression.

"I have some good news for you," he announced. "The interior police have an old black man in custody in connection with the shootings. He's singing like a bird."

"An *old* black man tried to kill my mother! Good Lord, why?"

"It seems that your mother created some powerful enemies during her short stay here. As I speak, a South African lawyer, Bryan Duval, whom your mother hired, and Captain Johannes de Klerk, the helicopter pilot who flew her to Tswanas in February of this year, have been taken into custody. The biggest surprise to all of us is that Lady Corrie Hallworthy, a social hotshot in these parts, has also been detained. They are all being charged with second-degree murder and attempted murder."

It took a spit second for the name to sink in.

"*CORRIE HALLWORTHY!*"

Marquand's eyes squinted suspiciously. "Do you know Lady Hallworthy?"

"I don't know her personally, but have heard the name."

His detective brain slipped into gear. "You need to explain."

"There's nothing to explain. I think I heard my mother mention it once, that's all."

His gut feeling told him she was lying, but he continued, "From Kelingo, the black man in our custody, we were able to deduce that it was Lady Hallworthy who arranged the shootings of both your mother and Anele Dingane."

"Why?"

"At the crime scene, I found some journals belonging to Lady Hallworthy hidden in your mother's suitcase. How these diaries came to be in your mother's possession is a mystery. But I will tell you this… your mother paid Lord Alan Hallworthy an unauthorized visit at the mental institution where he is still incarcerated for the murder a black prostitute many years back. It is my belief that when Lady Hallworthy found out, she blew her top… because… and I don't know how to put this delicately… apparently, from what I've read, your mother is Alan Hallworthy's illegitimate daughter."

Feigning surprise, Brianna blurted, "You've got to be kidding me! She told me her parents were dead!"

In a way, it was the truth.

"No, I don't think so. I ordered DNA tests on both Lord Alan and your mother, and I can say one hundred percent that she *is* his offspring."

Brianna's mind was reeling. Had that scurrilous Corrie written all the sordid details of her sick husband's appetite for young girls—including his daughter? Probably. Brianna had learned through her studies that sociopaths often felt the need to document their ghastly criminal behavior. There was no doubt in her mind now that Pieter Marquand knew everything there was to know about her mother. As did she. But Brianna was certainly not going to let on at this stage.

"I believe Lady Hallworthy hired the lawyer to get the job done," Marquand said. "But, I also believe he got cold feet. According to Kelingo, Durval promised him and the helicopter pilot big bucks to carry out the executions, and I'm pleased to say that less than an hour ago, Bryan Durval was apprehended at Durban airport with a bag of cash and a one-way ticket to Switzerland."

An angry bull facing a matador could not have snorted with greater derision. Brianna spat, "I hope they get the electric chair! But then even that is too good for those scumbags!"

Marquand didn't comment. Instead, he rose from his seat and said, "I have to go. I have a meeting with the DA. I'll keep you informed, *counselor*," he said respectfully, even though he was aware she'd not sat her final law exams, and ended with sincerity, "and I hope your visit with your mother goes well."

"Thanks, Detective."

Leaving Roberto to entertain himself at the hotel, Brianna left for the hospital. She could hardly wait to tell her mother the good news—but the news had traveled faster than the taxi.

A mob of reporters, recorders and cameras ready, thronged the hospital.

"Miss McTavish, how do you feel about Lord and Lady Hallworthy being involved in the shooting of your mother and the death of her companion?"

"No comment."

"Will you be attending their trial?"

"No comment."

Two burly security men rushed to Brianna's side. Using themselves as shields, they helped her past frenzied journalists, their tape recorders threatening to dislocate her jaw.

Shaking, she rushed for the elevator.

* * *

The curtains were open, and sunshine fell warmly on her mother's ashen face. Brianna kissed her forehead. "Mom, I've got good news.

They got the buggers! You *have* to get well now. Don't you want to see them fry, Mom?"

No response.

She cradled Lynette's swathed head in the crook of her arm and began singing an Irish lullaby—one her mother had crooned to her as a child. Brianna's tone-deaf rendition brought only wincing from the nursing staff. Then a fully cloaked visitor entered the room. "Hello," she smiled, extending her hand to Brianna. "My name is Sister Bertha. I've heard so much about you. I also loved your mother."

At long last, all the blank spaces in her mother's life became filled as the nun answered questions. She ended with, "I'd like you to have this…" she removed from her habit the same little crucifix that she had once tried to give Lynette. "Pray for her, my child. Shiya is much loved by the people of Tswanas. They miss her dreadfully. But there is someone special I'd like you to meet… the young man who saved her life." Bertha beckoned for Sliman to enter.

Brianna nearly winded the witchdoctor. "I don't know how to thank you. You are my hero."

He smiled, and then, tears rimming his dark eyes, he approached the bed and kissed Lynette. He bent and told her in Zulu how much he missed her company—laughter—feisty spirit—the loss he felt in his heart without her. There was no doubt—he had fallen in love. He turned from her to face Brianna and took hold of her hands. Instantly, she felt a tingling sensation, one she wasn't sure she liked. She quickly withdrew her hands.

"I would like to try something if it's agreeable to you?" Sliman asked.

"Try… *what?*"

"It is not conventional medicine, so to speak."

"If it will help my mother regain consciousness, go ahead."

"I would like you all to leave the room."

"No, I'm staying put," Brianna responded.

The nun peered over the rim of her bifocals and gave the witch-doctor a disapproving look, but nodded in compliance and left.

An icy shiver of uncertainty ran through Brianna as she sat on a chair. Hugging her chest, she watched Sliman remove a pouch from around his neck and empty a pile of stones onto the bed. The turquoise stones glistened under the neon lighting. One by one, he picked them up and placed each stone strategically around Lynette's prone body. Then he rested his hands on top of her bandaged head and began low chanting. Brianna would swear blind that she could feel the psychic vibrations.

After inaudible Zulu incantations, he spoke in English. "Shiya of Tswanas, feel the hands of the Great Spirit enter your broken body. Feel the warmth. Feel the love. Feel the healing. Open your eyes and come back to those who love you. Your time is not up on the mortal plateau. You must fight the hands that try to pull you into the place where evil spirits live, because I know your will to live is much stronger. I know this because I have I seen it. Open your eyes, wild child of Mother Earth's creations."

Nothing.

"Shiya, I know you can hear me," Sliman said. "Your daughter is here. She is crying for her mother. An invisible umbilical cord ties both of you together in this life and the next. If not for yourself, come back to earth for your beautiful daughter."

Nothing.

Brianna sighed. "I don't think my mother wants to live, Sliman. You see, I believe she wants to be with my father. She loved him more than me."

"No, sad child of Shiya. Your mother's love encompasses all. She no longer resides beside a silent ocean of sorrow—"

Brianna gasped as the window flew open, and a vagrant eddy whipped at the sheets.

A long strand of blonde hair escaping from the bandaging flicked across Lynette's face. The ashen pallor drained and a healthy flush replenished it. Super-glued to her seat, Brianna's mouth fell open. She could not believe what her eyes were seeing. Was she actually witnessing a supernatural event?

Lynette's eyelids opened, and sparkling emerald eyes stared at Brianna. She stifled a scream of joy by clamping her hands tightly over her mouth. It was true!

Her mother's green eyes were searching, looking for recognition.

"*Mom!*" Brianna's ecstatic shout echoed in the room.

"My precious daughter, is it really you?" Lynette had spoken nasally, the tubes in her throat and nose interfering with her speech. She looked at the IV in her hand, then at the bed, and over to the monitoring apparatus. "Why am I in the hospital? Did I fall or something?"

"Mom—" Brianna almost laughed. "You didn't fall. You were shot."

Disbelief widened Lynette's eyes. "*Shot! Why? And by whom? Where's my Anele.*"

A black nurse barging in the door ended the questioning. "Mrs. Martinez, you are awake. I'll go and get the doctor."

While she bustled away, Sliman broke the sad news about Anele. Lynette's sobbing could be heard throughout the ICU.

Dr. Cohen entered, and before he could say a word, Lynette grabbed his white coat. "Take these blasted drips out," she demanded. "I've got to go home to Tswanas. My mother is dead. I have to see her before they put her in the ground."

"Mrs. Martinez," the neurosurgeon cautioned. "You are in no fit state to be leaving this hospital. You have had a severe injury to the head—"

"I know my rights. Bring me the patient release form, and I'll sign the darn thing. That'll let you off the medical hook. Okay?"

Brianna could have shriveled into a ball but chose to defend the doctor. "Mom, don't be stupid. The doctor is right. Get well first, and Roberto and I will take you to Tswanas. You can put flowers on her grave."

The sour-faced doctor stomped out of the room.

"Who's Roberto?" Lynette asked.

"He's my fiancé. He flew here with me. He's a great guy, Mom. You'll love him."

"You never told me about him."

"I met him the day after my *father* died," Brianna emphasized the word.

Lynette looked deep into her daughter's teary eyes. "Oh, Brianna, I can't begin to tell you how sorry I am. I do hope that you will not hold it against me for the rest of your life."

"No, Mother. And I know that this is not the right time and place, but I have to tell you that I will never hold anything against you, especially what I heard on the tapes. I understand now that you did what you had to do."

Lynette sighed with relief then reverted back to her old self. This time the noisy sigh was one of defiance. "Wild horses can't keep me away from seeing Anele laid to rest. I owe her that much. Are you going to help me to get out of this hospital or not?"

It was Brianna's turn to sigh, but with resignation. "I suppose I have to put myself in your shoes. What would I do? Probably what you are going to do. Okay, I'll countersign the release forms. But Mom, I want you to come back with me to the hotel and rest while I make all the arrangements. Promise," she said, wagging her finger like a scolding parent.

Lynette nodded. "I love you, Brianna."

"I love you too, Mother. More than you will ever know. But if anything happens to you while you're in my care, I'll never forgive myself. And I'm not going to lose you for a second time."

"Nothing is going to happen to me. I've never felt healthier. And I know who I can thank for that."

Lynette winked at Sliman.

"Ah, no longer a doubtful woman, I see," he laughed. "I'm glad to hear that. Black—excuse the pun—the art of black magic is truly a gift from the spirit world."

Overhearing this as she came back into the room, Sister Bertha shot Sliman a disdainful "you-are-a-heathen" look but said nothing. How the black magician and the servant of Christian beliefs could stand side by side in this room was unbelievable to Brianna. But she had long learned that fact is stranger than fiction.

The nun and the seer said their goodbyes. They had many buses to catch to take them back to Tswanas. Lynette offered to fly them back as soon as she could make a telephone call.

"Thank you, but no," Sister Bertha said for her and Sliman. "We have our tickets, and we must leave now."

"I hope Anele hasn't been buried already?" Lynette asked.

"No," Sliman replied. "I told the burial women to keep her earth vessel preserved until you could make it back to Tswanas."

"You were awfully confident, weren't you?" Lynette smiled. "But then, why am I surprised?"

"See you in Tswanas, lovely lady." Sliman winked. "We will celebrate Anele's passing with good beer, singing, and dancing."

"God willing," the nun responded.

After they left, Lynette turned to her daughter, whose eyes had flown like darts between Sliman, the nun, and her mother.

"Now Lass," Lynette said. "It's time to make a move. Go and get the release forms from the not-so-happy Jewish doctor... get the nurse to remove these bloody tubes... pay the hospital bill. And please go and buy me some decent clothes at the nearest shop."

She sat upright. "Let's get the hell out of Dodge! I have a party to go to!"

Chapter 28

Monsoon-laden rain clouds hung low over Tswanas on the day of Anele's funeral. Six strong tribesmen hoisted the makeshift coffin, made from the wood of gum trees, onto their shoulders. Bare feet shuffling, they began the slow walk up the mountainside to the tribe's sacred burial site. Following in the pallbearers' wake, African drums strapped to their waist, young boys pounded out a traditional tune for the dead.

Brianna couldn't believe how many people there were.

As if attending a celebrity's burial, they followed: Father Samuel, Sister Bertha, relatives of the murdered girl Naomi, very old field workers and other former Hallworthy servants, and of course, the Tswanas tribe and some from the neighboring Mtunzini township. Also, there were media from Canada, Great Britain, and South Africa, their digital cameras and video recording devices working overtime. Winston Mandekana, who was the first to break the news of the shootings, was among them. The day he had bagged the story, he had used the oldest trick in the book to get it. He had lied:

"I was born in Mtunzini, your neighboring village. I am one of you," he had proclaimed to the Tswanas villagers. "You can trust me. The white woman... what was she doing here? How is she connected to the dead woman, Anele Dingane?"

The naïve tribe gave him what he wanted.

His story had been breaking news in London, England. The August edition of the *Mail On Sunday's* headlines read:

AFRICAN WOMAN IS MURDERED FOR SAVING THE LIFE OF A WHITE BABY IN 1945
By Winston Mandekana.

Typeset was the article written and wired by him to London. It read:

Lord Alan Hallworthy of South Africa (a direct descendant of the deceased Lord Nigel Hallworthy, a London-based architect, and cousin of Queen Victoria) and Lord Alan's wife, Lady Corrie Hallworthy, have both been named as persons of interest in this case...

The newspaper editor pleaded with Mandekana to follow up on this breaking story, but this was proving to be a problem. He couldn't get near the surviving woman of this tragedy.

Flanked by Detective Marquand and two of his policemen, Lynette and Brianna, holding hands, walked silently and unbothered between the armed officers. Held at bay with threats, the reporters were fuming, so they had to tell their stories from afar through constantly clicking ultra-zoom video and digital cameras.

At the burial site, the incessant hum of mosquitoes and other biting insects was soporific. Lynette was oblivious to the nasty pests tucking into everyone's exposed flesh. Groggy from pain medication and an excessive amount of brandy, she tried to focus on the coffin resting in the dirt below. She reached into the pocket of her black full-length dress and pulled out a folded piece of paper. It was a poem she had written the day after she and Anele had returned from the scared rock—the day the rare flower blossomed. Tears blinding her and sorrow choking her throat, Lynette swallowed and began to read what she'd written in English:

I tread the misty stairs, where there is no such word as time.
We can all be together there. I know we will be fine.
And under stars unfurled, will echo out our laughter.
Mother dearest, *Umama* Anele, we will be as one in this world.
Rejoined in the thereafter.
I love you. But I won't miss you. Because you will be forever locked in my beating heart.
Until we meet again in the Invisible Kingdom of souls.

For those who couldn't understand the English language, Sister Bertha translated. Dark faces beamed with appreciation for Lynette's poignant sentiments.

"Thank you, Sister," she said.

"My pleas—"

Eyebrows arched, the nun pointed, and Brianna jumped back. "Oh, my God! I hope it's not dangerous," she said, shrinking behind Roberto's back.

Undulating side to side, the most dangerous, arboreal, and feared snake in Africa slithered out of thick brush. The fast-moving bright green mamba, highly venomous and about 1.8 meters in length, continued slithering their way. Detective Marquand drew his pistol from its holder. Lynette blocked his aim with her hand. "Put your gun away," she demanded. "He's not going to harm anyone. He has come to see me." She turned away from the detective's *are-you-nuts!* stare and walked to the snake, which was hissing loudly. She bent low, lifted the slender snake to her chest, whispered something, and then dropped him onto the coffin lid. The mamba disappeared under the wildflower wreath adorning it.

Brianna said what the detective wanted to say: "Holy shit! Are you crazy, Mother! That thing could have killed you!"

"No, it wouldn't have. You don't understand, Brianna. Snakes and I are one."

"Now you're talking daft, Mom."

Sliman smiled.

But the biggest smile came from the mentally challenged Vimbela. She pushed her way through to Lynette's side. "Most beautiful daughter of Anele, *she* has heard your words. She will always be with you. See—" she pointed to the wreath. "*Umama* Anele sent you the green snake—"

All heads turned around at the sound of loud wailing.

Standing behind the reporters, a tall, slim female wearing a heavy veil, long black dress, and gloves, flanked by what can only be described as "rent-a-thug" beefy foreign-looking bodyguards, sobbed uncontrollably.

"Who is she?" Lynette asked Vimbela.

"I don't know, but she's not one of us. We don't wear such awful clothes."

When no one else seemed to know the woman's identity, Lynette walked away from the gravesite and, with Brianna and the police officers following, she approached the woman, who turned to flee. Lynette grabbed her arm. "Excuse me, I don't want to sound rude, but who are you? Obviously, you know Anele or you wouldn't be here."

The woman didn't reply.

But Lynette could feel her piercing glare from behind the heavy veil going right through her body. "Who are you? Do I know you?" Lynette asked again.

A muffled voice replied, "I should be in that grave, not her."

"Good Lord! What on earth do you mean by that?"

"If it wasn't for me, she wouldn't be lying in the cold earth."

"Okay, now you've lost me."

"She not only saved you… she once saved me."

"What the heck are you talking about? Who the *hell* are you?"

"I'm Maria… your *real* mother."

It didn't register in Lynette's fuzzy brain. "I'm sorry. What did you say?"

"My name is Maria Picasso. I'm your biological mother."

An emotion Lynette had never experienced before gripped her heart. She felt her legs give way.

Maria held her unconscious daughter in her arms for the first time. "I'm taking you home to Sicily. That's where we both belong."

"Over my dead body," Brianna hissed like the snake.

Epilogue

The Island of Sicily, That Same August 1998

"I need my head shrunk!" Brianna shouted. "What the friggin' hell am I doing here in Sicily?" She stood on the sea-facing terrace of Villa Favola, sitting peacefully in a small bay about 54 km from Palermo airport. A sea breeze from the Gulf of Solanto brushed her face as she looked impassively down at the lemon trees lining the steps past the heated pool to the sea. Any other time, she would have been thrilled with the splendor of this magnificent home and awesome views, but her tired mind blocked the spectacular vistas seen all around her.

Emotionally and physically worn out from the tragedies that seemed to be never ending, she was feeling chronically depressed. For the baby growing inside her, it was not a good start to life. She had blamed her missed period on nerves after receiving the phone call from Detective Marquand back in Canada. But an accurate urine-testing strip, bought at a pharmacy after her arrival in South Africa, had told her otherwise.

At the time, she had felt that the unplanned pregnancy would send Roberto over the edge. He had mentioned that, from having had to take unpaid leave to come out here, their financial affairs

317

could be at risk if they didn't return home soon. She reminded him about Lynette's money tucked away in her savings account. It would more than cover their traveling, hotel, and other expenses to and from South Africa and pay the rent and utility bills back home in their absence. That hadn't sat well with the Italian's "I'm the man of the house" attitude. Also, to Brianna, having her mother back in her life was one hundred million reasons not to rush into marriage. Roberto disagreed, and in the fight that followed, many cruel words were exchanged. The end result was: he packed his bags, called a cab, and as far as she knew, caught an earlier flight home.

He had walked out of her life without learning about his unborn child.

* * *

Thinking back to the funeral, she sighed with resignation as she recalled seeing Lynette fall to pieces after she discovered that the woman in the black veil was her natural mother. What did Maria expect after all these years? Open arms from the daughter that she had discarded like an unwanted mattress? Or to be welcomed by the villagers who had witnessed Anele's demise? None of these tragic turn of events would have happened if Maria hadn't started the ball rolling in 1945. Had the Tswanas tribe known who she really was, they most probably would have stoned her to death.

Immediately after being shoved aside by Brianna, Maria had fled with her "goons," and an aircraft was heard taking off. As if her appearance had been merely a mirage, the family returned to their respective hotels to pack, with a promissory agreement to come back for the pending trial of Bryan, Kelingo, and Lady Corrie.

What comes around does indeed seem to go around.

In a twist of fate, Brianna had learned from Marquand that Alan had slit his wrists and died about an hour or so into Anele's funeral. Brianna couldn't speak for her mother, but *she* couldn't wait to leave the country. At that time, she had remarked to Roberto. "What in the world was God doing when He created this Dark Continent, a country where violence has no soul."

"Life has to go on now, Sweetpea. *We*, as a couple, are important now. When we are married, I'll take care of everything, including the finances and any additional monies your mother may give us—" he laughed, showing his true colors, "—like a *big* wedding check to buy our first home."

That money-grabbing attitude had shaken Brianna's heart. She had half smiled at the man she *thought* was her soul mate. And now, after that final row, she knew it was never to be, but he would always have a special place in her heart. After all, he was her baby's father.

Packed and ready to leave the Edward hotel, the taxi waiting to take Lynette and her to the airport, Brianna went to her mother's suite and tapped on the door.

No response.

She knocked loudly.

No response.

"Mom, hurry up, the cab is waiting," she yelled through the door.

Still no response.

"Mom, open the door."

Thinking that her mother was taking a last minute bathroom break, she waited a minute, then rapped so hard her knuckles hurt.

Nothing.

A gut feeling told Brianna something wasn't right!

"Not again!" she muttered rushing to the elevator.

At the reception desk she urged, "Give me the key to Room 402. Hurry! It's an emergency."

Written on the hotel's stationary, the note on the unmade bed read:

Forgive me, Brianna. I can't go back to Canada with you. I have to finish the jigsaw puzzle that is my life.

I love you.
Mom.

Yet again, Lynette had disappeared—taken off without preamble or discussion. Once more she had asked for forgiveness. But now, Brianna had none to give.

* * *

A bitter and lost heart had brought Brianna all this way to Sicily. If it took her the rest of her life, she would find Lynette and Donna Maria… and then… then *what?*

Would she find closure? Or would the jigsaw puzzle remain incomplete?

Her journey was just beginning.

Brianna would never again set foot on North American soil.

Beside an Ocean of Sorrow

Her journey began as it would end buried in the earth,
A woman driven by abuse turned mad; tried to hide the birth,
As she escaped her captor she ran and ran and ran,
And this is where the story of another life began.
This one ran for a different course but followed the same ground,
She stopped awhile to catch her breath, that's when she heard the
    sound,
An animal she thought must be caught up in a snare,
She ran to where the sound was clear, horror she found there.
A first real breath was filled with dirt and her struggle here begins,
Because a life that's unwanted would be tortured by more sins,
A white raised by black begot looks of concern and surprise,
The color of a child's skin and eyes were the cause of much
    demise.
Troubles caused the child to flee to a world she never knew,
As time goes by her endless list of sorrows grew and grew,
She would make life so pristine and would settle in her new
    found home,
Where she would so proudly stand with her family; she did this
    on her own.
Upon return to her tormented past she found the life she'd lost,
She followed her leads to return to this place, but it was at great
    cost,
A mother of another color reveals to her how her life came to be,
A baby buried in the earth was found beneath a tree.
As everything in our world nothing is ever as it seems,
There's another woman, a white, which she only sees in dreams,
Her journey goes on as it never can end, she continues with great
    devotion,
Now this is where the story will end as it began, beside a silent
    ocean.

LaVergne, TN USA
26 March 2010
177245LV00003B/3/P